Seaview Inn

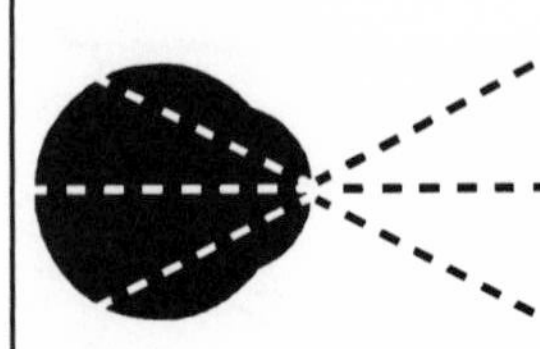

This Large Print Book carries the Seal of Approval of N.A.V.H.

Seaview Inn

Sherryl Woods

WHEELER PUBLISHING
A part of Gale, Cengage Learning

Detroit • New York • San Francisco • New Haven, Conn • Waterville, Maine • London

GALE
CENGAGE Learning™

Wheeler Publishing, a part of Gale, Cengage Learning.

Wheeler Publishing Large Print Hardcover.
The text of this Large Print edition is unabridged.
Other aspects of the book may vary from the original edition.
Set in 16 pt. Plantin.
Printed on permanent paper.

LIBRARY OF CONGRESS CATALOGING-IN-PUBLICATION DATA

Woods, Sherryl.
Seaview Inn / by Sherryl Woods.
p. cm.
ISBN-13: 978-1-59722-764-3 (alk. paper)
ISBN-10: 1-59722-764-1 (alk. paper)
1. Single mothers — Fiction. 2. Breast — Cancer — Patients — Fiction. 3. Florida Keys (Fla.) — Fiction. 4. Domestic fiction. 5. Large type books. I. Title.
PS3573.O6418S43 2008
813'.54—dc22 2008009602

Published in 2008 by arrangement with Harlequin Books S.A.

Printed in the United States of America
1 2 3 4 5 6 7 12 11 10 09 08

Dear Friends,

I doubt there are many of us whose lives have not been touched by cancer in some way. Though research has made great strides and there are many success stories, the diagnosis can be devastating. I'm a firm believer that a positive attitude can make a huge difference in the outcome, but how much more difficult would it be to maintain that attitude if one's own mother had died from the same disease just after your diagnosis?

That's the dilemma faced by Hannah Matthews in *Seaview Inn.* I hope her story will resonate with any of you who are currently in treatment or in remission or have loved ones who are. When I heard Elizabeth Edwards speak about the decision she and her husband had made to go forward with his presidential bid, what impressed me most was her very firm choice to *live* with

cancer on her own terms.

As I was writing the final pages of *Seaview Inn,* a very dear friend called to tell me that her breast cancer had returned . . . sixteen years after the original diagnosis. Two of her friends were also battling recurrences. So for Patti, her friends and all of you who might be facing this, my thoughts and prayers are that you, like Hannah in this story, will live in the moment and have many, many years of good times.

All best,
Sherryl

1

Hannah Matthews prided herself on being sensible and responsible. A single mom and a public relations executive handling several very demanding but fascinating clients, she was the person to turn to in any crisis. She claimed there wasn't a superstitious bone in her body, but she was beginning to wonder if there wasn't something to the old adage that things happened in threes, especially bad things. She was also losing her faith that God never gave a person more than they could handle, because she was definitely on overload.

Not quite three months past her final chemo treatment for breast cancer and less than a month after her mother's death from the very same disease, here she was back in a town she hadn't been able to flee fast enough, standing in front of the bed-and-breakfast that had once been her much-despised home. Worse, she was facing the arduous prospect of trying to convince her stubborn eighty-five-year-old grandmother that it was time to move into an assisted-living community and sell Seaview Inn. Life couldn't get much more stressful than this, or if it could, she didn't want to find out how.

"Hannah, why are you just standing out there daydreaming?" her grandmother demanded from behind the inn's screen door, her tone every bit as querulous and demanding as Hannah remembered from her last visit home. "As hot as it is, leaving this front door wide open is a waste of air-conditioning. And why weren't you here this morning? You *told* me you'd be here this morning. I've been sitting on the porch watching for you most of the day. The heat finally drove me inside."

Hannah bit back a sigh and grabbed the handle of her suitcase to pull it along behind her. "My flight was delayed, Gran. Remember, I called you from the airport in New York to let you know?"

Her grandmother's faded hazel eyes filled with confusion, yet another recent change from her once astute demeanor. "You did? Are you sure?"

"I'm sure, Gran, but it doesn't matter now. I'm here."

"And about time, too," her grandmother added with a little *humph.*

Hannah placed an arm around her grandmother's frail shoulders and gave her a peck on the cheek. "You look good, Gran. Are you feeling okay?"

Truthfully, her grandmother looked as if a strong wind would blow her away. She'd lost weight she could ill afford to lose. Her face, filled with eighty-five years of lines and wrinkles, was sallow. Losing her only child, Hannah's mother, had taken a lot out of her. Her friends in town had called Hannah to let her know that Jenny had rarely left the house since the funeral. She'd been skipping the meetings of her quilting circle and, more telling, Sunday services at church. They were worried about her.

"She's just going to fade away, die of a broken heart all alone, if you ask me," Rachel Morrison had said when she'd called.

Hannah hadn't missed the critical note in Rachel's voice, the unmistakable hint that Hannah had been irresponsible to run off right after her mother's burial and leave her grandmother to cope with her grief and Seaview Inn all on her own.

Though her family knew what she was struggling with, Hannah had been unwilling to share her own cancer crisis with any of these well-meaning neighbors. She'd been unable to defend her actions in any way that might have satisfied them. How could she possibly tell them that seeing her mom's quick decline and painful death while in the middle of her own treatment had left her terrified? She hadn't been able to get away from Seaview and the memories of her mother's final days fast enough. She believed that a positive attitude was an essential ingredient for surviving cancer, but it was almost impossible to maintain that attitude in the face of her mother's death from a recurrence that had come less than two years after she'd first been diagnosed.

So, instead of explaining, Hannah had succumbed to guilt and dutifully taken the remaining two weeks of leave she'd accumulated during years of ignoring vacation time and socking away sick days to come here. That two weeks was all that was left after the time taken for her mastectomy and then the chemo, which had knocked her for a loop despite her stubborn determination to pretend she was just fine. Her boss had grudgingly agreed to let her off, but he'd made it plain he wasn't one bit happy about the timing.

In less than twenty-four hours, she'd flown back to Florida, rented a car, driven for an hour, and then taken a ferry out to Seaview Key, a tiny island community of less than a thousand full-time residents just off Florida's west coast. Once there, she'd had to deal with traffic jams caused by winter tourists. All of which, given her current frame of mind, was trying, to say the least.

Worse, she had exactly fourteen days to convince her grandmother to sell the inn — which was also the family's longtime home — and move into a retirement community where she'd be well cared for. Since Grandma Jenny's parents had opened Seaview Inn when the island had been little more than a fishing village reached by boat, Hannah had a hunch her work was cut out for her. Her grandmother sometimes exhibited a tenacious streak of sentimentality that overrode common sense.

"I know it's only four o'clock, but we'll eat supper now," Grandma Jenny declared. "I missed lunch and I'm hungry. You can unpack your things later." She glanced at the suitcase Hannah had left at the bottom of the staircase that led up to the family's private quarters on the left and to the sprawling wing of guest rooms on the right. "Didn't bring much, did you? You having the rest of your things sent?"

Hannah stared at her blankly. "Why would

I do that?"

"Because you're moving home, of course." Jenny's tone was matter-of-fact. "I've told everyone in town who's been asking that we'd have the inn up and running again in another week or two, a month at the outside. While your mother was sick, we let a few things slide, but with the two of us working that should give us enough time to get things shipshape, don't you think so? There's still a couple of good months of the winter season left, and we'll draw some folks from the mainland in April and May. Of course, a lot of our regulars had to make other arrangements, but they'll be back with us next year, I'm sure."

There were so many things wrong with her grandmother's assumptions, Hannah couldn't decide where to start. It didn't matter, anyway, because Grandma Jenny hadn't waited for a reply. She was already heading toward the kitchen at a clip that belied the reported evidence of her declining health. In fact, Hannah very much suspected that Grandma Jenny would outlive her and do it with gusto.

All during their early supper of broiled snapper and fresh tomatoes and strawberries from the local farmer's market,

Grandma Jenny continued to bombard Hannah with her plans for reopening Seaview Inn as quickly as possible. She was as alert and strong-willed as ever.

"You can put that PR experience of yours to good use," she told Hannah. "Get some ads running up north. A lot of our regulars in Ohio and Michigan who come later in the season need to know our doors are open again. Maybe you can even do something on the Internet. I hear that's the best place to advertise these days. Or we can send postcards. I have the addresses for most of the customers who've stayed here in the past few years. Had 'em back to the beginning, but I figure those people are mostly dead and gone. What do you think?"

Hannah put down her fork and tried to find the right words to tell her grandmother that instead of spending time and money on advertising, they needed to be thinking about finding a good real estate agent. Then it occurred to her that a little renovating would give the place the kind of curb appeal needed to result in a quicker sale. Maybe she didn't have to discuss selling it just yet. She could wage that battle another day, when she wasn't quite so exhausted.

"I'll think about it," she said at last. "First thing tomorrow, you and I can take a look and see what needs to be done, okay?"

"Why wait?" Gran said, bouncing up, her eyes sparkling with enthusiasm. "Daylight might be scarce at the end of January, but we've got an hour or so till the sun goes down. We can check out the exterior first. I've been thinking a new coat of paint should be the first order of business, something bright and cheerful, maybe a nice turquoise with white trim."

Hannah winced, envisioning a garish result that would rob the inn of whatever tiny scrap of class it had.

"Well, come on," her grandmother called back. "Daylight's wasting."

With a sigh, Hannah followed her outside.

Over the years, the inn had grown from the original sprawling, two-story beach house that had been built in the thirties as a private home. Because of its size and her great-grandparents' enthusiasm for meeting people, they'd opened their spare rooms to paying guests. That first experimental season had been so successful, they'd officially named it Seaview Inn and expanded over the next few years, adding one section in the early forties, another in the fifties, operating much like the bed-and-breakfasts that had come along later.

Unfortunately, there hadn't been much

attention to architectural detail in the additions. Wings jutted out haphazardly, one on each side, angled so that the guest rooms on the right and the big formal dining room on the left, with its soaring windows and hodgepodge collection of antique tables and chairs, and the second-floor family quarters all had a view of the beach across the road. To Hannah's disapproving eye, it looked like a cross between a halfway decent home and a seedy motel. It would take more than a coat of paint, no matter the color, to fix it.

Her favorite part was the porch, which stretched across the front of the original house with a row of white rockers and a collection of antique wicker chairs with fading flowered cushions. In past years there had been hanging baskets of flowers, but this year neither her mother nor grandmother had had the time or energy to spare on such things.

As a child, Hannah had had tea parties with all her dolls on the porch. Sometimes her mom and her grandmother had joined her. Those afternoons had been the best. Later, as a teenager, the porch had been a place for sharing dreams and plans with her friends over sodas and snacks. Eventually her first kiss had been in the shadows on the porch.

Now, bathed in the light of a spectacular sunset, the inn didn't look as bad as it had at first glance. She could almost see its idiosyncratic charm and understand why her grandmother wanted to keep it open and in the family. The problem was that Grandma Jenny couldn't possibly do it alone and there was no one in the family to help her. Hannah didn't want to leave New York, especially with her team of physicians there, to say nothing of the demanding career she loved. Her twenty-year-old daughter, Kelsey, would probably wind up staying in California once she completed her studies at Stanford. Why keep the inn now, only to sell it to strangers in a few years, anyway? Her grandmother deserved to enjoy whatever years were left to her, not to spend them working her fingers to the bone waiting on strangers.

Hannah turned and caught her grandmother eyeing her speculatively.

"It's a good time of day, isn't it?" Grandma Jenny said quietly, her expression nostalgic. "Your grandfather and I spent many an evening out here watching the sunset with music drifting out the downstairs windows. And before that, my parents would spend their evenings doing the same thing. We didn't sit inside and stare at a TV screen the way folks do today. We talked, getting to know the people who stayed here. We enjoyed the beauty God gave us in this place." Her gaze met Hannah's. "You loved it, too, once. Do you remember that? There were nights we could hardly drag you home from the beach."

Suddenly Hannah remembered being maybe five or six and working all day on a sand castle, then being called inside. The next morning she'd rushed across the road to see her handiwork, only to discover that the tide had washed it away overnight. It had been her first hard lesson in the fact that some things simply didn't last, no matter how well built and solid they seemed. Sometimes it was the foundation that mattered, not the structure, and sand had a way of shifting underfoot, much as her own parents' marriage had crumbled a few years later.

As the years had passed and she'd developed more insights, there'd been little question in her mind that after the divorce her mother had felt trapped here by circumstances. What else could she do with a daughter not yet in her teens and no work experience beyond the family inn?

"I remember," she said at last, but it was said in a faintly bitter tone that drew a sharp glance from her grandmother.

"There *were* good times, Hannah, whether you choose to remember them that way or not."

"I wonder if Mom felt that way after Dad left. Wasn't there a time in her life when she dreamed of going away and doing something else? He got to run away from her and from all of his responsibilities, but she was stuck."

"What are you suggesting?" her grandmother asked indignantly. "That I kept her here when she wanted to go? Nothing could be further from the truth. She loved it here. She knew it was the best place to raise a child, surrounded by family and friends."

"Dad obviously didn't love it," Hannah said.

"Oh, Hannah, that's not so. Surely by now you've learned that relationships are complicated. Your parents were happy for a time, and then they weren't. It had nothing to do with Seaview Key or the inn."

Hannah didn't waste her breath trying to argue. How could she? She'd been so young, just on the verge of adolescence. It was entirely possible that she'd been totally oblivious to whatever rifts there had been in her parents' marriage. She relented now just to keep peace. "I suppose."

Her grandmother's shoulders seemed to sag. "I need to sit down," she said flatly, clutching the railing tightly as she climbed the steps to the porch. She sank into her favorite rocker as the sun slowly slid into the waters of the Gulf of Mexico, leaving the sky painted with streaks of orange and gold.

"Gran, are you okay?"

"Just a little tired. You go on in, if you want. Get yourself settled. I'll just sit here for a while and enjoy the evening. Leave the dishes. I'll do them when I come inside. Won't take any time at all."

"But we haven't even started the list of renovations you want to do," Hannah protested, feeling vaguely guilty for dampening her grandmother's high spirits.

"You said it yourself. Tomorrow's soon enough."

Oddly reluctant to go inside and leave her grandmother alone, Hannah stood in the doorway for a few minutes.

As twilight fell and a breeze stirred, the streetlight on the corner came on, illuminating the porch and yard. That was when Hannah noticed the tears glistening on her grandmother's cheeks.

"Mom, what on earth are you doing in

Florida?" Kelsey demanded when she called Hannah's cell phone later that night and woke Hannah out of a sound sleep. "I called your office earlier and your secretary told me you'd taken time off again to go to Seaview. I've been trying to call all day, but you must have had your phone turned off. When you didn't return my calls, I got worried. Is Grandma Jenny okay?"

Hannah sat on the side of the bed, almost regretting that she'd remembered to turn the phone back on before going to sleep. There had been five increasingly impatient messages from her boss and three from Kelsey. For once, she'd ignored them all, grateful that it was too late to call the office and deciding she really didn't want to discuss this situation with Kelsey just yet. Now she had no choice.

"You mean besides her delusion that I'm going to give up my career and move back here to run the inn?" she replied.

"Oh, boy," Kelsey muttered. "Is she serious?"

"She spent an hour at dinner talking about how we need to spruce this place up and get it open again in two weeks," Hannah said. "I'd say she's serious."

"But you're not going to do it, are you? You hate Seaview Key and the inn."

"Of course I'm not going to do it," Hannah said emphatically, then sighed. "Actually, I was thinking it might be a good idea to do a few renovations."

"But why, if she's not going to open the inn? You know she can't manage it alone."

Hannah hesitated. "I know," she said at last.

Kelsey sucked in a breath. "You want her to sell it, don't you? Mom, that will break her heart. You can't do that to her."

"What choice do I have?" Hannah asked defensively.

"None, I suppose," Kelsey admitted, "but I hate this, Mom."

"I know. So do I, but I can't stay here. I just haven't figured out how I'm going to explain that to your great-grandmother. You know how she is once she gets an idea into her head."

"A lot like you," Kelsey said.

"Yes, well, that is the problem, isn't it?" she said wryly. Suddenly it occurred to her that there had to be a crisis of some kind for Kelsey to be calling from college in the middle of the week. "Enough about what's going on here. I'll figure out something. Tell me what's up with you."

Kelsey hesitated. "Maybe this isn't a good time. We can talk about it when you're back in New York after you get things straightened out down there."

A sense of dread settled in the pit of Hannah's stomach. "Isn't a good time for what?" she prodded.

"You're sure you don't want to wait and talk about this another time?" Kelsey asked, sounding oddly hopeful.

"Now," Hannah commanded.

"Okay, then. Remember how I told you at Christmas that school pretty much sucks?"

"And I said you were just going through a rough patch," Hannah recalled.

"Well, it's more than a rough patch, Mom. Don't freak out, okay? I've really thought about this and it's what I need to do right now. I've decided to quit college, come home to New York and get a job."

Hannah's grip on the cell phone tightened. "In your junior year?" she said, her voice rising despite her best attempt to remain calm. "Are you crazy?"

"I knew you wouldn't understand," Kelsey said petulantly, sounding like a spoiled child rather than the responsible young adult she normally was.

"No, I don't understand. And unless you've got an explanation that includes full-time employment several steps above flipping burgers, I'm not likely to understand.

We had a deal. If I went into debt to get you into Stanford, the school of your dreams, you would stick it out and get your degree in graphic design, no matter what. Remember that?"

"I remember," Kelsey said meekly. "But, Mom —"

Hannah cut her off. "No, there is no *but, Mom.* You got into Stanford. I've paid for three years at Stanford, and you are finishing at Stanford. Period. You don't get to back out of the deal now."

"I can't stay here."

Years ago, after her divorce, Hannah had learned the value of being stern and unyielding. Otherwise, even as a toddler, her strong-willed daughter would have run roughshod over her. She called on that skill now.

"Of course, you can stay. If your courses are too hard, if that's what this is about, you can consider dropping one of them, but you're not dropping out, and that's final." She told herself all her daughter needed was a pep talk. She'd probably gotten something below an A on a pop quiz and decided she was heading for failure. "Come on, kiddo. You can do this. You're smart. You're more than halfway to getting your bachelor's degree. You just need to park your butt in the library and do whatever amount of studying it takes to get out of there next year with a degree."

"You don't understand," Kelsey said.

"Of course I do, sweetie. We all hit bumps in the road from time to time. We can't let them throw us off course."

"Mom, this isn't that kind of bump in the road. I'm pregnant," Kelsey blurted.

If Hannah hadn't already been sitting down, she would have fainted dead away and probably cracked open her skull when she hit the floor. Apparently things *could* get worse. And now she knew how.

2

Hannah had a splitting headache by the time she finally made her way downstairs to the kitchen in the morning. She'd replayed the conversation with Kelsey in her head over and over for the rest of the night, but not even her best editing skills could change the fact that her daughter was going to have a baby.

Grandma Jenny looked up as she entered the kitchen. "I thought you were going to sleep the day away," she commented, then took a closer look. "You don't look so good. Are you sick?"

Sick at heart, Hannah thought, but she kept it to herself. There'd be time enough to tell her grandmother what was going on after Kelsey arrived in the next day or two, as soon as she could get a flight from California. Hannah had made her promise not to make any big decisions or do anything drastic until they had more time to talk things through.

"I didn't sleep much," she told her grandmother. "A cup of coffee should perk me up, though."

"Good. Then we can get started with that list. I've got some help lined up, so we need to get ourselves organized."

The pounding in Hannah's head took on a more urgent beat. "As soon as I've returned a few calls from my boss," she promised, searching in a cupboard until she found a bottle of aspirin. She popped two of them. "He left a bunch of messages for me yesterday and I didn't get them until it was too late to call back last night."

A frown settled on Grandma Jenny's face. "Why's he bothering you? I thought you were quitting that job."

"No, Gran, I didn't quit," Hannah explained patiently. "I'm just on vacation for a couple of weeks."

"Well, you should give it up for good. This is where you belong. You'd be your own boss here."

No, Hannah thought, she'd be answering to her grandmother, and as annoying as Dave Harrow could be from time to time, he was easier to deal with than Gran.

"Let's not go there right now, okay?" Hannah pleaded. "I'm here for a couple of weeks and that's it."

Her grandmother waved off the explanation as if it were of no consequence. "But you're still down here on your own time, am I right? Your boss shouldn't be taking advantage of you like this. Anyone who works as hard as you do deserves to have a vacation that's really a vacation. A boss who appreciates you would know that."

"He's not really taking advantage of me, Gran. I left without much notice. There are a lot of loose ends that need to be tied up. Look, the call shouldn't take long. You start on that list of renovations and we'll go over it when I come back inside. I can get better cell phone reception on the porch."

"Well, you'd best hurry. Some of the things we're going to need aren't available on the island. We'll need to catch the eleven o'clock ferry if we expect to go to the mainland today."

Hannah grimaced. That was yet another reason not to live in Seaview. It was too inconvenient. If they missed the eleven o'clock ferry, there wouldn't be another one until four-thirty, too late to head over to the mainland to shop. In all there were only four ferries daily, these two, plus one that left at 6:00 a.m., mostly for people who worked on the mainland, and a final one at eight, which catered mostly to those who'd taken a day trip to Seaview Key, stayed for dinner and then wanted to head back.

"I'll hurry," she promised.

She took her cell phone and coffee out to the porch, choosing a comfortable wicker chair at the far end where the sun had created a pool of warmth on the chilly morning. She took a long sip of coffee, then turned her face up to the sun, wishing she didn't have to make the call. It wasn't going to go well. Dave hadn't been happy about her asking for this unplanned vacation, especially after all the months when her schedule had been totally unpredictable because of her chemo treatments.

Reluctantly, she dialed the direct line to his office. "Hey, Melinda, it's Hannah. Dave was trying to reach me yesterday, but I was traveling and had my phone off. Is he available now?"

"Yes," his secretary said, then lowered her voice. "But I should tell you he's on the warpath. Even though you briefed Carl before you left about the deadlines for the Parker account, he blew the very first one and Dave caught the fallout. Ron Parker was furious."

Hannah muttered a few choice words. Carl Mason was useless, but Dave kept giving him second chances. He'd insisted that Hannah turn her accounts over to him while she was away. It was his fault that things had gone wrong, but she was going to have to bail them all out.

"Look, don't put me through now. I'm going to call Ron and see if I can smooth things over. Then I'll call back to speak to Dave."

"Sure, hon," Melinda said, but before they could sever the connection Hannah heard Dave in the background.

"Is that Hannah? Put her through right this minute," he commanded.

"Sorry," Melinda murmured.

"Not your fault." She waited for Dave to pick up, then tried to do a preemptive strike. "Melinda filled me in on the problems with the Parker account. I was about to call Ron myself."

"There wouldn't be a problem with that account if you'd been handling it yourself," he grumbled.

Hannah barely resisted the urge to correct him and say there wouldn't have been a problem if Dave had assigned someone competent to fill in for her. She'd have been wasting her breath.

"Ron's not going to be pacified with a phone call," he told her. "You need to get back up here and do your job."

"You know I can't do that. There's a family crisis and I need to handle it."

"You've had a lot of crises lately," Dave said. "Maybe this job isn't as important to you as it once was."

Hannah gasped at his insensitivity. "Do you honestly think I chose to have breast cancer just so I could inconvenience you? Do you think I wanted my mom to die or my grandmother to have difficulty coping with that, so I could take more time off?"

He backed down at once. "I'm sorry. I shouldn't have phrased it that way. I know you've been through hell, but you're the best person on this team. When you're out of the office, it has an impact."

"Nice save," she said dryly. "Look, it's only for a couple of weeks. I gave Carl notes on every single thing that needs to be done, along with the deadlines. Maybe you need to look over his shoulder for the next couple of weeks and make sure he follows through. If that doesn't work, then I'm not the one to blame."

Dave sighed. "I know he's not pulling his weight around here. That's why I assigned him to work with you. I thought maybe your organizational skills would rub off on him."

"You always were a dreamer," she said

lightly. It was one of the reasons they'd always worked well together. She'd been his first hire after he and Lou Morgan had opened the firm fifteen years ago. He was a genius when it came to thinking up unique PR campaigns for their clients, but Hannah was the one who kept the projects on schedule, pacified nervous actors and authors and contributed her own share of creative ideas. He also counted on her not to mince words, so she didn't now. "Dave, you've given Carl more than enough chances. Maybe it's time to think about cutting your losses and letting him go. Get someone in that position who can cut it."

"You're probably right," he admitted with obvious reluctance. "If I hadn't promised my wife that I'd give the guy a break, I'd have fired him months ago. He's her nephew and she adores him. Do you know the kind of grief I'm going to get if I let him go?"

"Compare that to the grief you're already taking from clients like Ron Parker," she said. "Look, I'll call Ron now and fix this mess, but there can't be a next time, Dave. You know that."

"Yeah, I know it. Hurry back, okay?"

"Two weeks," she reminded him. "You'll hardly notice I'm gone."

"That's a joke. You weren't out the door

two minutes when we had our first crisis."

"Careful," she warned. "I'll start to think I'm indispensable and you'll have to give me a raise."

She hung up slowly, then spent several minutes tamping down her annoyance over Carl's screwup before calling Ron Parker and apologizing profusely. Fortunately, he was a reasonable guy, and the promise of a few perks on his next PR campaign calmed him down.

"I'm sorry Dave bothered you on your vacation," he told her. "I was still angry when I spoke to him, so I was blowing off steam. I was never going to take my business elsewhere. You're the best, Hannah. So is Dave."

"And we love working with you. We'll get together for lunch as soon as I'm back in town. You pick the place and it's on me."

"It ought to be on that idiot Carl Mason," he said. "Enjoy your vacation and don't worry about any of this, okay?"

"Thanks for understanding."

When she finally got off the phone, she felt drained. Her head was still pounding, though the caffeine and aspirin were starting to kick in. One more cup of coffee and she might be able to cope with Grandma Jenny and whatever she had in store to destroy her peace of mind today.

"I don't understand why you're going to Florida," Jeff told Kelsey as she packed her suitcase. "This is no time to go running off when we have so many things that need to be settled."

"Things *are* settled, Jeff. No matter what you say, I am not going to marry you, and that's final."

"But we're having a baby!" he said, as if she needed reminding.

"I'm the one having it," she retorted. "Not you. I'm the one whose entire life has to go on hold because we were stupid one night and had sex without a condom."

Jeff paled. "And that's my fault. I accept that. It was stupid, but no matter how many times I say I'm sorry, it won't change anything. Now we have to deal with where we are. I love you. I want to marry you. I want us to be a family. I wanted that before you got pregnant and I want it now."

"And I've told you that I'm not ready to get married," she said.

They'd been arguing like this for two solid weeks now, ever since she'd seen a doctor and told Jeff about the baby. Sometimes she wished she'd kept the news to herself, but she'd known how unfair that would be.

What she hadn't realized was how pressured she'd feel now that Jeff wanted to do what he saw as the right thing.

For him, the baby was only a tiny blip on a road he'd apparently mapped out when they'd first started dating last year. For her it changed everything. It took away her options and backed her into a corner. It wasn't that she didn't love him or that she didn't envision them having a future together . . . eventually. It was about being forced into making a premature decision, one far too important to be made in haste.

She was a child of divorce, and while her mother had done everything in her power to see that Kelsey never wanted for anything, Kelsey had never stopped wishing that she'd come from a two-parent home. She and her dad barely had any relationship at all beyond an occasional check at Christmas or for her birthday and even rarer phone calls. In the beginning she'd seen him at least occasionally, but then he'd remarried, had more kids and the kind of family life she'd always wanted.

Now, here she was, willing to deny her own child what she'd missed most during her own childhood. She understood the irony in that, but so far she hadn't been able to talk herself into backing down. She was convinced that if she rushed into marriage with Jeff because of the baby, they'd never have a real chance to make it work. She doubted she'd be able to hide her resentment, and that would poison their relationship.

Sighing, she sat down on the edge of the bed and pulled Jeff down beside her. Sitting thigh to thigh, even under these circumstances, she could feel the chemistry between them, chemistry that had been there from the time they'd first met. He wasn't like the preppy guys she'd always dated. He was offbeat, a little bit of a nerd. His dark brown hair was almost always in need of a cut, not out of rebellion, but simply because he forgot about it.

It was his eyes, though, that had drawn her in. They were like melted chocolate, and when they were focused on her, their intensity made her pulse scramble.

His wardrobe, while not totally atypical of that of all the kids around them, was a horror — faded jeans, T-shirts and ancient sneakers. It offended Kelsey's fashion sense, developed by associating with some of her mom's designer clients, but she'd seen beyond the clothes to the really good person he was. Only after they'd been dating for months had she learned that he was from a wealthy San Francisco family and that he was somewhat of a computer genius, who'd already amassed a small fortune himself with software he'd designed.

Sitting beside him now, she stared straight ahead, afraid that if she looked into his eyes, she'd give in and agree to marry him. It was the simplest solution to her predicament, but one she was determined to resist.

"You know that I'm not saying no because I don't love you, right?" she asked softly.

"You're saying no because you're stubborn," he countered. "We've been talking about marriage for months now. All this changes is the timetable."

"Exactly. We had that timetable for a reason. I wanted to graduate, to get established in a career before we took the next step in our relationship. I wanted to figure out who I am."

"I already know who you are, but I suppose that doesn't count," Jeff countered. "But you can still do all that. We'll hire a nanny. Or I'll take care of the baby while you're in school."

"You have classes, too," she reminded him.

He regarded her with an impatient expression. "Come on, Kelsey, we've been over this. I get what you're saying and why you're scared, but nothing has to change. If we didn't have a cent to our names, maybe there would be sacrifices, but trust me, we can afford a place to live and all the help we need. You'll have all the time and space you want to decide who you are and figure out what you want. In fact, it'll be easier because you won't be forced to take some nothing job just to pay bills. You can take your time after graduation and find the perfect job."

She heard the sincerity in his voice and she wanted desperately to believe things would be that simple, but she just couldn't. First thing she knew, she'd be Mrs. Jeff Hampton, a wife and a mother. She was scared to death that Kelsey Matthews-Ryan would get lost.

She also knew her fears were compounded because for years she'd been so certain about what she wanted — a career in graphic design. But now that she'd been studying for the degree that would get her that career, now that she'd proved she could handle it, the path she'd chosen had lost some of its luster. She feared the same thing could happen if she rushed into marriage. Maybe it was morning sickness, maybe it was hormones, but her world had tilted on its axis and left her reeling. She simply couldn't cope with a decision as huge as getting married right now.

"I can't, Jeff. I can't do it."

"You'd rather quit school and run home to your mom?" he asked incredulously. "That doesn't make any sense at all. You're actually giving up the very thing you claim you want."

"Temporarily," she insisted. "I'll go back to school after the baby's born. Maybe by then I'll have figured out if graphic design is what I really want, after all. Why get a degree in something and then decide it's not what I'm passionate about?"

"Okay, let's say you do take time off," he said reasonably. "How will you manage college a year from now or two years from now, especially if you decide you want a degree in something else and have to practically start over?"

Kelsey frowned. "I don't know exactly, but I'll make it work."

"Look at me," he commanded. "Kelsey, look at me. You're not still thinking about adoption, are you? Because I won't go along with it. I want this baby, even if you don't."

There was an unyielding note in his voice she'd never heard before. Why, when it came to this, did he have to change from an easygoing, come-what-may kind of guy into one determined to have his own way?

Tears stung Kelsey's eyes. How had things

turned into such a mess? A few weeks ago, her life had been totally on track. She'd aced most of her final exams. She was excited about her new courses, even though she was starting to question her career goals. She was with a guy she adored. And now, because of one careless moment, everything was at risk.

"You should go," she told Jeff. "We're not going to settle this tonight and I'm leaving first thing in the morning."

"But you're coming back?" he asked. "You're not going to disappear and do something behind my back, are you?"

"I can't believe you asked me that," she said, surprisingly stung. "You know me better than anyone. I promised you I wouldn't do anything crazy and I meant it. I promised my mom the same thing."

"Did she buy it?" he asked.

Kelsey sighed. "Not entirely. Look, whatever decision I make, I will come back here and I will tell you. That's the best I can promise."

"I suppose I'll have to live with that," Jeff said, then met her gaze. "For now."

"What does that mean?"

"It means that I have a stake in this decision, too. You need time right now, I'll let you have it. But not too much time, Kelsey, or I'll follow you and do everything in my power to make you see this my way."

Kelsey looked deep into his eyes and saw the determination there. She realized that Jeff's powers of persuasion were what scared her most of all.

Hannah used the twenty-minute ferry ride to the mainland to finally broach the subject that had brought her to Seaview Key. The waters were calm, the breeze balmy by mid-morning as they made the crossing. She and her grandmother stood by the railing and watched as the mainland grew from a distant speck to an impressive skyline.

"Gran, have you ever thought about living on the mainland?" she began carefully.

"Why would I do that when I have a perfectly good home where I am?"

"You'd be surrounded by more people your own age," Hannah explained, injecting as much enthusiasm as she could into her voice. "You could get involved in more activities. You'd be closer to doctors and a major hospital. The clinic on Seaview Key isn't prepared to cope with anything more than a minor emergency."

"Do you honestly think I would ever move into one of those retirement communities?" she asked derisively. "That's what you're talking about, isn't it? Putting me out to pasture like some horse that's outlived its usefulness."

"Not at all," Hannah said, doing her best to remain upbeat. "I think it would be great to be able to do so many things anytime you wanted to without worrying about the ferry schedule. Plus, you've spent your whole life catering to other people's needs. It's time for you to think about *your* needs."

"I don't have many needs and I don't worry much about the ferry schedule," Grandma Jenny replied tartly. "I have it committed to memory. Besides, now that I don't drive much, it's been months since I've needed it at all. Anytime I need anything from the mainland, I can find someone to fetch it for me. I'm not like you. I don't need to be on the go all the time. I'm happy right where I am." She gave Hannah a hard look. "Intend to stay there, too, so don't go getting any ideas."

Hannah dropped the subject for now. She'd check online to locate the best facilities in the area and call for brochures. Maybe on their next trip to the mainland, she could persuade her grandmother to at least look at a couple of them.

"Any idea where you'd like to go for lunch?" she asked, changing the topic to something neutral. "I think we should eat first, then run all the errands."

"I like that cafeteria well enough."

Hannah bit back a groan. The last time she'd tried a slice of pie there, the whipped cream on top had the texture of plastic foam. "I suppose you're going to want the liver and onions," she teased, resigned to choking down a tasteless meal.

"Of course. I learned a long time ago that I'd be wasting my time fixing that for you. You'd gag every time I set it on the table."

"Which ought to tell you something," Hannah said. "But if that's what you want, that's where we'll go."

Her grandmother gave her a knowing look. "Don't think buttering me up is going to work, young lady. You can agree to everything I suggest from now till Christmas and I still won't look at one of those retirement places."

"Whatever," Hannah said, then had to bite back a smile the instant the word was out of her mouth. She'd sounded exactly like Kelsey at her most annoying. Apparently the universe was intent on reducing her to a petulant child again, too.

"What did Gran have you doing today?" Kelsey asked her that evening.

"Picking out paint and looking at fabric for the cushions on the porch," Hannah told her. "We managed to get the paint at the first place we looked, but we had to go to four different fabric stores before we found anything that satisfied her. I looked at so many flowered prints, I came home dizzy."

"Have you told her yet that you're not staying?"

"I have," she said. "That hasn't stopped her from trying to change my mind. Now, tell me about you. Were you able to get a reservation?"

"My flight's tomorrow," Kelsey confirmed, then gave her the details.

"And your return flight?" Hannah asked.

Kelsey hesitated. "I just bought a one-way ticket in case I decide not to come back right away."

"Kelsey!"

"It's no big deal, Mom. I can always book the return flight as soon as I get there. Who knows? Maybe you'll decide that you and Grandma Jenny can use an extra pair of hands."

Hannah saw no point in arguing. "I'll pick you up tomorrow, then. Have a safe flight, sweetie."

"I will. Mom?"

"Yes?"

"Is it hard being there, you know, without your mom?"

Hannah wasn't sure how to answer. If she stopped for a second and let herself think, she'd say it was incredibly difficult, which was one reason she'd let her grandmother persuade her to do all these renovations. It left little time for thinking, especially about her mother's losing battle with cancer. And she had yet to walk into the suite of rooms that had been her mom's. She'd spent too many hours in there right before she died.

"I don't think I've let myself focus on that at all," she admitted.

"How can you *not* think about it?" Kelsey asked. "She was so much a part of Seaview Inn. You must see her everywhere you look, like those old sand pails she collected. They looked like rusty junk to me, but she'd get all misty-eyed when she told me about how they reminded her of when she was a girl."

Hannah choked back an unexpected sob. She could recall her mother's excitement every time she came across one of the tin litho sand pails with their colorful images in one of the antique shops she haunted. Her eyes would light up as if she'd just recaptured a hundred old memories, all good ones. Hannah had deliberately avoided looking at the shelves that held the prized collection. Only now did she see how much of the past two days she'd spent in denial.

"She loved them, all right," she said, when she could speak again.

"Oh, Mom, are you crying? I'm sorry. I didn't mean to make you sad."

"I think I've just been pretending since I got here that everything was normal, that she was just away on a trip or something. I haven't wanted to deal with the reality that she's gone forever."

"Maybe having me there will be a good thing, then, huh?" Kelsey said. "I can distract you."

"Given the reason you're coming, I'd say that's a sure thing," Hannah said wryly. "See you tomorrow afternoon."

"Bye, Mom. Love you."

"I love you, too," she said slowly, and disconnected, only to have the phone immediately ring again. She was tempted not to answer it, but given the work crisis she'd missed yesterday, she didn't want to risk another lecture from Dave about her inopportune absence. Glancing at the caller ID, though, she saw that it wasn't Dave at all, but Sue Nelson, who'd been her best friend since Hannah had arrived in New York nearly twenty years ago.

"I want to know why I had to find out

from your secretary that you've skipped town again," Sue demanded when Hannah answered.

"Sorry. The trip came together pretty suddenly."

"Jane said your grandmother was having a hard time coping without your mom. Is that why you went?"

"Pretty much. I'm hoping to convince her to sell the inn and move to a retirement community."

Sue chuckled. She'd met Grandma Jenny and could imagine her reaction. "And how's that going?" she asked.

Hannah laughed with her. "About like you'd expect. I didn't even get the words out of my mouth before she was warning me off in no uncertain terms."

"Then why aren't you heading home? I'd think being there right now would be really hard. Besides, don't you have a three-month cancer screening coming up?"

"I postponed it."

"Hannah!" Sue protested. "You can't do things like that. This is too important."

"Don't overreact. I only postponed it a couple of weeks. I'll go in the day after I get back to New York."

"Can I get that in writing? I know you're dreading it."

"Well, of course, I'm dreading it, but I'm not stupid. I know I can't put it off indefinitely."

"What's the new date?"

"Why? Do you think I'm lying?"

"I wouldn't put it past you, but that's not why I'm asking. I want to put it on my calendar, so I can go with you. I told you when you first got diagnosed that you're not going through any of this alone."

Hannah's eyes stung for the second time that night. "You've been wonderful and I will never be able to thank you enough," she said. "But you've spent enough of your time babysitting me through surgery and chemo. I can go to one appointment on my own."

"But why should you have to?" Sue asked. "Especially when we can go out afterward and splurge on an outrageously expensive dinner to celebrate that you're just fine."

"Hush. Don't say things like that. It's just asking for something to go wrong."

"I thought you weren't superstitious," Sue teased.

Hannah thought about how recent events had conspired to make her question that. "I'm reexamining my beliefs on that subject."

"Oh?"

"Long story, and you and John must be about to have dinner."

"He won't mind waiting for a few minutes," Sue said. "Tell me why you're suddenly leery of black cats and walking under ladders."

"It's not about cats and ladders," Hannah told her. "But trust me, bad things do come in threes." She paused, then announced, "Kelsey's pregnant."

"Oh, my God, you're kidding!"

"Not something I'd kid about," Hannah said.

"No, I don't suppose you would. When did she tell you?"

"Last night."

"How did you react?"

"You know me. I'm a control freak. I ordered her to come down here before making any decisions. I need to see her. I want to see for myself that she's okay."

"And she's coming?"

"Tomorrow," Hannah confirmed.

"Okay, now tell me how you're really feeling."

"I'm mostly numb, to be perfectly honest," Hannah replied. "I never expected this."

"I doubt mothers ever do, unless their daughters are wild ones, which Kelsey definitely is not," Sue said. "Is Kelsey okay or is she totally freaking out?"

"She sounded calm, but I know she's falling apart. She's definitely not thinking clearly. Right now her solution is to quit college and move back to New York with me."

"Oh, boy! I'm amazed I didn't hear your reaction to that all the way up here."

"So am I," Hannah said.

"Anything I can do?"

"Just knowing you're there when I need to talk is enough," Hannah told her.

"I could fly down there and mediate, if it would help," she offered.

"I'd have to give you combat pay," Hannah joked. "No, I'll muddle through this. Just start shaking the martinis the second I get back to New York."

"You've got it, and the minute you decide you need anything more, all you have to do is call."

"Thanks, Sue. I don't know what I'd do without you."

"Thick and thin, that was our deal all those years ago," Sue reminded her, then added dryly, "Too bad some of my marriage vows didn't last the way our friendship has."

"Only because you had extraordinarily bad taste in men before you met John. He's a keeper."

"Yeah, I think so, too, which means I'd better get in there and feed him. We miss you, sweetie. Hurry home."

"Thanks for calling."

Hannah disconnected the call with a smile on her face. She had other friends in New York, including Dave and his wife, and plenty of acquaintances, but Sue Dyer Martinelli Nelson was the best. If Hannah had said she needed her in Florida, Sue would have been here by morning, no questions asked. Knowing that was almost as comforting as it would have been to be sitting on the porch with her right now, a shaker of martinis between them.

3

The Seaview Inn looked like hell. Luke Stevens hadn't seen the place for twenty years and it was showing every one of those years with its fading paint, untended lawn, and half a dozen posts missing from the railing that wound around the sprawling front porch. In fact, it looked a lot like he felt, as if it had been tossed aside, a victim of neglect.

If the assessment of his life sounded bitter, he figured he had a right. Like too many other men returning from Iraq to find their old lives in tatters, he'd spent months in a rehab hospital in Washington, then faced the fact that going back to the life he'd left in Atlanta wasn't an option. His wife had filed for divorce two weeks before a car bomb had shattered his leg. The doctors had saved his leg, for which he'd be eternally grateful. Even so, he was a long way from being able to stand in an operating room doing the kind of orthopedic surgery that had been his specialty before he'd come out of military retirement and answered the army's call for doctors. Yeah, he was bitter and not one bit apologetic about it.

Sitting in a wheelchair during his recovery, staring out at the snow that had blanketed Washington one January morning a couple of weeks back, he'd suddenly had a yearning for the sunshine and palm trees he hadn't seen since leaving Seaview Key for college more than twenty years ago. Though his family had moved away from the island to live with his sister in Arizona, Seaview had continued to have a special place in his heart. It was home. It was where he'd fallen in love for the first time, where he'd learned to fish and swim, where he'd volunteered with the local rescue squad and discovered his passion for medicine. It was, he'd decided, the perfect place to heal.

There were no memories of Lisa, his soon-to-be-ex-wife, in Seaview, no images of his kids on the stretch of white sand there. After being gone for so long, he could only hope that no one there would remember him all that well. Most of the kids in his class had fled, chasing dreams of more excitement than the tiny town could offer. If he was right about that, there would be no pitying looks to bear, no questions to be answered, just the peace and quiet he craved while he figured out what to do with the rest of his life.

Twenty years ago, there had been only one place to stay on the island, Seaview Inn, a sprawling bed-and-breakfast run for three generations by the Matthews family. Hannah had been in his class, and like the rest of them, she'd been eager to flee. He had an image of a quiet, studious girl whose face lit up when she laughed, which was all too seldom. She'd been best friends with Abby Dawson, his first love, so they'd spent a lot of time on the inn's front porch, rocking for hours and talking about the future while sea breezes stirred the palm trees and stars sparkled like diamond chips scattered across black velvet.

He shook his head, struck by how simple life had been back then. His biggest problem had been trying to figure out how to rid Abby of her bra without getting slapped. He'd finally mastered the technique by the end of summer. He grinned as he thought of how well that skill had served him in college.

Once they'd all left for college, though, distance had taken its toll, and they'd lost touch. He'd met Lisa and stepped into his future, Seaview Key all but forgotten until recently.

With one call to Information, he'd found the number for the inn, but it had taken him days to get through to anyone. He'd found it odd and discouraging that there didn't even seem to be an answering machine, but he'd persisted just the same, unwilling to give up on the only plan that had appealed to him in months.

When the phone had finally been answered, it was by a woman who sounded ancient and annoyed. "What do you want?" she'd demanded without so much as a pleasant hello.

"Is this Seaview Inn?"

"That's the number you dialed, isn't it?"

He'd grinned despite her tone. Clearly old Jenny Matthews was having a bad day. He could relate.

"It certainly is," he agreed. "I was hoping to reserve a room."

"We're closed."

Luke decided to try another approach. "Mrs. Matthews, this is Luke Stevens. I don't know if you remember me —"

"My mind's not gone yet," she snapped. "Of course, I remember you. You're Mark and Stella's boy. Used to hang around here with that Dawson girl. She was all wrong for you, by the way. I sure as heck hope you had the good sense not to marry her."

"I don't know how much good sense was involved, but we didn't get married," he said, impressed by her memory.

"Good. Last I heard she was working in some bar up in Pensacola and hanging out with a rowdy crowd. Bikers, I suspect."

Luke chuckled despite himself. The last *he'd* heard, Abby had owned a restaurant in Pensacola and been married to a minister. He saw no need to debate the point with Mrs. Matthews. There would be plenty of time to settle the matter when he saw her.

"You said you're closed right now," he said, trying to get back to the point. "How soon will you be reopening?"

"That depends on Hannah."

Luke didn't even try to hide his surprise. "Hannah's still in Seaview?"

"No, Hannah's in New York, but I'm working on that. Once I get her back here, I figure I can convince her to stay. After that it'll take a couple of weeks to whip this place into shape for guests."

"I could help with that," he offered. "I don't know what you need, but I can manage some odd jobs for you."

"Not if you're a guest, you can't," she responded, sounding scandalized.

"I don't mind. It'll be good to do something useful. If you feel strongly about it, you can give me a break on your rates. I hope to be there for a few weeks at least."

She was silent for so long, he thought she was going to refuse, but then she asked, "When would you be coming?"

"The first week of February, if that would be okay with you," he said.

"Perfect," she muttered, more to herself than him. "Okay, Luke Stevens, you have yourself a deal and a reservation. You might have a fight on your hands with Hannah, but I imagine you'll be able to handle her. Goodbye."

She'd left him openmouthed then, just as the sight of the Seaview Inn had him openmouthed now. Apparently he'd been overly optimistic about just how idyllic this trip down memory lane was going to be.

Luke knocked on the front door of the inn, but when no one answered, he stepped inside and called out. "Mrs. Matthews, it's me, Luke Stevens. Are you home?"

He heard a door to his left bang open and then Jenny Matthews came bustling out of the kitchen and across the dining room, drying her hands on a dish towel.

"You're early," she said, making it sound

like an accusation. "I thought you weren't coming for another week."

"I was able to get away sooner than I expected. Since you mentioned having work to do around here, I figured the sooner I was here to help, the better. Is it okay?"

She looked troubled, but then shook her head. "Don't worry about it. I just haven't had a chance to explain this to Hannah." She shrugged, then gave him a rueful look. "Well, she'll get used to the idea soon enough, I expect. Let me show you to your room."

"You don't need to do that," he said, worried about her ability to negotiate all those stairs. "Just point me in the right direction. I can manage."

"Okay, then. I'll get you a key and you can take your things upstairs. Less running up and down I do, the better I like it." She went to a small desk in the foyer, pulled a key from the drawer and handed it to him. "Since there's no one else staying here right now, I'm giving you the room on the end. It has more space and the best view. Has a real nice bathroom, too. Hannah's mother talked me into putting one of those Jacuzzi things in there. Said we could double the price if we did that."

Luke thought of how wonderful that

would be for his bad leg, which still ached like the devil when he stayed on his feet too long or tried to walk too far. He couldn't seem to stop himself from testing his limits, though. Being incapacitated and less than his physical best bothered him more than he liked to admit. Being strong and athletic was as much a part of his identity as being a doctor.

"Thanks," he said. "I appreciate it."

"I dusted in there myself just yesterday. There should be plenty of clean towels, but if there's anything you need, let me know when you come back down. I'll fix some lunch for you. You can eat out on the porch, if you like. I imagine you'll find that more pleasant than sitting in the dining room all alone. Won't be fancy, but it'll be filling. Tuna sandwich, home-baked cookies and lemonade. How does that sound?"

"Perfect." He remembered her baking with the affection of a teenage boy for whom chocolate-chip cookies had been only a couple of rungs below stealing kisses on his list of favorite things.

"Will a half hour give you enough time to get settled?" she asked.

"More than enough. Thanks, Mrs. Matthews."

"If you're going to be staying here awhile,

you might's well call me Grandma Jenny."

"I'll do that, then," he said, and impulsively gave her a quick kiss on her cheek. "Thanks for taking me in."

"Oh, you'll earn your keep soon enough," she assured him. "Now, hurry along. You need to be settled before Hannah gets back."

He regarded her suspiciously. "Why is that?"

"Trust me, it's just better that way."

"You think she's going to want to kick me out, don't you?"

"Oh, I expect so," she said nonchalantly. "But don't worry too much about that, Luke. Despite what she thinks, I still have some say around this place. She hasn't sold it out from under me yet."

"Hannah wants to sell Seaview Inn?" he asked, astonished. "Why?"

"Because I'm old and she doesn't want to be bothered with it," she said succinctly. "I'd say that sums it up. Oh, she thinks I don't know exactly what she's up to, but I can read all the signs."

Luke didn't begin to understand the dynamics at work here, but he did know one thing. People shouldn't be forced into doing something just for someone else's convenience. He'd treated enough elderly patients with hip fractures to understand how many of them wound up leaving homes they loved because it put their children's consciences at ease.

Until he knew more about this situation, though, he needed to keep his opinions to himself. It would be wrong to leap to Grandma Jenny's side before he knew all the facts, as well as heard Hannah's perspective.

"Well, there's plenty of time to figure all of this out, I'm sure," he told her. "At least you and Hannah are agreed on fixing this place up, so as soon as I've had some lunch, you can put me to work."

"You're eager. I like that," she said approvingly. "Now, run along. Your lunch will be waiting on the porch as soon as you're ready."

"Will you and Hannah be joining me?"

"Not me. I have things to do," she said, looking vaguely guilty.

"And Hannah?"

"She's taking a walk on the beach. No telling when she'll be back."

Luke got it then. Grandma Jenny didn't want to be anywhere in sight when Hannah discovered that he'd taken up residence at the inn.

"You're a very sneaky woman, aren't

you?" he said, delighted by her spunk.

She grinned at him. "I have my moments."

Luke had a feeling that coming here was about to take some very interesting twists. Oddly enough, the prospect of a few fireworks intrigued him.

The salt air and cool waters of the Gulf of Mexico usually worked their magic on Hannah, but today it was going to take a lot more than a walk on the beach to settle her chaotic thoughts. Though she loved her daughter dearly and was anxious to see her this afternoon, she was dreading the battle to come over college.

Oh, who was she kidding? The real issue wasn't whether or not Kelsey remained at Stanford, but what she was going to do about the baby. Her daughter was *pregnant!* The thought still boggled her mind, at least when it didn't make her angry. Of all the careless, irresponsible things Kelsey might have done, this was one that Hannah had never even considered.

Sure, college kids in lust took chances, made mistakes, but Kelsey had always had a rigid, almost puritanical set of values. They'd talked about sex being best in a committed relationship. They'd talked about precautions, just in case a situation got out of hand. Dammit, it was the one subject about which they'd always been on the same page!

As close as she and Kelsey were, Hannah thought she knew everything there was to know about her daughter's life at school. She'd never mentioned any special young man, not even in answer to Hannah's direct questions about her social life.

"Sure, I go out, Mom, but it's nothing serious."

Hannah could recall her precise words. Well, she'd call a boy responsible for an unplanned pregnancy serious enough to qualify for a mention.

Spilt milk, she reminded herself sternly. She needed to stop thinking about all the dreams that might be going up in smoke. She needed to be calm and rational by the time she picked up Kelsey at the airport. The last thing her daughter needed was a barrage of judgmental, unanswerable questions the instant she stepped off the plane. Nor did she need her mother stepping in and trying to fix things, the way Hannah was always inclined to do.

Crossing the street from the beach, Hannah spotted someone sitting in a rocker on the porch, a very masculine someone who looked vaguely familiar and very much at home.

"Hey, Hannah," the man said, lifting a glass of lemonade in greeting. "Care to join me? Your grandmother left an extra glass."

She gave him another hard look, took in the dark brown buzz cut, the angular features on a face that was almost gaunt, the broad shoulders, the lips threatening to curve into a grin. It wasn't until she looked into his brown eyes, though, that she recognized him.

"Luke?" Her expression brightened. "Luke Stevens? How long has it been?"

"More than twenty years," he said, his gaze sweeping over her with the kind of masculine appreciation she wasn't accustomed to, from him. "You look good, Hannah. How's life treating you?"

"Don't ask. How about you?"

"Don't ask."

"You're not still living in Seaview Key, are you?"

"No. I haven't been back in years."

"Well, what on earth are you doing here now?" She heard how that sounded and quickly amended, "Not that I'm not glad to see you."

"I just came back for a visit."

"Well, isn't that an amazing coincidence?"

Amazing and a whole lot more, frankly. It was troubling to discover that Luke still had the same ability to rattle her and make her tongue-tied. Forcing herself to remember the way things had been — Luke and her best friend madly in love, rather than Luke at least noticing her — she deliberately asked, "Do you ever hear from Abby?"

He shook his head. "You?"

"Not since college. So, where are you staying?"

"Here, actually. I moved in about an hour ago."

Hannah, who'd been about to lean down and give him a friendly peck on the cheek, backed up so fast, it was only luck — and a sturdy railing — that kept her from sailing right off the edge of the porch.

"Here?" she said incredulously. "You moved in *here?*"

He chuckled and raised his glass of lemonade again. "Surprise!"

"But we're closed. Who said you could stay?" she asked, though the answer was obvious. Grandma Jenny wasn't taking any chances. Obviously she figured frugal Hannah wouldn't turn away a paying guest.

"I made the reservation with your grandmother a couple of weeks ago."

Hannah directed a sour look toward the

house. No doubt her grandmother was sitting right beside a window to get a perfect view of this encounter. "Really. For how long?"

Luke shrugged. "Hard to say. I have some things to figure out. I told your grandmother I'd help the two of you get this place spruced up a bit."

"Really," she said again. This must be the help Gran had said was on the way. "She never mentioned you. Did you and my grandmother make any other plans without sharing them with me?"

"Not me," he claimed. "I can't speak for her."

Hannah bounced up. "I think my grandmother and I need to have a talk." She was about to walk away, when her intrinsic manners kicked in. She turned around. "It really is good to see you again, Luke, but one word of caution."

"Oh?"

"Don't get too comfortable. In less than two weeks, this place will be closed, I'll be back in New York and my grandmother will be . . ." She faltered on that. "Well, she'll be somewhere. Right this second a psychiatric facility sounds like just the place."

She was about to storm inside and have it out with her grandmother when Luke stopped her.

"Hold it, Hannah. If me being here is going to be a problem, I'm sure I can find somewhere else to stay. I noticed a couple of new motels when I drove off the ferry."

She was about to take him up on the offer when she realized she was being absurd. There was no reason he couldn't stay in one of the guest rooms, even if having him underfoot was going to dredge up a whole lot of old memories of unrequited longing. It was only the fact that her grandmother had done this behind her back that grated.

She sighed and sat down in the rocker next to his. To buy herself a couple of minutes so that she didn't sound totally irrational, she poured herself a glass of the ice-cold lemonade and took a sip.

"Sorry about sounding so inhospitable," she said eventually. "You just caught me off guard. We've been closed since before my mother died a month ago. I had no idea that my grandmother had started taking reservations again."

Luke looked genuinely shocked. "Your mother died? I didn't know. I'm so sorry, Hannah. She was a wonderful woman. I always enjoyed talking to her. She really listened to all us kids."

Hannah blinked back a fresh batch of

tears. For a woman who'd always prided herself on keeping her emotions in check, since coming back here, she was turning into a regular waterworks.

"She was a good listener, wasn't she?" she said, a catch in her voice. "I remember how often you or one of the other kids would sneak off to the kitchen to spill some secret to her. I swear she always knew stuff about my friends before I did. I was halfway jealous of that."

"Your grandmother didn't say anything about her dying when I called. I thought your mom must just be away on a trip or something."

"Don't feel bad. I know she's dead and I feel the same way. I can't quite believe I won't turn a corner and bump into her."

He hesitated, then studied her with a gaze filled with compassion. "Do you want to talk about it or should we move on to another topic?"

"To be honest, I'm not ready to talk about it yet. She had cancer and things didn't go well, practically from the beginning, and . . ." She couldn't bring herself to say the rest, that she was terrified her own future was destined to follow the same path.

"It's an awful disease," he said quietly. "And it's really difficult to watch a loved one suffer."

"You have no idea," she said softly, then stood up abruptly. "Look, I have to catch the four-thirty ferry to the mainland and I really do need to talk to my grandmother about you staying before I go. Not that you being here is a problem, because it's not, Luke. Really. I just have to be sure you're not the tip of the iceberg and that hordes of other guests aren't descending without warning. There's a lot going on around here right now and, believe me, more unexpected visitors are not a complication I can handle."

"My offer to find another place is still good," he said. "I don't want to add to whatever stress you're under. I get what it's like when things start piling up. Big or little, it doesn't matter. Sooner or later, it's just too much."

Hearing the real sympathy in his voice, she fought back tears again. She shook her head, this time with more certainty. "No, stay. Please. Just be prepared for anything to happen. Once my daughter, Kelsey, gets here in a few hours, we may give new meaning to the phrase 'dysfunctional family.' "

He smiled at that. "You're not scaring me, if that's what you're trying to do. As it happens, I know quite a lot about dysfunctional families. I've recently taken a crash course."

She studied him curiously. "Do you want to talk about *that?*"

"Nope. I want to forget about it, at least for a little while."

"You realize we might not have much to say if we keep putting topics off limits," she said.

"Oh, I suspect we'll think of something. The weather's always safe enough."

She grinned. "At this time of year? The Chamber of Commerce brochures claim it's always sunny and mild."

"Except when it's wet and chilly," he countered.

"I'm pretty sure they never mention that."

"But you and I don't work for the Chamber of Commerce. We can be candid." His expression sobered. "You can be honest with me, Hannah. You're sure this is okay, me staying here?"

"I'm sure," she said, this time without hesitation.

The truth was that the more she thought about it, the more she wanted him to stay. She had a feeling that having another rational adult around might be the only thing that would keep her from going off the deep end before all these family crises were resolved. All she had to do was make sure her already prancing hormones didn't get any crazy ideas. Falling for Luke Stevens for the second time in her life — especially right now — would be so far beyond stupid there wasn't even an adequate word to describe it.

4

Instead of peace and serenity, Luke concluded he was smack in the middle of some Matthews family drama. He'd heard Hannah's raised voice not two minutes after she'd left him on the porch. Whatever she'd said, though, hadn't especially daunted her grandmother. Jenny Matthews had held her own. He couldn't hear the words, but they'd matched each other in heat and determination. He had to admire the feistiness in both of them, but especially in Grandma Jenny. Too many of his senior patients were cowed by family members. Clearly that wasn't the case here.

Ten minutes after the battle had died down, Hannah had stormed out of the house looking like a thundercloud, gotten behind the wheel of *his* rental car, which was almost an exact duplicate of *her* rental car, and tried to start the engine. Naturally the key hadn't worked. She'd gotten out, kicked a tire, then glanced at the car beside it and apparently grasped her mistake. A minute later she'd squealed out of the driveway at a speed that had him wincing. She hadn't acknowledged his existence with so much as a wave. He gathered things hadn't gone her way with her grandmother.

As soon as she was out of sight, the screen door opened and Jenny slipped outside. "That girl's going to get a ticket or run into a ditch if she keeps on driving like that," she said disapprovingly.

"She seems upset," he noted as the woman settled into the rocker beside his and poured herself a glass of lemonade, then grabbed the last cookie. Luke barely contained a sigh at the loss. He'd had plans for that cookie, even after all the others he'd eaten.

"I think her mood has something to do with her daughter," she said, glancing sideways at him.

Luke chuckled. "And *I* think it might have something to do with you. You trying to put something over on her, Mrs. Matthews?"

"I told you to call me Grandma Jenny," she said testily, then slanted a look at him. "Why would I be trying to put anything over on her?"

"That's what I'm trying to figure out. So far, here's what I've got. You want Hannah to come back here and take over the inn. She doesn't want to. You figured having a paying guest — me — would force her to stick it out here for a while, maybe start getting used to the idea."

Jenny didn't bother trying to deny it. "Think you're smart, don't you?"

"Far from it, but I know a con artist when I meet one. Is this just about you not wanting to sell this place because it's been your home for all these years?"

She gave him a scathing look. "It is not," she said emphatically. "I know that's what Hannah thinks, too, but this is about her. She's been living in New York for twenty years now, but she's not happy."

Luke bit back a comment. Hannah had seemed happy enough to him until she'd found out he was staying here. Then, again, they hadn't done a lot of catching up before that.

"Oh, she thinks she is," Grandma Jenny continued, "because she's busy every second of every day, dealing with all sorts of powerful clients and going out to fancy dinners and the theater and hosting elegant parties in the hottest clubs. She sends the clippings from the newspaper down here, so I'll be impressed with how successful she is, and I am. I'm real proud of her, but career success isn't all there is to life."

"Maybe not, but it doesn't sound like a bad life to me," he remarked. "Especially if it's the one she wants."

"It's bad, if at the end of the day she goes home to an empty apartment and a cold bed. Her daughter's clear across the country at Stanford. Her husband, who wasn't worth much to begin with, is long gone, every bit as irresponsible as her daddy. She's alone and she's forgotten who she is and what's important. She's chasing the almighty dollar, is what she's doing, and in the end, that's never enough to make a person truly happy."

Luke wondered what her assessment would be of *his* life. His view of success had matched Hannah's for a time. Money had certainly been high on his ex-wife's measure of success, as well. Now he saw Grandma Jenny's point. He'd made a lot of money, but he'd never been entirely happy, though he hadn't been able to say why. That was another part of the reason he'd come to Seaview Key. He wanted to believe he'd get his priorities in order while he was here, maybe get back to the values he'd been taught by his parents, to the love of medicine he'd had when he first went into practice.

"Do you think Hannah will rediscover herself here?" he asked.

"I'm hoping," she said. "I love this shabby old inn, no question about it. My parents built it and my husband and I had a good life running it and raising our kids here. Hannah had a good life here, too, though she's chosen to forget that. She was surrounded by family and a tightknit community, not millions of strangers who are scared to even look each other in the eye on the street. You must know what I mean. It brought you back here, didn't it?"

"Not to stay," Luke said softly. "Just to get my bearings."

She gave him a sly look. "Seems to me like the place you go to get your bearings ought to be home." She tapped her glass to his. "Something to think about, don't you agree?"

"You could have a point," he conceded. "And maybe I did come here because this was once home. I wanted to recapture a simpler time in my life." He met her gaze. "I'm not really sure it's possible to do that, though. Maybe all I'm doing is postponing dealing with reality."

"If you'd care to explain what you're talking about, maybe I could help you figure it out," she said. "Lots of folks think with age comes a little wisdom."

"I don't question that for a minute, and maybe one of these days we will talk more about what's going on in my life," he said.

She patted his hand. "Whenever you're ready to tell me, I'll be ready to listen. Now I need to start thinking about dinner. Kelsey — that's Hannah's daughter — will be hungry after eating nothing but airline food today. I'm thinking fried chicken and macaroni and cheese, good comfort food. How does that sound?"

"Like it'll clog all our arteries," he said. "And better than anything I've had in months." He watched as she struggled to her feet. "You want some help?"

Her expression turned indignant. "The day I can't get into this house on my own two feet is the day I'll walk away from it and check into that retirement home Hannah's so anxious for me to move into."

The show of spunk made Luke chuckle. "I meant with dinner."

"Now, that I can use. You know anything about cutting up a chicken?"

"I'm a surgeon. I think I can manage."

She gave him a startled look. "Well, I'll be. I hadn't heard that."

"My folks moved away before I went into

medical school, much less chose a specialty," he said.

Luke waited with dread for her to ask him a thousand and one questions about why he was hiding out in Seaview Key, instead of back home performing surgery.

Surprisingly, though, she just gave him a knowing glance and another pat on the hand. "Like I said, this is a good place for figuring things out."

Luke was counting on that. It was a far cry from the hospital in D.C., its hallways crowded with wounded soldiers whose souls were as shattered as their limbs. Compared to that or the hell that had been his life in Baghdad or the complications waiting for him in Atlanta, Seaview Key was pure heaven.

Iraq, a few months earlier

The calendar on the wall in Luke's quarters had big, bold *X*'s marked through the days. Practically from the minute he'd arrived in Baghdad, he'd begun counting down the time until he could go home again. He'd signed up for one year of active duty, partly out of patriotism and partly out of a sense of obligation. The army had paid for his medical degree, and though he'd already served the required amount of time in return, he still felt a moral duty to sign up for another tour when guys he'd served with were sent to Iraq.

He and Lisa had had a blowup of monumental proportions when he'd told her about his plan to volunteer for reenlistment.

"You got out of the military, Luke," she said, tears streaming down her face. "How can you even consider this? You've paid your dues. You have a family now. You have kids. Your medical practice is growing. We're finally financially stable. If you walk away from it now, what will that do to our income? Do you expect us to live on a soldier's pay?"

He'd lost patience with her then. "Plenty of other military families are forced to do exactly that," he'd told her. "Fortunately, we have a significant amount of money in savings and I'll work it out with Brad that a percentage of the money from the practice will continue to provide for you and the kids while I'm gone. Come on, Lisa. You're hardly going to starve and you know it. This is something I have to do. I have medical skill that's badly needed over there."

"And that's more important than your family?" she'd demanded angrily.

"Not *more* important," he'd said. "But sometimes you just have to do what you know in your heart is the right thing. If I can help to save just one kid's leg so he'll be able to walk again, then I have to do this."

He'd seen in her eyes that she just didn't get it. Maybe no wife would, especially when he was volunteering to put himself in harm's way. He'd only known that it was where he needed to be, what he had to do.

Though she'd eventually resigned herself to his decision, she'd been no happier about it by the time he left. She'd pulled out every stop, heaped on every bit of guilt she could think of, and when the day of departure had come, she'd refused to see him off. He'd said goodbye to her and his kids at home. There'd been no one waving a flag or blowing him kisses when he'd finally taken off. He'd tried not to let it hurt, but it had.

Once he was in Iraq, though, he hadn't had time for regret. He'd barely had time to sleep. The days flew by in a haze of misery and pain, too many soldiers, too many hours standing over an operating table, his back aching, his eyes blurring from exhaustion.

It was the successes that kept him going, and the e-mails from home. Lisa was good about that, at least, and so were the kids. As young as they were — Nate barely in kindergarten, Gracie only in second grade — they still managed to write, "I miss you, Daddy."

And every so often a package would arrive with home-baked cookies, photos of the birthday party he'd missed and drawings in crayon. The drawings went on the wall by the calendar on which he was marking off the days until he saw them all again.

"Doc, there's another chopper setting down," Kenny Franklin told him. "The OR's set up. You ready?"

Luke tore his gaze away from the latest picture of his kids. "I'm on my way," he told the young medic, already on his feet. He cast one last look at the snapshot, grinning at Nate's gap-toothed smile. He'd gotten a whole dollar from the tooth fairy, he'd told Luke in an e-mail.

He thought about that a few minutes later when he was examining the soldier whose face had been sliced to ribbons by the same mine that had ripped off part of his leg. Nate's smile would be whole in no time at all, the missing tooth replaced by another one. The boy on the table in front of him, not yet nineteen, according to his records, wouldn't be that lucky. He'd be lucky to live. Only a decade or so older than Luke's little girl, and this boy had put his life on the line for his country.

Luke had to steel himself against the tide of dismay washing over him as he snapped out orders and made his first incision. An hour later, it was over. The kid was dead. He'd lost too much blood and they hadn't been able to seal off all the bleeders fast enough.

"Sometimes there's nothing you can do, Doc," Kenny said.

"Yeah, I know," Luke responded. "That doesn't mean it doesn't suck."

On days like this it was hard to remember that he'd come here to save lives. It was hard, in fact, to remember why he'd left his home, his family, his life for *this.* If he thought about the devastation waiting for some family back home, if he thought about any of it, he wouldn't be able to function. All he could do was head back to his quarters and try to snatch a couple of hours of sleep before the next transport came in.

"Luke!"

The sound of Grandma Jenny's voice snapped him back to the present.

"Luke, are you okay? You're pale as a ghost. Sit down for a minute and I'll get you something to drink."

"I'm fine," he said, then realized he was standing over a chicken with a knife in his hand. "I'll just finish cutting this chicken up for you."

"I can do that," she said, nudging him aside. "Sit."

Suddenly too exhausted to argue, he sat.

"You want to tell me where you went just then?" she asked.

"Not really."

"Something tells me you ought to be talking to somebody about it. Bottling up the things that upset you isn't good."

"No, it's not," Luke agreed. But he'd talked this particular subject to death while he was in rehab and it hadn't made the memories fade. If anything, they were clearer and more deeply embedded in his mind than ever.

"So, talk. You said you're a surgeon. Where?"

"In Atlanta. At least, that's where my practice is."

"You have a family there?"

He got to his feet. "No offense, Grandma Jenny, but I can't talk about any of this right now. I'm going for a walk, if you don't mind."

She gave him a hard look. "You're not going to keel over the second you walk out the door, are you?"

He managed a faint smile. "I hope not."

"Then go." She shook a finger under his nose. "But don't think I won't still have the same questions tomorrow or the day after."

"I never doubted it," he said. "Right now, though, I need some fresh air."

"You'll be back for dinner, though, right?"

"I'll be back," he assured her.

He felt her concerned gaze on him as he left. There was something sweet about that. He couldn't recall the last time anyone had cared about his comings and goings. His ex-wife had stopped caring months ago, by his calculations. His kids, well, right now they were mostly confused. Very soon, when he felt more centered and sure of himself, he needed to fix that. They needed to know that he still loved them, that he was going to be there for them. To do that, though, to make that commitment, he had to figure out who the hell he was now . . . or who he wanted to be.

"So, have yourself a damn pity party, why don't you?" he muttered in disgust as he walked the few blocks into downtown, taking note of the many changes that had taken place since he'd left. Storefronts had been spruced up. There was more variety in the merchandise for sale. The tourists walking the streets tended to be families, rather than fishermen traveling solo. And a whole lot of people were riding around in golf carts, despite the fact that the nearest golf course was over on the mainland.

By the time he'd reached the small grocery store on the island, which was thankfully unchanged, he was in pain, but his mood had improved. He bought a half gallon of rocky road ice cream, which he vaguely recalled had once been Hannah's favorite. Or was it Abby's? At any rate, they'd eaten a lot of it way back when. Maybe it would be just the thing to put everyone in a good frame of mind tonight.

Then, again, that was asking a lot of a bowl of ice cream, no matter how big and decadent it was. Of course, at the pace he was walking these days, there was a good chance it would be soup by the time he got it back to the inn.

Kelsey took one look at the plate piled high with fried chicken and the huge bowl of creamy yellow mac and cheese and went running for the nearest bathroom. Morning sickness, which was a misnomer if ever she'd heard one, basically sucked. She hated heaving her guts out several times a day.

The doctor she'd seen assured her it would pass soon, but she wasn't counting on it. She had a feeling this baby was going to punish her from now through eternity for not wanting it. If it wasn't morning sickness, it would be something else . . . colic, or teething accompanied by cries of pain or, down the road, a teenage rebellion of monumental proportions. She figured she'd deserve every miserable minute.

Though she could hear the low murmur of voices from the kitchen while she was in the bathroom, the second she crossed the threshold, silence fell. Obviously they'd been talking about her. She hoped her mother hadn't filled her great-grandmother in on the news of her pregnancy yet. Grandma Jenny was going to have a lot to say about it and Kelsey didn't want to hear any of it. She'd made a mistake. She knew it. She was going to deal with it. What more was there to say?

Even her mom had known there was little to be said on the subject, because she'd been silent and withdrawn all the way from the airport to Seaview. Despite the careful silence, Kelsey had felt her judgmental stare every few minutes throughout the ride.

Now, as she glanced from her mom to Grandma Jenny, she caught a glimpse of someone else in the room who hadn't been there a minute ago. She turned to get a good look at the man hovering near the sink. He seemed intense. Dark and good-looking, but definitely intense.

"Kelsey, this is Luke Stevens," her mother said. "He's staying here right now. We were friends when we were kids."

Kelsey studied him curiously. All her visits to Seaview had been rushed and she'd rarely ever met anyone who'd known her mom years ago. As far as she knew, no one ever stuck around the island if they could get away. To hear her mom tell it, only losers stayed behind, but this guy didn't look like a loser.

"Nice to meet you," Luke said. "Seems as if you all have a lot to catch up on, so I'll just fix myself a plate and head up to my room."

"No," Kelsey said, as did both her mother and Grandma Jenny.

"Besides, you went out and brought home all that ice cream," Grandma Jenny added. "You need to sit right here and eat it with us."

Luke stared at them with amusement. "Gee, I've never felt so wanted."

Kelsey grinned, despite her lousy mood. "Every family needs a good buffer."

"Nice to know I can fill a niche around here." He stared pointedly at Grandma Jenny. "Though I thought I was here to do odd jobs for a couple of weeks."

Grandma Jenny shrugged. "I'd say being

a mediator for the three of us fits that, wouldn't you?"

"Just warn me ahead of time if I'm going to need a weapon or body armor," he said dryly.

Kelsey noted that even her mother had to fight a grin at that. As she munched on a handful of Saltines she'd managed to find in a cupboard, the rest of them dove into dinner. A few minutes later, Kelsey risked a little mac and cheese, then a chicken wing.

She looked around the table and suddenly felt the knot in her stomach ease for the first time since she'd found out about the baby. Maybe, like dinner, her life was going to turn out okay, after all.

Suddenly, acid burned the back of her throat and she bolted from the table.

As she wiped her face with a damp cloth after throwing up her dinner, she corrected herself. She was going to spend nine months heaving her guts out, the baby was going to arrive, and then things were going to get complicated, especially if Jeff refused to back away from his demand that they get married and keep this baby. In no scenario she could imagine would her life ever be okay again.

5

Luke didn't have to have a medical degree to know what was going on with Kelsey and why she'd come to Florida in the middle of the school year. She was pregnant. Hannah obviously knew it, which was why there'd been a pinched expression on her face when Kelsey had bolted for the bathroom for the second time since they'd arrived home from the airport. If Grandma Jenny knew, she wasn't giving anything away. She just poured a glass of ginger ale, set it down on the table at Kelsey's place and announced she was going to her room.

"Something tells me you and your daughter need to talk," she said to Hannah, then looked pointedly at Luke. "They could probably use some privacy, too."

Luke acknowledged the suggestion with a nod and stood up.

"That was subtle," Hannah murmured after she'd gone. "Are you sure you want to stick around here after tonight? I told you it was going to get messy."

"Do you want me to go?" he asked, studying Hannah's expression. "I mean now. Earlier both you and Kelsey seemed anxious to have a buffer. Maybe an impartial third party could help."

Hannah looked relieved. "To tell you the truth, I don't want to get into any of this tonight and I imagine Kelsey would rather postpone it indefinitely. Stay, please."

Luke acquiesced and sat back down, though not without some trepidation. "Does your grandmother know about the baby?"

"I haven't told her, if that's what you mean," she said, not bothering to deny that her daughter was pregnant. "But she knows. I'm sure she noticed the handful of crackers that Kelsey grabbed earlier. That's why she left that glass of ginger ale, too."

"You okay?"

She gave him a wry look. "I'm not the one who's still more than a year away from graduating from college and about to have a baby."

"No, but you are the mother of a young woman who's about to have one, and apparently without a husband, or am I wrong about that? Is there a wedding on the horizon?"

"Not that I'm aware of." She regarded him sheepishly. "Then, again, apparently I'm the last to know a lot of things. I didn't even know there was a man in her life."

"Maybe there's not," he said, phrasing his words carefully.

"Oh, I'd say a man's involved in this," Hannah retorted.

He grinned at the evidence that she hadn't entirely lost her sense of humor. "I meant anyone she's serious about."

"Are you suggesting she was just casually sleeping around?" she asked, her indignation stirring. "No way. I may not know much else, but I know that." She sighed. "Truthfully, we haven't broached the daddy factor yet. I just found out about this myself the night before last, right after I got down here. Kelsey flew here because I insisted. She's not thinking very clearly right now. She wants to quit school and move back to New York."

"And you disapprove?" He could read it in the set of her jaw and the tone of her voice.

"Strongly. Am I wrong?"

She gave him a surprisingly helpless look that made Luke want to fix this for her. He hardly had the right to even offer a suggestion, though. "Honestly, I don't know," he said eventually.

"Me, neither," she admitted. "I don't know if I have the right to push her to stay in school, or if it's even the right thing to do. I'm out of my league with all this."

"I don't think any parent's ever prepared for this moment."

"Do you have kids?"

"Two, but they're a lot younger than Kelsey. Thank God, I don't have to worry about something like this for a long time."

"Trust me, the time passes before you know it. A part of me still thinks of Kelsey in a frilly party dress, blowing out candles on a birthday cake, surrounded by a bunch of other toddlers. Instead, she's this amazing young woman whose life is about to be turned upside down. If she were a different girl, if she'd been flighty or reckless, I could understand how this could happen, but she's not. She's always been very much in control of everything."

The bathroom door opened and they fell silent. Kelsey looked pale and drawn, but she managed a wobbly smile.

"Sorry," she said. She spotted the ginger ale and took a tentative sip. "Where's Grandma Jenny?"

"She went upstairs," Hannah told her.

"I think I will, too," Kelsey said, avoiding

Hannah's gaze. "I know it's early, but I'm beat. I'd like to sleep for a week."

Hannah regarded her with disappointment. "I thought we could talk," she said, though it sounded halfhearted.

"In the morning, Mom, please," Kelsey said. "I'm just not up to it tonight."

"Okay, sure." Hannah was a little too quick to cave in, proving just how reluctant she was to have this conversation. "Get some rest, sweetie. I love you."

Kelsey bent down and kissed Hannah's cheek. "Love you, too. Good night, Luke. I swear I'll be better company tomorrow."

"Your company is just fine," he said.

She grinned. "You actually said that with a straight face. I think I like you."

Then she was gone and Luke was left alone with Hannah, who looked as if she were near tears.

"You're not going to cry, are you?" he asked worriedly. He wasn't sure what he'd do if she did. He could handle combat better than he could deal with a woman's tears. His wife had known that and used it to her advantage more times than he could count. The only time it hadn't worked had been when he'd reenlisted in the army.

"It's entirely possible that I'll bawl my eyes out before the night's over," Hannah admitted. "You can run for your life, if you want to."

Since she'd offered him an easy out, naturally he felt compelled to deny he wanted one. "Now, why would I do that? I'm just asking for advance warning, so I can get you some tissues. As for running me off, in general, let's just accept that I'm here for the duration, okay?"

"You are gallant, aren't you? Kelsey was right." She dabbed at her eyes with her napkin. "Just for that, I will not cry. I'll clean up these dishes and then make some iced tea. You want to join me for some on the porch?"

"Forget the tea," he said. "I want some of that ice cream. How about you?"

Her eyes brightened perceptibly. "I'd forgotten all about that. What kind did you get?"

"Rocky road."

She gave him a surprised look. "Was that a lucky coincidence or did you actually remember that was my favorite?"

He shrugged, his expression sheepish. "I remembered we ate an awful lot of it that summer I was hanging around here. It had to be somebody's favorite."

"Honesty. Wow, that's a rarity. Most men would grab the credit for being that thoughtful," she said.

"Only if they were trying to impress you, which I'm not." His gaze met hers and he felt something shift. There was an unexpected spark that took him by surprise. If Hannah's expression was any indication, she was as startled by it as he was. Talk about lousy timing. Both of them had way too much on their plates to consider adding another complication. Even so, it might be impossible to ignore this pull. It had been a long time since he'd been with anyone, an even longer time since he'd wanted a woman other than his wife. That had to explain this sudden spark between him and a woman who'd never been more than a friend. Whatever the reason, the reaction was undeniable.

"Maybe I should amend that," he said quietly.

"Amend what?" she asked, a faintly breathless quality in her voice as their gazes held.

"I'm not trying to impress you *yet.*"

The moment seemed to last an eternity before she grinned and the spell was broken. "Let me know when you're going to start trying," she said lightly. "I think I'd better be prepared. Something tells me you're a very dangerous man when you decide to throw yourself into something."

He chuckled, relieved to be back on more familiar footing. Teasing her had always been one of his favorite pastimes. "Hannah Matthews, are you flirting with me?"

She blushed furiously. "You started it. Now, scoop up that ice cream, Luke. It's gotten awfully warm in here."

He deliberately held her gaze a bit longer, then grinned. "Indeed, it has."

He retrieved the ice cream from the freezer, lingering with the door open in an attempt to cool down his overheated libido.

While he had his back to Hannah, he told himself he was an idiot. He was here to get his priorities in order. And her life appeared to be even more of a mess than his own. As much fun as flirting with Hannah — or a fling — might turn out to be, neither of them needed the potential heartache. He'd do well to remember that.

Besides, it had been years since he'd had a friend to confide in. That was the role he needed Hannah to play. This little *zing* he'd felt was an aberration. Tomorrow they'd go back to being pals the way they'd been years ago.

He was so busy formulating his plan that he didn't notice right away that Hannah was staring at him with amusement. When he did, he muttered, "What?"

"That's a lot of ice cream, even for you," she said, gesturing toward the bowl, which must have had a whole pint scooped into it.

He grinned and shoved the bowl in her direction. "Actually that one's for you. I recognize a woman in need of a chocolate fix when I see one." He doled out a huge dollop of hot fudge sauce to prove it.

She eyed the bowl skeptically, then picked it up. "You could be right. Come on out to the porch when you're finished."

Luke told himself he ought to be anywhere except on the porch tonight, but when he had his own bowl filled with ice cream, he couldn't seem to make himself climb the stairs to his room. Instead, he headed for the front door . . . and most likely straight for trouble.

"Why didn't you tell me your daughter is pregnant?" Grandma Jenny demanded the second Hannah wandered into the kitchen in the morning following the aroma of coffee brewing.

Hannah wasn't ready to have this conversation before she'd had caffeine. A lot of caffeine, in fact. She and Luke had been up way too late talking. They'd carefully avoided any repeat of the flirting that had gone on earlier, sticking to memories of old times, catching up on news of friends they'd each kept in touch with. He'd done a better job of that than she had. After a couple of hours of talking about old times and old friends — yet somehow avoiding any mention of Abby, who'd been so integral to both their pasts — they'd said a casual good-night and gone their separate ways. As they'd climbed the stairs, they'd kept a careful distance apart, pretending that the spark they'd both felt earlier had never happened.

Now Hannah deliberately ignored her grandmother, grabbed the biggest mug she could find and filled it to the brim with strong, fragrant coffee. Only when she'd had several sips did she dare to meet Grandma Jenny's expectant gaze.

"Why didn't you tell me about Luke staying here?" Hannah retorted, hoping to buy herself a couple of minutes, since she didn't have any real answers about the whole lousy situation.

"Don't try that with me," Grandma Jenny said. "I told you yesterday why Luke's here. Now I want to know why my great-granddaughter has shown up here with a baby on the way. And don't deny it. I'm not so old that I can't recognize the symptoms."

"I wasn't going to deny it," Hannah said.

"But to be honest, I haven't asked her a lot of questions yet."

"I left the two of you alone last night precisely so you could talk."

"Never happened. She went to bed. Luke stayed." She gave her grandmother a defiant look. "I asked him to."

"I see."

"I doubt it," Hannah replied. "I was so thrown when Kelsey told me about the pregnancy the other night, I couldn't think of anything to do except get her here so we could talk about it. Now that she's here, I don't know where to start."

"The father seems like a good place to me. Where's he in all this?"

Hannah shrugged. "Not a clue."

"Don't you think maybe you should ask?"

"I'll get around to it. With Kelsey, it's better to let things unfold at their own pace."

Her grandmother rolled her eyes. "Up to you, but I'd recommend you get answers before that child's due date."

"Grandma Jenny?" Hannah was surprisingly hesitant. This whole disaster was so far beyond her ability to control or fix, she honestly didn't know what to do next. "What on earth am I supposed to do?"

To her surprise, her grandmother pulled a chair up next to her and took her hand.

"You keep on doing just what you're doing. You're here for her. So am I. Together, we'll figure out what comes next," she said matter-of-factly. "To do that, though, we need to get all the cards on the table."

"You're not upset that I told her to come?"

"Don't be silly. This is your home as much as it is mine," her grandmother reminded her. For once it seemed as if she was merely stating a fact, not sending a pointed message. "And that makes it Kelsey's home, too. Where else should she go when there's a crisis?"

"When she told me, all I could think about was convincing her to stay and finish college. I didn't think for one second about how hard that would be or what would come later. She'll have a baby to raise all on her own. She's not ready for that."

"None of us are entirely ready for a baby, no matter what we like to think," Grandma Jenny told her. "Before your mama came along, I read every book. Made your grandfather read 'em, too, but it didn't do a lick of good. Every baby's different and every cry seems like a crisis until you get to know your own child. Eventually you just settle in and handle whatever comes along. Kelsey will, too. She's your daughter, isn't she? I imagine she has enough organizational skills and strength to get through this, even if the baby's father isn't in the picture."

"Am I wrong to want her to finish her education, no matter what?"

"Getting a good education is never wrong, but you won't know if now's the time for it until you sit down and really listen to her, will you? In the end, this has to be her decision."

"I suppose so." Hannah leaned over and rested her head on her grandmother's shoulder, taking comfort in the familiar rose scent of her cologne. "I love you, Gran. I know I came down here to bulldoze you into doing things my way, but I only did that because I love you and worry about you."

Her grandmother winked. "Then it's a good thing you're not the only one in this family with a stubborn streak, isn't it? I don't get bulldozed that easily. Now, go upstairs and talk to your daughter. You two need to start figuring things out. And if you run into Luke while you're up there, tell him he can take me to that hardware store on the mainland for some paint in an hour."

"Paint? We bought paint," Hannah protested.

"I've decided white's too boring for the outside of an inn on the beach. Don't know why I let you talk me into it."

"Boring?" Hannah repeated nervously. "Meaning what?"

"I'm going with the turquoise, after all. Thank goodness this isn't one of those silly towns that go all crazy about permits for this and that. Do you believe some places even have a boring color palette you're required to choose from? That's not for me. I want to breathe new life into this place. We should stand out from the crowd."

Hannah winced. "Are you sure?" She couldn't imagine a new buyer being drawn to a turquoise structure, but she supposed that was the least of her worries. Grandma Jenny clearly didn't intend to fall in with her plans for selling right now, anyway.

"I'm sure," Grandma Jenny insisted. "But I'll see if Luke agrees before I go wild." She gave Hannah a sly look. "He seems to have a good head on his shoulders. Have you noticed that?"

Hannah regarded her with suspicion. "You don't have some hidden agenda for Luke and me, do you?"

"I don't even know if the man's married," her grandmother said innocently. "If you want me to, I'll ask him while we're out. Get the lay of the land, so to speak."

Hannah groaned at the glint in her eyes.

"Leave it alone, Gran. I'm sure Luke will tell us anything he wants us to know."

"Some things it's better to know at the outset," her grandmother retorted firmly. "You deal with Kelsey. I'll handle things with Luke." She stood up. "Now that we have a plan, let's get going. We can't waste the whole day lollygagging around here."

Hannah glanced longingly out the window toward the gentle waves lapping at the shore a few hundred feet away. Lollygagging sounded a whole lot better than going upstairs and facing her daughter. She was tempted to sneak out of the house and head straight for the beach, but a knowing look from Grandma Jenny told her she'd never get away with it. "Okay, okay, I'm going upstairs," she said defensively.

"Now?"

"Now," Hannah agreed, though with a hefty amount of reluctance. When had she turned into a woman who hoped that ignoring problems might make them go away? When had she developed this powerful desire to stick her head in the sand and pretend that everything was okay?

It had to be the influence of Seaview Key, she thought as she trudged up the stairs. And that was just one more reason she needed to get back to her busy, organized life. In New York, she was "Go-to-Hannah." Down here, she was about to turn into someone who lacked motivation or drive or answers. Hannah, the slug. She shuddered at the thought.

Kelsey heard the tap on her door and knew it was her mom. "I have to go," she told Jeff. "I'll call you later." She turned off her cell phone and jammed it into a bedside drawer before telling her mother to come in.

"Who were you talking to?" her mom asked.

"Nobody."

"I heard your voice."

"Must have been the radio," Kelsey said.

Her mother's gaze narrowed. "You're lying, Kelsey, and you're not very good at it, so don't do it."

Kelsey winced. "It was just a friend from school."

"The baby's father?"

"Why would you . . . ?"

"You're actually talking to the father of the baby?" her mother continued as if Kelsey hadn't even attempted to deny it. "Why?"

"I never said —"

"Kelsey, how does this man feel about

your being pregnant? What kind of man leaves you to deal with something like this all alone?"

"Mom, you don't know what you're talking about, so drop it, okay?"

"After your father, I think I do know a thing or two about men who can't handle responsibility. You don't want someone like that in your life, Kelsey. Forget about him now. You have your grandmother and me. We can see you through this."

"This isn't your life, Mom, and Jeff isn't Dad. Far from it, in fact. I'm the one who doesn't want to get married. I'm the one who's having trouble facing all this. I don't want a baby now. I'm not ready. I'd have an abortion, but Jeff got furious when I even mentioned the possibility, so I promised him I'd think about everything before I did anything that drastic."

Kelsey felt awful when she saw the look of dismay that crossed her mother's face. "I know you don't believe in it, either, but how can I bring this baby into the world under these circumstances?"

"Sweetie, we don't always get to choose the circumstances, but a child is a blessing, no matter when it comes along."

"Really? Tell that to some poor woman who's been raped."

"Kelsey!"

"Well, it's true. There are circumstances when it's not a blessing, when the timing's all wrong or the people are all wrong together or a thousand other reasons. Shouldn't I have the right to say this is not right for me?"

She could tell her mother was struggling to be fair, to be impartial, even though she had very strong opinions of her own. And the truth was, after her initial desperate reaction to the pregnancy, Kelsey hadn't been able to see herself getting an abortion, either.

"You do have a right to make your own choice, but only when you've weighed this very, very carefully," her mom said. "This is one of those times when you can't go back and undo an impulsive decision. You have to live with it for the rest of your life. And, to be honest, I'm probably not the best one to help you decide. We're talking about my grandchild here. I might not have chosen this moment for him or her to come along, but that's life. Things happen. We deal with them."

Kelsey felt tears welling up. "I don't want to deal with them. I don't want to deal with *this,*" she said, and threw herself into her mother's arms. "How did I screw everything up so badly?"

"I think we both know the answer to that," Hannah said, a hint of levity in her voice. "Why don't you tell me about Jeff? That might be a good place to start. You've never even mentioned him before, but he must be important if the two of you are about to have a baby together."

Kelsey didn't know how she felt about Jeff anymore. A part of her loved him. Another part was furious with him for his role in this predicament. Because her feelings about him were so conflicted, she said, "Could we go for a walk on the beach, instead? I think that's what I need right now."

Her mom looked as if she wanted to insist that they sit right here and talk, but eventually she relented. "Maybe a walk will do us both good," she conceded. "Watching the waves come in, knowing they'll still be doing the same thing tomorrow and the next day and long after we're gone helps to put things in perspective. Problems never seem as huge and overwhelming by comparison."

Kelsey gave her mom a wry look. "I was just thinking that maybe for a little while it would make me feel like a kid again."

Hannah grinned. "Okay, that, too."

"I remember the last time I was here, not for Grandma's funeral, but before that. I was a junior in high school, I think, and you let me come down by myself during spring vacation."

"Hardest thing I ever had to do, watching you get on that plane," Hannah admitted as they slipped into sandals and walked across the street to the beach. "I knew you were old enough and responsible enough to travel alone, but it was terrifying for me. We'd never been separated for more than a couple of days before. I sat at the airport until the plane was in the air and then sat by the phone at home until you called me that afternoon. That was, without question, the longest week of my life."

Kelsey regarded her with surprise. "Really? I thought you were glad that I was spending time down here, getting to know Grandma and Grandma Jenny."

"I was. I wanted you to know the rest of your family, to feel that connection to them." She gave Kelsey a rueful look. "I think I was scared you'd fall in love with Seaview Key. A lot of people who leave New York in the middle of winter and discover it's possible to be warm in February develop an infatuation with Florida. And to someone who didn't grow up here, Seaview Key does have its charms."

"Like being able to walk to the beach from

your house and having everyone in town know who you are," Kelsey said, pausing to kick off her sandals and dig her toes into the cool sand at the water's edge. "I couldn't believe it when I went to the store with Grandma and every single person said hello and called me by name. They all knew who I was. At least, the locals did. It was kind of cool."

"I didn't think so when I was a kid and every one of those people would call my house if they saw me misbehaving," her mom countered. "I'd walk in the door and your grandmother and Grandma Jenny would be waiting for me, ready to let me have it."

"I guess that would suck." Kelsey grinned. "Did you misbehave a lot?"

"Enough," Hannah admitted.

"Tell me," Kelsey begged. "Come on, Mom, spill everything."

"I am not going to give you ammunition to use against me," Hannah retorted indignantly, but she was grinning.

"I'll just ask Grandma Jenny," Kelsey threatened. "I bet she remembers every bad thing you ever did."

"I don't doubt it. She always took great pleasure in telling me I'd messed up."

Kelsey's mood sobered. "Mom, you know

she and Grandma really loved you and were proud of you, right?"

Hannah stared at her. "What makes you think that?"

"They told me. When I was here, they asked a million questions about your job and your friends and all the places we'd been. I wish they'd visited us more in New York."

"I invited them, but they hated it the one time they came," her mother replied defensively. "I offered to send them plane tickets every single Christmas, but they always came up with an excuse and it always had something to do with the inn."

"It was their business, Mom," Kelsey said impatiently. "You, of all people, should understand about responsibility. Until you got sick, I don't think I ever remember you taking a real vacation."

"We traveled all the time," her mother protested.

"Only if you had to go somewhere for work. I hated those trips. When I was little, you'd leave me shut up in the hotel with some babysitter. When I was older you let me go sightseeing, but it was no fun doing that all alone while you were working."

"It wasn't like that."

"It was *exactly* like that," Kelsey insisted.

"Sure, we went to all sorts of exciting cities, but you never had any fun and I was always lonely."

Her mother looked crestfallen. "I'm sorry. I never realized you felt that way. I always thought how amazing it was that you were getting to travel to places I'd never even dreamed of when I was your age."

Kelsey felt guilty about ruining her mom's memories of those trips. "It wasn't all bad," she told her. "Room service could be pretty awesome. It certainly spoiled me for staying in your basic motel."

Her mom groaned. "Make me feel even worse, why don't you."

"Mom, I didn't say any of that to make you feel bad. I was just trying to make a point about you being as much of a workaholic as your mother and Grandma Jenny. I think you have more in common with them than you realize."

"I don't think so. We always argued about everything. You don't know what it was like."

Kelsey chuckled. "Really? Come on, Mom. Think about it. You and I have our moments. It comes with the territory. It wasn't until the past couple of years, when we've had some space between us, that we stopped arguing and started treating each other like actual people, instead of mother and daughter. You just moved away from here so I don't think that ever happened between you and your mom. She was actually pretty amazing."

"Well, I know that," her mother responded, that defensive note creeping back into her voice.

"Do you really? Did you know she was on her college swim team? Did you know that she was the first woman president of the Chamber of Commerce here?" Kelsey saw the flush in her mother's cheeks. "You didn't, did you?"

"No. How do you know that?"

"Because we talked, just like you and I are doing now. Every day I was here, we would walk on the beach and she'd tell me stories about this place and her life. And at night, on the porch, Grandma Jenny would tell me things about her past, too."

"Such as?"

"She won a prize once for doing the tango in a dance competition."

"Grandma Jenny? You have to be kidding."

Kelsey chuckled at her stunned reaction. "Not kidding. It's true. She and Great-Grandpa could really dance. He sang, too."

"In the church choir," her mother said slowly. "I remember hearing him when I was little."

"Not just in the choir. With a band. They played all over Florida. She showed me pictures."

Her mother turned to her with a bewildered expression. "How did I miss all this?"

Kelsey shrugged. "Maybe you never asked or never listened."

"Probably not."

"Let's never be like that, Mom, okay?"

"Never *again,*" Hannah said pointedly.

"I love you," Kelsey said impulsively, giving her a fierce hug.

"Love you more."

"Thanks for letting me come here. I know you'd be happier if I were in school, but I need this time to think and I needed to do that here. Not even in New York, but right here with you and Grandma Jenny."

Maybe on Seaview Key she could start to understand who she really was and where she came from in a way that would be impossible anywhere else. Maybe she could figure out what family was supposed to be, so the thought of creating one of her own wouldn't be so absolutely terrifying.

6

Luke managed to avoid Hannah for most of the day. First, he'd gone to the mainland with Grandma Jenny to exchange the paint she and Hannah had bought. When they got home late in the afternoon, he made an excuse about needing some time to himself and walked into town.

Seaview's official downtown, which was a few blocks farther away from the inn than the mom-and-pop grocery store he'd walked to the night before, had grown over the years, but it still wasn't much. There were two or three new restaurants, maybe half a dozen clothing boutiques and gift and antiques stores, and a couple of places that called themselves art galleries. He was no expert, but the works on display seemed more like some of the crafts his kids brought home from school than high-end art. Still, it made him smile to see that Seaview had gone upscale. In the old days, those spaces had sold bait and tackle and cheap T-shirts.

Though he'd had no particular destination in mind when he'd left the inn, he found himself in front of The Fish Tale, an unpretentious place that used to offer the best grouper sandwiches he'd ever tasted, along with ice-cold beer. The memory of that particular combination drew him inside.

He aimed straight for the bar and was stunned when he recognized the man behind it. Jackson Ferguson — Jack to his friends — had opened the place thirty years ago. Luke could remember the occasion as if it had been yesterday. As rustic as it was, it was the first real restaurant, besides the local diner and a couple of hot dog and hamburger stands, that catered to beachgoers. There'd been one bar that had catered to a rowdier crowd, but for too many years the full-time population of Seaview had been too small to support anything more.

There'd been balloons out front to celebrate The Fish Tale's opening, a small room with pinball machines off to one side to keep kids entertained, and a determinedly family atmosphere throughout. No one ever got drunk and unruly on Jack's watch. If anyone had a few too many before Jack caught them and put a stop to it, they were escorted outside and tucked into the island's only cab for a hasty ride home. If the cab driver — former New York cabbie John Blake — had gone home for the night, the cop on duty would provide the shuttle service.

Right now, Jack was busy at the far end of the bar, so Luke had a minute to study him. He still looked tanned and fit, though his face was more weatherbeaten than Luke remembered. He was filling orders with the alacrity and friendliness of someone who loved talking to people. When he spotted Luke, he blinked and then a grin spread across his face.

"Luke Stevens, I never expected to see you back in Seaview."

Luke reached across the bar and shook his hand. "I never expected to be here, either. How's Greta?" he asked, referring to Jack's beloved wife, who'd worked this place by his side.

Jack's expression fell. "Lost her last year," he said gruffly. "Heart attack. Damn near killed me, too, but this place doesn't run itself, and in the end, it saved me."

"I'm sorry. How about your kids? Are they still in Seaview?"

Jack pulled a draft and set it in front of Luke without asking if he wanted it. "Bill left right after high school, same as you. He had big dreams. Made good on 'em, too. He's a lawyer now. He works over in Biloxi. His home got hit hard by Hurricane Katrina, so the family came here for a couple of months, then went back to rebuild."

"And Lesley Ann?"

"You stick around tonight, you might see her. She's pregnant with her third baby and about two minutes from her due date, but that hasn't slowed her down any. She's over here once a day like clockwork to pester me about working too hard, telling me to hire more help." He shook his head. "That woman can nag worse than her mama."

Luke grinned. He'd had one memorable date with Lesley Ann and she'd done the same thing to him, nagged him from start to finish. Apparently some things never changed. "I'd like to meet the man she married," he said. "He must be very tolerant."

"That man worships the ground she walks on. He just lets all her talk roll right off his back. Maybe that comes with marrying later in life. They were thirty when they met, eloped two weeks later and never looked back." He shook his head. "Listen to me going on and on. Did you want something to eat to go with that beer?"

"You still have fried grouper sandwiches

and fries?"

"Put us on the map," Jack said. "Of course we do. You want a table, you'd better get one now. This place'll be crowded in another half hour or so."

"I'm good here," Luke said.

"I'll put in your order and check in on you from time to time."

"Thanks, Jack. It's good to see you."

The older man started toward the kitchen, then turned back. "You staying at Seaview Inn?"

Luke nodded.

Jack shook his head. "I feel real bad for Jenny. She loves that place, but I don't see how she's going to keep up with it now that her Maggie's gone. I hear Hannah's here now, but that she's not staying."

"That's my impression," Luke said.

"It's a shame when there's no one left to take over a family business. I'd figured on leaving this place to Bill, but ironically it's Lesley Ann who's taken to it. Once she has this baby, she'll be back here full time, pestering me to modernize this or to experiment with the menu." He shook his head. "I hope I don't live to see the day when she refuses to serve fried food. She already carries on about transfats."

Luke laughed. "I hear you."

"I'd best get your order in so you can finish it before she turns up. Otherwise, you'll be in for a lecture on what it's doing to your arteries."

Luke didn't waste time telling him he already knew — probably better than Lesley Ann — the dangers of fried foods. But some food was meant to be cooked that way and he figured he'd survive anything in moderation.

Once he was alone with his cold beer and his thoughts, he tried to make himself focus on the future, but all that came to him was an image of going back to Atlanta to a life nothing like the one he'd left behind. Atlanta was big enough that he and Lisa could probably co-exist and maybe even manage to be civil to each other for the sake of his kids, but going back to his medical practice was out of the question. The man who'd once been his best friend and business partner had moved in on his wife the minute his back was turned. Luke doubted he'd ever be able to see Brad Reilly without wanting to punch his face in. He could hardly practice medicine with him.

Just thinking about Brad with Lisa stirred his temper. He couldn't decide which of them he hated more. Betrayal, no matter how it happened, was devastating, but his best friend — the man he'd trusted to look out for his family while he was in Iraq — and his wife? He could still recall exactly how he'd felt when Lisa had told him in an e-mail. He could still feel the sense of shock as he read the words, the twisting pain in his gut as they sank in, and then the numbness that had followed.

What kind of woman told a man something like that when he was far from home, facing danger every single minute of every day? What kind of man blindsided a trusted friend by taking advantage of such a situation?

He knew the answer, of course. They were both self-absorbed. He'd known that about Brad since the day they'd met. Of every intern and resident he'd worked with, Brad's vanity had been legendary. Luke had looked past that and seen that he was a damn fine surgeon. Their partnership had been based on mutual respect of their abilities. Their friendship, apparently, had been built on quicksand.

As for Lisa, on some level he'd probably recognized the same trait in her, though it hadn't been exposed until the moment he'd told her about doing a tour of duty in Iraq. She'd made it plain just how unhappy she was, but he hadn't expected her to repay him by going out and having an affair with someone. He wondered if she'd gotten involved with Brad specifically because she knew that would cut out his heart.

Before he could sink all the way into a really good depression, Jack was back with his meal and another beer. He studied Luke intently for a minute.

"You need a side of conversation with that?" he asked, his expression concerned.

Luke forced a smile. "Not tonight, thanks."

"You change your mind, I'm always around," Jack said. "This job should earn me a degree in psychology. I've heard just about everything at one time or another."

"I'll keep that in mind," Luke promised.

"You going to stick around Seaview for a while?"

Luke nodded. "For a while."

"Okay, then, I'll let you get to your dinner before it gets cold. Holler if you need anything."

Unfortunately, Luke figured what he needed wasn't served in The Fish Tale, not unless Jack had a fortune-teller on staff that could offer him a clearer picture of the future than he'd seen for himself. The one he envisioned seemed pretty darn bleak.

■ ■ ■ ■

After her walk with Kelsey, Hannah returned to the inn determined to take advantage of the afternoon and evening to get a start on some of the cleaning and paperwork that had to be done. Kelsey might be here to sort through the decisions she was facing, but Hannah had flown down here to get this place ready to sell. Despite Grandma Jenny's strong objections, that was still the plan.

Dragging a vacuum cleaner, dust rags and furniture polish with her, she went from room to room in the guest wing, only to find that the rooms were already in good shape. Apparently her grandmother had gotten there ahead of her, either to prove she was still capable of running the place or in anticipation of reopening.

She approached Luke's room last, but couldn't seem to make herself open the door with her passkey. It felt too much like an invasion of his privacy. Or maybe she feared learning something about him she didn't want to know . . . such as whether or not there was a woman waiting for him back home.

"Stupid, stupid, stupid," she muttered

under her breath, and forced herself to go inside.

To her surprise the large room was neat as a pin. The few clothes Luke had brought with him hung in the closet. Towels had been placed on the racks in the bathroom, rather than tossed in a damp heap on the floor. The bed had been made with an almost military precision, sheets tucked in tight, the spread smoothed. If there was a speck of dust anywhere, she couldn't find it. Nor did she see anything personal beyond a snapshot of two kids — a gap-toothed boy and a girl — stuck into the frame of the mirror above the dresser.

Drawn to the view from the spacious room, she stood by the window and saw Luke's car turn into the driveway. Her grandmother emerged with several packages as Luke unloaded cans of exterior paint and set them on the porch. Hannah shook her head when she saw a sample streak of the bright turquoise color dabbed on the side of one can. Apparently Luke had approved of Grandma Jenny's choice.

Expecting to hear the sound of voices when they came inside, she slipped hurriedly from Luke's room and shut the door securely. To her surprise, she was greeted with silence following the familiar slap of the screen door swinging closed.

As she descended the steps, her grandmother glanced up with a startled expression.

"Hannah, what on earth are you doing?"

"I was going to clean the guest rooms, but they didn't need it."

"Well, of course not. I cleaned them just a few days ago myself."

"Gran, that's too much for you," Hannah protested.

"Don't be silly. Besides, Jolene Walker's girl, Macey, comes over once a week to help me. She scrubs the bathrooms and gets down on her hands and knees to dust around the baseboards."

"She does a good job," Hannah conceded reluctantly.

"Do you think I'd keep her on if she didn't?"

Hannah bit back a sigh. "How did your shopping trip go? I see you got the color paint you wanted."

Grandma Jenny's expression brightened. "Luke agreed with me that a little color was just what this place needed."

"Did he really? Or did you bully him into saying what you wanted to hear?"

"He's a man who knows his own mind. Besides, I was asking his opinion. Why would I bully him into anything?"

Hannah dropped the no-win subject. "Where's Luke now?"

"He went for a walk. He told me he'd get supper in town." She gave Hannah a sly look. "He mentioned something about The Fish Tale. You could join him if you wanted to. I can fix something for Kelsey. It'll give us a chance to talk. Maybe I can get to the bottom of what's going on with her." She paused. "Unless you managed to do that."

"We talked. She told me the baby's father wants to marry her, but she's not ready for that. Then she changed the subject."

"And you didn't push?"

"I thought it would be counterproductive," Hannah admitted.

"Well, I'm not so timid." She waved Hannah toward the door. "Go on now. Take a walk and see if you can find Luke. Maybe you'll have better luck figuring out what's going on with him than you had with Kelsey."

"What makes you think there's something going on with Luke?"

"He appears back here after all these years without any explanation. He's all alone. A man who looks as good as he does ought to have a woman in his life, a family."

"He has children, so there must be a

woman."

"Well, she's not with him, is she?" Grandma Jenny said. "Don't even try to tell me you're not curious. I saw you studying him the other night. And I remember the look in your eyes when he and Abby used to be over here every single day. You had a crush on that boy then, and something tells me it wouldn't take much to spark it again."

"You see entirely too much," Hannah muttered.

"And I can hear, too, so don't be making comments under your breath," her grandmother retorted.

Hannah chuckled, despite her annoyance. "Just stop matchmaking, okay? Promise me."

Her grandmother gave her a guileless look. "What can I say? It's second nature. Besides, you need a man in your life. A real man and not some ne'er-do-well who'll take off, rather than face his responsibilities."

Hannah didn't want another lecture on her ex-husband. That water was too far under the bridge. "I'm going to put these things back in the supply closet and then I'm taking a walk," she announced.

Her grandmother gave a nod of satisfaction. "Tell Jack I said hello."

"I never said I was going to The Fish Tale."

Grandma Jenny shrugged. "You're a fool if you don't, and I don't think we raised any fools in this house."

"You just finished telling me I made a foolish choice when it came to picking a husband," Hannah reminded her.

"You were young. It was a mistake. Now you have a second chance to do things right."

"Why are you so sure Luke would be right? You don't know anything about his life since he left here."

"I know enough," she replied. "And I've seen that look in his eyes before. He's seen his share of sorrows. A man who feels things that deeply has strength of character."

"If you say so," Hannah said doubtfully. "Are you sure you don't want me to stay and fix dinner?"

"I already told you I want some time alone with my great-granddaughter."

Dismissed, Hannah put away the cleaning supplies, washed her face and hands and brushed on a light coating of lipstick. As she gazed at her reflection in the mirror, she noticed that her cheeks had some much-needed color in them. Her hair, usually tamed with spray, was windblown from her earlier walk on the beach and had more curl than she was accustomed to. She looked almost carefree and relaxed. Which was a lie, given everything she had on her mind, but maybe for a few hours she could pretend that all was right in her world.

And her grandmother was correct about one thing: Luke was the most intriguing male distraction to cross her path in eons. She'd enjoyed talking to him on the porch last night. She'd enjoyed testing her out-of-practice flirting skills on him. If that was as far as things ever went between them, it would be enough to remind her that, cancer or not, her life wasn't over yet. She needed to live every moment that remained as if it might be her last.

Hannah strolled through town, assuring herself that The Fish Tale didn't have to be her destination. She could explore for an hour or so and go home. Luke would never have to know that she'd gone out intending to track him down.

She shook her head. She was acting like a teenager with her first crush. How many times had she and Abby plotted to run into Luke "accidentally on purpose"? More times than she could count. None of those encounters had had the desired result, though. It had taken something far more dramatic to finally catch Luke's attention.

Abby had nearly drowned and Luke had saved her. Afterward, he'd finally taken notice. From then on three of them had been inseparable. The situation had tortured Hannah, who'd developed her own crush on Luke but kept silent about it, especially after Luke had chosen Abby. Girlfriends didn't poach. Luke was as off limits to her as if he and Abby had had rings on their fingers.

When she reached The Fish Tale, she stood outside the door debating whether to go inside.

"The food's really good," a chipper voice announced behind her. "I can vouch for it. My family owns the place."

Hannah whirled around, a smile spreading. "Lesley Ann?"

"Oh, my gosh, Hannah! I can't believe it," Lesley Ann said, enveloping her in a hug made awkward by the size of her belly.

"You're having a baby," Hannah said, standing back to look at her. "And you're absolutely glowing."

"My third," Lesley Ann told her. "He's due any minute, so I'm not even supposed to be here, but I like to come down and check on Dad about this time every day. Since my mom died, he works too hard, but getting him to slow down is like talking to a wall. I imagine you're having the same problem with Jenny."

"Oh, yeah," Hannah confirmed.

"Come on, let's go in. I'll treat you to dinner on the house," Lesley Ann offered.

Hannah nodded, relieved not to be walking in alone.

Lesley Ann pulled open the door and stepped inside. "Hey, Dad, look who I found lurking on the sidewalk."

Just as she spoke, Luke slowly swiveled around on his seat at the bar and met Hannah's gaze. His lips quirked into a smile, though Hannah wasn't sure if it was meant for her or Lesley Ann.

"And look who turned up here earlier," Jack called back to his daughter, gesturing toward Luke. "Why don't you three find yourselves a table and catch up? I'll bring over some drinks. Hannah, what can I get you? A beer? Soda? Something to eat?"

"A beer and a fish sandwich," she said at once.

"Just some water for me, Dad," Lesley Ann said, then wove her way between the tables. "Let's take that empty table by the window, instead of a booth," she added, rubbing a hand protectively over her stomach. "This tummy of mine doesn't fit in the booths so well at the moment."

She led the way toward a table and pulled out a chair before Luke could get to it. He shrugged and gestured for Hannah to sit in the one he'd pulled out.

"Same old independent streak," he said to Lesley Ann.

"My mother taught me well," she retorted. "Now, tell me everything about yourselves. Hannah, you're living in New York, right?"

"Yes, and working in public relations."

"That sounds so exciting. Do you love it?"

"I do. It's everything I ever wanted," she claimed, then wondered why, if that was true, she wasn't happier these days. It had to be because of all the pressure she was under lately, not any dissatisfaction with her life.

"Luke, how about you?" Lesley Ann asked. "I haven't heard anything about you since your folks moved away while you were still in college."

"There's not that much to tell," he said tightly. His expression shut down momentarily, then turned to relief when Jack came over with their drinks and Hannah's sandwich.

Hannah took her first bite, then sighed. "It's every bit as good as I remembered."

Luke grinned. "I said the same thing."

"Well, of course it is," Lesley Ann said

indignantly. “It was Mama’s recipe and we don’t let anyone mess with it.”

“I hear you’re going to take over one of these days,” Luke said.

“I am, that is, if I can ever talk Dad into retiring.” She glanced toward the bar where Jack was once more chatting with a customer. “How can I push it, though, when this place is all that keeps him going now that Mama’s gone? You must know what I mean, Hannah. It must be like that for your grandmother since your mom died. Seaview Inn must mean more to her than ever.”

Hannah nodded slowly, hating to admit that Lesley Ann was right. “But I don’t see how she can keep up with it at her age.”

“Hire someone to help her,” Lesley Ann said matter-of-factly. “Or come back here yourself. I know you two were both anxious to get away from Seaview. I suppose we all were back then. But I have to tell you, I appreciate it now. It’s been a great place to raise kids and the slow pace is just right for me. Tourist season is a madhouse, but the rest of the year there’s plenty of time to catch my breath.”

Hannah didn’t want to cast a damper on her enthusiasm, but it was already the height of the tourist season, and by her standards, Seaview was as slow-paced and boring as ever. Sure, business was hopping here at The Fish Tale, but what else was there to do in town?

"I'm afraid I'd lose my mind living here," she admitted. "I'm used to going to the theater and concerts, to going out for any kind of ethnic food I want, and to spending an afternoon at a museum or an art gallery when I have the time."

Luke studied her intently as she spoke, then asked, "When was the last time you had the time? According to your grandmother, you're a workaholic."

Hannah winced but saw little reason to deny it. "Okay, yes, I am, but it's all there if I want to go," she said.

"It's wasted if you don't take advantage of it," he said.

There had been a time when she had, she remembered. She'd studied the endless list of gallery openings in the paper and chosen the ones she wanted to attend. She'd gone to free concerts practically every weekend, scraped up money for a balcony seat at the ballet or the latest Broadway musical. Even with money tight, she'd seen to it that Kelsey was exposed to every bit of culture that New York had to offer. When had that changed? Now she had enough money and sufficient contacts to sit front row center at just about anything in the city and she rarely took the time to go anywhere.

"Where do you live?" she asked Luke. "I'll bet it's not anyplace like Seaview. I'll bet it's a big city that's bustling with things to do."

"I was living in Atlanta," he said, suddenly looking distant again.

"Was?" she repeated, studying his expression for some clue about why he'd phrased it like that. "Aren't you going back there?"

"Maybe," he said, then shrugged. "Probably."

"Why so noncommittal?" Lesley Ann asked.

"Long story," he said succinctly. "And it's getting late. I need to get some rest if I'm going to start painting in the morning."

Hannah frowned. "You don't have to paint the inn, Luke. We can hire someone to do it."

"That was the deal I made with your grandmother," he countered. "She let me come even though the inn is closed if I would help with some of the renovations."

"I don't know what it is with you two," Hannah grumbled. "She lets you move in even though we're not taking reservations and you let her talk you into buying that awful turquoise paint."

"It's not awful," Luke protested, though his lips were twitching as he fought amusement. "It's cheery and colorful."

Hannah turned to Lesley Ann and rolled her eyes. "See what I mean? The two of them are in cahoots."

"I think it's sweet that Luke wants to help out," Lesley Ann said. "And the color does sound like fun. Let me know when it's finished and I'll bring Dad over to take a look. I've been pleading with him to let me paint this place a pretty shade of coral. I keep telling him it will make it look more beachy."

"It must be something in the air," Hannah muttered.

Luke laughed. "Could be. You walking back now?"

"I suppose so, as long as you don't try to sell me on that paint color while we walk."

"Wouldn't dream of it," he claimed, though his eyes were dancing with mischief. "I thought I'd fill you in on the color she wants to use in the dining room."

Hannah gazed at him with dismay. "What color?"

"I'll tell you on the way," he promised, giving Lesley Ann a wink. "Good night. We'll be back again, I'm sure."

"Good night, you two. Don't be strangers.

It's good to have you home again."

As they left and stepped outside, Hannah shuddered slightly, drawing an odd look from Luke.

"Cold?" he asked.

"No, I was just thinking about what Lesley Ann said. I haven't thought of Seaview as home in years."

"You can't deny where you came from," he said. "Like it or not, this is home."

"No, it's where I grew up," she said emphatically. "Home is New York."

"Other than people you work with, tell me half a dozen people in New York who know your name, much less your likes and dislikes," he challenged.

She was determined to rise to the bait, but it was harder than she'd expected. "The man in the bagel shop knows I like plain with extra cream cheese," she retorted finally.

"And his name is?"

She searched her mind, then came up with it. "Raul," she said triumphantly, then faltered. "Or is it Rafael?"

"You're obviously close," Luke commented dryly.

"Okay, I have a best friend I've known for years and lots of acquaintances. Are you telling me that it's any better in Atlanta? Is your life brimming with close friends?"

"No, but that's my point. There's something nice about being in a community where you can walk into a restaurant and the owners know you and your history and your family. Come on, admit it, Hannah. It felt comfortable being at The Fish Tale, seeing Jack and Lesley Ann again."

"Well, sure, for one night, it was good to catch up a little," she conceded. "But do you really think either one of us has a thing in common with them anymore?"

"We have a shared past, a ton of memories, friends in common. And they're not as isolated as we were when we were kids. The tourists who come through here now are from all walks of life and come from all over the world. I imagine Jack and Lesley Ann could carry on a lively conversation about just about anything. Talking to the customers is a necessary skill in a place like that."

"I think you've seriously overdosed on nostalgia," she said. "You'd be just as sick of this place in a month as I would be."

He turned and met her gaze. "I'm not so sure about that."

"You can't seriously be thinking about staying here," she said, stunned. "You have a life in Atlanta. Not ten minutes ago you said you'd be going back there."

"I said I'd *probably* be going back and I *had* a life in Atlanta," he said. "I'm not sure how much of it can be salvaged."

"Do you want to explain that?" she asked, her curiosity piqued. He'd sounded every bit as sad as her grandmother had claimed.

He shook his head. "One of these days, but not tonight. Let's just walk along the beach and enjoy the peace and quiet."

"There is no peace and quiet," she grumbled. "Have you ever listened to the waves?"

Beside her, Luke reached for her hand. "Hush, Hannah. You're making more noise than the waves."

She quieted at once, trying to decide how she felt about having her hand wrapped in his, his fingers entwined with hers. Twenty years ago, she would have given anything for a moment like this on a night like this with stars in the sky and a tiny sliver of a moon reflected on the water. Her heart would have filled to bursting if Luke had shown her even this much attention.

Tonight, though, with his declaration that he might stay in Seaview Key hanging in the air, the contact and the spark it stirred in her scared her to death. She could not fall for Luke Stevens a second time, only to have her heart broken again. If something was actually kindled between them this time, how could she possibly survive walking away? And walking away was inevitable because the life she wanted was in New York.

Then Luke lifted their hands to his lips and brushed a kiss across her knuckles. And in that second, it felt as if her world began and ended right here on this stretch of sand.

7

Sitting on the porch with Grandma Jenny, Kelsey rocked slowly. When she'd come to Seaview Key on her spring break back in high school, she'd discovered how soothing it could be to sit outside on a nice evening and rock, just listening to the sound of the waves and the birds and whatever music her grandmother and Grandma Jenny had chosen to put on the CD player that evening. Until then she hadn't realized how quiet it could be without the constant blare of honking horns and garbage trucks outside. Even in the middle of the night, New York was never really silent.

On that visit, she'd also liked listening to the stories the two older women told about their family history and about the guests who'd stayed at the inn over the years. She thought it was ironic that she and her mom lived in a huge city, crammed with thousands of tourists every single day, and they never met any of them. Yet down here, where the population was next to nothing, her grandmother and great-grandmother were actually getting to know people from all over the world, more than Kelsey had ever spoken to on all her trips abroad.

"Grandma Jenny, did you ever want to live somewhere else?" she asked, breaking the comfortable silence.

"Not even for a minute," she replied. "This is home, always was." She gave Kelsey a pointed look. "And it will be to the day I die."

Kelsey grinned at the firm declaration. "Has Mom been on your case about moving to a retirement place?"

"She's danced around the subject ever since she got here."

"Have you told her how you feel?"

"In no uncertain terms," her great-grandmother declared. "Doubt she's listened, though. Your mom came by her stubbornness naturally. Your grandmother Maggie was the same way." She grinned. "I'm worse."

"I don't think you should have to move if you don't want to," Kelsey said quietly. She'd been struck by an unexpected idea soon after she'd arrived. She wasn't sure exactly when she'd decided that it was the perfect answer for her right now, but once it had come to her, she'd embraced the plan wholeheartedly. Now seemed like as good a time as any to bounce it off Grandma Jenny. "I could stay for a while and help you out, you know, till the baby's born." She held her breath as she awaited her great-grandmother's response. To make the plan work, she needed Grandma Jenny on her side.

"Kelsey, you're a sweetheart to offer, but we both know that your mom thinks you should go back to school and finish your education."

Kelsey analyzed the response and decided it wasn't a total rejection of the proposal. "She's said that, like, a million times, but is that what you think, too?" she pressed. "Or are you saying what you think she'd want you to say?"

"I certainly agree with her that an education is important and I would hate to see you walk away from college and not go back," she replied.

Kelsey could tell she was choosing her words carefully. "But what do you really think?" she asked again.

"That it needs to be your decision, same as staying here should be mine," Grandma Jenny admitted.

"That's what I think, too," Kelsey said with a sigh. "I've tried explaining that to Mom, but she won't listen, so I've pretty much given up. I really would like to stay here. I'm glad Mom was here when I told her about the baby. Coming here was better than going to New York. In a weird way, it felt kinda like coming home. Do you think that's crazy?"

"Of course not. This *is* your home, even though you haven't spent much time here. Your family's roots are here. And one day, if you should ever decide you want it, this inn would be yours, too."

Kelsey's mouth gaped. "Really? It could be mine?"

"Well, who else would I leave it to? Hannah doesn't want it. I suppose if neither of you did, then you'd sell and split that money, but I don't want that to happen in my lifetime. It would hurt too much to see it in the hands of strangers, especially some developer who'd raze it and put up condos."

Kelsey sat back and fell silent. The thought of owning Seaview Inn someday had never crossed her mind. For years she'd been focused on having a career in graphic design because it was something she had an aptitude for, but her heart wasn't in it anymore. Not really. She liked people, liked talking to them to see what made them tick, cheering them up when they were down. What could be better than running a place where people came to relax and have a good time?

Besides, ever since that last visit, she'd felt a connection here to something bigger than herself. She'd had this nagging sense that this was where she belonged. Could it be that this unplanned pregnancy had happened simply to show her another option for her life? Wouldn't that be amazing?

She turned sideways. "Grandma Jenny, please let me stay here, at least until I have the baby. It'll give me time to figure things out."

"You mean like whether you really love the baby's father?"

Kelsey shook her head slowly. "No, I already know that I love Jeff. I'm just not ready to be married. I don't know who I am yet. And marriage is supposed to be forever, like you and Great-Granddad, not like my mom and dad. That's what I want, but how can I commit to something like that until I really know what I want out of life? Does that sound totally selfish?"

Grandma Jenny reached over and squeezed her hand. "No, I think you're much wiser than your mother and I have given you credit for," she said. "Of course you can stay here for as long as you want."

"Mom's going to be furious," Kelsey said, trying to imagine how that conversation was likely to go.

"Let me handle your mother. All she really wants is for you to be happy."

"That's all she wants for you, too," Kelsey reminded her.

"Then I suppose we'll both just have to show her what makes us happy," Grandma Jenny said matter-of-factly.

Just then faint voices rose over the sound of the waves.

"I bet that's your mother and Luke now," Grandma Jenny said. "They'll be here soon."

Kelsey wasn't anxious to have the serenity she was feeling broken. "Maybe we should go up to bed."

"Running away never accomplishes a thing, young lady."

"I was just thinking maybe they'd like some privacy. Admit it, Grandma Jenny. You're trying to get something going between them. I saw that gleam in your eye the other night when I first got here."

"You think you're so smart, don't you? Okay, yes, I'd like to see your mother find someone new. Everyone should have a special person in their life who cares about them."

"You never married again after Great-Grandpa died."

"That's different."

"How?" Kelsey asked.

"You saw how well we got along. We were together for more than sixty years and you don't get over something like that in the blink of an eye. I still miss him every single day and it's been four years now since he died. And it was just a couple of years after that when your grandmother got sick and all my time and attention were devoted to her. Besides, once you're my age, there aren't that many old coots around worth bothering with."

Kelsey giggled. "How about a younger man?" she teased. "You've still got a lot of spunk left in you."

"Now, that might be worth considering," Grandma Jenny said with a wink, "but most of them are chasing women half their age. No, I'm content with things the way they are. Your mom, though, is young enough to start over. And after the turmoil your dad put her through, leaving and coming back more than once before bailing completely . . ." She shook her head. "Well, she deserves to find real happiness with someone worthy of her."

"Do you really think Luke could be that someone?"

Her great-grandmother gave her a sideways glance. "Have you taken a good look at that man?"

"You know, there's more to a man than his looks, at least that's what Mom has always told me."

"Well, of course there is, but it's a fine place to start." She rose slowly to her feet. "You know, I think you had the right idea about going inside before they cross the street. Who knows what could happen between those two on a night like this if we're not around."

"Are you going up to bed or are you going to peek through the living room window to see what they're up to?" Kelsey asked.

"I would never do such a thing," Grandma Jenny retorted indignantly. "I am going to bed just as soon as I change the music to something a little more romantic."

"I could run inside and pour a couple of glasses of wine for them," Kelsey suggested, getting into the spirit of things.

"Too obvious," Grandma Jenny objected. "But you could leave a bottle and glasses on the kitchen counter where they'll be sure to see them. Then they'll think it's *their* idea."

Kelsey regarded her approvingly. "You're very good at this matchmaking thing."

"Oh, I've had my moments," she said, tucking her arm through Kelsey's. "Something tells me you're going to take after me."

Kelsey met her gaze evenly. "I hope so. I really do." Between her mom and Grandma Jenny, Kelsey thought, she couldn't have two better role models. She just had to get her mom to see that she'd learned the value of being strong and independent from them.

Luke left Hannah alone in a rocker on the porch and went inside to get them something to drink. When he spotted the bottle of wine and two glasses prominently placed in the center of the kitchen counter, he chuckled. He supposed they'd been left there as a subtle hint, but it might have been more subtle if the bottle hadn't been uncorked.

He grabbed the wine bottle by the neck and picked up the two glasses, then returned to the porch.

"Look what I found in the kitchen," he said dryly. "I'm fairly certain it was meant for us."

Hannah sighed. "I'm sorry. Grandma Jenny's determined to matchmake."

"Seems to me people only do that when they think their targets need help. Are we that pathetic?"

Hannah grinned. "I don't know about you, but I certainly am." She met his gaze. "Don't feel obligated to make a pass at me, though."

"Obligation might not enter into it," he said, realizing even as he spoke that it was true. He was attracted to Hannah. Walking hand in hand with her on the beach had felt comfortable. It had felt right. More than that, it had stirred feelings in him that he thought had died right along with his marriage.

"You probably shouldn't say things like that," Hannah said.

"Why not?"

"Because . . ." She faced him. "Luke, just how complicated is your life right now?"

He knew he owed her nothing less than total honesty. "Pretty complicated," he admitted.

"Mine, too. It's a really bad time to start something that can't possibly go anywhere, don't you think?"

"I suppose." He felt strangely disappointed, despite the logic.

"I'm sorry, though."

"Me, too," he said. He turned and waited till her gaze met his. There it was, that simmering heat just waiting for the right spark to set it ablaze. It seemed like a damn shame to waste it, but he didn't have the right to complicate her life, not when she'd made it plain it was chaotic enough. "Does that mean we can't just sit here as old friends and enjoy the wine and the evening?"

He thought he could see a faint smile on her lips as she shook her head.

"No," she said softly. "It doesn't mean that at all."

He supposed there were worse things than coming home and finding an old friend with whom he could share a few memories, some laughs and a quiet night like this. In fact, it was a pleasant surprise, like leaving his quarters in Iraq one day to find a wildflower determinedly sprouting through a crack in the concrete.

"In the name of friendship, do you want to tell me what's going on in your life?" he asked. "I assume Kelsey's pregnancy isn't the only issue."

"Not by a long shot," she admitted. "How about you? You want to tell me what's gone wrong in your life?"

He chuckled. "It could be sort of like, I'll show you my messed-up life, if you show me yours."

For an instant she seemed to consider the idea, then shook her head. "Nah," she said. "It's too nice a night to spoil it."

"Just remember that friends can share their problems, Hannah, okay? Anytime."

"Thanks. The same goes for you."

"And spoil the illusion that I'm perfect?" he teased.

"Only Grandma Jenny thinks that," she retorted. "You've already admitted to me that your life's messed up."

"Through no fault of my own," he felt compelled to say.

"Really? You sure about that?"

He thought about what had happened, thought all the way back to the beginning when he'd made the unilateral decision to go to Iraq in the first place. That was when it had started. Had he deserved what had happened? No. He would never accept that. But had he put it all in motion by not taking into account how strongly Lisa felt about him going back into the army? No question about it.

He sighed heavily. "I'm not sure how I feel about having a friend who can cut through the crap and call me on it," he said.

She regarded him with surprise. "Did I do that?"

"Yep, and it was damned annoying, if you must know, especially since you had no idea you were doing it."

She grinned at him. "Just think how much help I could be if I knew what on earth we were talking about."

"One of these days," he promised. "I'm just not ready to rip the scabs off the wounds yet."

She reached over to tap her glass against his. "To future revelations."

"And to healing," he added. Somehow he knew that Hannah had as much of that to do as he did.

"Grandma Jenny, guess what?" Kelsey called out excitedly as she ran onto the porch just before lunchtime the next day. She came to an abrupt stop and her expression faltered when she spotted Hannah standing in the yard painting the porch railing.

Hannah didn't miss Kelsey's suddenly guilty expression or Grandma Jenny's expectant one. She stood there and waited to see what the two of them were up to.

"What?" Grandma Jenny asked.

"I've booked five reservations this morning," Kelsey announced, avoiding Hannah's gaze. "Every single family I contacted made a reservation the second I told them we were reopening." She glanced at the sheet of paper she was holding. "The Van Dorns said to tell you hello, and the Johnsons said they need one more room this time because they have two new grandchildren and they want the whole family to come this year. They're booking four rooms in all. The Marshals, the Watsons and the Gradys are confirmed, too. Everyone's so excited to be coming back. A few of them are even canceling reservations they made at other places because they'd rather be here."

"That's wonderful," Grandma Jenny said enthusiastically. "Good work, Kelsey."

Hannah bit back the sharp comment that was on the tip of her tongue. Fighting to keep her temper in check, she asked quietly, "Why are you taking reservations, Kelsey?"

"It's an inn," she said matter-of-factly. "Renting rooms is what keeps us in business. People are thrilled to hear we haven't closed for good. It's really great, Mom. I heard so many wonderful stories this morning! People were telling me about how many years they've come here and how they look forward to it. You should have heard them."

"Whose idea was it to start calling people?"

Kelsey gave her a defiant look. "Mine.

Grandma said you hadn't done anything about sending out an announcement about the reopening, so I decided to start making calls to some of the regulars."

"Exactly when were the two of you planning to tell me about this?" she asked, not sure whether she was more furious that she'd been left out of the loop or that it was happening at all. How could they sell the place if it was filled to capacity? Or would that actually turn out to be a selling point? Maybe she was looking at this the wrong way.

"You know now," Grandma Jenny said with a touch of defiance. "I've said all along I wanted to get this place reopened as soon as possible. You were the one dragging your feet."

"Because you can't manage this place on your own," Hannah said, then caught the expression on Kelsey's face. A sense of dread settled in her stomach. "Go back inside, Kelsey. I need to speak to your great-grandmother."

Kelsey plopped down in a chair next to Grandma Jenny's. "No. This concerns me, too."

"Why on earth do you think that?" Hannah asked, again assailed by the feeling that she wasn't going to like the answer.

"Because I'm going to stay here and help Grandma Jenny keep the inn running," Kelsey said flatly.

"Over my dead body," Hannah said, her temper coming to a boil. She dropped the paint brush back into the bucket and marched up to the porch, scowling at the pair of them. Then she focused her attention on her grandmother. "What were you thinking putting such a ridiculous idea into her head? She needs to go back to Stanford, and the sooner the better."

"That's not what she wants to do," Grandma Jenny replied, her tone gentle. "Listen to her, Hannah. She wants to stay here, at least until the baby is born."

"And then what? Waste the rest of her life in this nothing little town?"

"I like Seaview Key," Kelsey protested. "And I want to stay here, at least for now, so that's what I'm going to do. I know you don't like it, Mom, and I'm sorry, but it's not your decision."

"We had a deal," Hannah argued, even though she knew the battle was lost. Kelsey was so strong-willed that any arguments would only solidify her resolve.

"I think our deal pretty much went up in smoke the day I found out I was pregnant," Kelsey said.

"Plenty of young women manage to attend classes while they're pregnant," Hannah said.

"I could probably drag myself around to my classes and maybe even pass them," Kelsey agreed. "But you've forgotten about the rest. Jeff wants to get married. He'll be in my face every single day and it will only get worse the closer I get to my due date. I can't deal with that kind of pressure, plus school. The one thing the doctor warned me about was stressing out. It's not good for me or the baby."

She stood up and looked Hannah in the eye. "Please, Mom, don't fight me on this. It's what I want, and in the end, I know it's for the best. This will give me the time I need to make a decision that's right for everyone — the baby, Jeff and me."

"Kelsey, staying here isn't the answer. You and Jeff should be working through this together."

"We can't," Kelsey said simply. "I know what will happen. I'll have a couple of bad days and he'll be right there, ready to make everything okay and I'll cave in because it's easier than dealing with all this alone. That's no way to start a marriage, not if I want it to last."

"Listen to how wise she's being, Hannah,"

Grandma Jenny chimed in. "You should be proud of her."

"I think you planted this idea in her head," Hannah accused her grandmother heatedly. They'd ganged up on her and she hated it. "You know I want to sell Seaview Inn, so you've enlisted Kelsey to help you keep it open. You've been determined to fight me on this and now you've found the perfect way."

"Mom, that's not fair," Kelsey said. "This was *my* decision. I came to Grandma Jenny with the idea of staying. In fact, I had to talk her into it, so don't blame her for any of this. I'm the one who screwed up and let you down."

Before Hannah could think of a single argument to convince Kelsey to go back to California, the girl was gone. Hannah sank into the chair Kelsey had vacated.

"This is wrong!" she said angrily. "It is so wrong."

"Not if it's what she wants," her grandmother said, her tone calm and reasonable. "You heard her, Hannah. She needs time to think, and what better place to do that than here?"

"She's barely twenty. She doesn't know what she wants."

"I think she does." Jenny regarded Hannah sympathetically. "I know how hard this is for you. Don't you think it killed your mother and me to have you announce that you wanted to move away from here and have nothing more to do with Seaview Key or the inn? But we let you go, didn't we? And we did it with grace. Don't you think Kelsey deserves the same consideration from you?"

Hannah eventually sat back in defeat. "Okay, you're right, I know you are. But how can I support this decision when it's going to ruin her life?"

"Because it's her life to ruin, her mistake to make," her grandmother suggested. "And who knows? She could prove you wrong. And it's not as if she's giving up college forever. She put a time limit on it, just until she has the baby. By then, she may hate this place as much as you do and be ready to go back to school. Or she may have found that this is where she wants to spend the rest of her life."

"I still think this works out awfully conveniently for you," Hannah muttered.

"Perhaps so, but I swear to you I had no part in planting the idea in her head. She was the one who came to me. Kelsey is a young woman who knows her own mind. You of all people should know that. You taught her well."

"Right now, I'm not feeling as if that's quite the compliment you meant it to be."

"It's going to work out. You'll see. Maybe you should focus on your own life and stop worrying so much about what will happen next with Kelsey."

"My life is just fine," Hannah protested, uttering the lie with total conviction.

"Really?" Grandma Jenny said, her skepticism as plain as Hannah's had been earlier. "Here's the way I see it. I know you must have a follow-up doctor's appointment soon and you must be scared to death. Who could blame you after the way things went with your mother? And I know you're not nearly as happy with your job as you want everyone to believe. You're successful, but you're at the beck and call of too many people. You have absolutely no time to enjoy your success. And I know that deep down inside, you wonder sometimes if you're truly living whatever time might be left to you."

Tears stung Hannah's eyes at the assessment. She'd had no idea Grandma Jenny could read her so well. Obviously she was stronger and more astute than ever. The problem was, Hannah wasn't ready to deal with any of it. These days her biggest accomplishment was putting one foot in front of the other and getting through each day.

"I don't want to talk about it," she said.

"You should. Burdens are always lighter when they're shared. Listen to me, Hannah," she said, then waited until Hannah turned to face her. "Not dealing with your fears, not doing whatever you can to reach for the things that make you happy, those are the real mistakes we make in life. And when our time comes, whenever that is, it's the things we didn't do that we regret the most."

"Do you have regrets?" she asked, because she didn't want to focus on her own.

"Only one, that your grandfather and I didn't find the time to take that cruise we'd been promising ourselves we'd take. We were always too busy and then it was too late."

"I never wanted to take a cruise," Hannah said.

"But what do you want to do that you haven't done?"

She thought about it for several minutes, then choked back a sob. It had been so long since she'd allowed herself to dream, she didn't even have one. How pitiful was that?

Even though she hadn't spoken, her grandmother gave her a commiserating look. "Take a page from your daughter's book. Use the time you're down here to think about it. Make some lists. Set some priorities. You had dreams once. You'll have them again, if you stop crowding them out with all the must-dos that aren't half as important as we make them out to be."

"You think so?" she asked, torn between hope and disbelief.

"I *know* so," her grandmother said. "Now, I'm going in to fix us all some lunch. Why don't you track down Luke and tell him it'll be ready in a half hour?"

"Luke Stevens is not my dream," she said, because she thought she ought to.

Grandma Jenny smiled. "He was once," she said complacently. "Fate, karma, whatever you want to call it, has brought both of you here. Second chances don't come along every day, Hannah. You need to seize them when they do."

That said, she went inside and left Hannah with way too much to think about, including the fact that her grandmother was happier and more alive than ever now that her beloved inn was going to stay open.

8

After her grandmother had gone inside, Hannah stayed where she was, immobilized by the sense that her life was spinning even further out of control. Despite Grandma Jenny's bracing talk that she could change things by making lists and prioritizing, she had a feeling she was incapable of getting any of it right. Just look at how badly she was bungling things with her daughter and her grandmother.

How had this happened to her? From the moment she'd been old enough to know her own mind, she'd set goals and met them. Heck, she'd *exceeded* most of them. She'd overcome every single obstacle that had been thrown in her path.

Determined to go to an out-of-state school, she'd won a scholarship that had allowed her to go to Columbia in New York City. Barely out of college and only recently married, she'd found herself pregnant.

She'd had Kelsey and still stayed on her career track, though the difficulty she'd had was just one of the reasons she was so worried about what lay ahead for her daughter.

When her husband had left for the third and final time after two roller-coaster years, she'd tightened the reins on her spending and managed to stay in the co-op apartment they'd bought together. She'd taken on freelance work to get the money she needed to put Kelsey in the best private schools in the city and start her college fund. For all of those years, she'd known exactly what she needed to do and how to accomplish it.

Now, suddenly, she was at a loss. She was losing ground at work because of her absences. Her friendship with Dave and her years of hard work could only carry her for so long. She couldn't control what was happening to her daughter. She couldn't control what was happening inside her own body. And all of it scared the daylights out of her. Grandma Jenny was right about that.

Admitting to the fear didn't accomplish one darn thing as far as she could tell. She needed solutions, but not a single one came to mind.

"You're looking gloomy," Luke said, coming around the side of the house wearing a pair of well-worn jeans and nothing else.

His broad shoulders, already starting to tan, were speckled with chips of the old white paint he'd been scraping off the inn. He looked sexy and way too appealing.

"It's been a challenging morning," she said. "Lunch should be ready any minute. I was supposed to let you know a little while ago."

"And yet you didn't," he said, climbing the steps to take a seat beside her, his body heat radiating to encompass her. She could barely resist the urge to lean into all that masculinity and draw on his strength. "What's going on? Is there something you want to talk about?"

Hannah had no idea where to begin. "Kelsey's decided she wants to stay here and help Gran run the inn."

"Sounds like a good idea to me," he said.

She frowned at him. "It's a horrible idea."

"Why? Because it's not what you want for her? Or what you had planned for your grandmother?"

She winced. "Okay, yes, that's part of it. I'm afraid she'll never go back to college and that Gran will make herself sick trying to keep up with this place."

"Kids always do better when they know what they want and where they're going," he suggested. "*We* did."

Hannah saw the parallel he was trying to draw. It was the same one Grandma Jenny had alluded to, that she herself had gone her own way. "Okay, you're right, but until now Kelsey had other things planned. When she was a little kid and came to work with me, she loved sitting with the graphic designers. By the time she turned ten, she could lay out a brochure that was as good as anything the pros did."

"That's what she was studying? Graphic design?"

Hannah nodded. "She has real talent, Luke. She could have a job at my firm the day after graduation. That's not just a proud mother talking. My boss has told her that."

"Maybe it's too easy," he said. "If she's been doing it since she was a kid, maybe she's bored with it and needs a new challenge. Or maybe what she needs now is just some breathing room. Being pregnant when she wasn't expecting it is more than enough to justify taking some time to reexamine things. Do you honestly want her to leap into a marriage she might regret or to waste money taking classes that no longer challenge or excite her?"

Hannah scowled. "Why do you have to be so darn reasonable?"

"It's a knack," he retorted. "It's *her* life,

Hannah. Not yours. She's not your little girl anymore. She's a grown woman. You can't make her choices for her, not about this any more than you could keep her from getting pregnant in the first place."

"Are you this calm and rational about your own problems?"

He smiled ruefully. "Of course not."

"Then let me have a crack at fixing something for you so I don't feel totally inept."

"I'm not fixing anything for you," he countered. "Just trying to give you another perspective." He stood up and held out a hand. "Now, let's go inside and have some lunch. You'll feel better. If you're very good, I'll take you into town afterward for ice cream."

"You're bribing me to leave my daughter in peace?"

"Maybe I'm just bribing you to spend some time with me," he said.

Since she hadn't had a better offer all day, she gave in and put her hand in his as she stood. "Ice cream sounds good. As hot as it is, though, wouldn't you rather have an ice-cold beer?"

"And miss the chance to watch you run your tongue over a scoop of ice cream? No way."

She saw the amusement dancing in his

eyes. “You’re flirting, Luke. Stop it!”

“No, I’m taking your mind off your troubles. There’s a difference.”

Maybe there was, she thought, but whatever he was doing, whatever his intention was, the result was a jittery sensation she had absolutely no idea how to handle. It was just one more thing to be added to the growing list of complications in her life.

Kelsey watched her mom warily all during lunch, waiting for another lecture about what a mistake she was making by staying in Seaview. She was ready once more to tell her to butt out, but her mom was oddly quiet. Luke and Grandma Jenny were the only ones talking.

“I’ll have most of the old paint scraped off by the end of the day tomorrow,” Luke said. “Then I’ll put on the primer.”

“What about the turquoise?” Grandma Jenny asked. “I can’t wait to see what it’s going to look like.”

“Me, too,” Kelsey said, casting a defiant look at her mother.

“We’re dealing with old wood. It needs this primer,” Luke said. “Otherwise, the boards will just soak up the paint. You won’t be happy with the results.”

“But you *will* be able to finish before opening day, won't you?" Grandma Jenny asked worriedly.

"You told me two weeks," he said. "Is that still the plan?"

Kelsey nodded. "Our first guests aren't due until March the first. I tried to give you a little bit of a cushion."

"Then we'll definitely be ready by then," he said. "Is the painting the only thing you need me to do?"

"What about those side steps, Grandma Jenny?" Kelsey asked. "A couple of them are loose. And I think the beach entrance where people hang their towels could use a fresh coat of paint. Maybe the floor could be painted the same color as the outside of the inn. The wood is pretty worn from all the sand that's been tracked through there. What do you think?"

Her great-grandmother regarded her with surprise. "I think that's a very good idea. Have you been making notes on what needs to be done around here?"

Kelsey shrugged. "Sure. That's part of my job, isn't it? We want everything to look great when people come back."

She noticed her mom frowning, but was grateful she didn't say anything. Another fight about this was pointless. And it was fun taking a fresh look at the inn and coming up with ideas to make it more appealing. None of the things on her list would cost much, either.

"I'm impressed," Grandma Jenny said. "Any other thoughts?"

"Do you have special menus and recipes? Should we look at those? Maybe I should practice some of them so I can help in the kitchen. I'm not a bad cook." She glanced at her mother. "Mom always hated cooking, so if I wanted to avoid having takeout night after night, I had to have meals ready when she got home."

"I didn't hate to cook," her mom protested. "I just never had time to do it right."

"There you go," Kelsey said. "You're a perfectionist about everything."

"If you're going to fix a decent meal for people, it requires more than the right ingredients," her grandmother said, taking her mom's side for once. "There's no point in doing it if you're just going to slap something together and put it on the table."

"Hey, everything I fixed was edible!"

"Well, most of it," her mom said with a smile. "There was that roast you charred to a cinder. And a couple of batches of biscuits that could have been used to build a house."

"Very funny," Kelsey grumbled, but she grinned back.

"Well, none of that matters, anyway," Grandma Jenny said, waving off Kelsey's culinary disasters. "I have someone who comes in to help with the cooking, but you do need to call her and let her know we're reopening. Last time I checked Merilee hadn't found another job. Her name and number are posted by the phone in the kitchen."

"Great," Kelsey said, checking that off the list she'd tucked into her pocket earlier. "I'll call as soon as we're finished with lunch."

"I love it that you're so eager," Grandma Jenny said. "But don't overdo it. You have to think about the baby. You'll need some rest every day. Working around here can be demanding."

Her mother's gaze snapped up at that. "Something you never would have admitted before you got Kelsey involved. You just waved me off when I said it was too much for you to handle."

"I never said I was going to run this place alone," Grandma Jenny retorted. "That was your assumption. I always knew I'd need help."

"You just thought it would be from me," Hannah said.

"I hoped it might be," Grandma Jenny admitted. "But I had a contingency plan.

There are plenty of people in this town in need of work."

Kelsey watched her mom clamp her mouth shut, then push her plate away.

"I'm going for a walk," she announced. "Luke, are you coming?"

He winked at Kelsey and Grandma Jenny, then followed her mom from the dining room.

"Well, that went well," Grandma Jenny said, breathing a sigh of relief.

Kelsey stared at her. "You could have cut the tension with a knife. Aside from making a couple of jokes about my cooking, it's pretty obvious that Mom is not happy about any of this."

"No, but she's trying to accept it. She didn't say half the things I expected her to."

"I suppose not," Kelsey said. "Do you think that's Luke's influence?"

"He does seem to have a calming effect on her." She grinned wickedly. "Or some other effect altogether."

"Grandma Jenny!"

"Hey, I knew the score about these things long before you were born, young lady."

Kelsey leaped up and gave her an impulsive hug. "Have I mentioned how much I love you and how glad I am that I'm here with you?"

"You can never say a thing like that too much. It goes both ways, too. Everything's going to work out with you and your mother. You'll see. She'll come around."

Kelsey glanced outside and saw her mom crossing the street toward the beach with Luke. "I hope so. She needs something good to happen in her life, so she's not worrying about her health and me so much."

"She will always worry about you, Kelsey. And she's right to be concerned about her health, too. Neither of those things means that there can't be something wonderful right around the corner."

Kelsey grinned. "Or in a room right down the hall."

Hannah was stalking down the beach at a pace that would have exhausted a drill sergeant. Luke's leg was already aching from climbing up and down a ladder all morning, so he gave up trying to keep up with her. When she eventually realized she'd left him behind, she turned, gave him a chagrined look and came back.

"Sorry. I guess I was trying to literally run away from my thoughts."

"Doesn't work, does it?"

"Not very well." She settled in beside him, then gave him an odd look. "You're limping. Are you okay?"

"Just a little overtired, that's all."

She stopped in her tracks. "Explain. Are you sick? Should you even be doing all that painting?"

Luke wanted to kick himself for opening this particular can of worms, but he doubted he could lift his leg high enough. "I'm not sick," he said, determined to minimize it to avoid her pity. "It's nothing. I just have a bum leg."

"Then you have no business going up and down a ladder all day. What were you thinking letting my grandmother talk you into that?"

He loved that Hannah was so quick to jump to his defense. Or maybe, he thought, she wanted one more thing she could blame her grandmother for. He wasn't going to be the cause of any more friction on that front. "Cool your jets, Hannah. She didn't talk me into anything. I need the exercise and I like being useful."

"What happened to your leg?"

"An accident," he said. "Stop looking at me like that. I've done rehab. I've been released. I'm perfectly capable of painting the inn."

"You should have said something. At least we could have *driven* into town."

"Are you kidding? There was no way I'd want you behind the wheel of a car in the mood you were in."

She grinned, her expression rueful. "Okay, I'm being a pain. I get that. I will be on my best behavior for the rest of the afternoon. Do you want to sit for a while? Go back home?"

"I told you I want ice cream. Let's just slow down the pace."

They walked along at a more leisurely pace for a few minutes. Eventually she turned to him. "How did the accident happen?"

Luke debated keeping the details to himself, but what was the point? His tour in Iraq might have been a bone of contention in his marriage, but he was proud of having served. There were men walking today because he'd been there to see that their injuries were properly treated.

"A car bomb in Iraq," he said succinctly.

Her eyes widened. "Luke! Good God, you could have been killed."

"But I wasn't," he said. "I made it home. A lot of others didn't. Save your sympathy for their families."

"Why were you in Iraq in the first place? Surely you didn't enlist."

"Actually, I did. I'd served in the army

before. They paid for my education, so when buddies of mine were sent over there, I reenlisted for a one-year tour of duty. I was only a few weeks from coming home when this happened."

"How long ago was that?"

"About six months."

"That long?"

"Rehab took a while."

She studied him with a narrowed gaze. "Something tells me you're minimizing what happened."

He shrugged but didn't deny it.

"What about post-traumatic stress disorder? Is that why you aren't with your family?"

Now they really were treading on turf he wanted to avoid. "No," he said tersely. "Look, let's not go there, okay?"

She looked hurt by his abrupt demand that they change the subject, but it was hard enough to see the sympathy in her eyes when she heard about his injury. He didn't want to see the pity that was bound to follow if he told her the whole ugly story of the disintegration of his marriage.

Just ahead, fortunately, he saw the road that intersected with the town's main street. Climbing over the dunes, they emerged onto a busy sidewalk. "Rocky road at the drugstore soda fountain or frozen custard from Lila's?" he asked.

"Frozen custard," she said at once. "Chocolate and vanilla swirled together."

He glanced at her, wondering how she'd remembered that it was his favorite. Or if she actually did.

"You brought me *my* favorite," she said, responding to the unspoken question. "Now it's my turn to treat you to yours."

"I'm surprised you remember," he said, studying her.

"I remember *everything* about those last two summers before we went away to college," she said in a way that made him wonder what she meant. What had made it so memorable for her?

Seaview Key, 1985

Just about everyone from the high school — sophomores, juniors and seniors — had turned out for the end-of-year party on the beach. The guys had dragged several picnic tables together early in the afternoon and those were now laden down with food. A couple of charcoal grills were glowing hot and the boys were taking turns fixing hot dogs and hamburgers, while the girls set out bowls of potato salad, macaroni salad and trays of home-baked cookies. Coolers filled with ice and cans of soda sat in the sand under the tables. Davey Roberts had brought his sound system and music was blaring. They'd chosen a secluded spot on the beach about a half mile from the inn, where no one would be disturbed by the noise.

Ever since sophomore year Hannah had had a crush on Luke Stevens, but he'd been unaware of it. Though they were both juniors now, they didn't hang out with the same crowd at all. Luke was a jock, who always had the most popular girls in school surrounding him. Hannah was focused on getting perfect grades, so she could win a scholarship to a school far, far away from Seaview. That didn't stop her from wishing that Luke would give her a second glance. Fortunately, no one, not even her best friend, had a clue about her infatuation, so there was no chance she'd be humiliated by someone pointing out the futility of it.

"Hey, Hannah, let's go for a swim," Abby Dawson shouted, waving at her from the water.

"I'll be there in two minutes," Hannah called back. "Just let me get the last of the food on the table."

She'd barely turned away, when she heard shouts from the water, but this time there was a frantic edge to them that had her whirling around and scanning the surf for Abby. Half a dozen kids were already running toward the last place she'd seen her.

Hannah dropped the bowl she was holding and ran after them. "Abby, where are you? Abby!"

She saw her friend's head bob above the churning waves, but then Abby went under again. Hannah started into the water, but suddenly Luke was there. He pushed her back. "Stay here. You're not a strong-enough swimmer. You'll wind up going under, too. I'll get her." He shook her slightly, his gaze locked with hers. "Hannah, are you listening? Stay here."

She nodded, tears streaming down her cheeks. "Just save her, Luke. Please, hurry."

While others waded more tentatively into the rough waters, Luke dove in and began swimming with clean, strong strokes. The next time Abby bobbed to the surface, he was only a few feet away. He covered the distance in less than a heartbeat, it seemed, but she was already under again. He dove down and seemed to be out of sight for an eternity. When he emerged, coughing and gagging, he was holding a limp Abby in his arms.

Towing her, he made his way toward

shore, then immediately lay her down and began performing mouth-to-mouth resuscitation. In moments Abby began to cough up water.

Hannah knelt down beside her, her heart pounding so hard she thought for a minute it was going to burst. "Abby, are you all right?"

"Has anyone called 911?" Luke asked, taking Abby's pulse. "I think she's okay now, but she should be checked out."

"They're coming," someone in the crowd said, and already the faint sound of a siren could be heard in the distance.

Clinging to her friend's hand, Hannah shook. "What happened, Abby? You're a better swimmer than I am."

"Stomach cramp," Abby murmured. "I went out too far, the cramp hit and then I was gulping water. Thank God for Luke."

When the EMTs arrived, they examined Abby and insisted that she go to the hospital.

"I'll go with her," Hannah said at once.

Abby gave her a grateful look, but then the EMTs suggested Luke go in and get checked out as well. He turned to Hannah. "I'll keep an eye on her, okay? You stay here and enjoy the party."

Hannah wanted to argue, but then she saw

the glint of adoration in Abby's gaze as it settled on Luke. She knew in that instant that something was going to happen between the two of them and she'd wind up being an outsider.

Abby reached for her hand and gave it a squeeze. "It'll be okay, Hannah. I'll call you as soon as I get home."

"Sure, fine," Hannah said, stepping back as they loaded Abby into the back of the ambulance. "Should I call your folks and tell them to meet you at the hospital?"

"Good idea," Luke said, his gaze never leaving Abby's face. He looked as if he'd been hit by a bolt of lightning, as if he'd never seen Abby before and had just discovered that she was this absolutely fascinating person.

Hannah stood by as the ambulance rode away. The other kids drifted away and then she ran the half mile up the beach to use the phone at the inn to call Abby's parents.

After she told them what had happened, she fixed herself a glass of iced tea, but when she started to pick it up, her hands were shaking so badly, she had to set it down again. Leaving it where it was, she went onto the porch, where her mother and grandmother were already settled in rockers for the evening, while her grandfather worked inside on the inn's books. For once, she craved the comforting familiarity of the routine.

"What are you doing back here so early?" her mom asked.

"Abby nearly drowned," she said, an unexpected catch in her voice. She covered her face and started to cry. "It was so awful, Mom. She got a cramp and she kept going under."

"Oh, no," her mom said, looking shaken. "She's okay, though? Someone got her out?"

Hannah nodded. "Luke Stevens saved her. He went with her to the hospital, so they could both get checked out. I just called to let her folks know."

"You must have been terrified," her mother said. "Are you sure you're okay? Do you want me to drive you to the hospital to check on Abby?"

Hannah shook her head. "Luke's there," she said wearily. "That's all she needs."

It was her grandmother who apparently caught the note of defeat in her voice. "Hannah, what's wrong? What is it you're not saying?"

She stood up, afraid she'd already let them see too much. "Nothing. Nothing at all. I'm going to bed."

"You don't want to go back to the party?"

her mother asked worriedly. “Maybe you should be with your friends tonight.”

“Abby’s my friend. It wouldn’t be any fun without her,” she said. And deep down inside, she wondered if the whole summer wasn’t going to be just as miserable as tonight had turned out to be.

The next day was the first full day of summer vacation and Hannah had managed to sleep away most of the morning. She dragged herself downstairs just before noon and wandered into the kitchen wearing shorts and a tank top, only to find Abby sitting at the table while Grandma Jenny made strawberry-rhubarb pies.

Hannah was relieved to see her, but a part of her was wary, too. “You’re okay? I got worried when you didn’t call last night like you said you would.”

Abby rolled her eyes. “Too much commotion then, but I’m fit as a fiddle, according to the doctors,” she said. “Otherwise, I doubt my parents would have let me out of their sight. They flipped out when they heard what happened, and they totally embarrassed Luke. They kept carrying on like he was this huge hero, and then they offered him a reward. Can you imagine? It was so embarrassing.”

“He was a hero,” Hannah said. “No one

else was diving in to save you. I was going to, but he stopped me. He said he was a stronger swimmer, and he was right."

Abby twisted the glass of tea she was holding around and around in her hands, her gaze avoiding Hannah's. "He was pretty great, wasn't he?"

"He was amazing," Hannah agreed. She hesitated, then asked, "So, are you going to see him again?"

Abby blushed. "He said he might stop by today. I told him I'd be here." She finally met Hannah's gaze. "That's okay, isn't it?"

Hannah forced a smile. "Sure. Of course." She was careful to avoid her grandmother's penetrating gaze when she said it. She had a feeling Grandma Jenny saw right through her and knew it was anything but okay.

"Why don't you girls go outside and sit on the porch and relax?" Grandma Jenny suggested. "I'll bring out something to eat. Abby, did you have breakfast?"

"No, ma'am," Abby said with a grin. "I came over here hoping you'd offer to fix us something. Now that my mom's working, at home all I'd have would be toaster waffles."

"I definitely think I can do better than that. Hannah, what would you like?"

"Whatever," she said.

"I'll make waffles, then. With peaches on

top. How does that sound?"

"Awesome," Abby said enthusiastically.

"It sounds great, Grandma Jenny. Do you need any help?"

"Not on your first day of vacation," she said. "Run along. And if Luke gets here, let me know. I imagine he'll want some, too."

Hannah slowly followed Abby outside and settled into one of the wicker chairs. "Are you really okay?" she asked Abby.

"Fine, thanks to Luke."

"Were you scared?"

"Terrified, but when I came to on the beach and saw his face, I knew everything was going to be okay."

"And now you're in love with him, aren't you?" Hannah said, her voice toneless.

Abby gave her an odd look. "I'm grateful to him and I think he's pretty incredible because of what he did, but he's never even noticed me. Last night was just an emergency."

Hannah had seen the look in his eyes the night before, when Abby had been lying on the sand. "You're wrong," she said. "Luke might not have noticed you before last night, but trust me, he's noticed you now."

"Well, half drowning will get a guy's attention," Abby said. "Hannah, why do you sound so angry about it?"

"I'm not angry. I'm glad he was there."

"Well, you're mad about something."

Hannah forced a smile. She was not about to reveal her crush now, when it was too late. "Am not. It's the first day of vacation. What's there to be mad about?"

Abby didn't look convinced. "That's what I want to know."

Fortunately before Hannah had to answer, her grandmother came out with two plates with waffles, glasses of orange juice and a pitcher of iced tea. And just as she set everything down on a table for the two of them, Luke strolled up the front walk. He acknowledged her grandmother with a nod and said a distracted hello to Hannah, but his gaze was riveted on Abby.

"You feeling okay?" he asked, his hands shoved in the pockets of his cutoff jeans.

To Hannah's disgust, Abby looked just as smitten as he did.

"Luke, if you're hungry, you can have my waffle," Hannah said. "I'll go fix myself another one."

She brushed past her grandmother and went into the kitchen. Grandma Jenny followed.

"It's hard, I know," she said as she spooned more batter into the waffle iron.

"Seeing your best friend with a boy you like."

"I don't like him," Hannah said adamantly.

"You sure?"

"Well, I can't like him, can I? He only has eyes for Abby and now she's falling for him, too."

"Sometimes it happens that way," her grandmother said sympathetically. "I'm sorry."

Hannah impatiently brushed at the tears welling up in her eyes. "Gran, please, don't say anything about this, okay? Promise me. They can't find out, not ever."

"Of course not. If you want to talk about it, though, I'm always here."

Hannah sighed. "I think the less said about this the better."

In fact, if God was merciful, she'd never even think about Luke that way again. But, of course, life almost never worked like that.

9

It was funny, Hannah thought as she and Luke sat on a bench now with their frozen custard cones, but as vivid as the memories of the past were, she didn't see the carefree boy in the man. She glanced sideways and studied him, trying to find some glimpse of the boy she'd been so crazy about, but it simply wasn't there.

Oh, he had the same twinkle in his eyes on occasion, the same dark blond hair that was already getting sparks of gold and red from being out in the sun, the same smile and dimple, but there was a sadness about him now that hadn't been there before. She imagined almost losing a leg to a roadside bomb had contributed to that, as had whatever had gone on in his marriage that had sent him to Seaview Key. She'd been infatuated with a boy. Now she was increasingly drawn to a man, with all of his complexities and secrets.

"Luke, do you ever wonder why your relationship with Abby didn't last?" she asked, recalling how powerful the attraction between them had been. They'd been inseparable that summer, all during the following school year and that one last summer after graduation. Once they'd gone away to separate colleges, though, the bond had been broken.

"We were kids," he said simply. "How long did your first real relationship last?"

"I didn't have a real relationship until I graduated from college," she said, faintly embarrassed to admit that. "I was too focused on my studies." And getting over her unrequited feelings for Luke, she added to herself. She'd dated from time to time, but not one of the men had been worth risking the achievement of her goals, and not one had come close to sparking the sort of feelings she'd had for Luke. For years she'd wondered if her feelings for him had been magnified simply because she couldn't have him or because she was so young, but based on how quickly they'd been rekindled lately, there had to have been something there.

"That surprises me. I thought one of the reasons you wanted to get away from Seaview was to meet guys who were smarter or more ambitious than the boys here."

She poked him with an elbow. "You make me sound like a terrible snob."

"Well, at the time I thought that, but in retrospect I can see that you were just being choosey."

"Did everyone think that?" she asked, horrified.

"Maybe not everyone, but I could name half a dozen guys who wanted to ask you out but were too scared to do it."

She stared at him in disbelief. "Name one."

"Tommy Wilder," he said at once, a wicked glint in his eye.

"Tommy Wilder could barely find his way from one end of the football field to the other, even with the team shouting at him," she said with an exaggerated shudder.

"But he thought you were hot. He even asked me to set the two of you up on a date."

"But you didn't even try," she recalled. "I would have remembered that."

"Abby said you'd never in a million years go for it," he said, then glanced over at her. "Was she wrong?"

"No. Abby knew me better than anyone. What did you tell Tommy?"

"That you were thinking of going into a convent, so you didn't date."

She poked him again. "You did not!"

"I did. I had to let him down easy. He was the best offensive tackle we had. I couldn't crush the guy. And the mention of a convent was all it took to scare off a good Catholic boy."

"You are so lying," she accused.

He grinned. "Didn't you ever wonder why all the boys at school were giving you a wide berth?"

"I'm not even Catholic," she said.

"Minor detail," he said blithely. "Sorry if I ruined your social life."

"Actually, you probably made me more intriguing than I deserved to be," she said, not especially bothered by the revelation that he'd deliberately put a damper on her social life. "And I had lots of time to study so I could keep my grades up."

"So, let's get back to my original question. How long did your first big relationship last?"

"Five-and-a-half years," she said. "And we were married for most of that time."

He whistled. "Kelsey's father?"

Hannah nodded. "Maybe if I'd been more experienced, I would have seen just how wrong we were for each other, but then, I wouldn't have had Kelsey. I can't regret my ill-advised marriage, because I came away from it with this amazing child."

He frowned slightly. "And there's been no one important since then?"

"No one worth shaking up the status quo," she admitted. "My judgment was so bad the first time around that I never quite trusted it again. Ironically, I chose someone just like my father, a man with no staying power. I figured the odds were that I'd do it again. Besides, Kelsey and I are a team. Some men couldn't deal with that. Some couldn't deal with my successful career. Either way, they wanted me all to themselves."

"Makes perfect sense to avoid a guy that selfish," he conceded. "Surely not every man in Manhattan is like that, though. And there have to be plenty who can deal with a smart, successful woman."

"Probably so, but as time went on I became more and more married to my career. I stopped looking." She gave a rueful shrug. "It drives my friend Sue crazy. She's set me up on so many blind dates and has such an agenda to see me happily married, it's a wonder any single man will go near her."

"Don't you know how challenging most men find an unavailable, uninterested female to be?"

"I thought all men hated and feared rejection."

"They do. They just don't believe it will happen to them. It's these oversize egos we're blessed with."

She studied him curiously. "You included?"

"Mine's taken a couple of hits, but basically, yes. I believe in myself."

Hannah wasn't entirely convinced of that. "Then why are you here?" she asked bluntly. "I get the feeling you're running away from something."

"Just taking some time off to get back on my feet, literally and figuratively," he claimed. He met her gaze. "So, tell me something, does it work?"

"Does what work?"

"Substituting a job for a life. Isn't that what you've been doing?"

She bristled at the suggestion, then sighed. That was exactly what she'd done. How could she even attempt to deny it? "I didn't mean to, but that's how it turned out. I'm not complaining, though. My career has allowed me to provide well for Kelsey and me. I get a lot of professional recognition."

"But you're alone at the end of the day. Who shares that success with you?"

Ah, that was the rub. There wasn't anyone.

Oh, Sue, of course. She was always ready to have a celebration. And the people at work always made a fuss when she landed a new account or pulled off a public relations coup for one of their clients.

"I see you don't have an answer for that," he said quietly. "And what happens now that Kelsey is grown and about to have a child of her own? Especially if she stays here in Florida or goes back to California?"

Hannah had no idea how to answer. The question was one she'd been asking herself a lot recently. Over the past couple of years she'd begun to realize that having Kelsey away at college was foreshadowing the loneliness of her future.

"I don't know," she confessed finally.

Suddenly she saw how deftly Luke had shifted the conversation away from himself. He'd barely answered her question about his breakup with Abby — or any of her other tentative personal questions — before turning the spotlight right back on her.

She was about to call him on it when the cell phone she'd stuck in her pocket out of habit rang. Glancing at the caller ID, she saw that it was Sue.

"I need to take this," she told Luke. "It'll only take a minute."

When she answered, Sue said, "I can hear

waves. Are you on the beach, you rat?"

Hannah smiled at her indignation. "No, but close. I'm sitting on a bench across the street and I've just finished a huge cone of frozen custard."

"I hate you. It's twelve degrees here and the wind is whipping down Sixth Avenue. I'm scared to walk outside for fear I'll be blown all the way to Staten Island."

"Sorry," Hannah said, but without much sincerity.

"No, you're not, and who could blame you?" Sue said. "When are you coming home?"

"Another week or so, I guess."

"You don't sound very sure of that. What's going on, Hannah? Is your grandmother balking at selling the inn?"

"She didn't balk. She flat-out refused. Worse, she's convinced Kelsey to stay here and work with her."

"Say that again?" Sue said, her shock evident. "Kelsey is giving up Stanford to stay in Seaview Key?"

"That's the plan," Hannah confirmed with weary resignation.

"Oh, brother. Do I need to come down there to keep you from killing her?"

"No, I'm restraining myself, for the time being, anyway."

"When are you coming home?"

"As soon as things are under control here, whenever that is."

"I thought your doctor's appointment was in eight days. You'll be back for that, right?"

"Hopefully," she said evasively.

"Hannah, you can't blow it off," Sue said urgently. "You know that. I don't care what's going on down there, this is too important."

Hannah rubbed her temple, where she could feel a headache starting. "I know. I'll be there, I promise. Even if I have to turn right around and fly back down here."

"You'd better be or I'll be down there the next day to drag you back up here myself."

She smiled, despite the added pressure she was feeling. Sue would do exactly that, if need be. "I'm not giving you an excuse to play hooky from work," she retorted. "If you want to come to Florida, just say so. You're always welcome."

"A few more days of this weather and I'll take you up on that." Sue paused, then asked, "You are feeling okay, though, right? And you're doing your self-exams?"

"Absolutely."

"Okay, then, I'll stop nagging for now. Love you."

"You, too," Hannah said. "Thanks for

checking in."

She shut off the phone and tucked it back in her pocket.

"You getting pressure from work to come back?" Luke asked.

"No, just Sue, the friend I mentioned earlier, calling to find out how things are going down here."

He studied her intently. "Are you sure? Because between Kelsey and me, things here are covered if you do need to go back."

"Are you trying to kick me out?"

"Heaven forbid!" he protested. "It would be a lot less interesting without you around. I just wanted you to know you could go back without worrying about Grandma Jenny or the inn. Or Kelsey, for that matter."

"Neither the inn nor my grandmother are your responsibility," she reminded him. "Neither is Kelsey."

"I'm just saying that if you need to go, I'm here."

She wasn't sure how she felt about him sounding so eager to be rid of her, then decided she was being ridiculous. He was merely offering to help out. She was the one twisting that into some sort of rejection. No wonder she didn't have a relationship. She couldn't even accept a simple act of kindness in the spirit in which it was intended.

"I do appreciate the offer," she said finally. "You really have been a godsend when it comes to getting the painting and repairs started. I know how much Grandma Jenny appreciates it. Despite what she says about all these people in Seaview looking for work, finding someone reliable isn't as easy as she makes it sound. Still, I don't want you to feel obligated to stay on or help out. You're going to want to get back to your own life one of these days."

"Hey, I'm in no rush. This has worked out great for me, too, so don't think I'm doing her any favors."

"You're the one climbing up and down a ladder, despite your injury," Hannah said. "That counts as a favor in my book."

He gave her an odd look. "Don't try to paint me as a hero, Hannah. Believe me, I don't qualify."

"Something tells me that there are a lot of people who would say otherwise, Grandma Jenny included, but if you want to be modest and humble, who am I to argue with you?"

"We should get back," he said tightly.

"You're not on a time clock," she reminded him, but she stood up, anyway.

"Maybe not, but your daughter has guests

booked into the inn in a couple of weeks and something tells me she's going to expect everything in perfect order when the first ones arrive." He glanced at her. "Does she get that perfectionism from you?"

Hannah nodded ruefully. "Probably."

"Don't say that as if it's a bad trait," he teased. "Just remember that sometimes relaxation is as important as getting it all right."

"You're not the first to suggest that I could use more balance in my life," she said. "It's a favorite refrain of Grandma Jenny's. What about you? Is your life in perfect balance?"

He laughed. "Hardly, but unlike you, I'm working on it."

"Can you actually *work* on relaxing? Isn't that an oxymoron?"

"No more than practicing taking deep, cleansing breaths," he said. "Breathing comes naturally. You have to teach yourself to do the other kind." He shrugged. "Or so I was told in rehab."

"I took yoga once," Hannah said.

"How'd you do?"

"I flunked."

"How can you flunk yoga?"

"The teacher said I was too intense. I was making the rest of the class nervous."

Luke chuckled. "I can actually see that happening. You probably tried to get everyone to breathe faster, so you could finish up and get back to work."

Hannah laughed with him. "Something like that."

"So how *do* you relax?"

She opened her mouth to answer, then suddenly realized that until the past few days, she couldn't recall the last time she'd done anything solely for fun or relaxation. She hadn't even taken a bubble bath in months, something she'd once savored. She was not going to admit that, though.

"I get together with friends," she said eventually.

"And talk business?" he inquired, amusement lurking in his eyes.

"Sure, sometimes," she said, then winced. "Okay, what about you? Are you any better?"

"Not much," he conceded. "But I have seen the error of my ways. I'm here right now, taking a walk along the beach with you, while there's painting to be done back at the inn."

"Well, heck, if that counts, I'm doing it, too."

"There you go," he said. "Maybe we're a good influence on each other."

"I think it's going to take more than one walk on the beach and an ice cream cone to drag us out of the ranks of the compulsive workaholic," she said dryly.

"Speak for yourself. I'm reformed," he insisted again. He took her hand and wove his fingers with hers. "I'll make you a deal. For as long as we're both here, we will do something just for fun every single day. How about it?"

Hannah couldn't immediately spot any drawbacks. "Sure. Why not?"

"It's a deal, then," he said, and lifted her hand to brush a kiss across her knuckles.

Heat shot through her at the contact, along with a sizzling awareness that had nothing to do with making an innocent pact. There it was, she thought with a shiver of panic. That was the drawback. She'd just committed to spending more time with a man who had the ability to distract her from all the things she should be dealing with. It wasn't good. It wasn't good at all.

Somehow, though, she couldn't seem to regret it.

Every single day, Luke's leg was a little less painful. He figured it was the combination of hard, physical work and taking walks on the beach with Hannah that kept it limber, and the slanting rays from the afternoon sun as he sat on the porch that soothed the aching muscles.

So far, five days after they'd made their pact, he and Hannah had kept each other honest and spent a part of each afternoon doing something relaxing. He'd challenged her to a croquet match one afternoon after setting the wickets up in the backyard in preparation for the inn's first guests after the reopening. The following day, they'd played a vicious game of badminton after he'd put the net up in the side yard. Hannah had beat the socks off him, though he'd blamed it on his injuries and dramatically limped away after the game. They'd walked on the beach and stopped for ice cream twice. Yesterday, he'd convinced her to take a bicycle ride around the island. He still hadn't decided what today would bring.

He glanced up as Grandma Jenny emerged from the house carrying two glasses of iced tea. She handed one to him.

"You and my granddaughter seem to be spending a lot of time together," she commented.

"She's good company."

"Yes, she is." She gave him a hard look. "But she has an awful lot on her plate right now. I'd hate to see her get mixed up in something that has the potential to hurt her."

Luke nodded slowly. "Warning duly noted. And just to reassure you, we've agreed that our lives are too complicated for anything serious to happen."

Grandma Jenny chuckled. "You've agreed. Now, that *is* reassuring," she said with tolerant amusement. "No wonder both of you are alone. You actually think you get to control these things. Trust me, Luke, if temptation's got a foot in the door, all the logic in the world can't fight it."

He knew she was right, knew how tempted he'd been on more than one occasion to haul Hannah into his arms and kiss her, despite their agreement. He'd seized a few too many opportunities just to touch her as it was.

"Are you saying we should avoid each other?" he asked.

"Not for me to say. I don't know what the complications are in your life, do I? I'm just saying if they're insurmountable, then don't start something with my granddaughter that will break her heart." She smiled. "Of course, if those complications are just something you've blown up out of all proportion, then you have my blessing to get on with pursuing Hannah."

Was that what he'd been doing? Pursuing her? Of course it was. He hadn't been married for so many years that he couldn't recall what it had been like to court a woman, to seek her out, flirt a little, relish the slow buildup of sexual tension. That was exactly what was happening with Hannah and more than likely, it was a huge mistake. She wasn't the kind of woman to have an affair and walk away unscathed, and he was in no position to offer more.

He stood up abruptly. "I think I'll walk into town, check out a few shops and have an early dinner at The Fish Tale," he said.

Her gaze narrowed. "I thought you and Hannah did something around this time every afternoon."

"We have been, but I think you're right. It's a habit we probably ought to break."

"Then you should be man enough to stay here and tell her that face-to-face. Don't leave it to me," she said.

"Come on. Give me a break here. I'm trying to do the right thing."

"Are you sure you know what that is?"

"I know what's right for this moment. Long-term? Not a clue," he admitted. He bent down and gave her a kiss on the cheek. "Thanks for the wake-up call."

"That is not what I intended when I sat

down here," she grumbled.

He grinned. "I know, but sometimes when you start a ball rolling, it's impossible to know where it will end up."

She shook her head. "You're starting to sound like me."

He winked at her. "Sometimes you're very wise," he said before turning and walking away.

An evening at The Fish Tale with some idle conversation with Jack, maybe a few minutes with Lesley Ann, and some time to figure out what the hell he was doing with Hannah, that was what he needed tonight. Tomorrow? Well, tomorrow would take care of itself.

Hannah flatly refused to let her grandmother see how disappointed she was by the announcement that Luke had taken off for town without her. Instead, she muttered something about having things to do and marched back inside and tackled the project she'd been putting off — organizing the inn's business files.

As she'd suspected, her mother had been no better at record-keeping than Grandma Jenny was. Both of them preferred the interaction with the customers to the business side of operating the inn. Other than annual tax forms, which were handled by an outside accountant, there wasn't a decent set of records since her grandfather had kept them. Receipts had been stuffed into file folders or envelopes, sometimes by year, sometimes by category, seemingly without any rhyme nor reason.

She found everything that appeared to pertain to the current year and spread it out around her in the middle of the floor. She was trying to sort through it all when Kelsey came in.

"What on earth are you doing, Mom?"

"Trying to make sense of all the bills and receipts for this place. Tax season is just around the corner. Since the inn was closed for most of the year, it should be simple enough to pull everything together." She shook her head in exasperation. "Or it would be if anything was ever filed properly."

"The inn needs a computer," Kelsey said. "I mentioned it to Grandma Jenny and she looked at me as if I was suggesting she make a pact with the devil."

"It's probably a waste of money," Hannah said. "You won't be here forever and she'll certainly never touch it."

"I could have my computer from school sent here," Kelsey suggested. "Jeff could do that. In fact, I really need to have him pack up everything and ship it to Florida. There's no point in paying rent for an apartment if I'm not going back."

"Or you could go back and get it yourself. If you're serious about quitting school, there are probably things you need to do."

"I can't leave now," Kelsey protested. "There's too much to do with the first guests arriving in a couple of weeks. Jeff can handle shipping the stuff and I can call the registrar's office about dropping out. I can probably do the paperwork online."

"Relying on Jeff is asking a lot of a man you refuse to marry," Hannah suggested.

"He won't mind."

"Does he even know what you're planning?"

Kelsey shook her head, her expression guilt-ridden.

"Why not?"

"Because he's going to be really upset about it," she admitted. "He says we can't resolve anything if I'm clear across the country."

"He's right."

"But it *is* resolved," Kelsey said earnestly. "I'm having this baby and I don't want to get married."

"But you love this boy," Hannah reminded

her. “That’s what you told me.”

“Yeah,” Kelsey said softly. “He’s a great guy.”

“Then I just don’t understand,” Hannah said with frustration.

“It’s too soon,” Kelsey said with finality. “I’m not ready to be anybody’s wife.”

“But you *are* ready to be someone’s mother?”

Tears welled up in Kelsey’s eyes. “Not that, either.”

“Sweetheart, what is it you’re not saying?”

“I want to give the baby up for adoption.” She put a hand protectively over her stomach. “It’s too late for anything else and I promised Jeff not to end the pregnancy, anyway. But I can’t raise a child. I’ve thought and thought about this, Mom. I’m not being totally selfish, even though it probably sounds that way. I’m trying to think about what’s best for the baby. I swear it.”

“How does Jeff feel about relinquishing his parental rights?”

“He says he won’t do it,” Kelsey admitted. “He wants the baby, no matter what.” She met Hannah’s gaze. “But I want the baby to have a dad *and* a mom. I just can’t be that mom.”

Hannah knew she had no right to try to

influence her daughter one way or another. This had to be Kelsey's decision, and Jeff's. All Hannah could do was make sure they weighed all the options carefully and thoughtfully.

Once again, she suggested, "Maybe you should fly back to California —"

"No way," Kelsey said before Hannah could even complete the thought.

"Just to pack up your own things and try to resolve all of this with Jeff."

"No," Kelsey said flatly.

"Kelsey, these are decisions the two of you need to be making together."

"I'll call him and tell him," she said. "It'll be better that way."

"Because it won't be as easy for him to talk you out of it if you're not face-to-face?"

Kelsey nodded.

"That should tell you something, then, shouldn't it? If your feelings for this young man are that strong, if your love and respect run that deep, then perhaps you should try to make this work."

"Haven't you heard a word I said?" Kelsey demanded in frustration. "I won't give up my chance to figure out who I am. Just me, as a person. Not as somebody's wife or mother."

"But you are going to be somebody's

mother, whether the timing's right or not," Hannah said. "You *are* responsible for the baby's well-being."

"I *know* that," Kelsey replied. "And the responsible thing is to give this baby to two people who desperately want a family."

She sounded so sure of herself, but Hannah knew she'd live to regret her choice. Maybe not right now when desperation had her grasping for an easy solution, but later when she thought about the child she'd given away.

"Why are you so determined not to marry a boy you love, if you're having his child? I don't think you've told me the real reason yet."

"I won't do it, because that's what you did when you married Dad," Kelsey blurted. "You got married too young. You had me too soon and just look how that turned out. It ruined everything for you."

She whirled around and left the room with her words still hanging in the air. Hannah stared after her in shock. That was what Kelsey thought? That Hannah's life had been ruined by her ill-fated marriage and by Kelsey herself? Nothing could be further from the truth.

But how on earth was she going to undo

twenty years of actions that had led to her daughter reaching that conclusion?

10

Since Luke had slipped away from the inn specifically to avoid Hannah and had spent the entire evening fighting valiantly to keep her out of his head, it was disconcerting to come home at midnight and find her on the front porch, staring morosely out into the darkness.

All of his resolve and good intentions went up in smoke. He walked over and took a seat beside her.

"I thought you'd be in bed long ago," he said, sliding a glance in her direction.

"Is that why you stayed out so late, to avoid me?"

"Pretty much," he admitted.

He caught her faint frown.

"Why?" she asked.

"Something your grandmother said earlier."

"Was she matchmaking again?"

"No, to the contrary, she was warning me

off. I have to admit it came as a surprise, since she'd clearly been advocating earlier for something to happen between us."

Hannah seemed as startled as he'd been.

"She's been trying to throw us together since you got here," she said. "I wonder what suddenly changed?"

"She said you had enough on your plate and that unless I was serious, I should steer clear." He shrugged. "Or words to that effect."

"And you actually took what she said to heart?" she asked, sounding incredulous. "You ran off because she told you to? That doesn't sound like you."

"Truthfully, I ran off because it seemed like the wise thing to do." He met her gaze, held it. "You should probably know that under other circumstances, I probably would have taken her warning as a challenge, tried my best to get you into my bed, preferably tonight."

Beside him, Hannah's lips curved. "Now I may have to kill her," she murmured.

Luke studied her, tried to decide if she was serious about wanting him. It would change a lot if she was. Though he thought he was getting to know Hannah well, he couldn't tell, so he gave her a rueful glance. "Please don't. She was one hundred percent right about one thing. I need to be fair to you. I don't know where this thing with us is going, if anywhere. To be honest, I don't know much of anything these days. I'm just getting to a point where I can look beyond the next hour."

"Well, join the club," she said with surprising bitterness.

He gave her a startled look. "What happened?"

"Apparently I have inadvertently given my daughter the impression that my life was ruined because I married young and then divorced her dad. Never mind that he had commitment issues and walked out on us more than once until I finally told him he had to stay or go for good. What stuck with Kelsey was that I had to raise her on my own with very little help from her father beyond child support."

Though Luke was relieved by the abrupt change of topic, he was stunned by what Hannah was telling him. "She said that?"

"Yep. She said that's why she flatly refuses to marry the father of her child." She regarded Luke with a bemused expression. "I worked so hard to make sure she had everything she needed, yet somehow she interpreted that as struggle and sacrifice, and she wants no part of it."

"She's young," Luke reminded her. "The world is just opening up to her. She doesn't know what she wants."

"So she's said, again and again. I've had to bite my tongue raw to keep from telling her how short-sighted and immature she's being."

"Maybe you should call her on it, if that's how you really feel," he suggested. "But I take it you didn't do that."

She shook her head, the slump of her shoulders revealing just how hurt she'd been by the whole conversation.

"I couldn't get my brain to kick into gear after she hit with me with that," Hannah admitted. "It didn't matter, anyway, because she took off as soon as she said it."

"Where'd she go? Timbuktu?"

"Of course not."

"Then why didn't you follow her? Straighten things out? I assume she had it all wrong."

"This from a man who slipped away to avoid talking to me directly about something that concerns me," she commented wryly.

"Guilty as charged," he agreed. "But why didn't you go after Kelsey? You're not a coward, Hannah. Everything about you tells me you confront most things head-on."

"I certainly used to," she said. "Lately, I

seem to be quite comfortable sticking my head in the sand. Besides, I didn't know where to start."

"The beginning's always a good place. You weren't pregnant when you married her dad, were you?"

"Of course not," she said, indignation putting a blush on her cheeks.

"Then you must have married him because you thought you loved him."

She nodded.

"Well, it seems to me that even when things don't work out, sometimes the beginning is as simple as that," Luke said. "Two people love each other. Marriage is a huge leap of faith based on hope as much as love. In reality, though, it doesn't mean they have the fortitude or the passion to make it work over the long haul, not with all the crises likely to crop up along the way. There are probably thousands of things — big and small — that can trip up a marriage and make it fail."

She turned toward him, her expression curious. "Is that what happened to your marriage? It couldn't withstand the separation of you going to Iraq? Or did you go to Iraq because there were already problems?"

For a moment, Luke was taken aback by her insight. As much as he hated admitting it, there *had* been problems. Maybe they hadn't pushed him toward the decision to reenlist, but they'd been there, lurking just below the surface of the mostly separate lives he and Lisa had begun to lead because of the demands of his work and her social nature. He considered not answering Hannah's questions, partly because it was so much more complicated than that and partly because he didn't especially want to reveal just how badly he'd been betrayed. Maybe he wasn't even ready to face the self-examination of his own role in what had happened.

"Did I touch a raw nerve?" Hannah asked, not sounding especially contrite about it if she had.

"Yes," he said honestly. "And we were talking about your marriage, not mine."

Her gaze locked with his. "Maybe we *should* be talking about yours. You've been awfully evasive when it comes to discussing anything the least bit personal. If Gran hadn't told me you're a surgeon, I wouldn't even know that much. Why is that, Luke?"

"I thought we were trying to figure out some way for you to make things right with your daughter," he said testily. "That's the more immediate problem."

"True, but maybe what I really need right

now is for you to tell me why it was so easy for my grandmother to warn you off of spending time with me. Are you still married, Luke? Is that it?"

He was dismayed that she even felt the need to ask. "No," he said at once. "The divorce is final."

"But you're not really over it? Are you hoping to win her back?"

"Absolutely not," he said fiercely. "But I do have two kids and I haven't figured out how to make all this work for them. I'm so angry I can't even imagine being in the same town with my ex-wife, much less in the same room."

"Anger implies that the feelings still run pretty deep."

Luke considered the comment. She was right. His feelings did run deep, just not the way she meant. At least he didn't think it was because he still loved Lisa. He was pretty sure anything he'd ever felt for her died the day she'd told him about her relationship with Brad.

"Okay, here's the condensed version," he said, avoiding her gaze. He stood up and began to pace, agitated just thinking about how his life had unraveled. "I decided to reenlist without talking it over with my wife. I suspect my motives were less clear-cut than I pretended they were. Our marriage was in trouble. I just didn't want to see it. I guess I thought a break would help and I did think I had a duty to do whatever I could in Iraq."

Hannah gave him a knowing look. "You ran away. I'm sensing a pattern here, Luke."

"Do you want to hear this or not?" he said, annoyed that she'd called him on his cowardice.

"Please," she said.

"Lisa was furious, which she apparently thought justified her having an affair with my business partner, Brad, and then asking for a divorce just two weeks before I was due to come home to my loving family. The request came in an e-mail." He clenched his fists, because just the memory of that made him want to break things. "She didn't even have the guts to try to reach me by phone or to wait a couple of weeks until we were face-to-face. She just laid it all out in an e-mail, how they'd fallen in love while I was gone and wanted to get married."

Hannah stared at him, her eyes filled with dismay. "Oh, Luke, I'm so sorry. How could she have done such a thing? Not just betraying you, but telling you like that?"

"I guess she thought it would be easier for me to come home without any expectations of picking up where we'd left off," he said, trying for once to see it from Lisa's perspective. He hated to think that she'd intentionally gone out of her way to add to the pain she knew she'd be causing him.

"How considerate of her," Hannah said sarcastically.

Luke liked the fact that she was immediately on his side. It felt good to know that someone was. "Yeah, that's what I thought," he replied. "Instead of being prepared, though, my anger consumed every waking minute. I think that's why I ended up wounded. I wasn't paying attention when I went outside the gates of the compound to treat soldiers who'd just been wounded by a car bomb. I didn't see the person sneaking into the middle of the chaos, didn't suspect a thing before he detonated *another* car bomb not fifteen feet away from where I was working on someone, trying to get him stabilized enough to take him inside. So, I suppose I blame Lisa and Brad for that, too. If I could lay blame for global warming on them, I'd probably do that as well."

Hannah's cheeks were damp with tears. She reached for his hand. "I am so, so sorry. No wonder you're angry."

"When I can see past that anger, I can

manage to count my blessings," he said. "For one thing, I'm lucky to be alive. And my leg's doing better than I had any right to expect when they first took me in. I think that was the worst part of all. I knew just how bad my injuries were. I knew it would take a miracle to save the leg. Ironically, I was the surgeon whose job it would normally have been to try. Thankfully one of the other docs had been working with me on some of the more complicated cases. He did just fine on his own. I owe him. Otherwise . . ." Luke couldn't even express what might have happened.

He waved off her sympathy before she could express it. "Hey, I'm here now. I'm almost back to a hundred percent. I have a lot to be thankful for."

"Have you seen your kids since you came home?" she asked.

"Lisa brought them up to D.C. while I was in rehab. We got to spend a couple of days together. It was awkward as hell, though. I couldn't really get around yet, so we couldn't go out and do stuff. Kids that age need to be active. They were just seven and nine the last time I saw them, but they've both had birthdays since then. Lisa offered to bring them back, but I told her not to. They don't need to be cooped up in some hospital room, especially when there's so much tension between their parents."

"But they do need to spend time with you," Hannah protested.

"We had e-mails and phone calls, at least for a while. The past couple of weeks I haven't been in touch. Lisa said they were getting too upset."

"Which meant she didn't want to keep having to explain things to them," Hannah said dryly.

"More than likely," Luke agreed. "They're too young to fully appreciate the whole situation. Meantime, back home, they've had to adjust to this new guy being around all the time, the man formerly known as *Uncle* Brad, though he's now acting as a surrogate dad. They don't know what to make of that, either. They're totally mixed up about where their loyalties should lie. They've always liked Brad, but now their dad is gone because of him."

He regarded Hannah with regret. "I get that they need my permission to be happy with the way things are now, but I'm sorry, I'm just not quite ready to forgive and forget." When she was about to speak, he held up a hand. "I know that I need to for their sakes, and I will. Just not today. Or even tomorrow."

"What a mess!" Hannah said. "I know marriages are complex and that there are two sides to everything, but this just seems flat-out wrong to me."

"Me, too," he said. "But I've stopped trying to analyze why it happened. I had a few minutes alone with Lisa when they came up to D.C., so I could have asked her, but I didn't. It was too obvious that it was over for her, that she couldn't wait to move on. Since it's too late to change anything, I need to figure out how to pick up the pieces and move on myself."

"I'll tell you what I told Kelsey earlier," Hannah said. "This may not be the best place for you to do that. She needs to be with Jeff, working things out. You need to be where your kids are. That's where the answers are."

"And I will be with them, eventually," he said. "However that works out."

"Meaning?"

He shrugged. "I wish I knew. I don't know what's going to happen next, Hannah. I don't know what I'm going to do or where I'm going to live, much less how to go about building a whole new relationship with my son and daughter."

"You didn't give your wife full custody, did you?" she demanded. "Please tell me you didn't do that. I asked for and won that from my husband, but now I see that it wasn't in Kelsey's best interests, any more than it had been when my mother got full custody of me after my dad left. If Kelsey's dad had been in her life more regularly, if I'd helped to facilitate that, maybe she wouldn't have such a skewed view of marriage and divorce. Ironic, isn't it? I knew what having my dad cut out of my life felt like, but I turned right around and did it to my own child. Now Kelsey's about to repeat the pattern by skipping the marriage altogether."

Luke gave her a penetrating look. "Hannah, we all do what we think is right at the time. You can't second-guess yourself now."

"Oh? The way you're second-guessing your choices?"

He sighed. "Exactly. But I did insist on sharing custody of the kids. I'll have liberal amounts of time with them once I get my life in order. And before you say it, I do know that needs to be sooner, rather than later."

"Good, because kids need to know they're loved. And they need to hear it and feel it day in and day out. It doesn't take much to shake their faith in that. Look at Kelsey. She was so affected by her father's abandonment that she can't envision holding a family of her own together. She doesn't even want to try. I guess we never see how the decisions we make as parents can reverberate years down the road."

"Which is exactly why I need to be careful with you. I don't want you to get caught up in my drama."

She gave him a wry look. "Isn't it ironic, then, that you're already caught up in mine?"

"Not the same," he insisted. "I have no idea where I'll be a month from now, Hannah. You already know you're going back to New York. You have a plan."

She laughed, though there was a nervous edginess to the sound. "I *had* a plan. It didn't anticipate my grandmother being stubborn, my daughter being pregnant or the two of them siding against me."

Beside her Luke smiled wryly at the frustration in her voice. "What's that old saying? Life is what happens while you're busy making plans?"

She nodded.

"So, welcome to life," he said wryly, then noted, "Sometimes it sucks."

"Amen to that."

Kelsey drew in a deep, satisfying breath as

she came outside with her cup of herbal tea. The morning was cool with a breeze from the north and blue skies were filled with faint puffs of clouds. It was perfect for working outdoors.

Setting the cup on a wicker table, she gathered all the supplies she'd need to fill the hanging baskets — potting soil, flats of flowers, a trowel and her watering can — then went to work, humming happily. She felt almost carefree.

When she heard her cell phone ringing, she ignored it. For one thing, her hands were filthy. For another, she knew instinctively it was Jeff. He'd been calling every morning at the same time — 10:00 a.m. here, 7:00 a.m. in California. It was the second day in a row she'd ignored his call. She knew she couldn't do it forever, but she was trying to buy herself a little time to gather the courage to tell him she wasn't coming back to Stanford.

Unfortunately her mom walked out the door while the phone was still ringing.

"Want me to get that?" she asked.

Kelsey shook her head. "He'll call back."

"Then you know it's Jeff?"

"Yes."

"And you don't want to speak to him

because he's not going to like what you have to say."

Kelsey nodded.

"Come on, kiddo. You know it's not fair to leave him hanging," her mom said quietly.

"I'm not going to leave him hanging forever," Kelsey said defensively. "I just need a little more time."

"For what? You told me you'd made your decisions about the baby and about staying here."

"That doesn't mean he's not going to fight me," she said, resigned to the arguments that lay ahead, just not ready to face them.

The phone finally stopped ringing and Kelsey breathed a sigh of relief. Once Jeff left for class, his day would be so busy, he wouldn't try again before nightfall.

"Sweetie, what are you *really* afraid of?" Hannah asked, starting on another planter, tucking in greenery and a few of the flowering vines. "If you're as certain of how you want to handle things as you say, then what makes you think Jeff can sway your decision?"

"He's pretty persuasive," she replied. "And I hate that I'm making him so unhappy, so yeah, I'm scared he'll change my mind."

"Okay, I know I've said this before, but it

bears repeating. If he can do that, then maybe getting married is what you really want, after all."

"No," Kelsey said adamantly. "This is what I want. I want to stay right here and have the baby here, then give it up for adoption."

"Do you intend to admit to the social worker that you know who the father is?"

She stared at her mother blankly. "What do you mean?"

"They're going to want to know who the father is."

"Why?"

"Because he needs to relinquish his parental rights, too. Otherwise, he could have grounds later to challenge the adoption. Will Jeff do that? Will he challenge it?"

The plant Kelsey was holding slid from her fingers. "No," she said, then sighed at the lie. "Yes. He says he will."

"If you know that, then why are you trying to go forward with an adoption?" Hannah fell silent, her expression perplexed at first, then dismayed as she seemed to grasp what was going on in Kelsey's head. "Please don't tell me you were hoping that you could give the baby up for adoption here and no one would even try to contact Jeff. Is that the reason you want to stay here?"

Kelsey hesitated, then sighed again. "Okay, yes, that's exactly what I was hoping." She hated how it sounded when her mom said it. It made her sound deceitful and sneaky, when what she really wanted was to do the right thing for her baby. "It's not why I wanted to stay here, but it is what I planned to do."

Hannah regarded her with disappointment. "Sweetie, you know that's wrong. Jeff could easily figure out where you'd had the baby and who'd handled the adoption. Can you imagine what would happen if he came here and the baby was taken away from people who'd already fallen in love with it? How is that fair to anyone?"

"It would be awful," Kelsey acknowledged. "I guess I just never got beyond thinking that the baby would be much better off with two parents who really, really want it."

To her surprise, Hannah's eyes filled with tears. "Was your childhood really so awful?"

Kelsey stared at her with dismay. "Mine? No, of course not."

"Really? Because it sounds to me as if you can't imagine any scenario in which Jeff could give this baby a good home on his own. I can't help thinking that's because you think I did a lousy job, that you needed two parents to be happy."

"I didn't mean it like that," she swore, filled with guilt. "And Jeff would be a great dad. Any child would be lucky to have him."

Her mom studied her with a perplexed expression. "Then what's really going on?"

Kelsey hesitated. The answer wasn't pretty. In fact, it was downright selfish, but it was the truth. "I'm scared that if Jeff takes the baby himself, it'll be the end of us," she said slowly, waiting for her mom to regard her with total disgust. Instead, Hannah merely waited, giving Kelsey time to say it all.

"How can we still be together if he's raising our child and I'm just this person who hangs out with them?" she continued. "That would be totally weird for everyone."

"So, if you give him the baby, you lose him, and that's not what you want?"

Again, Kelsey didn't like the way it sounded when her mom said it. It sounded ugly and mean and totally immature.

"I just want things to be the way they were," she said plaintively.

"Sorry, but that's not possible," Hannah said. She finished filling the basket she'd been working on, watered it, and then hung it from one of the hooks on the porch before facing Kelsey directly. "Sounds to me as if you have some more thinking to do. I'll leave you to it."

"Mom, I've been thinking so much, my head hurts. Just tell me what to do."

"Oh, sweetie, I wish I could, but, as hard as it is for me to stand by and watch, this is your life. You're an adult now. You have to make your own decisions. You're just figuring out that actions have consequences, sometimes consequences that can change everything. I will tell you one thing, though. Having you was the best thing that ever happened to me. Sure, I hadn't planned to get pregnant and your dad and I probably weren't ready for a child, but there hasn't been one single minute in all these years that I've regretted having you in my life."

"I'm just so afraid I *would* regret it," Kelsey said. "And sooner or later the baby would grow up and figure out that it was a mistake."

"Possibly," Hannah agreed, again in that carefully neutral tone. "Especially if you choose to see him or her that way. Or maybe you can start looking at this as an untimely and unexpected blessing. But if you really can't see it that way, then Jeff still has the right to make his own choice. You can't take that away from him, not if he's the decent young man you say he is."

Kelsey wished like anything that she could

look at this the way her mom wanted her to, that she could see the positive side of it, but right this minute, it just wasn't possible. And she hated the way that made her feel about herself and the kind of person she must be.

After her conversation with Kelsey, Hannah immediately went for a walk on the beach despite the wind that had kicked up. There was a storm brewing offshore, which meant she'd probably get soaked before she got back, but she didn't care. Right now the spray of saltwater felt good and the tumultuous waves matched the chaos of her thoughts.

She'd worked hard to hide her disappointment in Kelsey, but she suspected she hadn't been entirely successful. She recognized that her daughter was only twenty, still a child in some ways, and was struggling with a lot of conflicting emotions. Even so, it had been difficult to remain neutral when so much of what Kelsey had said sounded totally self-absorbed.

Hannah knew she had to refrain from using her own struggles as proof that things could work out. Kelsey obviously didn't see it that way. Despite Kelsey's denials, it was plain enough to Hannah that Kelsey thought she'd been shortchanged because of her mostly absent father. Whatever Hannah had done to make sure her daughter wanted for nothing, emotionally or materially, apparently hadn't been enough. The realization stung.

Suddenly a wave splashed ashore, drenching her, but the chilly water also served as an odd kind of wake-up notice, as well. Somewhere deep inside, where old emotions had been slumbering for years, she recognized Kelsey's feelings in herself.

Hadn't she been just as resentful of her mom after her father had gone? Hadn't she felt abandoned and cheated out of a real family? The love showered on her by her mother and her grandparents was more than many kids had, but it hadn't filled the empty space inside of Hannah.

The salty sea spray mixed with tears as she remembered how bereft she'd felt after her father had gone, how angry she'd been at her mother for not finding some way to keep him with them or bring him back. There had been one pivotal moment, when all of her fury had come bursting forth. She could recall it as vividly now as the day it had happened.

She'd been twelve, and her dad had only been gone a few months. She had come racing home from school, report card in hand, thrilled with her straight A's. She'd imagined the reward money she'd get and how she would spend it.

But when she'd shown the grades to her mom, there'd been hugs and lavish praise, but nothing more. It was her dad who'd established the tradition of giving her five dollars for each A she earned, her dad who'd always said that hard work deserved to be rewarded. In her mind it wasn't the money per se that she craved, but the acknowledgment in such a tangible form that what she'd accomplished was deserving of his respect. In a way, it was a contract between the two of them, and it had been broken.

She'd turned on her mother furiously. "Dad would have cared. He would have known how hard I worked for these grades. You don't love me the way he did," she accused. Then for good measure, she'd added, "I hate you for letting him go away. I hate you! It's all your fault he's not here anymore."

And then she'd run from the room, not caring about the stricken expression on her mother's face.

Later that night, it was her grandmother who'd come to her room. She'd sat gingerly on the edge of the bed and handed Hannah an envelope with six crisp five-dollar bills.

"I want to ask you something," she said as Hannah clutched the money, a sick feeling in her stomach. "Is that money more important to you than your mother's feelings?"

Blinking back a fresh batch of tears, Hannah avoided her gaze. "What do you mean?" she asked, though she already knew.

"I understand that you miss your father, especially on a day like today, but do you feel one bit better for having made your mother feel as if she failed you?"

It was the first time Hannah had realized that what she said could wound another person, especially an adult. Somehow she'd thought adults were immune to the words that spilled from her in anger. Or maybe she'd just thought they deserved them. Or maybe she hadn't really thought about it at all, just lashed out because there was so much hurt bottled up inside and it had to go somewhere.

"I'm sorry," she whispered.

"I'm not the one who needs to hear that," her grandmother said. "Tell your mother, but don't do it until you truly mean it, until you fully understand that sometimes she hurts just as much as you do because of the way things turned out with Clayton. And it's a thousand times harder for her, because she aches for you, too, not just herself."

Hannah had grown up a little that night. Not all the way, but enough to think before she spoke. And, amazingly, her resentment had died when she'd tried to look at the situation from her mother's perspective. Instead, she was able to view her as another victim of her father's abandonment, rather than someone who'd been responsible for it.

And now that she thought about it, that had been as instrumental in the outcome of her own uneasy marriage as her eventual divorce had been to Kelsey. She'd learned that a bad marriage wasn't necessarily better than no marriage at all. And when two people eventually walked away from each other, they did it because they had to, not to make life more painful for their children.

Kelsey apparently still had that lesson to grasp. Hannah couldn't help wondering if she would figure it out in time to make this life-altering decision ahead of her for the right reasons.

11

When Hannah returned from her walk, she was greeted by her grandmother, who held out her cell phone as if it were poisonous.

"You left this sitting on the kitchen counter," she said. "It's been ringing off and on ever since you went for your walk. You said it takes its own messages, so you probably ought to check them. Anytime someone calls that much, it has to be important. At least *they* think it is."

"Thanks, Gran," Hannah said, scrolling down the caller ID. Every call had been from her boss. "Looks like another crisis at work."

"You going to call back?" Grandma Jenny asked, studying her curiously as she set the phone aside. "What's going on, Hannah? You don't seem especially anxious to speak to your boss. Is he pressuring you about coming back?"

"No, no pressure," Hannah said. Mainly

because she hadn't been taking his calls.

"Then why don't you want to talk to him?"

Hannah wasn't sure she could explain. Maybe she was more like Kelsey than she'd realized. Maybe she, too, wanted to avoid awkward conversations. And this one was bound to be awkward. Her two weeks of leave would be up in a couple of days, but she was no closer to resolving things at Seaview than she'd been when she'd arrived. If anything, she had *more* problems to deal with. She couldn't go back yet and Dave was going to be justifiably furious about it.

"You said he hasn't been pressuring you, but he does want you back in New York, doesn't he?"

Hannah nodded.

"Are you going?"

"How can I? Kelsey needs me right now. So do you."

Her grandmother gestured toward a chair. "Sit down." She waited until Hannah had complied, then looked her in the eye. "I'm sure Kelsey appreciates your support, but as I've said before, your daughter needs to find her own solutions. I already know exactly what I intend to do, which is open this inn at the end of next week. I'm grateful you came running down here to check on me and I'm delighted that Kelsey's here. I'd like you to stay longer, because I'm selfish. But if you have obligations in New York, you can go back to them with a clear conscience."

Hannah didn't know why she wasn't eager to seize the chance her grandmother was giving her, but she was no happier about it than she had been when Luke reminded her that he was here to provide backup. "It doesn't feel right to go back right now with everything that's going on here."

"It's not because of Luke, is it?"

"No," Hannah said, and it was true. She and Luke did have a certain amount of chemistry that might be worth exploring if things were different, but things weren't. And she would never change her life or her plans for a man, anyway. "Luke and I are just friends, which I'm sure you know, since you played a role in making sure it stayed that way."

"Me?" Her expression was all innocence.

"Yes, you. You basically told him to stay away from me."

"I did no such thing. I just said he shouldn't start something he wasn't prepared to follow through on. That's nothing more than any parent — or in this case, grandparent — would tell a man who was sniffing around."

Hannah laughed despite her annoyance. "I am old enough to decide which risks are worth taking with my heart."

"Are you finally admitting you still have feelings for Luke after all these years?"

Hannah saw how neatly she'd been tricked into the admission. "Sure, I have feelings for him," she said, then added, "but they're not the same kind of infatuated-schoolgirl feelings I had years ago."

"Which means they have an even greater risk of causing you pain," her grandmother assessed.

"We're *friends,*" Hannah repeated.

"You can say that a thousand more times and I still won't believe that's all it is. I've been around a block or two and I know what's what."

A chuckle erupted before Hannah could stop it. "I love you, Gran."

A pleased expression crossed her grandmother's face. "And I love you, which is why I'm so worried. You have so much going on in your life, and you don't seem to be facing any of it. Look at how you ignored those calls from work. That's not like you."

"I know," Hannah agreed. "But I want you to stop worrying about me. You have enough on your mind preparing for this place to open." She stood up, putting an end to the conversation. "Tell me, what can I do to help?"

Her grandmother's surprise was evident. "You're really not going to call your boss?"

"Not right this second," Hannah said decisively, clicking the cell phone off so it would automatically go to voice mail. By her calculations that would be full soon, too.

Apparently Go-to-Hannah was on vacation, after all. The real shock, though, was that suddenly she felt darn good about it.

Hannah spent most of the afternoon painting the so-called beach room, which had been on Kelsey's list of must-do's before the first guests descended next week. The mindless task allowed her plenty of thinking time, which she didn't want, so she'd found a portable CD player that someone had apparently left behind and played a series of Jimmy Buffett songs, listening to everything from "Margaritaville" to "It's Five O'clock Somewhere," the hit duet Buffett had done with Alan Jackson. The laid-back tunes seemed to match her current, precariously happy mood.

She knew she'd pay for that when she finally checked in at the office, but for the moment she didn't care. For one day she was just going to let herself be a part of this family project to get the inn ready for guests.

She was dancing barefoot to one of the tunes, waving her paintbrush in the air, when she was startled by a tap on her shoulder. She whirled around, whipping off the earphones, and somehow in the process managed to leave a swipe of white paint across Luke's shadowed jaw.

"Oops," she said, then giggled. *Giggled.* Sweet heaven, what was happening to her? She never giggled.

She reached for a clean cloth as she stared into Luke's startled eyes. "Sorry. I'll get it off."

He caught her hand as she was about to reach for his face. "It's okay. It'll come off when I shower."

For some reason her breath seemed to be lodged in her throat. She swallowed hard, then managed, "Are you sure? It would come off much more easily right this second."

"Oh, I'm sure," he said, his gaze heated. "Having your hands on me right now would be a very bad idea."

She couldn't seem to stop herself from asking, "Why?"

"Because you've been on my mind today, Hannah. A lot," he said, the implication plain that the thoughts had been steamy. Apparently her grandmother's caution had only served to amp up the attraction, after all. "Then, finding you like this . . ." He gestured toward her shorts, her bare feet and the CD player. "You look sexy as hell."

"Oh," she whispered, unable to look away. It's because he's made himself unavailable, she told herself. That was why she suddenly wanted to lock lips with him. That's all it was, for both of them. Once more, she tried to steady her nerves. "Did you want something? Is that why you came in here?"

"I wanted to let you know that your grandmother, Kelsey and I have decided we all need a night out. It's Friday, and we're going to The Fish Tale for the seafood special. We'll leave in an hour. Can you be ready?"

For reasons that weren't entirely clear to her, she wasn't sure that was a good idea. Maybe it had something to do with that weak-kneed response she'd just had to Luke. After a couple of beers, she might not behave responsibly. She might just act on that instinct and worry about the consequences later. It seemed he, too, was in the same reckless mood.

"I should probably finish painting this room," she said.

"No," he said flatly. "You're coming with us. If you're determined to finish in here before we go, I'll help."

Hannah didn't think she could bear being in such a confined space with him for the time it would take them to complete the job. "No, never mind. It can wait until tomorrow."

"Then I'll help you tomorrow," he said, still gazing into her eyes.

"Not necessary," she said, then rushed from the room to take the brush outside to wash it out with the hose. She was such a ninny, she thought as she pointed the spray in her face, hoping to cool down her flaming cheeks. What was she, seventeen? And what had that whole scene been about, anyway? Luke was the one who'd put the brakes on days ago, so why had he been crowding her in there, deliberately kicking the sizzling chemistry into high gear? And why hadn't she been able to control her own responses, when she knew this was a dead-end street? Why were they playing such a dangerous game?

By the time she'd rinsed out the brush and left it to dry, Luke had gone upstairs for his shower. The paint can had been neatly capped and the drop cloth folded and put away. She sighed at the evidence of his consideration. She didn't need him being nice. She needed him to be an obnoxious pig. Otherwise, she might be in serious danger of falling for him, just as her grandmother feared she would.

After a quick glance at her watch, she realized she had only forty-five minutes to pull herself together. If she wanted to wash and dry her hair, that was cutting it close. She didn't bother examining why she wanted to look her best for dinner at a low-key Seaview restaurant. She had a hunch she wouldn't like the answers one bit.

Apparently the seafood special was the biggest draw on The Fish Tale's menu. The place was packed. Several people were standing on the sidewalk outside waiting for tables, which meant even the bar must be crowded.

"We'll never get a table," Hannah said, expecting to be relieved by the fact that she wouldn't have to spend an evening bumping into people she didn't especially want to see. To her surprise, though, she was vaguely disappointed.

"Not to worry," Luke said. "I called earlier. Jack said he'd hold a table for us. All we need to do is squeeze through this crowd and get inside."

"And then fend them off when they come after us," Kelsey said dryly. "Are you sure we should be cutting in front of the hungry hordes?"

"That's the beauty of making a reservation and of knowing the owner," Luke said, steering them inside.

Despite the chaos and noise, Jack somehow spotted them and came out from behind the bar to greet them, bending down to give Grandma Jenny a kiss on the cheek.

"It's good to see you out and about," he told her. "You need to come over here more, if only to visit with me."

"Jackson, you know how people love to talk in this town. Just imagine what they'll have to say if I start hanging out in your bar," Grandma Jenny said, though she looked pleased by the invitation.

Jack shrugged it off. "But just think of the customers I'd gain coming in here to catch a glimpse and decide for themselves what we're up to."

"I'm old enough to be your mother," Grandma Jenny said.

"You don't look it," he said, winking at her. "And I've always had a fondness for older women."

"You've only had eyes for Greta since the day she came to town," Grandma Jenny retorted. "Now, stop your foolishness and get us something to eat."

"Yes, ma'am," Jack said, grinning at her. "Your table's right over here. I've had to fight a few folks to keep it open."

"Thanks for doing that," Luke said. "And to save time, I think we're all agreed on the seafood special."

"Not me," Hannah said. "I'll have a Caesar salad."

"Me, too," Kelsey said.

"Since Jack looks swamped right now and there's no sign of Lesley Ann or another waitress, why don't I go up to the bar and get our drinks?" Luke suggested.

"Iced tea for me," Hannah told him. "And I'll come along to help you carry everything."

"Just water," Kelsey said.

"And I'd like a beer," Grandma Jenny said, grinning at their stunned expressions. "Well, I would," she added with a touch of defiance.

"A beer it is," Luke said.

Hannah squeezed through the path he created en route to the bar. When they got there, he nudged her until she was standing in front of him, then kept a protective hand on her shoulder as he placed their order.

He leaned down to murmur in her ear, "I

could have carried these by myself."

"I know. I just wanted to thank you for convincing me to come tonight."

"That's not what you were saying earlier."

"I realized that getting out has benefits."

He leaned in so close that his breath fanned across the back of her neck. "Such as this?"

Hannah trembled, then jolted when his lips brushed the same tender spot on the back of her neck. "What . . . Luke, what are you doing?" She turned enough to meet the smoldering heat in his eyes, then looked away. Stupid question. It was obvious what he was doing. He was going back on his word. He was tossing caution to the wind. Defying her grandmother. However she described it, she knew it was a very, very bad idea.

But it felt so good! It felt amazing to know she was desirable. Since her surgery she hadn't felt that way at all. In fact, she'd been terrified to even accept a date, because she'd feared what might happen next. She didn't want to see the look of dismay or, worse, disgust in a man's eyes when she told him about the mastectomy or, if he was brave enough to say it didn't matter, when he saw the scar where her breast had been.

Besides, it was too soon. Her body was

still healing, the scar still too vivid a reminder of what had happened and the uncertainty that lay ahead.

Oddly, though, none of those things seemed to matter with Luke. She had a feeling it was because she could almost pretend that she was the same person he'd known years ago, that he wouldn't look at her any differently because he knew who she was inside and that, at least, hadn't changed.

Not that it was going to go one bit further than these heated glances and stolen kisses, she told herself. Brave as she felt, she still wasn't strong enough to take the risk that she'd gotten it all wrong and he wasn't the kind of man who could see past the scar and its implication. Truthfully, she wondered if she'd ever see herself as just plain Hannah again, rather than Hannah who'd had cancer.

Right now he grinned at her. "You want to know what I'm doing? I'm making a pass at you, Hannah."

"But you said you wouldn't. You said it was a bad idea, and you were right," she said, sounding a little desperate even to her own ears.

He shrugged. "Changed my mind. I've done all this thinking about what happens next and the only thing I've figured out so far is that I can't imagine you not being a part of it. Couldn't we just for one night not think about the complications or what happens next, but just live in the moment?"

She gave him a rueful look. "That's exactly how my daughter wound up pregnant."

He chuckled. "I have an entire box of condoms in my room."

That startled her even more than the pass itself. "You were *planning* this? You intended to seduce me tonight? In front of my daughter and grandmother?"

"I intended to try," he admitted. He studied her intently. "Are you angry?"

She thought about it. How could she be angry that an incredible, gorgeous guy wanted to seduce her, even if the timing did suck?

For the second time that day, she decided to ignore what was smart and logical and go for what felt good. "You can try," she told him, giving him what she hoped was a flirtatious look over her shoulder as she grabbed a couple of drinks from Jack and slipped past Luke. She turned back with a grin. "Don't expect me to make it easy for you, though."

If Grandma Jenny had pinned him to a chair and threatened him with torture, Luke couldn't have said why he was breaking every one of the rules he'd made about steering clear of Hannah. There was just something about the way he felt when he looked at her. He felt young again and carefree, which was ridiculous considering all the baggage both of them had.

Spending time with her now, he couldn't imagine why he hadn't been drawn to her all those years ago, rather than Abby. Probably because he'd been young and stupid and more interested in the kind of fun Abby was likely to agree to. Even then, he'd known that Hannah wasn't someone to toy with, that she was worthy of respect and consideration, something of which he was incapable at seventeen with his hormones on a rampage.

He smiled at the irony. It seemed his hormones were on a tear once again, and he didn't even have a seventeen-year-old's good sense about ignoring temptation and keeping his hands off Hannah.

He assured himself he wasn't going to let this go beyond some heavy-duty flirting, partly because Grandma Jenny would skin him alive and partly because even he knew deep down that it was a bad idea. That didn't explain why he'd taken the ferry to the mainland earlier to buy those condoms, hoping to avoid the speculation that purchasing them on the island would have caused. Maybe he'd just realized that good intentions could easily go up in flames. Or maybe he knew his resolve wasn't worth anything when Hannah looked at him with the kind of longing that matched what he was feeling. Every now and again her careful composure slipped away, and he could read the same desire in her eyes that was turning his blood hot. They were adults. Despite what Grandma Jenny obviously feared, they could act on their feelings and do it responsibly. He hoped.

He was relieved when their dinners came and he could concentrate on the seafood instead of the woman sitting next to him.

"I haven't had shrimp this good in ages," Grandma Jenny declared.

"Me, neither," Luke agreed, then caught the expression in Hannah's eyes as she regarded her salad with distaste and his food with unmistakable interest. "You want a bite?" he offered.

"Would you mind?" she asked, already taking one of the shrimp off his plate. She ate that one and reached for a piece of fish. "This is good," she murmured. "Really good."

Luke shook his head and gestured toward

Jack, who came over a few minutes later.

"I seem to have lost my claim on my dinner. Could you bring another seafood platter and more fries?" He glanced at Kelsey, who was also eyeing the food with undisguised hunger. "You, too?"

She nodded sheepishly.

"Two more platters coming up," Jack agreed. "Don't know why you didn't order 'em in the first place, at least for Hannah. As I recall she was always stealing food off your plate when she was here with you and Abby."

"I was not," Hannah retorted indignantly.

"Were, too," Luke said, suddenly recalling exactly how she would always order a healthy, inexpensive house salad, then proceed to snatch food from his plate. He'd been so absorbed with Abby, he'd never paid much attention to it. "You'd wait until I had my back turned . . ."

She gave him an impudent look. "Until you and Abby had locked lips," she corrected.

"And then you'd take whatever you could get your hands on. I never understood why you didn't just order the burger in the first place."

Kelsey grinned. "Because, according to her, women are supposed to be dainty eaters, so men won't think they're pigs."

Hannah frowned at her. "I never taught you that."

"Yes, you did. I can't recall one single meal we ever had in a restaurant with whomever you were dating that you didn't order a salad and nothing else."

"Did you steal their food, too?" Luke inquired, barely containing a laugh. "Is that why you've never remarried, because all the men feared starvation because of you stealing their meals right out from in front of them?"

Hannah set the shrimp back on his plate. "I had no idea that taking a couple of shrimp was going to turn into this big a deal. You offered. Do you remember that?"

"I did, and that seafood is yours. Enjoy every bite of it. I have my own on the way."

"Oh, please, take this one back. I wouldn't want you to faint from hunger."

Grandma Jenny chuckled. "Now, children, stop bickering."

Kelsey gave her great-grandmother a high-five that had Hannah scowling. "Not you, too."

"Me?" Grandma Jenny asked. "What did I do, except try to bring some order to the table before people start wondering what the two of you are fussing about?"

"Lovers' spat, that's what I'm hearing," Kelsey teased.

Luke watched with fascination as color bloomed in Hannah's cheeks. "An interesting observation," he told Kelsey. "What about it, Hannah? Is that what's happening here?"

"Oh, go suck an egg," she retorted, spearing each and every one of them with a sour look as she grabbed his entire plate and finished the remaining fish.

Luke heard the edge in her voice and suspected they'd just tested her patience beyond its limits. Thankfully Jack returned with the rest of the food and the teasing died down as Luke and Kelsey started to eat.

"Jack," Hannah called after him. "Is there any apple pie left?"

"Just one slice and I was holding it for Luke. I know it's his favorite."

"Is his name actually on it?" she asked.

Jack gave Luke an amused look, then turned back to Hannah and shook his head. "No."

"Then I'd like it, with a scoop of vanilla ice cream on top," she said.

"Hey," Luke protested, then spotted the glint in her eye. "Never mind. Jack, bring the lady the pie."

"I'll have peach," Grandma Jenny said, then glanced at Hannah. "Unless you're planning to stake a claim on that, too."

Hannah beamed at her. "Nope, the peach is all yours. Luke, what about you?"

"Nothing for me yet. I'm just starting on my meal. I think I'll just see how this plays out."

Jack regarded them all as if they'd gone a little crazy, then went off to fill their dessert orders. When he came back and set them on the table, Luke watched as Hannah dug into the pie with gleeful enthusiasm that he suspected had nothing to do with her love of apple pie.

"Any good?" he asked, losing interest in his food.

"Delicious," she said. "Best ever."

He leaned forward until his eyes were level with hers. "Are you going to share?"

"I wasn't planning to," she said, deliberately taking another bite.

"How about if I ask nicely?"

Her expression turned thoughtful. "Maybe. Try it."

He tucked a finger under her chin and kept their gazes locked. "Hannah, please let me have a bite of your pie."

She swallowed hard, then blinked. "No, I

don't think so." Another bite went into her mouth.

"Ah, so you want me to beg," he concluded.

Her eyes lit up. "Begging would be great."

He opened his mouth as if to beg, then muttered, "Nah. The pie's probably cold by now."

"It is not," she protested. "It's warm and oozing with vanilla ice cream. It's perfect."

He laughed. "You really, really wanted to hear me beg, didn't you?"

"Yes, as a matter of fact."

He winked at her. "You will eventually," he assured her. "But it won't be for pie."

Kelsey giggled, but Grandma Jenny scowled at him and at Hannah. "Stop it, you two! There are others present."

"Sorry, Gran," Hannah murmured.

Grandma Jenny's stern expression wavered. "Well, all I have to say is thank goodness neither one of you was after my peach pie. I don't think my heart could have taken it." She stood up. "I'm going to pay the bill. Try to compose yourselves while I'm away from the table."

"Yes, ma'am," Luke said, though his lips were twitching.

"You two are very bad," Kelsey accused, after Grandma Jenny had walked away.

"What kind of example are you setting for the children?"

"And that would be you?" Hannah asked, then laughed. "Apparently I've already blown my chance to set a proper example for you. Come on, kid, let's go outside and wait for your grandmother. Luke?"

"I'll meet her at the bar and walk her out," he said. "I need to try to wrestle the bill away from her, anyway. I told Jack earlier I was paying. He already has my credit card."

Kelsey's expression brightened. "You and Gran are going to fight over the bill? That should be fun. We should stay, Mom."

"No. We're going outside in case there's bloodshed. It would be bad for the baby to hear your grandmother hitting Luke with some umbrella she grabbed from behind the bar."

"She's not going to hit me," Luke said. "She likes me."

"She also likes getting her own way," Hannah told him. "My money's on Gran winning this one. She's known Jack longer."

Sure enough, by the time Luke reached the bar, the bill had been paid — by Grandma Jenny.

"What can I say? She threatened me," Jack said.

"Here's your credit card, you sneaky

man," she said, handing it over. "Now, give me your arm. That beer has made me a little tipsy."

Luke tucked her arm through his and walked her out.

"Who paid the bill?" Hannah asked as soon as they emerged from the restaurant.

"I did, of course," Grandma Jenny responded.

Hannah immediately turned to Kelsey and held out a hand. "You owe me five bucks."

"You bet against me?" Luke asked indignantly as Kelsey handed over the money.

Hannah beamed at him. "No, I bet on a sure thing, but if you play your cards right, maybe I'll make it up to you before the night is over."

"Don't tease if you don't mean it," he warned.

Suddenly the entire clan of Matthews women seemed to be dedicated to making him edgy. And when he was, there was no telling what sort of outrageous thing he might do just to seize the upper hand once more. Lately he'd rediscovered the impetuous, reckless side of his nature, and something told him that he was about to give it free rein.

12

"Mom, the phone's for you," Kelsey called from the bottom of the stairs. "It's Dave."

Hannah froze in mid-stride. She hadn't counted on her boss calling the inn directly, rather than her cell phone, but of course he would. No doubt he'd tired of being ignored. Patience had never been one of his strong suits.

"Mom!"

"I'm coming," she shouted back as she left her room, then walked slowly down the steps to where her daughter was holding the portable phone.

"How does he sound?" she whispered.

"Ticked," Kelsey whispered back.

Hannah sighed and took the phone. "Good morning," she said cheerfully. "How are you?"

"I'm unhappy, that's how I am," Dave grumbled. "Don't you ever check your messages?"

"I lost track of my cell phone," she fibbed. "I know it's around here somewhere, but we've been so busy I haven't had time to hunt for it. What are you doing working on Saturday, by the way?"

"I'm trying to pick up the slack caused by having you take an unscheduled vacation," he said.

"I thought Carl was filling in," she said.

"Yeah, well, that hasn't worked out, just as you predicted. I spend half my time cleaning up his messes. I've had enough. I've given him two weeks' notice."

"Which is why you'd rather be in the office on a Saturday, instead of at home," Hannah guessed. "Just how furious is your wife that you cut her nephew loose?"

"Don't even go there," Dave said. "Bottom line, I need you back here this week. You are coming back on Monday, right? If I fill you in now, you'll have time to rough in some thoughts on these new projects and be ready to hit the ground running first thing Monday morning."

"Actually, I need to talk to you about that," she said, wincing at his uncensored curse, but plunging on, "I need more time."

"Hannah, no! Two weeks, that's what we agreed to. How long can it take to pack up your grandmother's things and move her?"

"A lot longer than I've had," she said dryly, "especially when she refuses to go."

Dave was a decent guy who'd been her friend almost as long as they'd worked together. Now he said, "She's not going into a retirement community? I thought that was the whole point of you rushing down there."

"Me, too, but she's flatly refused to go. I can't make her. She's not incompetent."

"So, what does that mean?"

"It means she's going to reopen the inn next week."

The announcement clearly stunned him into silence. When he finally spoke, there was a cautious note in his voice. "Has she dragged you into that?"

"I'm helping out a little. So is Kelsey."

"Kelsey's there? What about school?" he demanded, sounding more like a protective parent than an exasperated boss. He'd always taken a special interest in her daughter, treating her as if she were one of his own kids.

"She's decided to take some time off."

"Hannah, are you okay with that?"

"It seems I don't have a choice about that, either," she said. "I'm trying to adjust to the idea."

"No wonder you sound a little dazed. I hate to add to the pressure, but I really do need you back here ASAP. When you're not here, things fall apart."

"It's lovely to be considered indispensable, but we both know better. Dave, this is your business. You have plenty of competent people on staff. You just rely on me, because I'm usually handy. I've always been as much of a workaholic as you are."

"Exactly," he said. "I count on you, Hannah. Are you telling me you don't want the responsibilities anymore? Because if I train someone to take your place, there's no turning back. I can't dangle a promotion in front of someone else on the team, then yank it back once you decide you're ready to put in the time again."

The threat that she would lose her place in the hierarchy was unmistakable. She waited for sheer panic to set in, but it didn't. She had no idea why. Maybe it was because she thought he'd never follow through on it. Or maybe the real reason was within her. Maybe she honestly didn't care as much as she once had.

"Dave, you know I love you and the company, but right now being here has to be my priority," she said. "It won't be for much longer, but I know you can't run a business with that kind of uncertainty. Put me on unpaid leave and if and when things settle down here, we'll talk. If you don't want me back, then, well, that's just the way it will have to be."

"Hannah, you don't mean that!"

Her own amazement seemed to exceed his, but she didn't want to take the words back. "Actually I do," she said.

"Come on, let's talk about this. You need another week, even two, we'll manage."

"I can't promise that will be enough, and I don't want to let you down again," she said, her mind made up. Until things in Seaview seemed settled, until she saw whether or not the inn could operate without putting too much of a strain on her grandmother and Kelsey, she needed to stay here for her own peace of mind. If there were reasons beyond that, she didn't want to think about them now.

"How about a month?" he said, suddenly sounding desperate. "You can take a month's leave with pay, as long as you agree to consult by phone and e-mail when we need you."

The offer was more than she'd ever anticipated, proof of her worth to the company. She should have felt triumphant or at least gratified, but all she felt was more pressure. She knew exactly how it would turn out. Her days would be consumed with dealing with crises long distance. Her time wouldn't be her own. She'd be little help to Kelsey or to Gran. Her days of taking walks on the beach or doing something just for the sheer fun of it with Luke would be over as well.

"Come on, Hannah, it's a good offer and you know it. Say yes," Dave pleaded.

"I'm sorry," she said, feeling oddly euphoric as she uttered the words. "I can't, Dave. I'll call as soon as things are under control here and we'll talk. If you need to move on in the meantime, I'll understand."

"Dammit, I am not letting you quit!"

"I don't believe I ever said anything about quitting," she reminded him. "I'm on an unpaid leave of absence with my return subject to negotiation."

"Oh, spin it however you want to," he grumbled. "You're not coming back. I can hear it in your voice. I don't know what's going on down there, Hannah, but you're losing your edge. You need to get back here before it's gone for good."

She laughed at his frustration. "How can you possibly say I've lost my edge? You just made me a dream offer, one you never would have considered when you made this call. I'd say that gives me the upper hand, even though technically I'm not even negotiating."

"Whatever," he muttered, then fell silent. When he spoke again, there was real concern in his voice. "Hannah, is this about the cancer? Are you suddenly scared that you don't have time left? Is that what this is about? Are you trying to make the most of every minute?"

"No, Dave, it has nothing to do with the cancer," she said honestly. "It's about my family. Right now, they need me and I need to be here for them."

"You're sure?"

"I'm sure."

He sighed heavily. "Okay, then. Call me when you're ready to come back."

"I will," she promised.

"I love you, babe. Forget anything I said before. There will always be a place for you here."

Suddenly her eyes filled with tears. "Thanks, Dave."

"I'll be in touch. I'm not going to let you forget about us and the fact that I want you back."

"Bye," she said, because her voice was suddenly too choked to say anything more.

She clicked off the phone, then sank onto the bottom step. Kelsey suddenly appeared, which made Hannah wonder how much of the conversation she'd overheard.

"Mom, are you really okay?" she asked, sitting down beside her. A worried frown knit her brow. "You weren't lying to Dave, were you? Your cancer's not back, is it?"

Hannah draped an arm over her daughter's shoulders and pulled her close. "Nope. This is just where I belong right now, that's all. While I was talking to him, I just saw it all so clearly, that you and Gran need to be my priorities right now."

Kelsey leaned into her. "I saw things more clearly once I got here, too. Isn't it weird how things turn out sometimes?"

Weird wasn't the word Hannah would have used. *Ironic* was the one that came to mind. Never in a million years would she have imagined herself choosing Seaview Key over New York, even for a minute, much less weeks, but she just had. And even though it was temporary, it didn't make the decision any less unexpected or disconcerting.

Kelsey set out for her afternoon walk with her mom at a brisk pace. For one thing, the doctor she'd seen had told her that walking on the beach was good exercise, but she liked it because she could clear her head out here. It was as if the sea breeze blew away the cobwebs and let her see things more clearly. She wondered if her mom had suddenly realized the same thing and that's why she was staying in Seaview for the time being. Had she started to appreciate Seaview in a whole new way?

Whatever her reasons, though, Kelsey was glad her mom was going to be around for a while longer. She liked taking these afternoon walks with her. Sometimes they never said a word, like now. Sometimes they talked about the past, all the things — good and bad — her mom remembered about living here as a child. At those times, Kelsey felt the ties to her ancestors in a way she never had before coming here, especially when she surprised her mom with stories that she claimed she'd never heard. Kelsey suspected she'd always been so anxious to leave, she'd never really listened to all the reasons that Seaview was someplace worth staying.

"You're awfully quiet today," Hannah said, glancing her way. "Is there something on your mind?"

"Not really. I was just thinking about how glad I am that you're staying longer."

"Me, too."

"Really?" Kelsey said. "I figured you were doing it because you felt obligated or something."

"That's part of it, I suppose," her mom said. "But like I told you earlier, it seems as if this is where I belong right now. Maybe I need to get in touch with the person I used to be."

"When you knew Luke?" Kelsey asked, curious about the relationship. It was plain as day they were attracted to each other, but she had no idea if they'd been involved years ago. "Did you used to date?"

"No, he dated my best friend."

"But you liked him, didn't you? Those sparks between the two of you now can't be something totally new."

"He was the hottest jock in high school, so I suppose I was just as infatuated with him as every other girl in school. But he only had eyes for Abby. He never even gave me a second glance."

"Well, he's glancing now," Kelsey said. "And then some."

Even though her mom hadn't admitted that there was anything between them, Kelsey couldn't miss the pleased expression on her face.

They continued on in silence, Kelsey stopping every so often to pick up a unique seashell or a piece of sea glass to add to the collections she was creating for display in the inn.

"Sweetie, can I ask you something?" Hannah said, sounding surprisingly hesitant.

"Sure."

"Have you talked to Jeff lately?"

Kelsey bit back a sigh. "I finally called him back last night," she said.

"How did it go? Did you tell him you're staying here?"

"I told him," Kelsey said.

"And?"

"He was pretty angry." She glanced at Hannah. "I didn't expect that. I thought once I explained everything, he'd get that this was the best decision. Usually he's this really laid-back, go-with-the-flow kind of guy, which is one of the things I love about him. He's like the anti-Dave, if you know what I mean."

Her mom grinned. "I know exactly what you mean."

"Well, he wasn't like that last night. He started issuing all these ultimatums and telling me he wasn't going to let me give his child away to strangers."

"How did you respond to that?"

"I told him he wasn't the boss of me and hung up," she admitted with a rueful grin. "Real mature, huh?"

"No, but understandable. It's obvious, though, that you two do need to see each other and work this out face-to-face."

"I already told you I can't do that. I'll cave."

"I think you're stronger than you give yourself credit for. If you cave, as you put it, it will be because on some level it's what you want. Maybe there's a compromise you haven't even thought of yet."

"I don't think so. I think he'll win because he'll just wear me down."

"You could invite him to come here. You'd have all of us as moral support," Hannah suggested.

"No," Kelsey said at once. "I don't want him here."

"Well, if you change your mind, it would be okay with Gran and me."

"You've talked about this?" Kelsey asked, suddenly indignant. "What are you doing, plotting behind my back? Are the two of you picking out wedding dresses or something?"

Her mom just stared at her as if she'd gone off the deep end.

"Don't be ridiculous," Hannah said finally. "If either of us wanted to plot behind your back, we'd have called Jeff ourselves and invited him here. I'm just saying that we'll support you, no matter what you decide about asking Jeff for a visit or about putting the baby up for adoption or anything else, okay?"

Kelsey's temper cooled at once. "Thanks. Sorry I snapped at you."

"It's okay. It comes with the territory." She linked her arm with Kelsey's. "Now, we'd better get back before Gran decides to climb a ladder to change light bulbs or something."

Kelsey grinned. "You caught her doing that, too?"

"Oh, yeah. The woman doesn't know when to quit."

"Tell me about it."

At least that was one thing they could agree on, she thought as they turned and headed home.

From the front porch, Luke watched mother and daughter walking on the beach. They'd been doing the same thing for days. He couldn't help wondering what mother-daughter secrets they shared on those walks, but he never asked. Since until recently he'd kept more than enough secrets of his own from Hannah, he could respect their right to theirs.

Not that he had much time to wonder about what those two talked about. Grandma Jenny had him so busy he didn't have a lot of time to sit and ponder his own life or anyone else's. He'd taken some rare time off this afternoon and he intended to enjoy it. He'd leave his future on the back burner for another hour. Or maybe another day. Who knew, as contented as he was feeling right now, maybe even longer.

He closed his eyes and let the sun soak in. The warmth made his bad leg feel better, especially after he'd put too much stress on it trying to keep up with all the chores Grandma Jenny had for him. He could have told her the truth about his injury and begged off, but he'd liked feeling useful too much to risk having her cut back on the assignments out of pity. If she'd noticed him limping more at the end of the day, she'd never mentioned it, and he'd liked that, too. He appreciated that Hannah apparently hadn't revealed what he'd told her, either, leaving it to him to decide how much he wanted Grandma Jenny to know. He didn't want anyone hovering over him.

"You catching a catnap before Gran puts you back to work?"

Hannah's teasing words snapped him awake. He grinned at her. "Don't tell, okay? The woman's wearing me out."

She perched on the railing opposite him, her slim legs tanned and fit from the long walks she'd been taking, the color high in her cheeks, her hair streaked with blond highlights. She looked younger and more relaxed than when he'd first arrived.

"Me, too," she confided.

He asked a question that had been on his mind for a couple of days now. "Aren't your two weeks up now? You going back to New York?"

"I should be," she said, sounding resigned. "But you know I can't. Gran has her heart set on reopening the inn. I can't bear to disappoint her. And then there's Kelsey. Her life's in chaos at the moment. I told my boss this morning that I was going on an indefinite leave of absence."

He regarded her with surprise. "You're staying indefinitely?"

"That's the plan," she said, then added, "Not forever, though."

He smiled. "Just so I'm clear about it, huh? Or are you saying that for your own benefit?"

"Okay, sure. I do have to keep reminding myself that this is just temporary. It makes it bearable."

"You know what I think? I think you like being here more than you expected to. It works that way sometimes. When we're young, all we care about is growing up, being independent and moving on. Then we discover that being out there in the cold, cruel world is not all it's cracked up to be, and home doesn't look so bad, after all. Admit it, Hannah, Seaview is starting to grow on you again."

She shrugged. "Maybe a little," she conceded. "And right now, being here is good for Kelsey, too. I've managed to buy myself a few weeks of unpaid leave, but then I absolutely have to go back or I can kiss my career goodbye."

"You said that being here is good for Kelsey. What about you? Why won't you admit that it's been good for you, that staying is about more than obligation? You look a lot more relaxed than you did when I first got here."

Her expression turned thoughtful. "I'm annoyed at being conned into staying."

"Conned?" he inquired.

"Okay, it was my decision," she admitted. "But I am frustrated that I can't get Gran to see my point of view. I still hate Seaview." Her eyes sparkled, despite the litany. "But, yeah, it's been good for me, too," she said, the concession grudging. "How about you? You making any progress on all those heavy decisions you need to make?"

"Your grandmother's kept me so busy, I

haven't had much time to think. You know what, though? That's okay. I thought I needed to think things through, force myself to make some decisions, but I think I'd been doing way too much of that during all those months of rehab. I was just going around in circles. I needed to just be for a while, get in touch with myself again." He smiled. "I know it all sounds a little touchy-feely, but you know what I mean."

"Yeah, I think I do," she said.

Just then his cell phone, which he'd stuck in his pocket out of habit, rang, something it hadn't done for days. He pulled it out, glanced at the caller ID and winced. "I have to take this."

Hannah started to move away. He put his hand on her bare thigh, then yanked it back.

"You don't have to leave. I'll only be a minute. Stay, okay?"

He held her gaze until she turned and sat down in the rocker next to his and closed her eyes, soaking in the sun as he had been moments earlier. He wasn't sure why he wanted her there, maybe because her presence helped to ground him.

"Hello," he said curtly when he finally took the call.

"You haven't called the kids for weeks,"

Lisa announced, dispensing with any pleasantries.

"You're exaggerating, as usual. It's been less than two weeks," he said, immediately on the defensive. "Besides, my impression was that you thought that would be for the best. You said when I called, it only upset them, and you wanted them to adjust to having Brad in their lives."

"Well, I was wrong. This is upsetting them more."

"Then I'll call tonight," he promised. "I never intended to stay out of their lives forever, Lisa. You know that. This was just a break until I could make some decisions and things started to get back to normal."

"Where are you, anyway? I called the hospital and they told me you'd been discharged two weeks ago. Are you back in Atlanta?"

"No."

"Then where are you?"

He didn't want to listen to the sarcastic comments she'd make if she knew he'd gone running back to Seaview, so he avoided telling her. "It doesn't really matter. You have my cell phone number. You can reach me if you need to."

"Are you coming back eventually? What should I tell Brad? He's wondering what to do about the practice."

Luke could think of a few choice things she could tell his one-time best friend, but he refrained. Words couldn't change the fact that Brad and his wife had hooked up while he was in Iraq. Well, God bless 'em. They deserved each other. His kids, however, deserved better.

"Actually, I've changed my mind, Lisa. I'm not going to call the kids tonight. I'm going to drive up tonight and get them first thing tomorrow morning."

"Get them? What do you mean? I have custody. That was settled when the divorce went through."

"Actually, we have joint custody and I have visitation privileges even when they're with you," he reminded her. "Quite a liberal amount of it, in fact. Let their school know that they'll be spending the next week with their dad, who's just home from Iraq and out of rehab. I don't think anyone will have a problem with that, you included, am I right?" He didn't even try to keep the challenging note out of his voice. He was spoiling for a fight and he wanted her to know it.

"But you said you're not in Atlanta. You don't even have a place to stay here, do you?"

"We won't be staying there. We're going on a long-overdue vacation."

"Luke, I don't like this. I don't like it one bit."

"There are plenty of things lately that I haven't much liked, either, but I had to deal. You'll get over it. I'll see you tomorrow. And don't even think about trying to fight me on this."

"Come on, Luke, be reasonable. Nate's playing ball. He has games scheduled."

"He's not in the pros, Lisa. He can miss a couple of games. Any other excuses?"

"Not right now, but we will discuss this further when you get here," she said icily.

He ignored her tone. "Okay, then," he said. "That's settled."

"It is *not* settled," she countered.

He pretended she hadn't even spoken. "Oh, there is one more thing, Lisa. Make sure Brad is nowhere near the house tomorrow when I get there. The first time he and I cross paths, it will not be in front of the kids." He hung up without waiting for a reply, his jaw clenched so tightly it ached.

"Luke?"

His head snapped around. He'd forgotten all about telling Hannah to wait. Now she'd heard firsthand just how bad his relationship with his ex-wife was.

"I need to get inside to pack an overnight bag and then I should probably hit the road," he said without meeting her gaze. "I should get in a couple of hundred miles today, so I can be in Atlanta first thing tomorrow."

"Are you planning to bring your children here?" she asked.

He realized then that he'd made a huge assumption, when he should have at least had the courtesy to ask first. He wasn't even sure if the inn was fully booked. He raked a hand over his head. "I'm sorry. I didn't think. I should have spoken to you and your grandmother before I made these plans. Will there be room for the kids?"

"Don't be silly. It's fine. I'm glad you're bringing the kids here. And if the guest rooms are taken, we have room on our side of the house. I just wondered how many rooms we should get ready."

Relief flooded through him. "You're sure it's okay? They're eight and ten, a boy and a girl. They're used to having their own space, so it's probably best if they have that here, too. Their lives have been in turmoil for a while now, so there's no telling what kind of acting out we might be in for."

"Hey, do you see anyone who passes for normal around here? They'll fit right in.

They need to be with their dad. That's the only thing that matters."

"Thanks."

"Don't thank me. I think I'll sit right here, though, while you go inside and tell Gran that we're about to have our first official guests before she's finished dusting everything for the thousandth time."

"What about me? Don't I count as an official guest?"

"Anybody who paints, fixes leaky faucets and unclogs the bathroom drain qualifies as family in my book. I don't know why Gran wants me around. You're the one who's qualified to run this place." She gave him a knowing look. "Of course, it would be quite a come-down from surgery. Or are you planning to change careers in mid-life?"

He shrugged. "You never know." One of these days he was going to have to take a hard look at the future and what he wanted from it. Right now, all he knew for sure was that he wanted to spend some time with his kids and maybe some intimate time with Hannah one of these days. Maybe that would be the first step on his path to a new life.

And he wanted Hannah, Grandma Jenny and Kelsey to share in this reunion with his children. Maybe it was as simple as wanting a buffer, just as they had when he'd arrived in their midst. Maybe it was a whole lot more. One of these days he'd have to figure that out, too.

"Luke," Hannah prodded. "Forget what I said before. Just go. I'll talk to Gran about your plans. You need to get on the road. Something tells me your kids have waited long enough to see their dad."

Luke was about to walk away, but before he could, he was drawn back. He leaned down and pressed his lips to Hannah's. He'd meant the kiss to be nothing more than a quick thank-you, but it turned into something else entirely. Cupping her face in his hands, he stayed to plunder, tasting her, letting the heat that had simmered for days stir to a boil.

Finally, reluctantly, he drew away, more shaken than he cared to admit. His gaze met Hannah's. She gave him a wobbly smile, her eyes dazed.

"That was . . . interesting," she said, sounding breathless.

"If I had more time, I imagine I could improve on it," he taunted.

"Any improvement, you'd have to scrape me up off the floor," she said.

Luke grinned. "I'll see you in a couple of days," he promised.

Again, he started away, then turned back. "Hannah, don't spend all that time reminding yourself why this thing between you and me is a bad idea, okay?"

"I won't, if you won't," she said.

He nodded. "Then we have a deal."

Of course, with his two kids underfoot, he had a hunch their opportunities for pursuing anything were going to be extremely limited. Then, again, he'd always enjoyed a challenge and that's exactly what finding time to be alone would be — an incredibly tempting challenge.

He grinned. Just thinking about that ought to give him the incentive and strength to face whatever lay ahead in Atlanta.

13

Gran was amazingly upbeat about the prospect of having Luke's children underfoot for a week. "It'll do 'em good to spend some time in the sunshine just being kids," she declared at breakfast the morning after Luke had left for Atlanta. "And if you ask me, Luke needs them more than he's been letting on."

"Gran, how much do you know about Luke's situation?" Hannah asked.

"About the same as you, I guess. He's divorced. It was an ugly situation."

"Do you know he was injured in Iraq?"

Gran looked taken aback. "I knew there'd been an accident of some kind. His leg still bothers him. That's obvious. That's probably why he's not doing surgery."

"Do you really think he's not well enough?" Hannah asked. "Look at everything you've had him doing. Surely surgery can't be any more physically demanding than that. I think he's hiding out here because he can't face going back home."

Grandma Jenny shrugged. "So what if he is? Can you blame him? Seems to me he has a right to take some time to get back on his feet, literally and figuratively. And it's perfectly natural that he wouldn't want to work with that awful man who stole his wife." She gave Hannah a speculative look. "You're not suddenly unhappy about having him around, are you?"

"Of course not. I'm just concerned that he's not really accepting what's ahead for him. The life he's come home to is a far cry from the one he left. Do you really think it's okay that he's down here painting and doing other odd jobs, instead of facing reality? Isn't this some kind of extended denial? What if he just goes on drifting?"

"What if he does?" Gran said.

"He's a surgeon. That takes years of training. It's a skill that shouldn't just be tossed aside in favor of lazing around on the beach, especially at his age. He'll never be satisfied with that kind of life."

"Have you seen Luke lazing around for more than a minute or two since he's been here?" her grandmother demanded, clearly indignant on Luke's behalf. "That man's worked as hard as anyone in this house and he's done it without complaining or using his injuries as an excuse to slack off."

"I know," Hannah said, feeling duly chastised. "I wasn't being critical. I'm just concerned that the longer he hides out down here, the harder it will be for him to pick up whatever pieces are left of his life."

"Just because you can't imagine a life without some high-powered career doesn't mean everyone feels that way," Gran suggested. "Maybe he doesn't want to go back to that life. Maybe he wants a fresh start. He wouldn't be the first person to make a change after a tragedy."

"He has two children. He has to take that into consideration," Hannah argued.

"He's gone to get them now, hasn't he? What's this really about, Hannah? Are you afraid Luke might decide to make a life for himself here, and then, because you've fallen for him, you'll once again be forced to choose between this place and your life in New York?"

"It has nothing to do with me," she insisted, but her grandmother had hit on the truth. There was something between her and Luke, no matter how often they'd warned themselves not to get too involved. That kiss had been proof enough of that. It would be one thing to pursue that if he was back in Atlanta and another thing entirely if he chose to remain right here in Seaview Key. She had too many unresolved issues from the past to ever come back here for the long-term.

"It does if you're in love with him," Gran said. "The same way it's going to be a problem for Kelsey if she really does love this young man and he insists on going back to California and starting their family there."

"How is that the same?" Hannah asked. "Kelsey loves California."

"Haven't you been paying attention at all?" Gran asked. "Your daughter is crazy about this place. She wants the inn to be hers one day. I know it's impossible for you to understand how that could be, but it's true. Kelsey feels a real connection to the inn. She loves everything it stands for — family history, relaxation, meeting interesting people."

"She's just staying here to avoid the baby's father," Hannah said.

"I can't deny that's part of it, but there's more. Open your eyes, Hannah. Watch the way her face lights up when she talks about the inn and the improvements she wants to make. Her future is here. I think I knew that the first time she spent any time here. She asked enough questions about what your mom and I were doing to fill a textbook on managing an inn. She loved sitting on the porch and chatting with the guests as much as your mother and I did."

Hannah knew her own view of the inn was colored by her desperate desire to get away from it when she was Kelsey's age, so she couldn't imagine that Kelsey saw it differently.

"She's just excited because this is new and different," she said defensively.

"No, she's excited because this is a part of her history," her grandmother countered. "I think she's found what she was meant to do." She frowned. "If I'm right about this, I hope you won't try to dissuade her just because the decision doesn't suit you."

"I would never do that," Hannah said. "There's nothing I want more than for Kelsey to be happy."

Just then an unfamiliar car turned into the driveway, and a young man with long hair pulled back into a ponytail, jeans and a T-shirt for some heavy metal band climbed out from behind the wheel. Hannah swallowed hard and turned to her grandmother. "You don't think . . . ?"

"I don't know what to think," Grandma Jenny said with a shake of her head. "You deal with him. I'll go inside and get the phone so I'm ready to punch in 911 at the first sign of trouble."

As the young man approached, rolling a suitcase along behind him, Hannah's tension evaporated. Despite the black shirt and long hair, he looked more like a scared kid than any kind of troublemaker.

"You're Kelsey's mother?" he asked.

Hannah nodded.

"I'm Jeff Hampton," he said, swallowing hard. "You probably hate me and I know Kelsey doesn't want to see me, but I came, anyway." He lifted his chin with a touch of defiance. "How are we supposed to work this out if she's all the way across the country?"

Hannah had to admire his determination, if not his unscheduled arrival. "Tell me something, Jeff. Do you love my daughter?"

"Yes," he said without hesitation, his gaze holding hers. His nervousness seemed to evaporate. Now he was all earnest conviction. "I love her and I want to marry her and I want us to have this baby. But even if she says no, even if she wants to give up the baby, I'll take him because he's ours, you know what I mean? A baby deserves to know that at least one of his parents really, really wanted him."

"Sometimes giving a child up for adoption is the mature, caring thing to do," Hannah said before she could stop herself. She'd vowed to leave this decision to Kelsey and Jeff. It was theirs to make, but maybe she could at least make him view Kelsey's viewpoint from a different perspective.

He stared at her with shock. "You think I'm being selfish? That I'm just some idealistic kid who has no idea how hard this will be? I'm not. I can give this baby a good home. Heck, my family has more money than some small countries, not that I intend to take anything from them. I sold a software program last year and I'm doing okay all on my own. It's not like we'd have to struggle. Kelsey has this crazy idea that she'd be giving up on her entire future, but she wouldn't. She could do anything she wants to do. The baby and I wouldn't hold her back."

"Maybe she just doesn't love you enough," Hannah suggested gently, though given some of the things Kelsey had said, she had to wonder if that was entirely true.

"I think she does," Jeff insisted, not backing down. "I just think she's scared. Heck, so am I. Having a baby is a big deal. Getting married is a huge commitment. But I want all that, you know? And I want it with

Kelsey. I knew it the first time I saw her."

Despite her prior inclination to hate the young man who'd thrown her daughter's life into turmoil, she liked Jeff Hampton. She liked that he'd come here to fight for what he wanted. She liked that he was eager to take on the responsibility of a wife and a baby. She liked that he'd looked her straight in the eye when he'd declared that he loved her daughter, that he wouldn't back down in the face of her skepticism.

Unfortunately, she wasn't the one he had to impress. And Kelsey, she knew from years of experience, was going to be a much tougher sell.

"She's taking a walk on the beach," she told him, reaching for his suitcase. "I'll take this inside for you. If you head north, you'll probably run into her, though she said something about stopping off in town before she came back. If you don't see her on the beach, check the frozen-custard stand."

A boyish grin spread across his face. "Thanks."

"Don't expect this to be easy," she warned.

"Hey, I'm a complicated guy. Easy would bore me."

That said, he trotted off toward the beach, as eager as a puppy, even in the face of likely rejection. Watching him, Hannah sighed and hoped her daughter wouldn't break his heart.

Gran emerged from the house as soon as Jeff was out of sight. "Was that him? Was that the boy who got our Kelsey pregnant?"

Hannah nodded. "And you know what? I like him. Despite the awful clothes, there's something reassuring about him. He's surprisingly mature and grounded. Best of all, I believe him when he says he loves her."

Her grandmother regarded her skeptically. "Really?"

"Yes. He said it with real emotion and conviction. And he really, really wants this child."

"Isn't it what Kelsey wants that matters? At least to us?"

"Of course," Hannah said. "But I'm still feeling relieved that he's not a total jerk." She stood up. "Now, I think we'd better get inside and decide where we're going to put all these unexpected guests. For once I'm actually glad to be living in an inn. We can separate the various combatants."

"It could be that young man will expect to stay with Kelsey," her grandmother suggested.

Hannah grinned. "Then isn't it a good thing you and I are here to gang up on him and tell him otherwise? In fact, I think I'll put him right next door to Luke so we can be sure there will be no shenanigans."

"Luke won't be back until tomorrow or the day after," her grandmother reminded her.

"Which is why I'm going to sleep with my ear pressed against the wall to Kelsey's room. If Jeff sneaks in or she sneaks out, I'll know about it."

Gran shook her head. "Don't you think you're worrying about a horse that left the barn some time ago?"

"Probably, but it makes me feel better," Hannah admitted. She picked up Jeff's surprisingly light suitcase and carried it inside. When her grandmother didn't budge, she called back to her. "Aren't you coming?"

"To do what? Install a dead bolt on your daughter's door and give you the only key?"

Hannah stopped in her tracks. "Do I sound that ridiculous?"

"No, you sound like a mother who's trying to protect her child. All I'm saying is that it's a little late for that kind of protection. What Kelsey needs from both of us now is our unconditional support and whatever words of wisdom she asks us to impart. And, if you ask me, those two need to spend as much time together as possible. If she loved that boy enough to risk getting pregnant, then she probably loves him enough to take the next step. She just has to find her way to that decision on her own."

"But what if she doesn't?"

"Then she'll have us," Gran said without hesitation. "I can't say I'd mind having a baby underfoot again. How about you?"

Hannah hadn't really allowed herself to think much about the baby — her first grandchild — mostly because Kelsey had been so adamant about giving it up for adoption. She remembered how it had felt to hold Kelsey in her arms in the hospital and realize her part in creating such an amazing tiny human being. It was the first time she'd truly believed in miracles. It would be nice to capture that feeling again.

"No, I wouldn't mind that, either," she said softly. "In fact, it would be incredible." Then she sighed. "But we can never tell Kelsey how we feel. She shouldn't be influenced by what the two of us want."

"Of course not," Gran said, but there was a glint in her eye that suggested she wasn't above using her powers of persuasion to get exactly what she wanted.

Kelsey had gone for her walk alone today,

because her mom had been huddled with Gran talking about Luke's unexpected decision to go to Atlanta and bring back his kids. Kelsey wasn't sure why they were making such a big deal about it. She thought it would be kind of cool to have a couple of kids running around. The inn was meant to be filled with families and noise and laughter. This would be the ideal test run. They'd have a few days to make sure everything was working as it was supposed to before the first paying guests arrived.

She was so excited, in fact, that she'd made a stop in town at the discount store and picked up a bunch of plastic beach toys for the kids. It was the kind of stuff they needed to have on hand — beach balls, brightly colored floats, swim rings for the smaller kids and plastic pails. She thought the antique tin sand pails her grandmother had collected were more fun, but these were more durable. She'd also picked up some extra beach towels, bottles of suntan lotion and a big, floppy straw hat, which she was wearing now to keep the sun out of her face. She was beginning to get freckles on her nose, which was kind of cool actually, but probably not too smart.

Her purchases were a lot heavier than she'd anticipated and the sun had gotten hotter than she'd expected. She was walking along the edge of the water lugging everything when she spotted Jeff. He was strolling toward her, looking out of place in his jeans and his favorite black shirt. He thought it made him look dangerous, which was a joke, given what a sweet, quiet nerd he was. Just looking at him, she felt her heart skip a beat.

He picked up his pace the instant he recognized her. "What were you thinking?" he scolded. "You shouldn't be carrying all this stuff."

He tried to take some of the bags, but Kelsey held on tight. "I can manage," she insisted.

"Oh, would you just give it up and let me help," he said impatiently. "I know you're strong and capable and that you can do anything you want to do. That doesn't mean you can't let me carry some of this for you."

She sighed and relinquished a few of the bags. She started to ask what he was doing here, but she already knew the answer to that. In fact, to be honest about it, she was a little surprised it had taken him this long to show up.

He gave her a knowing look. "You don't seem that surprised to see me."

She shrugged. "You didn't like the answers

I was giving you. Of course you'd fly all the way across the country to try to change my mind." She gave him a defiant look. "But my mind is made up, Jeff."

"Okay," he said simply, and fell into step beside her.

Kelsey halted in her tracks. "Okay? Just like that?"

He grinned. "You're stubborn as a mule. Arguing with you will only make you dig in your heels."

"Then why did you come?"

"Because you're here," he said.

Kelsey frowned. "What about school?"

"I dropped out for the time being."

Her jaw dropped. "You've left school? That's crazy."

"No crazier than you doing it," he said indifferently. "I can do my computer stuff anywhere, and that's what's going to pay the bills for both of us and the baby. I'm having all that stuff shipped here, by the way. Mine and yours."

"You can't just show up here and expect to move in," she protested.

"You live in an inn. I'll rent a room."

"We're all booked," she told him proudly. "At least as of next week."

"Then I'll rent a room until the other guests show up."

"And then what?"

He grinned at her. "Maybe by then you'll be used to having me around and you'll let me move in with you."

"Under my mom's watch? Good luck."

"I think your mom already likes me," he said.

"You met my mom? For what? Like five minutes?"

"It felt like longer," Jeff said. "But maybe that's because she was interrogating me. I think I held up okay."

"You didn't meet Grandma Jenny, did you?"

He shook his head. "I think she was standing just inside, though, ready to call the cops if she didn't like what she heard. At least, she had a phone in her hand." He grinned. "I never saw her dialing, though, so I must have passed some sort of test with her, too."

Kelsey grinned back at him. That would be just like Gran, ready to turn Jeff in to protect Kelsey from him.

"So, do I get to stay or not?" he asked, looking around. "This place is kind of cool."

Despite her trepidation about spending too much time with him, Kelsey couldn't help sharing her enthusiasm about the inn. "Just wait until I take you on a tour of the inn, Jeff. It's so amazing. We've been working like crazy to get it ready to open. I've been trying to pull some of the paperwork so it can be computerized, but I haven't got it all figured out yet. I want to create a Web site."

"I could do that for you," he offered.

"Would you?"

"Of course."

"I've sketched out all these ideas, but I don't have enough experience to make it look right online. I'll show you after I've given you the grand tour."

His steps slowed. "Kelsey?"

"What?"

"You really like what you're doing here, don't you? It's been a long time since I've seen you this excited about anything."

"I do," she said. "I feel as if I'm part of something that goes back for generations. I feel this amazing connection to this place that I never felt in California or even in New York."

He nodded slowly. "Okay, then. I guess you'd better take me on that tour. If this is where we're going to live, then I should know everything there is to know about it."

"Jeff —"

He cut her off before she could complete the protest. "No arguments, okay? I'm not going to push for getting married right now, but I'm not leaving, either."

"Just like that?" she asked, astounded. "You would stay here just because it's what I want?"

"Of course."

His response didn't settle everything, not by a long shot, but it went a very long way toward putting her mind at ease. Maybe there was hope for the two of them, after all. How many men would change their lives at the drop of a hat to please a woman? That had to count for something.

A couple of hours ago, if anyone had told her that Jeff was going to show up and announce he was here to stay, she would have felt nothing but panic. Now, here he was, and what she felt was hopeful.

Hannah was exhausted by the time they'd finished dinner and dessert. She'd sent Gran off to bed and Kelsey and Jeff out to the porch.

"I'll do the dishes and clean up," she told them, shooing them out of the house.

She wanted the time alone to recover from the tension of waiting for an explosion that had never come between Jeff and Kelsey. Instead, they'd acted as if his arrival were nothing unexpected. Not one word had been said about the future or marriage or the baby. In fact, all of the talk had been about a new Web site for the inn, which Jeff was apparently going to create. The whole meal had been surreal.

When the phone rang, she grabbed it, eager for anything that might distract her from the latest turn of events.

"Hannah?"

Her heart skipped a couple of beats. "Luke, hi. Where are you?"

"At a motel just outside Atlanta. Traffic was awful. I got in later than I expected, so I'll pick up Nate and Gracie tomorrow morning. Hopefully we'll be able to drive straight through to Seaview." He paused. "Are you still sure you're up for this?"

"Hey, it'll be a great distraction from our other guest."

"What guest is that? I thought no one was due to check in until next week."

"This isn't that kind of guest. Jeff turned up to plead his case with Kelsey."

"How's that going? He's not pressuring her, is he?"

"Only if kindness counts," she said. "He's already pitching in around here. She has him designing a Web site. I gather he's some kind of computer genius who creates software, something she'd neglected to mention. He's also heir to a family fortune, which he claims doesn't interest him. And he looks as if he just rode in with a biker gang, at least until you look into his eyes and realize he's just a kid who's wild about my daughter."

"You like him, don't you?" he asked. He sounded astonished.

"Yes. I'm actually on his side. He's smart, too, by the way."

"You mean because of the whole computer thing?"

"No, I mean because he's apparently picked up on Kelsey's love for this place and is making himself a part of it, instead of fighting her. I gather we now have two dropouts on our hands."

"Maybe you should stop thinking of either one of them as dropouts and think of them as entrepreneurs."

"An interesting spin," she said glumly. "I'll try." Because she didn't want to discuss Kelsey and her uncertain future, she turned the tables. "How do you feel about seeing Lisa? Are you nervous?"

"Not nervous. It will be strange. I've known her for twenty years, but she's not the same woman I fell in love with."

"What about your medical practice?"

"What about it?" he responded, a distinct edge in his voice that should have warned her off, but didn't.

"Will you stop by? Make any decisions?"

"I'll never walk into that office again," he said.

"Luke, you can't just turn your back on it. I may not know much about the medical field, but you invested a lot of your life in building that practice, I'm sure. It's not right to walk away with nothing."

"Which is why I will eventually have to hire an attorney to sort out the dissolution of the practice," he said. "But I can't think about that now. Right now, my focus is on the kids. I hope they're not angry with me."

"For leaving them to go to Iraq?"

"Yeah."

"Luke, even if they are angry, they'll get over it. I mean, what kid can resist being happy with endless hours to play on the beach?"

"I hope you still have that positive outlook a couple of days from now," he said.

"I will," she told him. "I promise."

"I'm counting on it, Hannah," he said. "I really am. I should get some sleep, if we're going to get on the road really early."

"Do you think you'll make the last ferry?"

"I'm planning on it. I'll call if we don't."

Her heart accelerated in anticipation, which probably wasn't a good thing. "See you tomorrow night, Luke. Drive safely."

"Night, Hannah."

She hung up slowly, then stepped outside to gaze up at the darkening sky. One lone star winked at her. "Let this be okay for him," she whispered. In fact, let it be okay for all of them.

14

Luke arrived at his former home before dawn, anxious to pick up the kids and get on the road. If there had been any way to avoid it, he would have skipped an encounter with his ex-wife, but he could hardly sit in the driveway and honk the horn until the kids came out. Reluctantly he crossed the manicured lawn and rang the doorbell. Since every light in the house was blazing, there was no chance he'd be waking anyone up.

When the door opened, Brad was on the other side, his expression wary. "Luke, you look good," he said with forced geniality. "Come on in."

Luke's hands instinctively balled into fists. Lisa hadn't even done him the courtesy of keeping Brad away as he'd requested. Any other time, any other place, he'd have punched the man out. Because his children were undoubtedly close by, he restrained himself. "No thanks. I'll wait right here. Are the kids ready to leave?"

"Just about," Brad said. He hesitated, then added, "Look, I'm sorry, man. I never meant for any of this to happen."

"I don't want to hear any of your excuses or apologies," Luke snapped. "Tell the kids I'll be in the car when they're ready."

"Come on, don't do this," Brad pleaded. "We need to find some way to co-exist for Nate and Gracie's sakes. And you and I have a business relationship."

"Not anymore, we don't," Luke said. "Do you think I could ever trust you again?"

"Look, I know this is bad. Lisa and I, we didn't plan any of this. I was doing what you asked me to do, looking out for them, you know?"

"And by your interpretation that included sleeping with my wife?" Luke inquired.

"Of course not," Brad said. "It just happened. We certainly didn't mean to hurt you. You and me, we go back too far to throw our friendship away."

Luke stared at him incredulously. "You can't possibly be that naive. As if we could ever be friends again. I don't even want to share office space with you." He held up his hands. "Forget it. I'm not having this conversation with you. You're both adults.

You knew exactly what you were doing and what the fallout would be, so don't pretend to be all broken up about it now. I'll be in the car. Just send the kids out."

He whirled around and walked away before he succumbed to temptation and bloodied Brad's aristocratic nose.

Five minutes later, Lisa emerged from the house with Gracie and Nate trailing behind her, obviously reluctant. For two kids who were normally eager for any excuse to skip school, they didn't seem especially happy about this unexpected vacation in sunny Florida.

Luke forced a smile for them and opened the back door. "Hop in, guys. This is going to be a real adventure. I can't wait for you to see Seaview Key."

Gracie gave him a surprisingly bored look. "Whatever," she said.

Nate said nothing.

Luke turned to Lisa, who'd rolled two suitcases up to the car. They didn't look as if they'd hold enough for an overnight visit, much less a week. "You sure they have everything they'll need?"

"I've packed shorts and T-shirts and bathing suits. We're talking Seaview Key. They won't be dressing up."

"No, but they're kids. They will be getting dirty."

"Doesn't this inn have a washing machine? If not, I'm sure you can spring for a few more things from the nearest discount store. They do have some kind of dollar place there, don't they?"

Her attitude snapped the last thread that was keeping his temper in check. He took a step closer and whispered in her ear, "When did you turn into a first-class bitch?" He made sure his voice was low enough that the kids couldn't overhear him.

"The day you started making all the decisions for all of us," she retorted.

"Don't even go there," he said, nudging her a safe distance from the car. "We are not having this conversation now. You wanted out of our marriage, Lisa. You got it. Let's not rehash old news. And maybe, while the kids and I are away, you can come up with some way for the two of us to be civil to each other. And it needs to start with keeping Brad out of my face."

"How am I supposed to do that? He lives here now."

"Find a way," he said grimly. "I'll have the kids call you once we get in tonight."

"Any idea what time that will be?"

"Why don't we just say they'll call around

six? That way it won't matter if we're held up. You'll know when to expect the call."

"Actually, I'm meeting Brad at six. We're having dinner with friends."

Luke kept a tight grip on his patience. "Then they'll call you on your cell phone. Make sure you keep it turned on."

He could tell from the expression on her face that she wanted to find something wrong with that plan, too, but she remained silent.

"Okay, then," he said with forced cheer as he walked back to the car. "I guess we're ready to hit the road." He leaned inside. "All set, guys?"

Neither child responded.

"Tell your mom goodbye," he said.

Nate and Gracie both stared accusingly at Lisa as if she were sending them off to Siberia, rather than to a winter break at the beach. Neither said a word.

"Love you," Lisa said to them, anyway. "I'll see you in a week. Have fun in Florida."

Luke finally forced himself to meet her gaze. "I'll take good care of them," he told her.

Her chin wobbled slightly. "Oh, Luke, don't you think I know that? I am so sorry . . ." Her voice shook. "You know, about everything."

“Yeah, I know,” he said tightly.

He got behind the wheel and turned on the engine to drown out whatever else she might say. He didn’t want to hear apologies or excuses from her any more than he’d wanted to hear them from Brad.

He waved one last time as he pulled out of the driveway, then didn’t look back. What would have been the point? That woman, that house, that life were all behind him now.

Luke hadn’t known what to expect when he picked up the kids earlier in the day, but he definitely hadn’t anticipated the total silence that had greeted him at the house or the sullen expressions he’d been dealing with ever since they’d hit the road. He wasn’t the one who’d betrayed his family, but clearly he was paying the price for a decision that had been out of his hands. If today was any indication, this was going to be a very long week, and any progress toward healing the rift between him and the kids was going to be made by inches, not leaps and bounds.

“Want to stop for pizza before we go out to the inn?” he asked. Pizza had always been a sure-fire hit. “We have about an hour before the ferry.”

His ten-year-old daughter's sunny disposition was nowhere to be found in the scowl that greeted his question. Eight-year-old Nate glanced at his big sister hopefully, but then sighed and remained stubbornly silent.

"Okay, then," Luke said, trying his best to remain determinedly upbeat. "I want pizza, so I guess that's what we'll have."

"I'll stay in the car," Gracie said, crossing her arms over her chest.

"Afraid not, kiddo. We're all going in."

Her scowl deepened. "Well, I'm not eating!"

"Okay with me," Luke said. "How about you, Nate? Are you hungry? I'm thinking a pepperoni pizza."

Nate gave an almost imperceptible nod, then looked down as if embarrassed that he'd caved at the prospect of his favorite pizza.

Inside, Luke ordered a large pizza and sodas — three of them despite Gracie's claim that she didn't want a drink, either — then led the way to a table by the window.

"Want me to tell you about Seaview Key?" he asked, keeping his attention focused on Nate, who'd shown at least a tiny sign of mellowing. "When I was your age, it was a great place to live. I spent all summer long swimming and fishing."

"There are sharks in the water," Gracie declared. "I'm not swimming with sharks!"

"I'm not scared of sharks," Nate piped up, shooting a defiant look at his sister. "And I love to swim."

Finally, a breach in their united front, Luke thought triumphantly.

"Gracie's just a big baby," Nate added.

"Hey, that's not a nice thing to say about your big sister," Luke scolded. "I'm sure there are just things she would rather do. You used to like to read, Gracie. Do you still go to the library every week? There's a great one on Seaview. We can go tomorrow and you can pick out some books."

He thought he caught a glimmer of interest in her eyes, but she shut down almost immediately, her scowl firmly in place.

"I brought my own books," she told him.

"Well, if you read all those, the library will be there," he said, still determinedly upbeat.

When the pizza came, Luke maintained a mostly one-sided conversation. Nate ate as if he was starved, but Gracie continued to stare at the food with disdain and flatly refused to touch it or her soda.

"One last slice, Gracie," Luke said eventually. "It would be a shame to let it go to waste. Are you sure you don't want some?"

"If you don't, I'll take it," Nate said eagerly.

"And then you'll hurl in the car," Gracie retorted, grabbing the slice as if she were determined only to save them all from that fate.

Luke had to hide a grin. Gracie had his pride and her mom's stubborn streak, but she'd finally found a way to eat and save face at the same time.

"Okay, you two, when we get to the inn, I want you to remember your manners. These people were kind enough to let us stay there, so let's not make them regret it."

"If it's an inn, that means you're paying them, so we can treat them however we want," Gracie said, her imperious tone sounding a whole lot like her mother at her worst.

"No, actually these are friends, and we are not paying them for your rooms. Grandma Jenny insisted that you be her guests."

Nate looked puzzled. "Is she our grandmother?"

"No," Luke said.

"Is she yours?"

"No, it's just what she likes to be called. She does know your grandmother and grandfather, though, from when they used to live in Seaview Key."

"Well, I'm not calling her that," Gracie said. "I have three grandmas already."

"Three?" Luke queried.

"Uncle Brad's mother wants us to call her Grandma, too," Nate explained, making a face. "You know, once he and mom get married." He sighed dramatically. "But she's mean. She's not a very good grandmother. She has too many rules. Does Grandma Jenny have a lot of rules?"

Luke honestly didn't know the answer to that, but he had a suspicion that once Grandma Jenny saw how unhappy his children were, she was going to do everything she could to spoil them both rotten. Probably best, though, if these two master manipulators didn't know that.

"I'm sure her rules are the same ones you're already familiar with," he told them.

"Like what?" Nate asked.

"Like no running in the house," he began, then winked at him. "And no putting frogs in your sister's bed."

"Oh, gross," Gracie said. "Are there frogs?"

"Well, I have to admit that I haven't seen any since I got there, but you never know."

"What other rules are there?" Nate asked worriedly. "Do we have to go to bed early?"

"Not while you're on vacation," Luke assured him. "But that doesn't mean you can stay up half the night. We'll figure that out once we're there and see how tired you are after playing on the beach all day."

"The sun's bad for my skin, so I won't play on the beach, and I'm going to bed at nine, like always," Gracie said. "Mom said so."

"I don't think your mom will mind if you stay up a little later, since it is vacation," Luke said. "But if you're tired at nine, then it's fine to go to bed. And we'll slather you with sunscreen for the beach."

"Do we have to eat vegetables?" Nate asked.

"I'll bet there's spinach every day," Gracie said with resignation. "Or collard greens or something yucky like that."

"Haven't had any so far," Luke said. "But I have had some strawberry-rhubarb pie. Most days we take a walk and get ice cream or frozen custard in the afternoon."

Nate's eyes widened. "Really? Every day?"

"Just about."

"Cool."

"Mom would be really mad if we ate ice cream that much," Gracie predicted.

"Vacations have different rules," Luke insisted. "Just remember that when you're in Atlanta, Mom's rules have to be followed."

"I think vacation's going to be fun," Nate announced, glancing defiantly at Gracie.

She crossed her arms over her chest and scowled back at both of them. "We'll see."

Luke bit back a laugh. What was it about the women in his life lately? They all seemed intent on tossing challenges his way. He just prayed he was up to meeting this one.

Hannah stood on the steps of the inn and watched as Luke's children emerged from the back seat of the car. The boy — Nate, if she remembered correctly — took one look at the beach across the street and let out a whoop of pure joy. He was about to dart across the road, when Luke snagged the back of his shirt and hauled him back.

"Hold on, son. Let's get our stuff inside and then I'll take you to the beach."

"But, Dad, it might be dark by then," Nate protested. "I really want to see the ocean."

"It's not the ocean. It's the Gulf of Mexico," Hannah corrected, then grinned at Luke. "And he's right, it will be dark very shortly. If you expect to do any wading, now's the time."

"Thanks for backing me up," Luke said

dryly. “Nate, Gracie, this is Hannah. Her family owns the inn. She grew up here, just like I did.”

“But I don’t live here now,” Hannah said a little too quickly. “I live in New York.”

Gracie regarded her with a spark of interest. “We went to New York once. My mom took us to see the ballet.”

Nate rolled his eyes. “I liked that history museum better.”

Hannah laughed. “Yes, well, New York does have things to do for just about every taste.” Glancing across the street, she noted that the sun was about to slip below the horizon. “Time’s running out, guys. Anyone want to see the beach?”

“I do,” Nate shouted eagerly.

“Gracie, what about you?”

The little girl looked torn. Hannah suspected she’d resolved not to enjoy anything on this trip.

“I guess,” she finally said, as if she were granting them all a favor by agreeing.

Luke shot Hannah a grateful look. “Okay, then, we’ll take everything inside when we get back.”

At the edge of the road, he pointedly stopped and hunkered down to look directly into his son’s eyes. “No running across the road until what?”

"Until we've looked both ways," Nate said dutifully.

"Okay, and here's one more rule," Luke said firmly. "You only go to the beach if an adult is with you."

That one surprised Hannah, until Luke added, "Neither of you has much experience with swimming, so I don't want you going in the water unless you're with a grown-up. Got it?"

Nate sighed dramatically.

"Got it?" Luke repeated, still gazing into his son's eyes.

"Yes, sir," Nate mumbled.

The four of them crossed the street, but the second their feet touched the sand, Nate kicked off his shoes and ran straight for the water's edge. Gracie trailed along behind, but unlike her brother she stayed well back from the gently lapping waves.

"She's still unhappy with me," Luke confided to Hannah. "She barely spoke all the way down here and she's taking every opportunity to let me know she's furious."

"Give her some time," Hannah said. "All of this is so new to her. Her mom with Brad. You away from home. This place. It's bound to be unsettling and she's expressing her confusion the only way she knows how."

"That's just it. She's not expressing it. If

she'd yell at me, we could talk things out. Instead, she's just punishing me with silence. I know you'll find this hard to believe, but Gracie's always been the one with the bright smile and easy-going nature."

"She was Daddy's girl, I'll bet," Hannah said, regarding him sympathetically.

Luke nodded.

"Well, it's tough to be Daddy's girl when Daddy hasn't been around. I was the same way. I adored my dad. When he left, I took it really hard. For a long time I blamed my mom, but eventually I turned the blame where it belonged, on him. I'm not sure what I would have done if I'd ever seen him again, but I suspect I wouldn't have run into his arms first thing. I would have made him *earn* back my love."

"But I never abandoned my kids," Luke protested. "I was in touch every single day I was away. I was always coming back. I thought they got that."

"They're kids. A few weeks is an eternity. A year is almost incomprehensible, especially when their mom is turning to someone else. And then you were injured and a year turns into eighteen months. I'm sure they thought you'd never be back, no matter what you said. Now it's just going to take some time to prove to them that they haven't lost you, that you will always be back, that you will always be their dad, no matter how often you're separated or for how long."

Just then Nate came running across the beach toward them. "Dad, can we go swimming?"

"Not tonight," Luke said. "It's getting too dark, but we'll go first thing in the morning."

"Promise?"

"I promise," Luke said solemnly.

Nate studied him closely, clearly trying to gauge the worth of the promise, then finally nodded. "Okay."

"We'd better go back now," Luke said. "Gracie, come on, honey. Let's go see your room and get you settled."

Once again, Gracie dragged her heels about coming with them, her scowl still firmly in place. Hannah saw Luke frown at her, but wisely he kept silent.

Grandma Jenny, Kelsey and Jeff were waiting for them on the porch.

"My goodness, look at you two. You're the spitting image of your daddy," Grandma Jenny declared when she saw them. "And I imagine you both could use some cookies and milk after such a long trip."

Nate's expression brightened at once.

"Cookies?"

"Chocolate chip, baked fresh this afternoon," Grandma Jenny told him, then instinctively turned to Gracie. "Maybe you'd like to help me bring them out here, so we can enjoy them on the porch."

For just an instant, Gracie looked as if she might balk, but then she sighed dramatically. "I guess so," she said.

"Kelsey, why don't you come along, too?" Grandma Jenny suggested. "Jeff, you could take their bags inside."

"Sure thing," Jeff said eagerly. "I'll set 'em in the hallway so they can choose which room they want when they come upstairs."

Luke turned to Hannah. "What's she up to?" he whispered after they'd all gone.

"Forming allegiances, I guess," Hannah said. "She always could recognize when someone needed extra attention."

"Your mom did that, too, didn't she?" Luke recalled. "She always knew when one of us wanted to talk but didn't want to do it in front of other people. She'd come up with some excuse to ask for our help in the kitchen."

Hannah grinned. "Worked like a charm, too, didn't it? You leave Gracie to Grandma Jenny. My mom learned from a master."

"Dad, can I go see where they went?"

Nate pleaded. "I'm really, really hungry. I can help, too."

"Go," Luke said. "Just remember —"

"I know," Nate said impatiently. "No running."

Hannah grinned as the screen door slapped shut behind him. "Want to bet how long he remembers that?"

"Until he's halfway across the dining room, I imagine," Luke said, then slowly faced Hannah. "I missed you."

Her breath caught in her throat at the heat in his eyes. "You hardly had time to miss me. You were only gone two days."

"But that kiss right before I left was pretty memorable. Maybe we should try it again to see if my memory did it justice."

Hannah felt herself swaying toward him, but in a belated attempt to be sensible, she jerked herself back. "Bad idea."

"Oh? Are you having second thoughts about where that kiss might lead?"

"No, I'm just very much aware that there are two already confused children on the premises."

His gaze narrowed. "So what? No more kissing till I take them back to Atlanta?"

"Seems prudent to me," she said.

"You don't sound very disappointed about that."

Hannah thought about his analysis. "Let's just say I have mixed feelings."

"Meaning?"

"The part of me that wants to throw myself into your arms is very, very disappointed," she admitted. "Another part of me thinks we probably need this time to let common sense weigh in."

Luke laughed. "Would it matter if I said to hell with common sense?"

"It would be a huge boost to my ego," she assured him. "But it wouldn't change the decision."

"You always were the sensible one," he said. "I suspect Abby and I would have gotten into a lot more mischief without you along to point out the pros and cons of anything we were contemplating."

Hannah winced. "Was I always that much of a wet blanket?"

"No, it wasn't like that. You were smart and cautious and both of us respected you enough to listen." A smile tugged at his lips. "Most of the time, anyway. Sometimes I was persuasive enough to overcome the voice of reason whispering in Abby's ear."

"Too much information," Hannah protested, not wanting to think about exactly what Luke might have persuaded Abby to do.

He reached over and tucked a stray curl behind her ear. "Are you still that same sweet, cautious girl, Hannah?"

Not when he was touching her, she thought as a shiver ran through her. "Pretty much," she insisted, anyway.

His gaze locked with hers. "That's good," he murmured, his fingers trailing along her cheek.

"Good?" she whispered.

"Maybe it'll keep us from getting in way over our heads here," he said. He rubbed the pad of his thumb across her bottom lip, practically daring her to run the tip of her tongue over it. He smiled slowly. "Then, again, maybe it won't."

Hannah's knees were so weak she was surprised she could remain standing without reaching out and clinging to his broad shoulders. Only the sound of little feet thundering across the dining room floor amid peals of laughter kept her from reaching for Luke and breaking every rule she'd just set.

She smiled as Nate skidded to a stop just inside the door in a last-second attempt to avoid being caught misbehaving. He cast a guilty look toward his dad as he came outside holding a fistful of cookies.

"Want one?" he asked, giving Luke and

Hannah an appealing grin as he held out the cookies.

"I would love one," Hannah said, accepting the offer.

Nate handed it over with obvious reluctance, then looked to his dad. "There's one more."

"You keep it," Luke told him. "I'm sure there are more on the way."

"Grandma Jenny's bringing a whole big plate of 'em," Nate confirmed.

Luke gave him a stern look. "Did I hear you running a minute ago?"

"I started to, but I stopped," Nate said. "Because I remembered what you said."

"Good for you," Hannah said, trying to prevent a lecture the boy obviously didn't need. He understood the rules.

So did she, she thought ruefully. But apparently Nate wasn't the only rule-breaker at the inn. She was on the verge of breaking a few herself, and in her case the consequences could be devastating.

15

"My dad is going home to live with my mom," Gracie announced the next morning, her chin jutting out. Her dark eyes, so much like her dad's, sparked with defiance. Even at ten, she was already showing signs of the strong-willed beauty she would become. In temperament at least, she reminded Hannah of Kelsey at that age.

From her place beside her on a blanket that had been spread on the sand, Hannah regarded Gracie evenly, not rising to the bait. "Really?"

"You can't stop him," Gracie continued, her tone a warning, or maybe a challenge.

"I would never try to stop him, if that's what he wants to do," Hannah assured her.

She had no idea why Gracie felt the need to confront her. Maybe she had sensed some of the undercurrents between Luke and her, despite their best efforts to avoid any intimate contact in front of the children.

Although she'd vowed to stay out of the family's relationships, Hannah decided perhaps she could help to smooth things over between Luke and his daughter. She justified it by reminding herself that Gracie had been the one to approach her, choosing to sit beside Hannah, rather than joining her dad and Nate in the water.

"I imagine you missed your dad a lot while he was away," she said casually.

Gracie regarded her suspiciously but nodded.

"I know he missed you, too. He told me how much the e-mails and pictures you sent meant to him."

"Yeah, sure," Gracie said, her skepticism plain.

"It's true," Hannah confirmed. "You know, you and I have something in common, Gracie. A very long time ago, my dad went away and I was really, really angry at him."

Gracie's eyes widened. "You were? Did you tell him?"

"I never had the chance to tell him, because he didn't come back, so for a very long time I just had to keep all that anger bottled up inside."

"Did he die?" Gracie asked, her voice dropping to a whisper.

"No, he just left, and I never saw him or heard from him again. You're so lucky that your dad is back home. You can tell him how you're feeling and work things out. I would have given anything for a chance like that."

Gracie sighed. "It's not the same. He's not really back. He's down here and we're in Atlanta." As if she realized what she'd just admitted, she added, "But he *is* coming home."

"And, just as important, you're together right now," Hannah pointed out. "That's something you should enjoy, but I know it's hard to do that when you're still mad. But there is a way to get rid of all that anger."

Gracie looked interested but perplexed. "What is it?"

"You could tell him everything you're feeling," Hannah replied.

"I don't think so."

"Why? Because it's hard?"

Gracie nodded. "And I'll hurt his feelings."

"He's your dad. He can take it. But if it will help, you can tell me first. Just say whatever you would say to your dad if you could."

Gracie hesitated, her expression uncertain.

"It's okay," Hannah said. "I won't tell him."

"You promise?"

"Of course. This will be between you and me. It'll be *your* decision about when you tell him."

Tears welled up in Gracie's eyes. "He . . . he could have *died* in Iraq," she said, her voice choked. "He went there and he could have *died.* He almost *did* die. Stuff about Iraq was on TV all the time and Nate and I saw it. Every single time a soldier died and they showed it on the news, I thought that could be my dad, but —" her voice broke "— he didn't think about that at all. Or about what we'd do if he didn't come back. We didn't even *matter.*"

Hannah wanted to reach out and enfold Gracie in her arms, but she sensed the girl wouldn't welcome the overture. She also had a hunch Gracie was saying something she'd heard her mother say, probably more than once. The suggestion that her dad didn't care about any of them had clearly made an indelible impression. Hannah felt heartsick.

"Oh, sweetie, I can imagine how scary that was for you, but please don't ever think your dad didn't worry about how his decision would affect you. There is nothing that matters more to your dad than you and Nate. Nothing in the whole world."

"Then why did he go?" Gracie asked.

"Because he knew he could help some of those soldiers who'd been injured. That's what he was trained to do, to help people with serious injuries. He couldn't turn his back on them. You should be proud of him, Gracie, for being so brave, for putting himself on the line for his country."

"I guess," Gracie responded. She leaned against Hannah, clearly needing whatever comfort Hannah had to offer, after all. "Do you really think he missed us?" she asked, her expression hopeful.

"I know he did," Hannah said emphatically, putting her arm around Gracie and giving her a reassuring hug. "Maybe you need to focus on the fact that he's back home. That's something to be very grateful for, don't you think so?"

"Yes." Gracie sniffed.

"You know what, though? I think it would be okay for you to tell your dad how upset you are about everything that's happened. Tell him exactly what you told me about how angry you are and how scared you were. I know he feels really bad that you're mad at him, and if you talked about it, just the way you did with me, you'd both feel better."

"He doesn't love us," Gracie said miserably. "If he did, he'd come home."

"You're wrong about how much he loves you, and you're old enough to understand why he can't come back home," Hannah told her. "He does love you, Gracie. He loves you and Nate more than anything, and he wants you to be happy."

"I don't believe it," Gracie said stubbornly. "If he did, he'd come back to our house."

"I'm afraid there are a lot of reasons why that might not happen, but it has nothing to do with you and Nate. Wherever he is, you will still be the most important people in the world to him."

Gracie gave her a look that was entirely too knowing. "More important than you?"

Hannah smiled. "Way more important than me. Your dad and I have known each other since we were kids. We're friends."

"He doesn't look at you like you're a friend. He looks at you the way Uncle Brad looks at our mom."

Hannah was rapidly getting out of her depth. When had ten-year-old kids gotten wise to the nuances of a look between grown-ups? She needed to get the focus back on Luke's relationship with Gracie and Nate. "Just talk to your dad, okay? Don't spend this whole week being mad when the two of you could be having so much fun together. Will you at least think about that?"

Gracie heaved another dramatic sigh. "I guess."

Hannah bit back a grin. "Good. Want to race me to the water? Looks to me as if your dad and Nate are having a great time without us."

Gracie stood up, then regarded her hesitantly. "Are there really sharks in the water?"

"Sometimes, but they're usually way offshore. If any have ventured in closer, I imagine your dad and Nate have scared them away with all the noise they're making."

"They're just being guys," Gracie said with world-weary resignation. "That's what mom always says."

"And guys can be a nuisance," Hannah replied. "But all in all, they're pretty nice to have around."

Gracie grinned shyly. "Especially if they chase away the sharks."

"Definitely if they chase away the sharks," Hannah agreed.

Luke finally got the children settled down

for the night, then grabbed a beer in the kitchen and headed for the porch, anticipating some quiet time with Hannah. After four days of nonstop activities to keep the kids entertained, he was coming to treasure these brief late-night encounters, even if they never discussed anything more important than the next day's plans.

"Hey, you," he said, dropping a chaste peck on her cheek, which was the most she'd permitted since the arrival of the kids.

"Hey," she said, glancing up at him. "Kids tucked in?"

"Finally. I had to read two stories to Nate, then Gracie wanted to talk."

"About?"

"She finally admitted how mad she's been at me." He glanced sideways at Hannah. "How'd you convince her to do that?"

"What makes you think I had anything to do with it?"

"I saw the two of you talking on the beach. You looked very intense."

"I just told her it was okay to be mad, but that she should talk about it to you so you could make it right."

"Anything else?"

"Nope. That pretty much sums it up."

"Really? Because I got the feeling from her that she might have told you that I was off limits," he said, watching Hannah's face closely. She smiled.

"Yeah, she did warn me off. She said you were going home to her mom."

"Wishful thinking," he said, then frowned. "You didn't listen to her, did you?"

"I recognize wishful thinking, Luke."

"Yet I hear a *but* in there somewhere."

"The truth is, neither of us knows what's going to happen, not between you and your ex-wife or between you and me."

"Oh, I know the answer to part of that. There is no going back for Lisa and me, period."

"Because you're hurt and angry," Hannah said.

"No, because it's over. She's moved on. So have I."

She gave him an anguished look. "I'm not sure either of you have the right to move on without doing more to save what you had. Those kids in there deserve better. They love you to pieces, Luke. And they need you in their lives."

He stared at her in shock. "What are you suggesting?"

"That you go home and try to make things right with your wife and your family. It's not like you to walk away from anything without a fight. Don't you owe at least that much to your kids?"

"You want me to go back to a woman who's fallen in love with my best friend and intends to marry him?"

"I don't want any of this," she retorted. "But I'm trying to make you see what's for the best. Earn your way out of the marriage, Luke. Make Lisa earn her way out of it, too. You've made it too easy for her, and neither of you has thought about what it's doing to your children."

"The outcome will be the same," he insisted. "The marriage is over. Why prolong it and put the kids through even more heartache? Giving them false hope would be cruel."

"Well, sure, if that's the attitude you take into it, it *will* be a waste of time. But what about going in with an open mind and an open heart? Give the wounds some time to heal."

Luke studied her, trying to figure out what was behind this sudden pep talk for his marriage. "What's this really about, Hannah? Are you scared of what's happening between us? Are you worried about the complications that lie ahead?"

"I'd be a fool if I weren't," she admitted. "But when I was talking to Gracie earlier, all I could think about was how I felt when my dad left all those years ago. I don't want that for Nate and Gracie."

"But you lost your dad forever. You never had contact with him again. I'm still going to be around," he said. "I will never abandon those kids."

"You just won't go back and fight for the one thing they want more than anything."

"Because it's too damn late," he said heatedly. "That ship has sailed, that train has left the station. It's over, Hannah. Brad's living under my roof now."

She almost smiled then. "And he's too big and tough for you to kick out?"

"No, actually he's a wuss, but you're missing the point. I don't want to go back, not to that house, anyway. Not to Lisa. I get all the stuff about forgiveness and second chances, but some betrayals are just too huge to be forgiven. What happened forced me to take a hard look at our marriage. It was broken before I even left, Hannah. Fixing it is out of the question."

She leveled a look into his eyes. "If you don't want to fix your marriage, then what do you want?"

Luke started to answer, then sighed. That was, indeed, the million-dollar question. One of these days very soon, he was going to have to stop drifting and figure out the answer. He had a hunch that Hannah was going to turn out to be part of the equation. Right this second, though, he had to wonder if she'd be pleased about that.

Kelsey stood in the doorway between the kitchen and the dining room and studied the layout of the room. It had been bothering her for days, but she couldn't quite put her finger on what seemed out of place.

Though she'd never waited tables in her life, she didn't think it had anything to do with the access the waitresses would have between the tables. The aisles were wide enough, even if someone had a chair sitting too far back from a table.

Most of the room's dozen or so tables had a clear view of the beach. Each seated four people, though they could easily be pushed together for larger groups. The linen tablecloths and matching napkins were striped in blue and sage-green, almost the exact shades of the sea glass collection she had started in a large glass vase on a table in the foyer. Next week each table would have a small green or blue vase on it with fresh flowers. She'd already spoken to the florist about delivering long-lasting blooms once and possibly twice a week, at least during the busy winter season.

Slowly she walked around the perimeter of the room, trying to figure out what was bothering her. When she almost bumped into an old oak sideboard in which they stored extra table linens and clean flatware, she got it. The heavy piece fit perfectly with the room's decor and was great for storage, but it was totally inconvenient. The staff had to cross the entire width of the dining room if they needed to replace napkins or a fork during a meal. If it were across the room, closer to the kitchen, it would not only be more accessible, it could also be used for pitchers of ice water and tea, which would save the staff from having to go back to the kitchen to refill glasses.

She took another survey of the room and saw the perfect spot for it. She started moving tables and chairs out of the way and was just about to shove the awkward piece across the room when Jeff walked in.

"Kelsey, what are you thinking?" he said, sprinting to her side and nudging her away from the sideboard. "This thing is too heavy for you to move. And who shoved all those tables around?"

She frowned at him. "I did. I'm not helpless, you know."

"Of course you're not helpless," he said impatiently. "But you *are* pregnant. If you wanted something moved, you should have called me or Luke."

"Why, when I was perfectly capable of doing it myself?"

He frowned back at her. "Because you're having a baby, that's why."

"And according to the doctor, I'm healthy as a horse. I wasn't trying to lift the stupid sideboard. I was just pushing it across the room. It's on rollers, in case you haven't noticed."

"Still, you should have asked for help," he said stubbornly.

She barely resisted the urge to roll her eyes. "Jeff, you really need to stop hovering over me."

"Was I hovering? I wasn't even in the room. I was on my way to the kitchen to get a bottle of water and here you were moving furniture. Excuse me for thinking that wasn't very smart."

"Smart?" Kelsey echoed, her voice turning to ice.

He backed down at once. "I didn't mean you're not smart," he said. "Of course you are. It's just that this whole baby thing is new to you. Maybe you don't even realize what your limits are."

"Limits?" The temperature of her voice dropped below freezing.

He stopped pushing the sideboard and stared at her. "Are you going to make an issue about every word I use?"

"I am if they're demeaning. I'm every bit as smart as you, Jeff Hampton, and there are no limits to what I can do." She stepped up until she was in his face. "And the fact that you don't realize that is exactly why I don't want to marry you. This whole baby thing has turned your brain to mush. You don't give me credit for anything anymore."

"Oh, for Pete's sake," he muttered in frustration. "Most women want the men in their lives to care about them. You act as if it's some kind of crime for me to be concerned about you and the baby. Even your grandmother told me she thought it was sweet that I worry so much."

"Yeah, well, you're not telling her what to do all the time, are you?"

"Are you saying this stuff just because your hormones are all out of whack, or do you honestly believe it? Do you really think I'm trying to control you?"

He was lucky that she wasn't a violent person, because that crack about her hormones would have sent some women over the edge. "My hormones are just fine, thank you very much," she snapped, then burst into tears.

Jeff blinked hard, then pulled her into his arms. "Hey, it's okay, Kelsey. Everything's going to be fine."

She clung to him and let her tears soak his T-shirt. "Sure," she murmured. "In about seven-and-a-half months."

She swore she could feel his lips twitching against her cheek. "I swear if you're smiling, I will hit you," she said with a sniff.

"Not smiling," he assured her.

She pulled back and saw that he was struggling to keep his lips turned down into a frown. She punched his arm. "You are, too. Stop it."

"I love you," he said, rubbing her back until she finally began to relax against him. "And I worry about you. I can't help it. But I promise I will try not to hover."

Against his chest, her sensitive breasts began to tingle. His hands, moving innocently across her back, were stirring up an unexpected maelstrom of sensations.

"Um, Jeff," she said, her voice ragged.

"Sshhh. It's okay. Everything is okay."

She pulled back again and looked into his eyes. "Jeff, I think we ought to take a break."

"A break?" he repeated blankly.

"While everyone's gone over to the mainland," she said.

She watched with amusement as understanding dawned.

"Oh, *that* kind of a break," he said. "Are you sure? Is it okay?"

"If you ask me if it will harm the baby, I swear —"

"I just meant is there enough time before they get back?"

"It's barely noon. The ferry doesn't get back for hours." It was one of the advantages of living on the island, she thought. Comings and goings were fairly predictable.

A grin spread across Jeff's face. "Hours, huh?"

"So," she said, studying him speculatively. "How's your stamina?"

"A match for yours, I'll bet," he said, taking her hand and leading her toward the stairs.

She drew to a halt before they started up. "This doesn't change anything. I just want to be clear about that. I'm still not ready to marry you."

"Just ready to have your way with me," he said.

She nodded.

He shrugged, then grinned. "I can live with that."

"Are you sure?"

"I'm sure," he said. "For now."

■ ■ ■ ■

Hannah knew she couldn't put off making the call to her doctor's office any longer. She'd been dreading the lecture she was bound to get when she told them that she was canceling her appointment yet again. Since it wasn't a call she wanted anyone to overhear, she'd waited until they made this trip to the mainland, then found an excuse to run a few errands of her own while Luke, Grandma Jenny and the kids stocked up on supplies like toilet paper at the discount store.

She found a bench in a small park across the street from the restaurant where they'd agreed to meet for lunch and took her cell phone from her purse. Drawing in a deep breath, she found the doctor's number and hit speed dial.

"Good morning, Oncology Associates," Beth McBride said cheerily.

Beth was the perfect receptionist for an office that dealt too often with death. Compassionate and friendly, she managed to make every patient feel better, no matter how dire their circumstances were. At first Hannah had been put off by all that unrelenting good cheer, but she'd finally seen the sincerity behind it and appreciated the lift to her spirits.

"Hi, Beth, it's Hannah Matthews."

"Hannah, how are you?" Beth asked. "You back from Florida?"

"Actually, no. I'm not going to be back for a while yet, so I need to change my appointment again."

"Oh, Hannah, are you sure about that? Dr. Blake is going to want to talk to you. Hold on a sec."

"Beth, no," she protested, but it was too late. She was already on hold.

Less than a minute later, Anthony Blake was on the line. "Hannah, I understand you're postponing your appointment again."

"It can't be helped. I'm still in Florida dealing with some family issues."

"Issues that are more important than your health?" he asked. "Or are you hiding out down there because you're afraid of what these tests might turn up?"

She sighed heavily at the question. Was that what she was doing, hiding out because she was scared? More than likely. There was certainly no question that she was terrified about the possibility of a recurrence. "Maybe," she admitted finally.

"There's an excellent chance everything will come back clear," he told her. "Then you'll have worried all these extra weeks for nothing."

"Or I will have had a few weeks of tranquility before another diagnosis of cancer hits," she countered.

"Okay, I'll make a deal with you," he said. "And it's my final offer."

"What deal?"

"You reschedule today for the end of next week here, or I will find someplace there for you to have the screening done and the results sent to me. Take it or leave it."

She grinned at his tough-guy attitude. Anthony Blake was a sweetheart who somehow always found time to listen, no matter how jam-packed his waiting room was. "What if I leave it?"

"Then I'll call in the big guns. I'll send your friend Sue down there after you."

She laughed at the threat. "You've already spoken to her, haven't you?"

"Just yesterday. She called to find out if you'd rescheduled. Beth spoke to her and then I called her back. We're rallying the troops, Hannah. You can't hide from all of us."

It should have made her feel better to know how much they all cared, but instead she just felt pressured. The next thing she knew they were going to draw Kelsey and

Grandma Jenny into their plot to make her face facts. That was the last thing she needed.

"I'll be back next week," she promised.

"No excuses, okay?"

"No excuses."

But the second she disconnected the call, she realized that next week the inn was reopening. There was no way she intended to miss that. The screening could wait a few more days, just until she was absolutely sure that Grandma Jenny and Kelsey had everything under control. A few days couldn't possibly make any difference, she told herself.

She looked up when Nate shouted her name. He was already running across the grass in her direction, followed at a more sedate pace by Gracie. The sight of Luke with Grandma Jenny's arm tucked through his as they made their way toward the bench made her smile, and just for an instant she forgot all about her cancer follow-up.

Beside her now, Nate ripped open the bag he was carrying and started pulling out plastic action figures. "How cool are these?" he asked. "Dad says we can play with them on the beach later. You wanna come?"

"Sure," Hannah said, ruffling his hair. "What did you buy, Gracie?"

Shyly she opened her bag and pulled out a collection of barrettes and hair ribbons in every color of the rainbow. "Grandma Jenny said she'd help me fix my hair in French braids. She said she used to do it for you when you were my age."

Hannah smiled at the memory. "She did, at least until I got tired of it one day and cut my hair as short as a boy's."

Gracie looked horrified. "You didn't!"

"Oh, yes, I did," Hannah assured her. "It was pretty awful."

"Did Grandma Jenny yell at you? Were you grounded forever?"

"No, she and my mom agreed that looking really, really bad until it grew out was punishment enough. It was the last time in my life that my hair was short."

Gracie gave her an odd look. "But it's short now," she said.

And then Hannah remembered. This time it hadn't been a matter of style or even impulse. Her hair was short because it still hadn't completely grown out after she'd lost it during chemo. Suddenly it was all she could do not to cry.

"Hannah, did I say something wrong?" Gracie asked worriedly.

"No, of course not, sweetie. Sometimes I just forget."

“How can you forget that your hair’s short?”

There was no good answer to that. She could hardly explain to a ten-year-old that she barely spent five seconds in front of a mirror these days because she couldn’t bear to see the ravages left behind by her treatments. When she had caught a glimpse of herself recently, she had noticed that her color had improved, that her hair was growing back with some unexpected curl to it and that her eyes were clear and bright. Maybe one of these days, she would even recognize herself again.

16

"Any idea where my children are?" Luke asked Grandma Jenny as he snatched a freshly baked cookie from the tray she'd just removed from the oven.

"I think they walked into town with Hannah. Didn't they invite you to go along?"

He tried to hide his reaction, but apparently she caught his disappointment.

"They didn't, did they? I'm sorry, Luke. I thought things were better."

"Most of the time they are," he told her, grabbing a carton of milk from the refrigerator and pouring himself a glass. He gestured to her. "You want some?"

"Sure," she said. "I'll join you. I could use a break."

A minute later they were sitting at the kitchen table. Grandma Jenny was watching him expectantly. Finally she gave him an impatient look. "Are you going to ask for my advice or not?"

He chuckled. "I figured you'd offer it when you were ready."

"I don't butt in where I'm not wanted," she said piously, then shrugged. "Okay, that's a fib, but it is nice to be asked for an opinion now and again."

"What do you think I should do?" he inquired dutifully.

"I think you should decide what you're going to do with the rest of your life and get busy doing it. Children don't respond well to uncertainty. You keep telling Gracie and Nate that you intend to remain an important part of their lives, but you haven't told them how. I'm not sure you even know yourself."

"I don't," he conceded.

"Do you even know where you intend to settle down?"

He shook his head.

"Or when you're going to go back to practicing medicine?"

Luke winced at all the relevant questions he was unable to answer. "Not really," he admitted.

She shook her head. "Well then, I'd say it's time you came up with a plan. Drifting is all well and good for some stray branch floating along with the tide, but it's no way to live your life."

He smiled despite her serious tone. "An apt analogy," he told her. "I am drifting, but I don't seem capable of making a decision."

"Do you suppose that's because you're finding it hard to live with the consequences of the last big decision you made — the one to go to Iraq?"

He stared at her, stunned that she'd pegged it exactly right. He'd been so sure that reenlisting in the army had been the right thing to do, and just look how it had turned out. Maybe he was scared to make another decision and risk having it turn out as badly. Not that he regretted going to Iraq. What he regretted was the impact that decision had had on the rest of his life. He'd lost his family and very nearly lost his leg.

Grandma Jenny regarded him with a smug expression. "Nailed it, didn't I?"

"On the head," he said.

"Well, the only way I know to get over fear is to face it. Make a list if you need to. That always works for me. Write down all the decisions you have to make, then pick one and make it. Start small, if you need to."

"All the decisions that matter are huge," he said.

"Tell me," she commanded, as if she hadn't gone over them herself only moments before.

"Okay, my medical practice, for starters," he said.

She gave him a wry look. "Not where I would have started," she chided. "Besides, I thought you'd made that decision. You said you wouldn't work with that partner of yours ever again. Can't say that I blame you for that, by the way. I don't know much about how things like that work, but can't he just buy you out?"

Luke grinned at the simplicity of her suggestion. Of course, it could be that easy. He didn't have to wrangle with Brad. In fact, he'd never planned to handle the details himself. He just needed to make the call to an attorney, tell him what compensation he wanted to give up his share of the practice and get the ball rolling. It would be the first step toward getting his life back into focus. "You're pretty smart. You know that, don't you?"

"I have my moments. What's next?" she asked eagerly.

"Going back to Atlanta or not, I suppose."

"Your kids are there," she said at once.

"That's the plus," he said. "Maybe the only one."

She regarded him quizzically. "You weren't happy there? You lived there for how long?

Twenty years?"

"Something like that."

"Why didn't you do something about it, then?"

He thought for a long time before he replied. "I'm not entirely sure," he admitted eventually. "It's all twisted up with my marriage, though. Somehow it was all about striving for more — a bigger house, a fancier car, better private schools for the kids — all to keep my wife happy. Lisa had a right to expect all that and I wanted to give it to her, but none of it mattered to me."

"None of that has anything to do with the city," she said.

"In a way, it did. Lisa wanted to live in Atlanta because it actually has 'society,' and that's in quotes. If there was an important charity function, she wanted to be on the board, not to make a difference, but to make the contacts. I suppose that's one reason she and Brad are so well suited. He's very big into networking, too."

"And you're not?"

"I just wanted to practice medicine."

"I imagine there are plenty of people in Atlanta in need of a doctor whose focus is on his patients." She gave him a sly look. "Truth is, though, we could use a doctor right here in Seaview. Doc Langley is getting up in years. I hear he's been looking for someone to take over his clinic. Of course, with your specialty, you'd have more to do over on the mainland. You have options, Luke. You just have to decide which one is most appealing."

"I can't stay here," he said, but even as he uttered the words he wondered why not. He felt at peace in Seaview in a way he never had in Atlanta. Since he'd come back, he'd assumed it was simply because this was an escape from the real world where all the tough decisions awaited him, but maybe it was more than that. Maybe Seaview had a hold on his soul he'd never recognized before.

As for practicing medicine in Seaview, it would require some changes, but he'd always enjoyed the interaction with patients far more than the intricate and delicate surgeries he'd performed. He'd been adept at them, and as a result, his professors and Lisa had pressured him to work toward an orthopedic surgery specialty. The professors had admired his skill. Lisa had been more attracted to the financial rewards. Somehow along the way, he'd lost his own enjoyment of keeping people healthy or helping them through an illness.

Still, he couldn't stay here without figuring out what that would mean for Gracie and Nate. Today had proved once more that they hadn't totally forgiven him. They'd gone off with Hannah without even suggesting that he come along.

Grandma Jenny reached over and patted his hand. "It will work out, Luke. The answer will come to you. If not today, then tomorrow." She stood up. "Now, I'm thinking that I would like some frozen custard. How would you feel about escorting an old lady to Lila's?"

"Now? I should finish up the last little bit of painting," he said.

"That can wait," she declared decisively. "Come on. Let's go splurge and forget all our worries."

"You have worries?"

"At my age, it's hard not to."

"You want to talk about them? You've been listening to me. I owe you."

"Another day. Now the only thing I want from you is a trip to Lila's."

"Then it would be my pleasure," he told her. "Want me to drive?"

"It's just a few blocks," she said. "If I can't walk that far, I shouldn't be eating frozen custard."

"Okay, then, let's go."

Outside, as if to prove her energy was

high, she set off at a brisk pace. It took only ten minutes to arrive at Lila's, which had evolved from the small frozen custard stand along the beach it had once been, to an actual old-fashioned ice cream parlor with a soda fountain and Formica-topped tables, trimmed with chrome. From what Luke could see through the huge plate-glass window, the place was packed. He noted the helium-filled balloons floating around the room.

"Looks as if there's a party going on," he commented. "Maybe we should go for ice cream instead."

"Nonsense. If there's a party, it's bound to be for someone we know. Let's go in."

Luke shrugged and opened the door for her. A minute later, as he stepped inside, a shout went up. "Surprise!"

He blinked and stared around the room just in time to see Nate and Gracie bolting in his direction.

"Are you surprised, Daddy?" Nate asked.

Gracie was bouncing up and down, a grin splitting her face. "Are you, Daddy? Are you really surprised?"

He stared at them blankly. "This is for me?"

"It's your birthday," Gracie reminded him. "Did you forget?"

Nate stared at him incredulously. "How could you forget your own birthday? It's when you get presents."

Luke finally glanced up and spotted the banner over the soda fountain. It had been painted in bold colors by unsteady young hands: *Happy birthday, Daddy!* Beneath it on the counter was a pile of presents.

He turned to Grandma Jenny. "You were in on this," he said.

She beamed at him. "Of course. They couldn't have done it without me to keep you occupied. I felt real bad for you when I saw how disappointed you were at being left behind this afternoon. I figured this would make up for it, though."

"Indeed it does." He grinned at Nate and Gracie, who were still bouncing with excitement.

Gracie grabbed his hand. "Come see your cake," she said. "Hannah baked it."

He searched the room until he spotted Hannah sitting on a stool at the counter. "I had no idea you could bake."

"Wait until you taste it before you decide if I can," she said dryly.

Only then did Luke realize that he knew all the people crowded into Lila's. Jack was there, as well as the still-pregnant Lesley Ann and her family. So were Kelsey and

Jeff and Doc Langley, whose presence was highly suspicious, considering the conversation he'd had earlier with Grandma Jenny. There were old neighbors of his family's, a handful of classmates from high school, and of course, Lila, who'd been running this place since taking it over from her father thirty years ago.

He couldn't help thinking that a birthday celebration in Atlanta would have been orchestrated with caterers and a band and everyone decked out in designer clothes. This impromptu gathering had a whole lot more to recommend it, especially with a jukebox playing music he remembered from his teens.

He hunkered down in front of his kids. "This is the very best birthday party I've ever had," he told them.

"It's not fancy like the ones Mommy always had," Gracie said worriedly.

"And that's exactly why it's the best," he assured her. He stood up. "Now, who wants cake?"

"I do, I do," Nate said eagerly.

"Me, too," Gracie said, though she was more sedate. "And then presents."

He scooped each of the kids up for just an instant and gave them a kiss. "I already have the best present of all. You guys are here to share this with me."

The truth was, he hadn't celebrated a birthday in a way that meant more to him in years.

"You are a very sneaky woman," Luke accused, slipping an arm around Hannah's waist and dragging her into an alcove by the restrooms. Not the most romantic place in the world, but at least it gave them a moment's privacy. He tucked a finger under her chin and kissed her, tenderly at first and then with unmistakable hunger. "God, you taste good," he murmured.

"Better than cake and frozen custard?" she asked, her cheeks pink and eyes shining.

"A thousand times better," he confirmed, dipping his head to prove it with another deep, soul-searing kiss that stirred a demanding arousal.

Hannah was the first one to move away. "The kids," she reminded him with obvious reluctance.

Luke sighed and linked his hands behind her waist so she couldn't go too far. "So, tell me how you pulled this off without giving me a hint?"

She grinned. "Fortunately, you're a typical man. You were oblivious to all the whispering the kids and I were doing. And Grandma Jenny did her part by keeping you distracted the past couple of days."

"Now that you mention it, there was a definite increase in the number of odd jobs she dreamed up. How did you even know it was my birthday, though?"

Hannah didn't want to admit that she'd recalled the exact date because she'd helped Abby plan a celebration for him all those years ago. "The kids mentioned something about it when they first got here," she said, which was only a slight fabrication. She'd mentioned it first and Nate and Gracie had immediately gotten into the spirit of planning the surprise party, though Gracie had been skeptical that they could pull it off.

"Thank you for going to all this trouble," he said. "It was great seeing so many familiar faces." He tucked a strand of hair behind her ear. "Whose idea was it to include Doc Langley?"

"Grandma Jenny's. Why?"

"I think your grandmother is scheming," he said.

"Scheming how?"

"Right before we walked over here, she mentioned that he's looking for someone to take over his clinic."

Hannah stared at him. "But you're an

orthopedic surgeon."

He grinned. "I did go to medical school to get that degree."

"But you can't just switch specialties at the drop of a hat, can you? Besides, you haven't said a single word about staying in Seaview. She shouldn't be putting that kind of pressure on you."

"Hey, slow down," he soothed. "I'm not feeling pressured. It was just an idea. And you're right, I'd have to be recertified in family medicine, but it is possible."

Hannah was still indignant. "She shouldn't be poking her nose into your business like that. I'm sorry."

"I asked for her opinion about some things," he responded. "She was just tossing out options."

"But she insisted I invite Doc Langley here," Hannah said. "So he could get in your face, at your birthday party of all things."

"He never got in my face. In fact, the only thing he and I talked about was fishing. We're going out together tomorrow and taking the kids. You're invited, too, as long as you don't try to dump him overboard if he mentions medicine in my presence."

Hannah regarded him sheepishly. "Am I overreacting?"

"Just a little. How about it, though? Want to go fishing tomorrow? Grandma Jenny's given me time off. She says Jeff can pick up the slack around the inn."

"Jeff would gladly clean out the gutters and paint the whole inn again, if she asked him to. He's trying desperately to make an impression on Kelsey."

"I don't think he needs to make an impression on her," Luke said. "It's obvious she's head over heels in love with him. Didn't you see how those two were looking at each other when we got back from the mainland the other day? Even someone as oblivious as you claim I am could see that something was going on with those two while we were away. Jeff just needs to hang loose and wait for Kelsey to figure that they belong together."

"I suppose you've passed on that advice," Hannah grumbled.

"Nope. Nobody's asked for my opinion. I'm not the one in this crowd with the matchmaking gene."

"That makes you a rarity around here, then. Everyone else seems to toss out opinions and advice at the drop of a hat."

Grinning, Luke touched a finger to her lips. "Fishing, Hannah. Do you want to go or not? I'll even bait your hook for you."

She hadn't been out in a boat in years. At one time, when her dad had been around, she'd loved it. Those times the two of them had shared had been so special to her. The loss of those memorable trips had been one more thing for which she'd blamed her mom.

"I'll go," she said at last. "But you're cleaning any fish we catch."

"Deal."

"And no one's giving anyone any advice," she said. "The boat is an opinion-free zone."

"Unless it pertains to fishing," he corrected.

"Okay. I can live with that. Though I have to tell you that I may know more about fishing than you and Doc Langley combined. My dad was really, really good and he taught me everything he knew."

"Then I promise to ask you and only you for any advice I need," he told her, his lips twitching.

Hannah nodded. "Good. That will be a pleasant change."

Doc Langley apparently harbored a secret desire to be the Dale Earnhardt Jr. of the fishing-boat circuit. He headed out to sea at a dizzying clip. The kids were bundled up in their life vests and clinging to the railing for dear life, but Hannah had to admit they looked happier than they had since arriving in Seaview. She, however, was feeling a little nauseated.

"Want me to tell him to slow down?" Luke asked, sitting down beside her.

"And make me the sissy?" she said. "No way."

"According to his GPS system or sensor or whatever fancy piece of equipment he's monitoring, we should be in prime fishing territory any second now."

"Thank God," she said fervently. "Fishing with my dad was nothing like this."

Luke stared out to sea. After a couple of minutes of silence, with the salt air rushing into their faces, he said, "Tell me something, Hannah. Did you ever think about trying to find him?"

"Who? My father?"

Luke nodded.

"I probably thought about it a million times right after he left, but I was just a kid. I had no idea how to go about it. And then I got angry and decided if he didn't love me enough to come back, why should I care about him? Eventually I stopped asking about him, which obviously relieved my mother and my grandparents."

"I think that's pretty much where Gracie

and Nate stood before I brought them down here."

"Are you suggesting it was a childish reaction?"

"Not in a bad way," he assured her. "After all, you *were* a child. What about now, though? Do you ever wonder what happened to him?"

"Sometimes."

"Did you ever ask your mother if she had any idea where he'd gone? Or your grandmother?"

Hannah shook her head. "At first, but they claimed not to know. Like I said, eventually I stopped asking. Mentioning him clearly upset my mom."

"I can see why it might have been upsetting for your mother, but Grandma Jenny's another story. She's pretty tough. Maybe you should talk to her about it sometime before it's too late."

Hannah understood what he was saying, but she didn't like thinking about Grandma Jenny dying. Right now she could barely cope with the reality that her *mother* was gone. Besides, what would be the point of rocking the boat at this late date? Wherever her father was, it was pretty clear there was no room in his life for her or he would have made the effort himself to contact her long ago. Besides, she'd finally made peace with the way things were — that is, if total avoidance of a very sore subject counted as making peace.

"Just think about it," Luke urged. "I have a hunch that he's one of the reasons you have such strong feelings against Seaview."

"You're probably right," she admitted, recalling the comment she'd made to Grandma Jenny when she'd first arrived a few weeks ago. As a child she'd thought that Seaview's limitations were one of the reasons her father had left. Then somehow she'd managed to twist that into a belief that her mom had felt trapped into staying. Grandma Jenny had insisted that neither of those things was true. So maybe, if Hannah asked now, her grandmother would be willing to shed some light on what had *really* happened. Hannah wasn't entirely sure why that mattered all these years later, but perhaps, as Luke had said, her dad leaving had caused her deep resentment toward this island.

Would knowing the truth change anything? Probably not. But perhaps she could finally put the past to rest once and for all.

Though it was hard to focus on Hannah with two rambunctious kids on a boat, Luke managed to keep an eye on her during the morning. Ever since he'd suggested she speak to her grandmother about her father, her expression had been thoughtful and just a little sad.

Maybe he'd been wrong to prod her into asking questions about something that had happened years ago, but he was pretty sure it had shaped the woman she was today in ways she might not realize, such as the way she viewed marriage and relationships.

"Daddy, I got a fish!" Gracie shouted exuberantly, snapping Luke's attention away from Hannah.

He moved behind her and helped her brace the rod against the pull of the fish. It was giving her one heck of a fight. "Want me to reel him in?" he asked.

"No, no, I want to do it," she insisted, drawing an amused look from Doc Langley.

"Got yourself a real fisherwoman there," Doc said as Gracie strained to hold on to the rod. Even with Luke's help, it was bobbing and weaving dangerously.

"We need to give him a little slack in the line," Luke coached her.

"No, he'll get away," Gracie protested, holding tight.

Suddenly the rod was ripped from her hands, throwing her off balance. She fell hard. There was a sharp cracking sound in the arm she used to catch herself, and she screamed at the top of her lungs.

Luke knew before he even touched the arm that she'd broken a bone. Gently he tried to feel her forearm, but each touch elicited a shriek that tore at his heart.

"Simple fracture," Doc said decisively, proving he'd seen his share of such injuries even among a population as small as Seaview's. He was already heading for the wheel to turn the boat around. "We'll X-ray it back at the clinic, but an expert like you shouldn't have any problem setting it right here. No need to go to the mainland. I'll have us back at the dock in no time."

Luke wanted to protest that he wanted better for his little girl, but he knew Doc was right. Unless the X ray turned up something unexpected, this would mean a few weeks in a cast and nothing more.

"Daddy, it really hurts," Gracie said, her eyes filled with tears.

"I know, sweetie. We'll give you something for that as soon as we get to the clinic."

Hannah appeared at his side and immediately sat down next to Gracie. "Why don't you lean against me?" she suggested gently. "And I'll tell you a story while we're heading back to shore. It's about a mermaid named Gracie."

For just an instant Gracie seemed to forget about the pain as her gaze turned to Hannah. "Really?"

"Yep. And she was the most beautiful mermaid in the entire ocean. She was a really good mermaid, too. All the fish loved her, because she was so kind and cheerful, but she was lonely. She really, really wanted someone to love."

Luke's gaze caught Hannah's over Gracie's head. "Thank you," he mouthed silently.

She smiled, but went right back to telling the story. Nate slid over until he was next to her, too, as captivated by the story as Gracie was.

Relieved that Gracie had been distracted from her pain, Luke made his way through the boat to join Doc at the helm. "How much longer?"

"Five minutes, maybe ten if there are too many boats in the harbor. How's she doing?"

"Hannah's keeping her occupied for now."

"The kids seem really taken with her," Doc observed. "How about you? You have your eye on her?"

Luke glanced back at the picture Hannah made sitting on the deck of the boat with his kids snuggled up beside her. He tried to imagine Lisa being as calm and soothing under the same circumstances and couldn't. She would have been hysterical, blaming him for putting Gracie into a dangerous situation.

He had to stop this, he told himself sternly. Making comparisons might be inevitable, but they weren't fair to either woman. He noticed that Doc was still eyeing him speculatively.

"Hannah and I are friends," he told him. "We've known each other since we were kids."

"As I recall, you didn't appreciate her back then. You only had eyes for that Dawson girl. Next to her, Hannah sort of faded into the woodwork." He grinned at Luke. "Can't say that now, can you? She's a real beauty."

"I suppose," Luke said, thinking how he'd been captivated by her inner beauty, the woman she'd become. Of course, now that his gaze had settled on her mouth, he couldn't seem to tear it away. And he couldn't stop thinking about how much he'd enjoyed kissing her.

He shook his head and deliberately turned away, hoping to banish the thoughts, which were entirely inappropriate when his daughter was sitting there with a broken arm. If he was going to be obsessed with something, that would be a good place to start.

No sooner had he mentally lectured himself about that than Doc pulled the boat into the marina, maneuvering it into its slip with impressive precision. He reached into his pocket and handed Luke a set of keys. "These'll get you into the clinic. The little key will get you into the cabinet with pain medication. You use whatever you need in there. I'll finish here and bring Hannah and Nate along with me."

"Thanks," Luke said, then went to gather up his daughter. "Let's go, sweetie. We'll have that arm fixed up in no time."

"Can Hannah come, too?"

"She'll be along in a minute with Doc."

To his surprise, Gracie latched onto Hannah's arm with her uninjured hand and clung to it. "No, I want her to come now!"

"Of course I'll come," Hannah said at once. "I'll sit in the back and hold you while your dad drives, okay?"

Luke nodded. "Sounds like a plan. Nate, will you be okay helping Doc?"

"Sure!" Nate said eagerly.

Minutes later, Luke, Hannah and Gracie were inside the clinic. He turned on the X-ray machine and took the films he needed. "It'll take a couple of minutes for me to process these. Gracie, you want some of that pain medication now? You've been really brave, but it will help when it comes time to set that arm."

"Do I have to have a shot?"

"Afraid so."

She gazed at Hannah trustingly. "Is it going to hurt?"

"Not for more than a second," she promised. "I imagine your dad knows how to give shots that barely hurt at all. Think of it as a fairy kiss. There and gone in the blink of an eye."

"Thanks for the vote of confidence," Luke said. He'd never had to administer a shot to one of his own children before, but his time in Iraq had prepared him to handle far worse emergencies. He glanced into Gracie's eyes and saw that she was regarding him with complete trust, thanks to Hannah's faith in him. He wiped the upper part of Gracie's arm with alcohol, then gave her the shot. "All finished," he announced.

She beamed up at Hannah. "Just like a fairy kiss."

He walked into the processing room and had to lean against the door. How the hell had he done this kind of thing for a living? Somewhere along the way, even before the mind-numbing pace of treatment in Iraq, he'd been so focused on the procedure and the outcome that he'd forgotten there was a scared patient before him. Gracie had brought that home to him. He vowed never to forget that again.

When the films were developed, he brought them out and put them on the light board. As he'd anticipated and Doc had predicted, it was a clean break that could be easily set right here.

He worked with practiced skill to set the bone and fit Gracie with a plastic cast. "There you go, kiddo. When you go back to school, you can have all your friends sign your cast and then you'll have a souvenir from your first fishing trip in Florida."

Gracie studied the bright pink cast on her arm, then sighed. "It would have been better if I'd caught the fish."

17

Gracie was reveling in being the center of attention when they got back to the inn around two. Hannah grinned as Gracie regaled Grandma Jenny, Kelsey and Jeff with her version of the events as she stuffed herself with ice cream, while Nate ate cheese, crackers and then ice cream.

"Can I be the first to sign the cast?" Jeff asked.

Gracie beamed. "Sure. You, too, Kelsey."

"I'd be honored," Kelsey said, and went in search of a good pen.

When she returned, they made a major production out of the signing ceremony, then Luke studied his daughter and announced, "Time for a nap, sweetie. You, too, Nate."

"But I'm too old for a nap," Gracie protested.

"Not when you've been out half the day on a boat and come home with a broken arm. I think anyone would want a nap after that. Then I think we should call your mom and tell her what happened, okay?"

Gracie studied him worriedly. "Do you think she's going to be mad?"

"At you? No way," Luke said. "If she's upset with anyone, it will be with me for letting this happen to you."

"But it wasn't your fault," Gracie protested. "It was that big ole fish's fault."

"The fish was just doing what he had to do to survive," Luke told her. "Now, scoot. You need some rest."

Gracie turned to Hannah. "Will you come upstairs with me and tell me another story?"

"Sure," Hannah said, following her.

Gracie crawled under a sheet, already yawning. "I liked the story about the mermaid," she murmured sleepily. "Tell that one again."

Hannah repeated the story, adding some embellishments along the way. She watched as Gracie's eyes finally began to drift shut.

"That's a good one, Hannah," she murmured sleepily. "You should put it in a book."

Hannah chalked the comment off to stress and exhaustion. For years she'd made up stories for Kelsey to keep her entertained on long flights. Kelsey had suggested a time or two that Hannah write them down, but she hadn't taken her seriously, either.

But a few minutes later, after Gracie had fallen asleep and she was on her way back downstairs, she actually thought about Gracie's suggestion. She'd spent most of her career writing press releases and coming up with catchy phrases. Why had she never considered turning her writing skill in another direction? Probably because it had seemed too chancy for a mom with a child to support. Or maybe because it hadn't seemed important enough, making up stories to entertain kids.

When she got downstairs, Luke was waiting for her. "You're looking awfully thoughtful," he said, studying her curiously. "Did something happen with Gracie?"

"She told me I should put the mermaid story in a book," she said, watching his face closely for any hint of disdain.

"That's a great idea!" he enthused. "It was a terrific story."

"Come on," she protested. "It was just something I made up to keep her distracted, so she wouldn't think so much about being in pain."

"And it worked," he said. "Do you think any boring old story would have worked as well? And Nate was captivated, too."

"You're just glad she stopped screaming."

"That, too," he conceded. "But think about it, Hannah. Have you ever considered writing children's books?"

She shook her head. "Not really. Every mom makes up stories for her kids. It doesn't mean any of them have what it takes to be an author."

"You won't know if you're one of the exceptional ones unless you try, will you?"

She couldn't believe he was encouraging her to try something so crazy, but he seemed totally serious. "Publishing's a tough business," she countered. "I have a few authors as clients and I know what they go through."

"Ah, but think of the advantage you'd have over them," he said. "You know exactly how to put a marketing plan together."

She laughed. "There is that. How about a glass of wine? I could use one. It's been quite a day."

"You go outside and I'll get the wine. Maybe I can rustle up something to eat, too. I don't know about you, but I'm starved. We forgot all about lunch. Grandma Jenny fixed Nate a snack before he went upstairs, and Gracie ate all that ice cream, but we haven't had a bite to eat."

"I think there's some cold chicken in the

fridge. You could make sandwiches with that."

"You just relax. I'll find something."

Hannah settled herself into a rocker on the porch and closed her eyes. It had been a long, eventful morning. She'd been impressed with how well Luke had kept his cool with Gracie, fixing her up with the kind of skill that ought not to be allowed to languish idly when good doctors were so hard to come by. She had a feeling the time had come when he needed to go back to work, but the thought of him leaving Seaview depressed her. So, in its own way, did the thought of him staying here and taking over for Doc.

But what saddened her most was knowing that their days together were drawing to a close. She'd enjoyed having someone with whom she could compare notes at the end of the day, someone who found her attractive and made her feel like a woman again.

When Luke finally came back outside with two thick sandwiches made on Grandma Jenny's homemade whole-grain bread, along with chips and wine, she turned to him.

"Luke, how much longer are you going to wait before you make a decision about going back to work?"

"What is this?" he grumbled. "Are you

and your grandmother conspiring to push me back into an operating room?"

"It's just that I saw for myself today how good you are."

He shrugged off the compliment. "It was a simple break, Hannah. Any competent doctor could have done as well. I imagine Doc has set his share of bones right here in Seaview."

"Are you trying to tell me you're just ordinary? I don't believe it. If you were, you wouldn't have been qualified to treat the kind of injuries you faced in Iraq."

"What's your point?"

"You're wasting your time here."

"Am I really? I thought I was reconnecting with my kids," he said brusquely. "And with you."

"And that's great, all of it," she said with total sincerity. "But it's not real life, Luke. Real life for you is back in Atlanta."

"I had no idea you were that anxious to get rid of me."

She frowned at his edgy tone. "You know I didn't mean it that way. Having you here, and Gracie and Nate, has been wonderful. It's the best time I've ever spent in Seaview, but it can't last."

His gaze locked with hers. "Are you so sure about that, Hannah? I like it here. I was impressed by Doc's clinic. It's modern and well equipped for a community of this size. He can certainly handle most minor emergencies and some major ones, too, if he can't get help from the mainland fast enough. Working there would be a challenge."

She didn't even try to hide her skepticism. "For how long? Luke, from what you've told me, you're used to doing complicated orthopedic procedures. Setting broken arms and treating the sniffles would bore you silly."

He shook his head. "I don't think so. I think it would be great to have time to really connect with patients."

His enthusiasm for Seaview, when her own feelings were so mixed, dismayed her. "Then you've made a decision?" she said, her tone flat. "You're going to stay here?"

"No, I haven't made any decisions," he said impatiently. "But I *am* evaluating all the options. Unlike you, I'm not scared to try something new."

The accusation stung. "What does that mean?"

"You dismissed the possibility of writing children's books without a moment's thought, just as you've dismissed coming back here to help run the inn."

"Because I have a career I actually love!" she snapped. "Why would I look at alternatives?"

"If you love it as much as you say you do, why are you still here? There's nothing keeping you in Seaview, Hannah. The inn will open in a few days with plenty of people to help. As far as I can tell, your grandmother is both physically and mentally capable of staying right here for the immediate future. That's my medical opinion, as well as the opinion of someone who cares about her. Kelsey's thoroughly enjoying the challenge of running this place and Jeff is right here to do whatever either of them needs. So am I. You're free to go back to the life you claim to love."

Hannah didn't have a ready answer to any of that. The fact that he was so willing to see her go hurt. So did the implication that her presence wasn't needed by anyone. Her whole adult life she'd been working hard to make herself indispensable. She'd been the touchstone in Kelsey's life, the go-to woman in her office. At the end, even her mother had needed her to help with her care. For a couple of days she'd even envisioned herself as Grandma Jenny's savior, rushing in to see that she was living someplace safe.

Now she realized with dismay that none

of that was true. Kelsey was managing her own life, perhaps not as Hannah would have preferred, but she was on her own path. Grandma Jenny was as capable as ever. Even her boss was managing without her, because she'd forced him to. What had she been thinking? Who would she be, if no one needed her anymore?

She stood up, almost upending the table beside her in her need to get away. "I'm going for a walk," she said, taking off down the steps and all but running to the beach.

She heard Luke call after her, but she pretended not to, and kept going. She didn't think she could stand it if he tried to placate her, after inadvertently making her see how empty her life really was.

Besides, she needed solitude to think about what was going to happen next. How ironic that she'd started that whole lousy conversation by trying to make Luke think about his future and now, suddenly, she saw just how bleak her own future was. Add in the specter of that cancer screening hanging over her, and all she felt like doing was sitting down on the warm sand and bawling her eyes out.

He was an idiot! Luke cursed himself six ways from Sunday for saying what he'd said to Hannah. He'd seen the hurt in her eyes and immediately felt like a jerk, but it had been too late to take his words back or try to make things right. She'd run off, and though he'd wanted to follow, something told him to stay right where he was until he could come up with an apology she'd actually believe.

He thought he knew why she was so touchy. She was no more settled about what tomorrow should bring than he was. The difference was that he'd come here searching for answers and she'd come here thinking she already knew them. He'd already faced the fact that changes were inevitable. She was just discovering that change might be more alluring than she'd ever imagined. And, knowing Hannah and her stubborn streak, she was going to fight making that change no matter how appealing she might find it.

"Where's Hannah?" Grandma Jenny asked, joining him on the porch.

"I ran her off," he said ruefully.

"How'd you do that?"

"I asked her why she was still here if she was so committed to her life in New York."

"Yes, I can see how that would do it," she said wryly. "Hannah doesn't like being reminded that her actions and her words don't always match. How much do you remember about her from high school?"

Luke thought back to the girl he'd known back then. The truth was he'd hardly noticed her when Abby was around. What he remembered most was her determination to leave Seaview. It had been unwavering.

"She really wanted to go to college and make her mark on the world, preferably someplace far away from this island," he recalled.

"Exactly. And she's done that. From what I know, she's widely recognized in her field. She's won all sorts of awards. Made good money, too, enough to support herself and Kelsey in a city where it's not cheap to get by. That's how Hannah's defined herself, by her success. She's not likely to admit that it's not enough." She cast a glance in his direction. "Sound familiar?"

He frowned at her. "Let's leave me out of this for the moment. You got Hannah down here thinking you could convince her to stay," he said.

"I hoped she'd come to view saving the inn and protecting her heritage as a challenge. She hasn't embraced it the way I hoped," she admitted. "Kelsey's the one who's done that. Hannah's just hiding out."

Luke was struck by her choice of words.

"What makes you say she's hiding out? What does Hannah have to hide from?"

Grandma Jenny gave him a sharp look. "She hasn't told you?"

"Told me what?"

"As close as the two of you have gotten, I was sure she would have said something."

"Tell me," Luke said.

For once the usually talkative Grandma Jenny clammed up. "It's not my place. This is her information to share." She gave him a pointed look, then added, "Or not."

Luke studied her intently. He could think of only one reason she'd be that evasive. "Is Hannah sick?"

She smiled at his persistence. "Talk to her, Luke. Make her tell you why she hasn't left. And if she tells you it's all about looking after me, don't believe it." She stood up. "I think I'll go and lie down for a little while before I start fixing supper. Everyone will be hungry when they wake up from their naps."

Luke let her go. He knew her well enough by now to know that she'd said all she was going to say. She was probably very pleased with herself that she'd revealed just enough to make him curious, but no more than she should have.

He left the porch and crossed the street to

the beach. After he'd climbed over the dunes, he could see Hannah in the distance. She was trudging back toward home, still looking as if the weight of the world was on her shoulders. Even so, she was beautiful with her short hair curling chaotically around her face, her cheeks flushed, her arms and legs lightly tanned and as slender as a girl's.

He started toward her, then stopped and waited for her to come to him.

"I'm sorry for what I said before," he said when she drew closer.

Despite the apology her expression remained wary.

Luke tucked a finger under her chin and gazed into eyes still shimmering with tears. "I really am sorry. I never meant to imply that we didn't need you here."

"It's true, though," she said. "I'm not making any real contribution to getting the inn up and running again. Kelsey and my grandmother have that totally under control. You've done all of the repairs. I should go back to New York."

Because she looked so sad, Luke kept his hand against her cheek. "Why haven't you?"

She swallowed hard, her gaze avoiding his.

"You can tell me, Hannah. Is it your job? Are things not going as well as you've led everyone to believe?"

"No, work is great," she said.

"Then what is it? Is there a relationship you haven't mentioned?"

She shook her head.

He forced her chin up until her eyes met his. "Tell me," he said softly. "I'm male. I'm no good at this kind of guessing game."

Her lips twitched slightly at that, then she sighed. "I'm scared," she said at last. "Not the way you said earlier, but I am scared."

Nothing she might have said could have surprised him more. "Scared of what?"

She was silent for so long, he thought she might not answer, but then she looked away and blurted, "I have breast cancer. Or I did. They did surgery and radiation and chemo and supposedly it's all gone, but that's what my mother thought, too, and hers came back less than a year after her supposedly successful treatment." She sucked in a breath, then added, "And then she died."

Luke swallowed the rush of words on the tip of his tongue. He knew all the sympathetic platitudes and he suspected Hannah had heard them all so often they were meaningless.

"How long has it been?" he asked matter-of-factly, determined to hide his own dismay.

"I'm due for a three-month checkup," she said.

He frowned. "That's the appointment you've been postponing, the one your friend has been calling about?"

She nodded.

"Oh, Hannah," he murmured, reaching for her and pulling her into his arms. He rested his chin on her head and held her, trying to find the right words. The doctor in him wanted to insist she go back tomorrow and have those tests. The man who was falling in love with her wanted to hold her and pretend that everything was all right, that it would be all right as long as there were no test results to say otherwise.

He tried to imagine how terrified she must be. Any cancer survivor dreaded these follow-up appointments, but how much worse they must be for a woman who'd just lost her own mother to the same disease. Putting off the tests, though, was no solution. He knew that. So did she.

"Want me to come to New York with you?" he asked, his arms tightening around her. "You can come with me to take the kids home tomorrow, then we can fly up from Atlanta the next day."

She pulled back to look at him, amazement written all over her face. "You would do that?"

"Absolutely," he said without hesitation. "Just say the word."

She shook her head. "No, though I can't tell you what it means to me that you would offer to do it. This isn't your problem, Luke. It's mine. I have to face it."

"You don't have to face it alone," he argued.

"I *won't* be alone. Sue will be there. We've always been there for each other."

"I'm glad you have a friend like that, but it couldn't hurt to have someone else in your corner, especially someone who gets all the medical mumbo-jumbo."

She smiled at that. "My doctor's pretty good at speaking plain English."

Oddly disappointed that she didn't want him at her side, he forced a smile. "Okay, then, when is the appointment?"

Once more she avoided his gaze. "I haven't exactly made it yet. It was supposed to be this week, but the inn's reopening on Friday. I should be here for that."

"If you flew up with me from Atlanta on Monday, you'd be back for the opening," he countered.

She frowned and backed away. "I knew telling you was a mistake. Now you're going to hound me, too."

He nodded unrepentantly. "Yeah." He pulled her back in his arms, determined to settle this. "Let me face this with you."

"Why?"

"Because I have a stake in those test results, too." He looked deep into her eyes. "You matter to me, Hannah. There are still a lot of questions both of us need to answer, a lot of decisions we need to make, but I think there's some amazing potential here."

She frowned, which wasn't the reaction he'd been anticipating.

"You think there's potential with a woman who's just told you she may not even live another year?"

"That is *not* what you told me," he said emphatically. "You have a follow-up exam, Hannah. You were all clear just three months ago. There's every reason to believe that the results will be negative this time, too."

"They weren't for my mom. She was in remission for a grand total of five months and then the cancer came back even more aggressively than before and there was nothing more they could do."

"You're not your mother."

"Genetically you're only half right," she said.

"Pessimism doesn't become you, Hannah. I know I'm out of my field of medical expertise here, but I believe that a positive attitude can play a big role in how these things go. You've always been a fighter. Has there ever in your life been a more important battle for you to fight?"

She covered her face with her hands, then moved away and shoved her hands in her pockets. She started pacing back and forth as she spoke. "Look, I know you're right, and honestly, I was doing okay until my mother died. I was the most upbeat, determined patient in the universe until I had to sit beside her bed and watch her die."

"So what? You decided you were just like her, that your fate was inevitable, too?"

"Pretty much."

"That's ridiculous. Maybe your original diagnosis was earlier than hers or it was a different type of cancer cell. And for all you know there's never been any cancer on your father's side of the family. You have those genes, too. Maybe those, along with all that chemo and radiation, are enough to keep you in the clear from here on out."

She stopped pacing, sighed wearily and rested her head against his chest. "You're a pretty good cheerleader, you know that?" she murmured.

Despite himself Luke laughed. "Sorry, sweetheart. I don't have the legs for it."

At his comment, she chuckled, then started to laugh, the sound almost hysterical. Luke folded her in his arms and held her again as she wept. When she was done, though, he brushed the tears from her cheeks. Her skin was petal-soft to his touch. Being totally male, he couldn't stop himself from wondering if she was that soft all over. Then he dragged his thoughts back to more important things.

"Enough," he commanded. "You call and make the appointment. Get the tests done this week as scheduled and then we deal with whatever lies ahead. We do that together."

"Why would you do that?" she asked, her expression mystified.

"I told you why, because you matter to me and one way or another we're going to have a future together. I refuse to think otherwise."

Her lips curved into a faint smile. "Oh well, then, if you won't think otherwise, then that's the way it will be."

"Nice to have you agreeing with me for a change," he told her. "Now, let's go back to the inn and you can book that flight to New York. If you insist on going alone, then fly out tomorrow morning. I'll drive you to the airport when the kids and I head out for

Atlanta."

"I probably can't get on a flight at the last minute," she said.

"Wishful thinking," he said. "There's bound to be one seat on one plane tomorrow. Put Jeff on it. He's the computer whiz. He'll find it."

He held her hand as they walked back to the inn, then paused when they reached the steps.

"I know you're scared, Hannah, and you don't want to do this, but focus on one thing. If you fly up tomorrow or even Monday and have the tests done right away, you'll be back here by midweek and so will I. We can celebrate."

She tilted her head, her eyes brightening. "Celebrate how?"

He gave her a long, lingering look. "Oh, I imagine we'll be able to think of something."

To his relief, Hannah laughed.

"Now, that could be an incentive to hurry back," she said. "If you upped the ante just a bit."

"I can do that," he said confidently.

He leaned down and covered her mouth with his. Hunger and heat and uncertainty gave the kiss an edge of desperation that made him want more. A lot more.

Hannah leaned into him, her hands on his

face. “I need you, Luke,” she murmured. “I don’t want to, but I do.”

“Now’s a fine time to tell me,” he said, his lips curving into a smile. “We’re right out here in plain view and my kids are back at the inn.” He gazed into her eyes, regretting that a kiss would have to do for now. “Next week, Hannah. Next week we’ll make up for lost time. I promise.”

It was a provocative promise of what could be. It was also a terrifying reminder of how much he could lose.

18

Donovan's on New York's Upper West Side had always been a favorite of Hannah's and Sue's. The decor was warm and welcoming, the staff accommodating. It was *Cheers* with a touch of class — a mahogany bar, etched-glass mirrors and seductive lighting. It was the perfect spot for celebrating the fact that Hannah's three-month screening was behind her. It would be days before all the results were in, but Dr. Blake hadn't found anything that alarmed him in the physical exam or in the mammogram taken by his radiologist.

"See, you went through all of that anxiety for nothing," Sue said, lifting her glass of champagne in a toast, though she took barely a sip, then set the glass aside.

Hannah refused to let herself rejoice too soon. "We don't have all the results back yet," she cautioned.

"Hey, enough with the pessimism. They're

going to say the same thing, that you're still free of cancer," Sue predicted, then studied her friend. "Have you called Luke yet to tell him?"

Hannah frowned. "No. I'll see him tomorrow night."

"Don't you think he might like to know now? He is the one who finally kicked your butt and got you up here, isn't he?"

"Yes, but he's in Atlanta delivering his kids to his ex-wife," she said, then added emphatically, "And I don't intend to say anything to Luke until we have *all* the results, not just these preliminary ones."

"A confrontation with the ex-wife?" Sue shuddered dramatically. "All the more reason to call. He'd probably like to hear a friendly voice."

"He'll call me when he's free," Hannah insisted, then determinedly tried to change the subject. "Tell me everything that's going on here. How's John? How's work?"

Sue took a deep breath, then beamed at her. "My life is just about perfect," she exulted. "And I have news. I was waiting to see you so I could tell you in person. I wanted to see the look on your face."

Hannah had never seen Sue more excited. She was almost giddy. "Tell me. What news?"

"I'm pregnant!"

Hannah's mouth dropped open. If Sue had announced she was taking up sky-diving, she wouldn't have been more stunned. "Pregnant? As in having a baby?" A dozen different thoughts scrambled through her head at the same time, memories of conversations about motherhood in which Sue had dismissed the whole notion as not for her. "But I thought you never wanted children. You're happy about this?"

"I was never with anyone before who was good father material," Sue said, "but John is. I didn't realize how much I wanted this until it happened. Now I can hardly wait."

Hannah was still grappling with the magnitude of the change that was about to occur in her friend's life. "I probably shouldn't ask this, but we've known each other too long for me not to. Did you plan it?"

Sue nodded. "But I didn't want to say anything until I was sure I could even get pregnant. I'm forty-three and I know my age is an issue, but the doctor says I'm in good health and shouldn't have any problems. We'll probably do the whole amniocentesis thing to be sure the baby's okay, but, Hannah, I am so thrilled! I can hardly wait to start decorating a nursery. I've already bought half a dozen little outfits, suitable for a boy or a girl, of course. When you get back from Florida for good, we're going on a major shopping spree, though. I'm already clipping out pictures of baby furniture in magazines. Thank goodness we never turned the guest room into an office. Now it'll be just right for a nursery. It gets lots of sunlight. I'm thinking it ought to be painted yellow. Don't you think that would be cheerful? And it wouldn't matter then if the baby's a boy or a girl."

She was so filled with plans, it left Hannah's head spinning. "How does John feel?"

"He's over the moon. Of course, he already has two grown children and they're not quite as excited as we are, but who cares? They'll deal. They want their dad to be happy. Once they know he's not going to cut them out of the will, they'll be fine."

Hannah grinned at her. "Just think, your baby and Kelsey's will be practically the same age. How wild is that?"

Sue blinked rapidly. "Boy, that is a wake-up call, isn't it? I watched that girl grow up. She should not be having a baby of her own yet, much less at the same time I am." She gave Hannah a wicked look. "Then, again, if things go well for you and Luke, who knows? Maybe her baby will have a younger aunt or uncle."

"Are you crazy?" Hannah demanded.

"Nope. I just know how I felt once I had a man like John in my life. Suddenly I was ready to be a mom, to do the whole family thing. It could happen that way for you, too."

Hannah refused to let herself even *think* about such an outrageous thing. She could barely think about tomorrow, much less about a future that included another child.

"I really don't think that's in the cards," she told Sue.

"We'll see," Sue murmured. "Now, tell me how things are with Kelsey and Jeff?"

"If you ask her, she still says she is absolutely, positively not going to marry him." Hannah grinned. "If you ask me, they'll be married two seconds before they wheel her into the delivery room. Even I can see how much they love each other. Fortunately Jeff is smart enough to just wait her out and let her figure things out for herself."

"Okay, then, Kelsey's life is coming together. I'm having a baby. Now, let's get serious about you and Luke," Sue said. "What's going on there?"

Hannah wasn't sure what to say. "It's complicated. He says he has feelings for me."

"And you? Are you crazy about him? It

certainly sounds as if you are when you talk about him, and you positively glow when his name comes up."

"I don't glow," Hannah said.

"Yes, my dear, you most certainly do. So, tell me about these complications."

"I think he's going to decide to stay in Seaview."

"Uh-oh," Sue said. "I can just imagine how you feel about that."

Hannah remained silent.

Sue studied her incredulously. "You *aren't* upset?"

"It was a shock at first, and I had my usual knee-jerk reaction, but now . . ." She shrugged. "Not as much as I expected to be," she admitted. "To be honest, being there has been . . . different. Every now and then that old familiar knot in my stomach loosens and it actually feels pretty good to be there. I like being with Kelsey and Gran. It's nice having family around. I feel — I don't know — grounded, maybe. I can't describe it."

"And Luke?" Sue persisted. "Is it nice having him around?"

Hannah could hardly deny it. "Yes."

"But could you really go back there for good? What would you do?"

"A week ago, I would have said it was

impossible, that I'd lose my mind if I had to give up my job and stay there, but you know something? I don't miss work as much as I thought I would. Oh, I did for a few days, especially with Dave calling constantly, but then I kind of fell into a new rhythm. I like taking walks on the beach. I like sitting on the porch in the evening and talking to my family."

"And Luke," Sue prodded again.

"Okay, yes, Luke is at the center of a lot of this, which is probably a really lousy idea."

"Why, if he intends to settle there, too?"

"How can I get involved with any man, but especially the father of two young children, when my future is so completely uncertain?"

Sue immediately got it. "The cancer."

Hannah nodded. "Even if these tests come back clear, that doesn't mean the next ones will or the ones after that. I'm going to be living under a cloud of uncertainty for a long time to come."

"Sweetie, you can't live your life based on what-ifs. No one would expect you to. Luke obviously knows the risks as well as you do, but he seems willing to explore where things could go."

"But can I ask those kids to do the same

thing? They're an important part of his life." She smiled just thinking about how much fun they'd had during their visit to Seaview. "You should see them, Sue. They're wonderful and quirky and funny. It would break my heart if I got sick and ruined that."

"Ruined it?" Sue said incredulously. "It's not as if you'd be doing it on purpose."

"I know, but it would rob them of their childhood to watch someone they love die. Even if they spend most of their time in Atlanta, there will always be a place for them with Luke. What if we get close and —" she swallowed hard and forced herself to say it "— I die?"

"Do you know how few guarantees there are in this life?" Sue demanded. "I could have this baby on a Monday and get hit by a bus — or one of those maniac bicycle couriers — three days later. There's no way to predict the future."

"But mine's more uncertain than most," Hannah insisted. "I have to take that into account. Nate and Gracie have already been through too much." She waved Sue off when she would have interrupted. "Look, we're getting way ahead of ourselves, anyway. Who's to say Luke and I will ever do much more than have a wild fling for a few weeks?"

Sue's expression brightened. "A wild fling? Sounds like the perfect place to start. Go for it."

Hannah thought about Luke's kiss the day before she'd left. It had stirred feelings she hadn't had in years. She wanted that much — the anticipation, the excitement, the hot, steamy sex. After that, well, she'd just have to wait and see.

Sue stood up, the expression on her face mischievous. "Finish that champagne," she ordered. "We have places to go and things to do."

"Such as?" Hannah asked, even as she dutifully downed the last few sips of champagne.

"Follow me. You'll see."

Ten minutes and a few blocks later, Sue led the way into a fancy lingerie boutique. "Anything you want, on me," she announced. "You cannot start a wild fling in cotton panties and boring bras."

Hannah looked around at the displays of skimpy thongs and lacy, seductive bras. "I can't wear this stuff. I'd feel ridiculous. Besides, it looks uncomfortable." She held up a bra that was totally unsuitable for a woman who'd had a mastectomy. "Sue, really. Try to imagine how I'd look in this. It would be pitiful, especially without my prosthesis in place. I'm not sure I'm ready for Luke to see me in revealing lingerie."

Sue grinned at her. "Oh, sweetie, you've been celibate way too long. Trust me. If you play your cards right, you won't be wearing any of it that long."

The next evening Hannah squirmed as she waited on the porch for Luke to return to Seaview. Why she'd let Sue talk her into that lingerie was beyond her. She'd been right. It *was* uncomfortable.

But she did look amazingly sexy in it, she thought, still trying to come to terms with that and with the idea that Luke might actually see her in it. She told herself a doctor would be able to overlook the scar, but what if he couldn't? She'd know soon enough.

Though he'd missed the last ferry, he'd found someone willing to bring him over to the island. He'd called to let her know that he'd be there soon. He'd go back for his car in the morning. When he strolled up at last, it was nearly 11:00 p.m. Everyone else had gone to bed.

"You waited up," he said as he crossed the lawn.

"I told you I would," she said. "I missed you."

Surprise and what she hoped was pleasure

darkened his eyes. "Really?" He leaned down and kissed her, teasing her lips with his tongue. "I missed you, too."

"How did it go in Atlanta? Were the kids glad to be back home?"

His expression turned troubled. "They didn't want me to leave," he said, settling into the rocker next to hers. "Gracie really carried on. She acted as if she'd never see me again. Believe me, the tears were a whole lot worse than the silent treatment. It caught me off guard. I thought we'd worked through a lot of this stuff while they were here."

"But they need specifics, don't they?" she said, resigned to seeing him head back to Atlanta, after all.

He nodded.

"How soon will you go back?"

"Next weekend," he said. "I rented an apartment before I left. It's a couple of miles away from the house. It has three bedrooms, so they'll have their own rooms with me. We'll pick out furniture when I go back."

Hannah struggled to hide her disappointment. He'd made the right decision, the only decision a loving father could make. "I see," she said softly. "I know they'll be glad to have you close by."

Luke regarded her with a puzzled expression. "You say that as if we'll never see each other again."

"We have to be realistic. If you're living in Atlanta and I'm in New York, how much time would we get to spend together? It's good that we didn't let this relationship go any further than it has."

"Hold it. You've gotten this all wrong. I'm not moving back to Atlanta. I'm still going to talk to Doc about taking over the clinic from him eventually."

She stared at him, not comprehending. "But the apartment?"

"I need a place where Gracie and Nate can spend time with me. I'll fly up at least one weekend a month, maybe more. On vacations they'll come here. When I finally understood the impact that the uncertainty was having on them, I worked it all out with Lisa. I actually think she's as relieved as the kids to have a plan."

Hannah could barely hide her own relief. "I see."

"Of course, there is still the issue of a plan for you and me," he said, reaching for her hand and linking their fingers together. His touch was warm, reassuring. "Especially if you're going to be in New York. Sounds like I'm going to be spending as much time in the air as I am on the ground. And speaking of New York, how did your trip go? What did the doctor have to say?"

"So far, so good, but some of the test results won't be back until next week," she said.

"How did it feel being back in the city?"

"Great!" she said, injecting as much enthusiasm into her voice as possible. It was too soon for him to know she was wavering about going back permanently. And she certainly didn't want him to think her decision would have anything to do with him. "Sue and I went to our favorite neighborhood bar for champagne after my appointment and then we went shopping." She grinned. "And guess what? She's pregnant. This will be her first, though her husband has two grown children."

He studied her with a thoughtful expression. "You're not going to want to miss any of that, are you?"

"If you're asking if I'm going back after the opening here, the answer is probably yes."

A glimmer of hope sparked in his eyes. "Probably?"

She'd thought a lot about that since her conversation with Sue. "At least for a while," she confirmed. "Until I know what's going to happen with the cancer."

"You can't let your life be controlled by that," he said.

She reached over and touched his hand. "I won't let that happen." Determined to change the subject and the mood, she said, "You didn't ask what I bought when I went shopping."

"Do I really want to know?"

"I'm wearing it."

He frowned at that. "I've seen that blouse and those shorts before."

She gave him what she hoped was a provocative look. "But not what's underneath."

His expression brightened. "Who knew you had a wicked streak, Hannah?"

A smile spread across her face. "I'm just discovering that myself."

"Well, personally, I think coming home to a fashion show would make that long drive today and the money I spent to charter that boat to get here tonight worthwhile. What do you think?"

She stood up. "I thought you'd never ask." She hesitated just inside the door. "One thing, though. We probably don't want Grandma Jenny to catch us."

"It's been a lot of years since I've had to sneak around with a woman," he said. "It might be kind of fun. Want me to carry you, so the only sound will be the weary traveler trudging upstairs to his room? That'll throw her off."

"A romantic idea, but I don't want you collapsing halfway up and requiring paramedics. That would pretty much spoil the whole plan. Let's just be really, really quiet."

She tiptoed up the steps with Luke on her heels. Just inside his room, he backed her against the wall and covered her mouth with his as he shoved the door closed with his knee.

"Lock it," Hannah whispered when she could catch her breath.

"Do you really think your grandmother is going to come in here to check on what all the commotion is?"

"Better safe than sorry. And there can't be that much commotion."

He stared at her. "You have rules for sex?"

"No, I have rules for noisy sex, at least under this roof."

"Now, there's an interesting challenge if ever I've heard one. I hope to hell the bed springs don't squeak."

Hannah grinned at him. "They don't. I bounced on them earlier."

He chuckled. "Do you have any idea how much I love you? You're amazing."

She froze for a second at his admission that he loved her. She wanted to savor the words — then analyze them to death, more than likely. Because there were far better options right in front of her, she bunched his shirt in her fists, stood on tiptoe and kissed him.

Suddenly filled with need, she reached for the buttons on his shirt, shoving it out of her way as she went. "You're pretty amazing yourself," she said, her gaze riveted on his chest. He still had those six-pack abs she'd coveted years ago. She'd known that from watching him work shirtless, of course, but this was the first time she'd had a chance to touch him, to feel the combination of heated skin and hard muscles. She was reveling in the sensation, when Luke reached for the buttons on her blouse. For an instant she stilled, filled with sudden panic.

He tucked a finger under her chin and met her gaze. "It's okay, Hannah. I swear it will be okay."

She released a sigh, then nodded. She wanted desperately to believe him, and when his clever hands touched her, when she saw herself reflected in the darkening passion in his eyes, she did.

■ ■ ■ ■

"Did you hear Mom sneaking out of Luke's room this morning?" Kelsey asked Jeff over breakfast. She couldn't seem to contain a grin.

Jeff regarded her blankly. "What was she doing in his room?"

Kelsey gave him a disbelieving look.

His eyes widened. "Oh? Wow! I had no idea."

"You really do need to look up from your computer screen once in a while. This has been coming for some time now."

"Do you think it's serious?"

Kelsey sobered at once. "I hope so. Mom's been through so much. She needs someone in her life who'll really appreciate her. I think Luke does."

Before Jeff could reply, her mom breezed into the kitchen humming under her breath, a smile on her face.

"Good morning, you two. It's a lovely day, isn't it?"

Kelsey giggled. She couldn't help it.

Hannah just stared at her. "Okay, what's that about?"

"You seem especially cheerful this morning. What put you into this good mood?"

Kelsey inquired innocently.

Jeff stood up, his cheeks flaming. "I'm out of here before you answer that, Hannah." He brushed a kiss across Kelsey's brow. "I'll have that reservation system up and running this morning. You need to check it out."

"I'll be there in a little while," Kelsey said distractedly, her gaze riveted on her mom's sheepish expression. When Jeff was gone, she said, "Okay, Mom. Spill it. What's going on with you and Luke?"

"I have no idea what you're talking about."

"I saw you sneaking out of his room this morning."

"Um . . . I was just checking to see if it needed dusting."

Kelsey laughed. "It was 6:00 a.m. Try again."

"Do you really want details?" Hannah asked.

"No, probably not. Just tell me one thing. Are you happy?"

"Very."

Kelsey could see the truth of that in the sparkle in her eyes. "I'm glad."

Hannah's expression turned stern. "Now, do you want to tell me what *you* were doing in that wing of the inn at 6:00 a.m.? I don't suppose you were dusting Jeff's room, were you?"

Kelsey chuckled, then shrugged. "Okay, you caught me. We're even."

"Do you think Grandma Jenny knows all these shenanigans are going on under her roof?"

"If you ask me, she's been counting on it," Kelsey said.

Hannah looked taken aback, then nodded. "Probably so, but just the same, I really don't want to have a conversation like this with her. It would be too weird."

"Agreed," Kelsey said with a shudder.

"Mind if I ask something? If you're so sure you don't want to marry Jeff, why are you sleeping with him?"

"Because I love him," Kelsey said simply. "And I can't very well get pregnant again."

A worried frown spread across her mother's face. "Oh, Kelsey, you're playing with fire. You know that, don't you? Jeff adores you. He's a really good guy. Don't break his heart. Don't let him start to think that you've changed your mind about marrying him or giving the baby up for adoption, if you haven't."

"I won't," Kelsey said automatically. "I haven't."

"There's something else we've never talked about," Hannah said. "How do his parents feel about all this?"

Kelsey flushed. "I don't think he's told them. He said if they knew, they'd just add to the pressure, and he wants to protect me from that. I guess they'd completely freak out at even the possibility that their grandchild might be given up for adoption."

"More than Jeff's freaked out?"

Kelsey nodded. "He said they'd drag lawyers into the mix, and after that he and I and what we want would get completely lost."

"I'm glad he's protecting you from that. It's just one more indication of how much he loves and respects you."

"I know," Kelsey agreed.

"You need to show him the same respect and not send him mixed signals, Kelsey."

"I'm trying not to do that," Kelsey replied.

But even as she said the words, she knew they weren't entirely accurate. She knew Jeff was probably drawing his own conclusions about their relationship these days and she'd been saying less and less to contradict those impressions. The reality was that with every day that passed, she was less and less certain about what she wanted — from Jeff, the baby, her whole future. All she really knew was that she still loved Jeff, loved him more than ever, in fact, for coming here, making himself a part of the inn and her life in Seaview, and not making any demands. What had ever made her think she could walk away from a man like that? Why had she even wanted to?

19

Hannah watched her daughter with amazement. Kelsey had a clipboard and checklist and was going through the inn from top to bottom and from kitchen to porch, making sure no detail had been left unfinished with the first guests due to arrive in the afternoon. Hannah recognized her own organizational skill in Kelsey, along with a joy in what she was doing, something Hannah hadn't felt for longer than she could remember.

The whole inn smelled of baking bread and miniature fruit tarts, a combination that had Hannah's mouth watering. But when she went into the kitchen to beg for a sample, Grandma Jenny and Merilee Wilcox, the inn's part-time cook, shooed her out.

"All of this is for the guests," Grandma Jenny declared. "Hands off until it's time for our welcoming tea this afternoon."

"We have a welcoming tea?" Hannah asked incredulously. "When did that happen?"

"It was Kelsey's idea. She did some research on the computer about what other inns offer, and the fancy ones always have afternoon tea."

"But we're not fancy," Hannah protested, trying to imagine their usual guests sipping tea from china cups, rather than pop from a can.

"Tell that to someone who's biting into one of Merilee's tarts," Grandma Jenny retorted. "Trust me, the queen herself couldn't have anything tastier. Our guests will appreciate this and tell all their friends. Business will be booming. Pretty soon we'll have to build another addition."

Just then Luke came in from the beach entrance. "Grandma Jenny, do you want to take a look at those hooks I put up for the beach towels? Make sure there are enough and that they're where you want them?"

"I trust your judgment. Is the paint dry on that bench Kelsey asked you to build underneath?"

"Dry as a bone," he confirmed. "Any other chores on your list?"

"Not on mine," Gran told him. "Check with Kelsey. That girl has lists of her lists."

"Will do," Luke said, then winked at Hannah. "Want to come with me?"

"And risk having my daughter put me to work? I don't think so."

"And here I intended to make it worth your while," he teased.

Hannah's cheeks flamed and she cast a guilty look toward her grandmother, but Gran's lips merely quirked slightly at Luke's innuendo.

"Scoot, both of you. Merilee and I have work to do. With half the town turning out for the official grand reopening this afternoon, we don't dare slow down."

"What's on the menu besides the tarts?" Hannah inquired after Luke left as ordered.

"Merilee's sour cream pound cake and banana bread, plus little tea sandwiches."

"I could help with those," Hannah offered.

Her grandmother gaze her a skeptical look. "You sure about that? When was the last time you made tea sandwiches?"

"Never, but at least I could cut the crusts off the bread," she said, feeling useless.

"No need," Gran said. "You run along and relax. Your vacation will be over soon."

Hannah drifted out of the kitchen, feeling oddly left out of the commotion. She knew the others had their reasons for not putting her to work. Gran had concluded she wasn't interested in being a part of the grand reopening. Gran was also well aware that Hannah was essentially mystified by cooking and baking. Kelsey not only liked doing things herself, but she was also being protective about Hannah's health. And if Jeff and Luke thought it odd that she wasn't taking a more active role in the family business, they were too polite to say so.

Feeling disgruntled, she changed her mind and went upstairs in search of Kelsey. Surely there was *some* contribution she could make to ensure that the inn was ready for guests.

She found Luke and Kelsey huddled together over her daughter's multipage checklist. He was jotting down notes on his own pad of paper, which he stuck back in his pocket.

"Okay, got it," Luke said, glancing up and catching sight of her. "You changed your mind about taking a break with me? Or about pitching in?"

Though a break with Luke was infinitely more appealing, Hannah knew he wouldn't take one as long as there was work to be done. "I came to offer myself for slave duty. What can I do to help, Kelsey? I've already been kicked out of the kitchen."

Kelsey grinned. "Yeah, me, too. Merilee likes her space. As long as she keeps baking stuff that smells so heavenly, I can live with that. My mouth is already watering over tomorrow's breakfast menu. The stuffed French toast sounds totally decadent. Gran says it's been a favorite here for years, but I don't think I had it when I came to visit."

"Me, neither," Hannah said. "So, what can I do?"

Kelsey glanced at her list. "How about arranging flowers in the dining room? I checked the delivery earlier. There should be enough for one big arrangement on the sideboard and for all the little vases for the tables. You used to do amazing flower arrangements."

"But it's been years," Hannah protested.

"Mom, nobody's expecting anything elegant enough for a New York party. You know flowers and you know color. Go for it."

"I'm on it," Hannah agreed, then walked downstairs with Luke as they went to tackle their assignments.

"Kelsey has taken to this business as if she's been doing it all her life," he commented.

"She really has, hasn't she?" Hannah said with a sense of wonder. "The most amazing part of that is that she actually seems to be having fun. I always knew she was smart and organized, but she seems to be excited about every aspect of running this place. And her talents are a natural fit with Jeff's. He's brought the reservation system, the billing and accounting systems and the Internet marketing into this century. He's as excited about today as Kelsey is."

"He'd be happy about sweeping a parking lot, if Kelsey was the one asking him to do it."

"I know and that worries me," Hannah confessed.

"Because?"

"I'm afraid Kelsey's taking advantage of his feelings for her, because it suits her right now."

Luke shook his head at once. "No way. For one thing, she's crazy about him, too. For another, Jeff's smart. I had a talk with him the other day. The guy knows exactly what he's doing."

"Which is?" Hannah asked warily.

"Fitting in to Kelsey's life, proving to her that she doesn't have to give up anything to be with him, that he will always support what she wants. He's convinced she's beginning to get that."

"I don't suppose there was any mention

of marriage in this guy-talk you two were having," Hannah said.

"His cards are on the table. It's up to Kelsey. You know your daughter better than I do, naturally, but it makes sense to me that if she's half as stubborn as her mom, the only thing to do is wait her out."

Hannah's gaze narrowed. "Is that what you're doing with me? Waiting me out?"

He gave her an innocent look. "I wasn't aware we were at odds over anything. Are we?"

"Staying in Seaview comes to mind," she said. "I'm committed to going back to New York. You're committed to staying here."

"Have you heard me ask you to change your mind and stay here?" he asked.

Hannah frowned. "No, but I thought . . ." She cut herself off, embarrassed at having made any assumptions. Just because they were sleeping together didn't have to mean that Luke was looking beyond today. "Never mind. I need to get busy with those flowers."

She'd taken two steps when Luke caught her arm and whirled her around, bringing her body tight against his. At least there was no mistaking the attraction between them.

"Okay, maybe I am waiting you out," he admitted. "I want you to come to your own conclusions about staying here and what we could have. I don't want to back you into a corner. You'll head straight back to New York at the first hint that I'm issuing some kind of ultimatum, am I right?"

She shrugged, then nodded. "Probably."

"So, lips zipped," he said with a grin. "No pressure. Jeff has convinced me that the technique works on the stubborn Matthews women."

"And you trust the word of a guy in a T-shirt promoting some heavy metal band we've never heard of?"

"As a matter of fact, I do." He gave her a hard kiss that took her breath away. "Gotta go. I don't want Kelsey to catch me slacking off on her big day."

"Probably another wise decision," Hannah confirmed. "See you later?"

"Count on it," he said.

The heat in his eyes seared her all the way down to her toes. Who was she trying to kid? She'd fallen for Luke every bit as hard as Kelsey had fallen for Jeff. The only thing left to decide was whether she'd have the courage to walk away so Luke and his kids would never have to go through what she'd faced when her mother had died — the endless hours at her bedside watching her get weaker and weaker, seeing her suffer with agonizing pain as her body wasted away and she hardly even looked like herself, all things that could easily be in Hannah's future.

Instead of her relationship with Luke getting simpler now that they both knew how deep their feelings ran, the relationship was a thousand times more complicated and the stakes were higher than ever.

Kelsey was ecstatic. At the last minute she'd had the idea to invite some of the locals to the grand reopening tea, so she'd spent half the morning making calls to ensure word got around. Thankfully Gran and Merilee had baked enough food for an army, because everyone had wanted to come for a peek at the changes they'd made. Between the locals and the guests, the inn had been hopping for several hours. There had been a buzz of happy chatter in the dining room, and laughter had floated from the porch through the open windows. It had gone so well, in fact, she couldn't help wondering if she'd set the bar too high. It couldn't always be like it had been earlier in the afternoon.

Now most of the guests were in their rooms and everyone from here in town had left. Gran had gone upstairs for the evening, her mom and Luke had gone for a walk, and she was on the porch with her feet propped up and a glass of lemonade at her side, trying not to obsess about what tomorrow might bring. Would she feel a letdown now that her initial mission had been accomplished? Would the fun of running this place start to wear thin after the novelty wore off? She didn't think so, but the only way to tell would be to see how it went next week, next month or even next year. Right now she simply felt the contentment of a job well done.

She heard the screen door slap shut and glanced in that direction. Jeff was heading her way with a tray of sandwiches — real ones thick with ham and cheese, lettuce and tomato, not the fancy little tea sandwiches they'd served to their guests.

"Don't argue with me," he said before she could protest. "I know you never ate a bite during the party. You have to take care of yourself. And once you've eaten something, you should go to bed and get some rest."

"You're probably right," she admitted with a yawn. "I'm beat."

He stared at her with an astonished expression. "Say that again."

"I'm beat," she repeated.

"No, the part before that, when you said I was right."

She laughed. "Well, you are. This time,

anyway." She met his gaze. "Maybe a lot of other times, too."

He put his hand on his chest in a dramatic gesture. "Be still my heart."

She laughed at his antics. "Stop it! I know I probably haven't said it enough, but I really am glad you're here. You've been a huge help getting this place ready to reopen. And the perks of having you around weren't bad, either."

"I knew it," he said with an exaggerated sigh. "It's always been about my body."

"Your body is pretty amazing," she conceded. "But it's more than that, and you know it. I love how you care about me."

"I *love* you," he corrected.

She gave him an impatient look. "Will you just listen? I'm trying to tell you something important."

"Sorry," he said contritely.

"The past few weeks have been eye-opening for me. I think I've found what I was meant to do. I love this place. I love being close to Gran. I loved getting it ready to open, and coming up with new ideas, and helping Merilee with the menus. I can't wait to get to know the guests better." She leveled a look into his eyes, trying to gauge his reaction. "It's exactly what I want to do with my life, Jeff."

"You're not telling me anything I haven't figured out for myself," he said.

"But do you know what one of the best parts of this has been?" she asked.

"What?"

"Doing it with you. We make a good team."

He studied her closely. "So . . . what? You want us to work together?"

"No, I'm trying to tell you that I think maybe we can make this thing work between us, after all. You came here with a mission, but you didn't try to shove anything down my throat. You let me find my own way. And I think maybe you actually approve of the new me that I've found here."

"It's not a question of me approving of anything. You're happy doing this. That's all I care about, all I've ever cared about."

"I know that now, and I am more grateful than I can begin to tell you."

"Kelsey, is this your roundabout way of saying that you're ready to reconsider marrying me?"

That was exactly what she'd been trying to do, but now that the words were out there, she froze for an instant. Then she thought about all the strength she'd discovered within herself since coming to Seaview. She would never lose who she was if she married Jeff, not now or ten years from now. Partly because she wouldn't allow it, and partly because he would never ask that of her.

"I suppose what I'm saying is that *if* someone were to actually ask the question again, I *might* have a different answer this time," she said.

He frowned at her. "Don't tease me."

"Don't make me be the one to get down on one knee," she countered. "I'm a traditional girl."

He raised a brow at that.

"Okay, maybe not so traditional, but some traditions shouldn't be tampered with."

A smile tugged at the corners of his lips. "Then you're going to have to wait," he said.

She stared at him. "I beg your pardon?"

"You want tradition, you'll get tradition. That means I get to pick the time and the place to do any asking that's going to be done."

"Jeff!" she protested.

His smile spread. "Waiting's hell, isn't it? Just giving you a taste of your own medicine."

"You're a rat."

"That's not what you were saying five minutes ago."

"Five minutes ago I loved you."

He stood up, scooped her into his arms, then settled back down on the wicker love seat with her on his lap. "Trust me, you'll love me even more if I do this up right."

"I don't need an elaborate production."

"No, just tradition," he said. "I get it."

"Now would be better than later," she said.

"This will be worth waiting for," he promised. "You were."

Kelsey sighed and rested her head on his shoulder. "Just keep in mind that the baby's due in seven months. I'd like to still be able to waddle down the aisle."

"I'll keep that in mind."

She yawned and let her eyes drift shut. Today had been one of the most perfect days of her life, even without the proposal she'd been counting on. And the best thing was, she still had that to look forward to.

Several days after the inn's reopening, Luke sat on a stool at The Fish Tale sipping a beer and waiting for Doc. It was time to figure out if he really could take over the clinic, as several people had urged him to do. Though plenty of people thought Doc was ready to retire, Luke hadn't heard him express any desire to do that in the immediate future.

"Those stools are hell on my back," Doc

announced when he joined Luke. "Let's get a booth."

"Fine with me."

When they were settled in a secluded corner with their drinks and fish platters, Doc gazed at him speculatively. "I'm pretty sure you didn't invite me here just for the company, so what's this about?"

"I keep hearing a rumor that you might be thinking about retiring or at least cutting back," Luke said. "Is that true?"

"I'm seventy-four and have a lot of fishing I'd like to do. What do *you* think?"

"What's stopping you then?"

"No one's come along I thought would fit in here. Seaview Key's not a big town, but you know that. I've spoken to a couple of young doctors who are fresh out of their residencies, but they're so wet behind the ears I wouldn't trust my patients with 'em."

"There's a lot to be said for someone young and eager to establish a practice," Luke suggested. "For one thing, they're up on all the latest treatment options and medicines. For another, they're energetic."

"They also have a mile-high stack of bills from medical school," Doc said. "They're not going to make the kind of money here they'd make in a big city. Trust me, none of them would stick around more than a year or two. Then where would this town be?"

"Good point," Luke said. "What about me? How would you feel about me taking over for you at some point down the road?"

Doc's expression brightened. "You serious? This is the first you've brought it up."

Luke nodded slowly. "I had a lot of thinking to do when I first got here, but I think I'm ready for this. I like being back here. And my orthopedic practice was too limiting. I think I'd like to expand my knowledge, brush up on family medicine and get recertified."

"Working with me would give you a crash course in what you need to know in no time," Doc said.

"You willing to stay on while I go through the recertification process, show me the ropes and maybe phase into full retirement a couple of years down the road?"

"That would suit me fine. I've done this for so long that I'm not sure I'd know what to do with myself if I made a clean break from the clinic. I'd like keeping my hand in, so to speak, for as long as you'd have me. Maybe hang around a few hours a day or a day or two a week eventually, until even that gets to be too much for me. You sure having me underfoot wouldn't cramp your style?"

Luke laughed. "I'm not sure I have a style.

I do think I could benefit tremendously from your wisdom and experience."

"You don't have to flatter me to win me over. I'm already sold. I've had a dozen people or more ask me why I wasn't begging you to do this. Seems to me you're an answer to a prayer, for me and for Seaview."

For the first time in years, Luke was starting to feel excited about medicine again. He shook his head. "No, Doc. I think it's the other way around."

"How do you want to do this? Should we call Tim Morrow and ask him to draw up some paperwork to make it official?"

"Why don't we sit down again in a few days and hammer out the agreement we want, then we can get Tim to make it all nice and legal?" Luke suggested. "I need to get an attorney in Atlanta to dissolve the partnership I'm in there and I have to look into all the certification I'll need down here. That could take a few weeks, maybe even months if I need to take some classes."

"That's no problem. You do what you need to do. Call me when you settle things in Atlanta and want to schedule that meeting to work out our arrangement." He hesitated, then asked, "How does Hannah fit into this plan of yours to make Seaview your home again? You two seemed pretty close the day we went fishing and you have been staying at the inn for a while now. Rumor has it that there's something going on between you two."

"The rumor mill in Seaview is not known for its reliability, but in this case there might be some truth there," Luke admitted. "Only problem is that Hannah still has some issues about coming back here."

"Because of her mom, I imagine. That wasn't an easy time for any of them. And those two always did have their differences. I'm not sure they ever got past Hannah's dad leaving. She blamed her mom for that, irrationally, as it happens. I know why Clayton left. He got tangled up with a waitress on the mainland and she wound up pregnant. She was threatening to go after him and the inn."

"Blackmail?" Luke asked, stunned.

"That's exactly what it was," Doc confirmed. "Clayton divorced Hannah's mom and married the little tramp to shut her up in a totally misguided attempt to save the inn. There was more to it, of course. There always is in a situation like that. He made a pact with the devil, in my opinion, but he told me it was the only thing he could think of to do. The inn would have folded or they'd have had to sell it to pay the bills if there had been a costly legal battle. Add in his concern about the child the woman was expecting and he felt he had no choice. I think he realized too late that the woman wasn't all that stable, and he feared what would happen to the baby if he weren't around to protect it."

"Did Grandma Jenny or Hannah's mom know that?" Luke asked. "Certainly no one's ever said anything about Hannah having a half brother or sister somewhere."

"Well, Jenny may have put two and two together, especially after a few locals spread rumors that they'd seen Clayton around Clearwater or St. Petersburg with another woman and a child. But Hannah's mom, she knew, because she started staying close to home. Maggie said something to me once about how humiliating it was to have people talking about her husband that way. Said she couldn't bear it, so she hardly left the inn."

"I don't remember that," Luke said. "She was always great with any of us who were hanging around there."

"Probably because you'd all been too young to hear the stories or to understand them if you had," Doc said. "I think Hannah was protected from all that talk. She was young, for one thing, and folks tend to want to leave kids with their innocence as long as possible. And everyone knew how she'd idolized Clayton. They weren't going to say a bad word about her daddy right in front of her."

"Hannah should know about this," Luke said. "For one thing, the man she adored may be living no more than an hour or two away from here. Aside from that and the fact that she has a half brother or sister, it might also change her view that the inn was this huge albatross that drove her dad away. He obviously loved it and her mother enough to do what he thought he had to in order to protect her and the inn that had been in her family for so long."

Doc looked skeptical. "Luke, I don't know that this is something you should share with Hannah. It all happened a long time ago."

"And it changed everything for her. Knowing the truth could give her peace."

"And change the way she views Seaview and the inn," Doc concluded. "Is that what you're hoping?"

"Probably," Luke conceded.

"It's your decision, and you know Hannah better than I do these days. In the end, I know you'll do what you think is right," Doc said with confidence. "Just think it through first, that's all I ask. Maybe talk it over with Jenny. She might have an opinion about the truth coming out after all these years. There could be a reason she and Maggie kept Hannah in the dark."

"I'll do that," Luke promised.

And maybe he'd do a little investigating on the mainland before he went up to Atlanta at the end of the week for another visit with the kids. Perhaps he could locate Clayton and see how his life had turned out and whether or not he was someone Hannah would want back in her life after all these years.

20

Hannah stood outside the door to her mother's suite of rooms and tried to work up the courage to go inside. Now, while Luke was in Atlanta, was the perfect time to confront one of her biggest demons. She needed to go in there and face the fact that her mom was dead. She had to face all those awful memories of her final days and somehow make herself believe that she wasn't going to share the same fate.

It was also time to put to rest the years of pent-up resentment she'd felt toward her mom, first for the breakup of her marriage that had sent Hannah's father away and then for settling for life here in Seaview. Though she'd been here during her mother's final illness, it had been out of duty and obligation. They'd never fully reconciled, because Hannah could hold a grudge with the best of them, even when she understood that it was time to let it all go and move on.

As she stood there immobilized, her hand on the doorknob, she felt Kelsey slip up beside her.

"Mom, you don't have to do this," she said. "I can clean out Grandma's room. I just haven't had time to get to it yet."

Hannah shook her head. This was about more than throwing away some old clothes or going through her mother's personal papers. "No, sweetie, I need to do this myself. I think that's why Gran hasn't done it. She knew I needed to make peace with the past."

"At least let me help," Kelsey pleaded.

"No, I really do think this is something I have to do alone," Hannah insisted. She gave Kelsey a hug. "Thanks for offering, though."

"You'll call me if you need me, though, promise?"

"I will," she assured her daughter. "Don't you have things you need to be doing? Now that there are guests on the premises, there's almost always a crisis of one kind or another. I remember that much from living here. Our time was never our own."

"Everything's under control," Kelsey assured her, ignoring the bitterness Hannah hadn't been able to keep out of her voice. "Jeff's been handling a lot of it. And he's the only one who seems to be able to persuade Grandma Jenny to sit down and rest." She grinned. "He's really sneaky about it, too. Right now he has her studying this huge pile of motel brochures he got from a travel agent. He says he needs her input before he can design our brochure. Next he swears he's going to get her online to look at Web sites."

"Your great-grandmother in front of a computer," Hannah said in amazement. "Now, that's a sight I can't wait to see."

"Me, too," Kelsey said. "But Jeff will pull it off. Not even Gran seems to be able to resist his charm." Once again, she regarded Hannah worriedly. "You're sure you're okay? This can wait."

"I'm fine. Now, go and do whatever you need to do."

After Kelsey had run down the stairs, Hannah grasped the doorknob once again and forced herself to turn it. Expecting to find the suite musty from being closed up, she was surprised to find the curtains billowing and a sea breeze filling the rooms with fresh air. Grandma Jenny's work, no doubt. She should have known her grandmother wouldn't avoid the suite as Hannah had, even if she had left everything in place for the day Hannah would be ready to face her demons.

Stepping inside the sitting room with its cozy, chintz-covered chairs, she quietly shut the door behind her, then closed her eyes against the tide of memories flooding her. Some of them went back to childhood, when she'd run in here to share her sorrows or to get a hug. She tried to cling to those, the good memories of sitting on the edge of the bed in the attached bedroom watching her mother brush her long hair, of jumping onto the bed between her parents on a lazy Sunday morning, while her grandparents were downstairs dealing with the guests.

But those memories faded too quickly and all that was left behind were the recent memories of her mother lying propped up against pillows, her face gaunt, her hair thin and limp, her skin so pale and dry that Hannah had feared it would crumble at a touch like dried leaves. That image was seared in her mind.

"Oh, Mama," she whispered, tears stinging her eyes. "I'm so sorry."

Even as she murmured the apology, she wasn't entirely sure what it was for. Was it for being so judgmental? For not making amends? Or simply because now they would never have the chance to recapture the warmth and closeness that had once existed between them?

Overwhelmed when she finally stepped into the bedroom, Hannah moved quickly to the overstuffed chair by the window and breathed in the room's lavender-and-sea-breeze scent. For one fleeting moment she was able to imagine that her mother was still in the room and think of all the things that should have been said. Why hadn't she realized in time just how much she was losing by holding on to so much bitterness and anger?

"Mama, I am so sorry I judged the choices you made," Hannah whispered. "I'm sorry for holding you accountable for a decision that Dad made. I wish I'd been a better daughter to you, the kind of daughter that Kelsey's been to me. We had that relationship once and I let it slip away." No, the truth was, she had carelessly thrown it away.

For just an instant, the scent of lavender seemed to be stronger and a breeze fanned her cheeks, drying her tears. Then the scent faded and the breeze stilled, leaving her feeling more peaceful than she'd felt in years. It was impossible to explain the sensation that she'd been forgiven. Perhaps, in reality, she'd simply forgiven herself.

Either way, she felt comforted. Brushing the last of the tears from her cheeks, she stood up and began emptying drawers, creating piles of clothes to be discarded and another of things that could be donated to the church thrift shop. From time to time, she lingered over a remembered sweater or a favorite scarf, setting some of those things aside for herself or for Gran or Kelsey.

When she found the drawer filled with papers, she almost closed it again to leave that chore for another day. Something, though, kept her from doing that. She took the neatly bundled papers and spread them on the bed, trying to determine if there was any rhyme or reason to them.

Some were related to the inn, papers that should have been in files. Hannah set those aside to take to the office downstairs. Some, amazingly, were her old school papers — essays and tests on which she'd gotten an A, report cards all the way back to elementary school, even a few drawings she'd done in crayon.

Next she came across an envelope marked "Hannah's stories." Puzzled, she opened it to find half a dozen amateurish attempts at writing children's stories, along with accompanying sketches. As she read through them, she winced at the awkward writing, but to her amazement, the stories themselves weren't bad. She recognized that they were stories she'd made up for Kelsey, then written down at her daughter's urging. How they'd gotten here was beyond her. Had Kelsey brought them with her and left them behind? And why had her mother saved them? Why had she saved any of these mementoes after the way Hannah had abandoned her with hardly a backward glance?

As she sat there fingering the old pages, she thought she understood. After all, she herself was a mother, and no matter what happened between Kelsey and her in the future, there were a thousand and one things she would treasure. In fact, she had papers just like this back home in New York. She still had a framed childhood drawing of Kelsey's on the wall in the hallway leading back to their bedrooms, right alongside signed and numbered prints from rising stars in the New York art world. Saving things like that was just something mothers did, and it made her feel a fresh connection to her own mom.

Reaching into the drawer for the final packet of papers, she saw at once that these were letters — *unopened* letters. And they were all addressed to her. Shaking, she studied the handwriting and knew at once who they were from: her dad.

Two seconds ago, she'd let everything from the past go and now this. This was fresh evidence that her mother had withheld letters meant for her, letters that might have made everything right. She felt queasy just looking at the small bundle tied with a pink ribbon. Ironically, she remembered that exact ribbon from a dress her mom had made for her for her sixth birthday, a day her dad had brought a pony home for all her friends to ride. It had been the most memorable birthday she'd ever had. Somehow seeing *that* ribbon around *these* letters made it even worse.

Unable to stay in the room another moment, she bolted for the door, the letters clutched in her hand. She ran down the stairs and out onto the porch, pausing at the top of the steps to catch her breath.

"Hannah, what is it?" Gran asked, starting to rise from her rocker. "Hannah, are you okay?"

"Not now, Gran. Not now." She forced herself to keep walking, crossing the street to the beach, then plodding through the deep dunes until she reached the hard-packed sand at the water's edge. She kicked off her shoes and, still clutching the letters, kept going. The cold water was a shock on her bare feet, but at least it told her she was still alive. That was better than the dead-inside feeling that had come over her when she'd realized what the letters meant — that her dad had tried to stay in touch, but her mother had prevented it.

The worst thing about making the discovery now was that there was nothing she could do about it. She couldn't scream at her mom over the betrayal. For all she knew it was even too late to find her father and make things right with him.

After she'd been walking for nearly an hour, she finally began to feel calmer. She turned slowly and headed back toward home, but when she was about to pass a bench in the park at the end of Main Street not far from Lila's, she decided what she needed most was a few more minutes alone to really think about her discovery. She had just enough money stuffed in her pocket for a cherry snow cone from Lila's. She bought one, and with that refreshing treat in hand, she sat on the bench and set the letters next to her, eyeing them with a mix of curiosity and dismay.

Eventually, she tossed the snow cone wrapper in the trash, then picked up the letters and untied the ribbon. It was a long time, though, before she could bring herself to open the first one, after making sure that she would be reading them in chronological order.

"Hi, Hannah Banana," she read, and found herself tearing up again at the nickname only her dad had ever used. "I don't know if or when you'll read this, but I just want you to know that I love you and miss you. Someday, when you're old enough to understand, I hope your mom will explain why I had to go away. I hope when you know the whole story, you'll forgive me. Love you. Dad."

There were only five letters in all, the first two written months apart right after he'd gone. The rest had been sent over a span of years. She'd been eighteen when the last one had been sent. The theme was always the same, that he loved her and hoped she'd forgive him.

Though there were no return addresses on any of them, Hannah studied the postmarks. She was stunned when she realized that most had been mailed from nearby cities on the mainland, cities she'd been in hundreds of times as a child and even a few times recently.

Tying the letters back together, she practically ran back to the inn, ignoring Gran for a second time as she raced inside shouting for Jeff.

"Mom, what on earth?" Kelsey said, coming out of the office with Jeff on her heels. "What's happened?"

"Can you find someone online?" she asked Jeff. "I mean, I know it's possible, but can *you* do it? I'd do it myself, but my hands are shaking and I can't even think straight."

"I can try," he said at once.

"Mom, what's going on?" Kelsey asked. "You look as if you've seen a ghost."

"In a way, that's exactly what's happened," she said, holding out the letters. "These are from your grandfather. Today's the first time I've ever seen them."

She heard a gasp then and turned to see Grandma Jenny grab onto a chair, her complexion ashen. Hannah stared at her in shock. "You knew about the letters?"

Kelsey went to her great-grandmother and helped her to a chair, scowling at Hannah. "Mom, not now!"

"When, if not now?" Hannah said, beyond being reasonable. "For years I thought my dad left and forgot all about me. Now I discover that there are letters that have been stuffed into a drawer for years."

Gran brushed off Kelsey's attempt to help her. "Did those letters tell you one single thing that your mother and I hadn't told you?" Gran demanded. "We told you over and over that your dad loved you, that his leaving had nothing to do with you."

"How can you say that? He was my father and he was gone. That had *everything* to do with me."

"Would it have helped to see a piece of paper with a few words on it?"

"Yes," Hannah said. "Yes!"

Gran sighed. "You don't know what you're talking about. It would have raised more questions than it answered. Next you would have wanted to know where he was, when he'd be back, why you couldn't see him or talk to him."

"Of course I would have wanted to know all that," she said.

Gran's jaw set stubbornly. "You were too young to understand any of the answers."

"What about later?" Hannah demanded heatedly. "Would I have been old enough at sixteen? Or when I graduated from high school? After college? When I got married? Last week?"

"Mom, stop it," Kelsey said. "None of this is Grandma Jenny's fault."

"She knew about the letters and she went along with keeping them from me."

"Your mother and I thought we were doing the right thing," Gran said, the lines in her face deepening with anguish. "We really did. After a while, when you stopped asking about your father, we were even more convinced that it had been the wise decision. You'd moved on with your life."

Jeff had listened to most of this in silence, but then he turned to Hannah. "What was your father's name? Not Matthews, right, because your mother took back her maiden name after she'd divorced your dad and she changed your name, as well?"

"His name was Clayton Dixon," Hannah said. "Do you think you can find him if he still lives in the area?"

"I already have," Jeff told her.

All three women stared at him in shock. Hannah felt as if the breath had been knocked out of her.

"You have? Why?" Kelsey asked.

"Luke came to me right before he left and asked if I'd do an online search. He never said who the person was. He just gave me a name. I found this Clayton Dixon in Clearwater Beach."

"So close," Hannah murmured, "my God, all these years and he's been right under my nose."

"And yet he never came looking for you," her grandmother said quietly. "Maybe before you cast blame on me or your mother, you should ask yourself about that.

Other than that pitiful handful of letters right there, what effort did your father make to settle things with you?"

"He probably thought I'd never forgiven him because . . ." Her voice faltered when she realized he'd never given her a phone number to call or an address where she might find him. Maybe Gran was right. Maybe he hadn't wanted to be found, hadn't wanted anything more than to be able to tell himself that he'd tried to keep in touch. Perhaps that had been enough to absolve him of guilt in his own eyes, if not Hannah's.

"Hannah, I'm sorry," Gran said. "It was complicated. Sometimes even your mother and I had a hard time making sense of it."

"Making sense of what?" Hannah asked. "Why did he leave?"

"That's not for me to say," her grandmother told her.

"But you know?"

She nodded.

"Then tell me," she pleaded.

"I think if Jeff has located him and he's so nearby, then you should see him for yourself. Let him tell you his side of it. That way you'll never question whether I've told you the whole truth or some version of it that suits me."

Hannah could see the sense of that, but she wanted to know now. Suddenly the importance of something that Jeff had said struck her. "Why was Luke looking for him? Had you told him about my father?" she asked her grandmother.

"No. Luke never mentioned him. Not to me."

Hannah turned to Jeff. "Did he tell you why he wanted to find him?"

"Not a word, just that it was important," Jeff replied.

"And you told Luke that you'd located my father before he left for Atlanta?"

Jeff nodded.

Hannah wondered if that had anything to do with Luke's decision to leave earlier that Friday morning than he'd originally planned. Had he gone to see her father en route to Atlanta? If so, why?

"I need to speak to Luke," she said, leaving them to go in search of her cell phone. It was ironic that something that had always been within reach was now missing when she needed it the most. She found it tossed in the drawer of her nightstand, but when she called Luke's number, it went straight to voice mail.

"Luke, call me when you get this, please," she said. "It's important. No, it's urgent!"

She tossed the phone back on the bed and paced around the perimeter of the room. The sensible side of her nature told her to wait for that call, not to do anything rash. If Luke had found her father, she needed to know what he'd learned before blundering into a situation she might not understand.

The need-to-know-now side of her overruled the sensible part.

Grabbing the cell phone and her car keys, she ran back down the steps.

"I'm going out," she called out to anyone in the vicinity.

"Hannah, wait!" her grandmother commanded. "You're not going anywhere."

"You can't stop me," she said.

"Fine, go," her grandmother said dryly. "You won't get far. The last ferry left an hour ago."

"Well, damn and hell," Hannah muttered in frustration.

"Watch your language," Gran said automatically.

"Sorry."

"I thought you were going to talk to Luke, anyway," Gran said.

"I couldn't reach him."

"Well, he'll check in before the night's out, I imagine. In the meantime, why don't we go inside and fix dinner for the two of us?

All the guests are settled down for the evening. Kelsey and Jeff left a few minutes ago to walk into town. They probably won't be back for hours. They said something about going to play bingo at the Catholic Church, just the way we used to do when you were little." She smiled hesitantly. "Do you remember that?"

Hannah had forgotten that half the town played bingo at the church or at the fire department or wherever else it was being played on any given evening of the week. These were Seaview social events as much as fund-raisers for various organizations. She'd won a few prizes, including a treasured doll which was still in her room.

"I remember," she said at last. "Maybe we should go with Jeff and Kelsey." The last thing she wanted to do was sit across the kitchen table from her grandmother and be forced to bite back all the questions on the tip of her tongue. Gran had already made it plain that she was through talking about Hannah's father, and that was the only thing Hannah wanted to discuss.

Disappointment spread across her grandmother's face. "You go if you want to. I'm not up to going out tonight."

The rare admission forced Hannah to drag herself out of her own misery to take a good look at Grandma Jenny. She did seem paler than usual. Instantly guilty, she said, "I'll stay here, but why don't I go in and fix something? You've been on your feet most of the day. I'll call you when it's ready."

Gran looked skeptical. "You're going to cook?"

"I don't know where you got the idea that I'm totally incompetent in the kitchen. Kelsey and I never starved."

"The way I hear it, she taught herself to cook, and before that the two of you survived on takeout."

"It was not that bad. Actually, I fix a fairly edible omelet and I think there are some of Merilee's biscuits left. How does that sound?"

"Filling," Gran responded with a smile. "And it's hard to talk with a mouthful of biscuit."

Hannah smiled back at her. "My thought exactly."

Somehow she'd manage to hold off asking all those questions about her father until she was with someone who might actually be willing to answer them.

Luke had two urgent messages from Seaview. The first was from a highly agitated Hannah, but it was the second one from

Jeff that was most disturbing. Jeff admitted he'd told Hannah about finding her father for Luke. That explained Hannah's message that had come in not two minutes earlier. He turned off his cell phone and tried to decide what to do. He could call Jeff and try to find out what was going on down there, or he could just call Hannah and face the music. She hadn't sounded happy.

There was also a third choice, of course. He could ignore both calls and deal with the whole situation when he got back to Seaview. By then, perhaps he would have more news. His attempt to speak to Clayton Dixon on Friday had been fruitless. No one had been home at the address Jeff had given him. A neighbor said the Dixons were away for a few days but expected back on Sunday. With luck they would be there when Luke drove back from Atlanta on Monday morning. Yep, he liked that option the best. He'd already had his fill of messy confrontations since arriving in Atlanta.

Brad had been home when he'd arrived late Friday afternoon to pick up Gracie and Nate. This time he refused to back down when Luke told him to get out of his face.

"We need to have this out," Brad said. "Not for me or you or even for Lisa, but for the kids. This house can't be a battleground every time you turn up."

"It doesn't have to be," Luke told him. "You just need to clear out when I'm expected. I'll be civil to Lisa, because she's the mother of my children, but I don't owe you a damn thing."

"But we were —"

"Don't say it," Luke said. "Maybe we were friends at one time, but that didn't stop you from hooking up with my wife while I was in Iraq. Maybe I can even understand that from her point of view. She was furious with me. You were handy. Who better to have an affair with and then throw it in my face? But what had I ever done to you, Brad?"

Brad paled. "Nothing," he admitted. "There's no excuse for what happened. And, honestly, I'm sorrier than you'll ever know, but it's too late to turn back. I love her. And I'll be good to her and to Nate and Gracie."

"Just as long as you remember that I'm their father," Luke said tersely. "That will never change, no matter where I'm living."

Brad regarded him with surprise. "You're not staying in Atlanta? I thought since you rented an apartment that meant you intended to come back here."

"No, that apartment is so Nate and Gracie have a place to stay with me whenever I come to town. I'm going to be living in Seaview and going into practice there."

"And *our* practice? What do you intend to do about that?"

"My attorney knows my intentions. He'll be in touch."

"I'll be more than fair," Brad said. "I owe you that."

"And a hell of a lot more, when it comes down to it," Luke said. Rather than belaboring the conversation another second, he shouted upstairs. "Nate, Gracie, let's go."

The kids had thundered down the stairs so quickly, he couldn't help wondering if they'd been eavesdropping, but neither of them mentioned anything about the confrontation as they drove away. Gracie had been a little quieter than usual during dinner, but Nate had filled the silences with nonstop chatter about school and signing up for baseball.

Now, as Luke sat in front of the TV with the sound on mute, Gracie came into the living room and crawled onto the sofa beside him.

"Can I ask you something?" Her expression was worried.

"You can always ask me anything," he told her.

"If you're living in Seaview, will you forget

about us?"

"Never," he said at once. "Not in a hundred million years!"

"Do you promise?"

"Of course I promise. You and Nate will be coming down there every chance you get and I'll be up here at least once a month."

"Mom says you'll get busy like you did before and we'll never see you."

"Well, Mom is wrong about that," he assured her, tamping down his annoyance with Lisa for planting this latest fear in Gracie's mind. "I know that I used to spend a lot of time at work before I went away, but that's all changed now. I have my priorities in order."

Gracie's brow knit in a frown. "What does that mean?"

"It means that nothing is more important to me than spending time with you and your brother. Nothing!"

"Then why can't you live here?" she asked wistfully. "Like before."

Luke tried to think of a way to explain it that Gracie could understand. "Do you remember what you used to tell me about going to the library?"

She frowned. "That I liked it because it was so quiet and peaceful?"

"Exactly," Luke said. "That's how I feel in

Seaview. It was my home for a long, long time, and I feel better there, like it's where I belong. And Doc is getting older, so he needs someone to help him at the clinic."

"But Nate and me need you here," Gracie protested. "You said we were important, not Doc."

"And you *are* important. If you ever need me — really, really need me — I will be here in a heartbeat. As it is, I'll be here so much, you'll probably get sick of me." He nudged her gently in the ribs. "You'll have to give me your undivided attention, even when you'd rather be hanging out with your friends, even when you're old enough to date and would rather be with a boy."

She giggled then. "Daddy, it's going to be years and years before I'm old enough to date."

Luke grinned at her. "I'm thinking thirty would be a good age."

To his relief, she giggled again. "You're being silly," she accused.

"I am," he agreed. "But I am serious about one thing. I love you, Gracie, and that will never, ever change. Okay? Don't ever let anything or anyone convince you otherwise."

She held his gaze for a long time, then nodded. "Okay. Do I have to go back to bed or can I stay here with you for a while?"

"You can stay here," he said. "Close your eyes, though. It's way past your bedtime."

She yawned widely and leaned against him. She'd taken a bath using some kind of strawberry-scented soap. It brought back a hundred memories of getting soaked from head to toe as she splashed in the tub pretending to swim. At four and beyond, she'd always had half a dozen toys in the water with her, including a swim ring that he'd bought her on a trip to the beach. She'd come out of the water with her cheeks rosy, her skin shiny with moisture, and he'd wrap her in a towel. As a toddler she'd invariably pulled free and run through the house, naked as a jaybird until he or Lisa caught up with her.

There had been such an innocent joy about her then. He wanted that for her again, but maybe it wasn't possible. Maybe, like too many children of divorce, she'd been forced to grow up too soon, to try to understand things that were too complicated for a ten-year-old.

That made him think about Hannah and how she must have felt all those years ago. At least Gracie and Nate still had him in their lives, but she'd been abandoned with very little explanation. Maybe it was years too late for those explanations, but he wanted them for her. And Monday, he intended to get them.

Until then, he wasn't ready to have the conversation that he knew from her messages she wanted to have. He wanted to give her answers when they spoke, not to have an argument about his interference in her life.

21

In the commotion stirred up by the discovery that her father was living nearby, Hannah had forgotten all about her test results. When the call came in from Dr. Blake's office, it was a shock. As she waited for him to come on the line, her palms began to sweat. She clutched the phone in a death grip, and a familiar knot formed in her stomach.

"Good news," he said as soon as he picked up. "Everything's clear, Hannah. None of the tests showed any trace of cancer."

Relief made her knees weak. She sank onto a chair at the kitchen table, aware of the concerned glances from Gran and Kelsey.

"You're sure?"

"A hundred percent sure," he told her. "I'll want to see you again in three months, though. No postponing again, okay? Will you be back in New York by then?"

She hesitated. "I'm not sure about that, to be honest. Things here are a bit more complicated than I'd expected, but I will come there for the tests. I promise you that."

"I'll hold you to it," he said. "Congratulations, Hannah! Enjoy yourself."

He sounded as if three months were a worry-free eternity, when in truth she would have a few days, maybe a few weeks before anxiety would start nagging at her again. Still, days or weeks were better than nothing. She needed to find a way to enjoy that time — to live each day to the fullest — and shove cancer out of her mind.

"Thanks, Dr. Blake. I'll see you in three months."

Slowly, she put the receiver back on the hook.

"You're okay?" Kelsey asked, studying her with concern.

Hannah forced a smile. "For now," she confirmed.

"Oh, Mom, that's wonderful," Kelsey said, smothering her with a hug.

"It's great news," Gran said. "We should celebrate. When Luke gets back tonight, let's have dinner at The Fish Tale."

"Sounds good," Hannah agreed. "And I hear that Lesley Ann finally had the baby last week and has been bringing him in every evening for a few minutes to show him off. We should run out and buy a present."

Kelsey's eyes lit up. "Absolutely. Let's do that now, Mom."

Hannah regarded her curiously. "It won't bother you to be looking at baby things?"

"No, it'll be fun," Kelsey said, as if the thought of giving her own baby up for adoption had never once crossed her mind.

"Did I miss something? Are you and Jeff going to keep your baby?" she asked.

Kelsey flushed but nodded. "We saw the baby on a sonogram last week and I knew then that adoption was out of the question. There was this whole little person that Jeff and I created right there inside me. It was awesome. I think I would have made the decision to keep the baby right then even if Jeff hadn't practically passed out with excitement." She hesitated, then added, "It's a girl." She literally glowed when she told them. "She's still so tiny, but she's perfect, at least that's what the doctor said." Her hand rested protectively on her stomach as she spoke.

Gran clapped her hands together. "Another Matthews girl! Won't that be wonderful?"

Hannah's eyes filled with tears. "It will be, won't it?" She wanted to ask if it would, indeed, be a Matthews girl or if it would be a Hampton, but she managed to silence the question. One step at a time, she told herself. Kelsey and Jeff were on the same page about keeping their daughter and that was huge. For now, it would have to be enough. The question of marriage could wait for a while longer.

"I think I'll call Jack and tell him to hold a table for us," Gran said. "What time do you think Luke will get here?"

"I imagine he's going to try to make the five o'clock ferry," Hannah said. At least if he wasn't held up trying to make contact with her dad. She was still annoyed that he hadn't returned her call. She'd had to content herself with knowing that he'd be back today and that she'd have her answers then.

"I'll make the reservation for seven, so he'll have time to rest a little," Gran said, then gave her a pointed look. "And so you can ask him all those questions that are plaguing you."

"Thanks, Gran."

"I just hope he has answers you want to hear," Gran added direly. "I don't want to see your heart broken all over again."

Hannah bristled, even though she had the same concern herself. "I'm ready to handle just about anything."

She said it emphatically, but down deep she couldn't help wondering if it was true. She wanted a happy ending and, as life had already taught her, sometimes those were few and far between.

On Monday, Luke pulled his rental car into the driveway behind a ten-year-old car with fading paint and a dented back fender. The house was modest, but well kept with a small patch of carefully tended lawn.

As he rang the doorbell, Luke wasn't sure what he was expecting, but when the door was opened by a slim, fit-looking man in his mid-to-late thirties, wearing shorts and a golf shirt, it took him aback.

"Mr. Dixon? Clayton Dixon?"

"I'm Clay Dixon," the man said. "My Dad's Clayton."

Of course, Luke thought. This was the child he'd had with the other woman. This was Hannah's half brother. He thought he could see a bit of a resemblance around the eyes and in the color of the hair. He couldn't help wondering whether Hannah would be shocked by that or pleased.

"Can I help you?" Clay asked, regarding him with friendly curiosity.

"Sorry for staring," Luke said. "You

remind me of someone. Does your father live here?"

"He does. He went to the store for groceries. We've been away for a few days."

"I'm Luke Stevens, from Seaview Key."

The man's eyes brightened perceptibly. "Really? Did you know my dad when he lived there? He talks about it all the time, but for some reason we've never managed to make the trip over there. Mentioning Seaview upsets my mother," he confided.

Luke wondered how much this man knew about his father's past. It wasn't up to him to reveal it, though, so he settled for asking, "Any idea why that might be?"

"Something about a relationship from Dad's past," he said with a shrug. "You know how women can be. My own wife got all weird when we went to my high school reunion and ran into a couple of my old girlfriends. Hadn't seen them in years, but that didn't matter to her. Needless to say, it was the only reunion we ever attended."

Luke regarded him sympathetically. "I can imagine. Would you mind if I waited for your father?"

"No, of course not. Come on in. Like I said, he should be here any minute."

"What about your mother? Is she around?"

"No, we dropped her off at church. She has a ladies group that meets every Monday morning. I'm just waiting for Dad to get back with the groceries and my car. I don't like him driving that old rattletrap of his any more than he needs to. I had a few chores to do for them here, so I told him to take mine. You want a glass of tea or something? Mom always keeps a pitcher in the fridge."

"Sure," Luke said.

"Follow me. We might as well sit on the patio and wait. Around here it pays to enjoy the outdoors when you can. The humidity and heat will get oppressive soon enough."

"Don't let me keep you from your chores," Luke told him.

"No problem. I finished a while ago." Clay settled onto a chair beside the small pool and set his tea on an old aluminum table with peeling paint. "So, tell me about Seaview. You must like it there. Dad says in his time there most young people didn't stick around."

"He's right about that. Actually I'm just in the process of moving back. I grew up there, then went off to college, married, you know how it goes. Now I'm getting divorced and suddenly discovered that my roots really are in Seaview." He barely kept himself from uttering an invitation to visit. That was going to be up to Hannah's father.

"Hey, Clay, whose car is that in the driveway?" a man yelled, just as a door slammed. "There are more bags of groceries in the car. Can you give me a hand?"

"That's Dad," Clay said unnecessarily. "I'll send him out here."

"Thanks."

A few minutes later, a man emerged, his expression wary. His gray hair was still thick, and like his son, he was slim and fit.

"Clay tells me you're Luke Stevens," he said as he crossed the patio and held out his hand. "I know that name."

"I grew up on Seaview," Luke said quietly. "I'm a friend of Hannah's."

The color drained out of the man's face, leaving his complexion ashen. He sat down hard. "I see." Eventually he met Luke's gaze. "How is she?"

"She'd be a whole lot better if you'd kept in touch, maybe let her know that you still care about her," Luke said harshly.

"I *did* keep in touch," Clayton said defensively, then sighed. "I wrote a few times over the years, just so she'd know I was thinking of her."

"You couldn't have called?" Luke asked, unable to keep the judgmental, condemning note out of his voice. "Or stopped by? You're not living on the other side of the country, you know. It's going to come as a shock to her that you've been this close all along."

"It was better this way," the older man said. "You don't know how it was."

"Tell me," Luke suggested, just as Clay called out from the kitchen.

"Dad, I'm taking off now."

"Okay, son." He looked at Luke. "Does Hannah know you're here?"

Luke thought she might, but he couldn't say that with certainty, so he shook his head. "I don't think so. I'm not even sure if she knows you're still alive. She certainly doesn't know about this other family of yours. I gather Clay doesn't know he has a half sister, either."

"No," he admitted. "Believe me, I know how that sounds, but it was for the best. My wife, Clay's mother, is not an easy woman. Years ago, when she got pregnant, she made threats. She wanted me or money. She figured I had plenty because the inn was successful. She's . . ." He hesitated, then said, "She's not stable. For years now she's struggled with depression. I was afraid for our child and what she might do to destroy my family."

Luke couldn't help drawing comparisons

with how blasé Brad had been about destroying Luke's family. "So you decided to split the difference and just let her destroy your family," he said scathingly.

"Something like that," Clayton Dixon agreed solemnly. "Hannah's mother and I talked about it. We considered fighting her, but I knew how important the inn was to her and to Jenny, and I couldn't ask them to risk it to borrow the money to pay this woman off. I was the one who'd created the whole mess, so it was up to me to solve it. And there was the baby to consider. Lucy simply wasn't up to raising a child. I suppose I could have fought for custody and probably won, but I couldn't ask Maggie to raise another woman's child. I'd already asked too much of her. I'd begged her for forgiveness one too many times. We divorced and I remarried."

"And forgot all about the broken-hearted child you'd left behind," Luke accused. "How did Hannah fit into this scenario? Or did you consider her at all?"

"Of course we did. The inn was her legacy. Do you think it was easy for me to walk away, trade one child for another? Believe me, it wasn't. There's a hole in my heart where that child belongs. I thought about her on every birthday, every Christmas, on her graduation day."

"But you did nothing to get in touch. How do you think that made her feel?"

"It was better than the hell she would have gone through if my wife had discovered we were having any contact. Lucy's a hard woman. She had a tough life before we met. I guess when she got pregnant, she saw her chance for something better and she took it. She saw the inn as her ticket to a better future. It was worth a fortune, even back then."

"Didn't she know it wasn't yours?"

"I told her," Clayton said. "But like I said, she wasn't rational. In the end, I saw how messy it was going to get and I couldn't put my family through the humiliation. They had to go on living in that town and it would have been years before anyone in Seaview let them forget about the scandal. Maggie made me see that when she showed me the door."

"So, this was all altruistic on your part?"

"Hardly," he admitted. "This was Maggie's decision as much as mine. She'd had enough and I could hardly blame her."

"What about now? Do you still think walking away was your only choice, or would you do things differently?"

"I've thought about that through the

years," Clayton said. "But honestly, I don't see that I could have."

"And Hannah? Haven't you wanted to see her, to know how she is, to know what's going on in her life?"

"I haven't earned the right to any of that," he said with what sounded like genuine sorrow.

"What if she wants to see you? Will you allow her to come? Or meet her elsewhere? What if she wants to know her half brother?"

Clayton closed his eyes, his expression weary. "I would sell my soul for that," he said. "I would, but I don't think it would have the happy ending she probably wants. Clay, he might be okay with it. He's a friendly, easygoing guy. His wife's the same way. But *my* wife? She'd make it hell on all of us. She's better now, takes her medications the way she's supposed to, and to tell you the truth we've made a decent life for ourselves, better than I had any right to expect, given how it started. That doesn't mean she can handle the upset of having my daughter come into our lives."

Luke tried to muster an ounce of sympathy for him, but couldn't. "I know Hannah," he said slowly. "She's not going to let that stop her. You should probably prepare yourself and your son — even your wife, for that matter — for the fallout."

Despite Luke's warning and his own obvious misgivings, Clayton nodded, a glimmer of hope in his eyes. Maybe he was happy about the likelihood that the decision would be taken out of his hands, just as Maggie had taken the final choice about their divorce away from him.

"You'll tell me ahead of time if she's coming?" he asked.

"I will if I know about it," Luke promised. "Hannah tends to be independent. There's no telling what she might do or when. I'll do my best, though."

"Thanks. I'll walk you out."

"It's okay. I can find my own way."

Outside, he drew in a deep, cleansing breath. In one way he didn't envy Clayton Dixon the potential disaster that lay ahead. In another, he thought the man would only be getting what was coming to him.

He also saw with vivid clarity what the outcome might have been if he'd followed his first selfish instinct and stayed away from Atlanta and his kids forever. Luckily he'd known practically from the beginning that he couldn't have lived with himself if he'd done that. Not only would it have affected Nate and Gracie as Clayton Dixon's abandonment had affected Hannah, but he would have wound up spending the rest of his life filled with regret and loss.

Hannah was waiting on the porch when Luke arrived. The others were all inside resting before their planned celebration, except for Jeff, who'd gone out and bought a fancy crib, which he was now struggling to put together as a surprise for Kelsey. He was so thrilled about their decision to keep the baby, he told Hannah he simply couldn't wait.

"I know it's too soon, but as you can see furniture assembly isn't my strong suit. This could take months," he'd said with a self-deprecating grin.

Hannah had been forced to leave the room to keep from chuckling at his inept handling of a screwdriver and muttered curses as he tried to interpret the instructions. Thankfully Luke would be here soon to help him finish. Otherwise that crib would be almost certain to collapse the first time they put the baby in it.

Now, as she watched Luke emerge from the car, her heart did a little stutter-step, her annoyance forgotten.

"Welcome back," she called. "How was your trip?"

"Interesting," he said, his expression wary

as he came up the steps. He leaned down to kiss her, lingering over it until heat stirred inside her. "How are things here?"

"Interesting," she said, mimicking him. "We're going to The Fish Tale tonight for a celebration."

"Oh? What's the occasion?"

"My cancer results came back," she said. "I'm still okay."

Luke's eyes brightened and Hannah thought she detected a hint of relief in his expression. "That is definitely worth celebrating. What time are we going?"

"Gran made a reservation for seven."

"Perfect. That'll give me time to run inside, shower and change."

He would have walked right into the house then and there, leaving Hannah frustrated and curious, but she halted him with a command. "Sit, Luke. We need to talk."

He looked vaguely guilty, which just proved he had things to hide. Still, he did sit down.

"Sure," he said. "What's up?"

"As if you didn't know. Did you see my father or not?"

"I did," he admitted without hesitation. "But I think we should talk about it later. There's a lot to absorb and I think it'll go down better on a full stomach."

Hannah considered the suggestion. Though her impatience for answers argued against waiting one more minute, there really wasn't much time before their dinner reservation. Maybe waiting would be best.

"Okay, but the minute we get home, we talk."

"Absolutely. Now, let me go inside and get ready. I'll be back down in a flash."

Again, he was on his way to the door when she stopped him. "Luke, just tell me one thing. Is he okay?"

"Other than being shocked that I'd found him, yes, he's fine."

"Did he ever miss me, even a little bit?" she asked, unable to keep the wistful note out of her voice.

"Every day," Luke said emphatically.

"Really?"

"That's what he said, and I believed him."

A single tear slid down her cheek. "Thanks for telling me that."

It wasn't much, but it was more than she'd dared to hope and certainly enough to carry her through a couple of hours until Luke could tell her the rest.

Luke kept a close eye on Hannah all through their celebratory dinner. For a woman who'd just been given a clean bill of health, she seemed oddly subdued. He knew that was because of this whole situation with Clayton Dixon. Discovering that the father who'd abandoned her had lived nearby all these years had to have thrown her for a loop. He still had no idea how she'd found out, but it didn't surprise him that she had. Jeff might have inadvertently revealed something about the search Luke had asked him to conduct. Or maybe Grandma Jenny had suddenly come clean after all these years. She might not have known precisely where her former son-in-law was living, but she knew enough, including the details about why he'd left. Luke noted that she was as subdued as Hannah all through dinner. Only Kelsey and Jeff seemed oblivious to the undercurrents.

When they excused themselves along with Grandma Jenny to take a present to Lesley Ann's new son, Luke turned to Hannah. "Something changed with those two? Kelsey and Jeff, I mean."

"They've decided to keep the baby," she told him, then grinned. "And it's a girl."

"You looked pleased."

"How could I not be? Kelsey's happier than I've ever seen her. I'd like to see a ring on her finger, but I just keep hoping that will come in time."

"Oh, I think you can count on that," Luke said. "I told you that Jeff is determined to make it happen, and he seems to understand your daughter well enough to know not to push her."

"By the way, I think you're going to be enlisted to help him put a crib together. He bought it as a surprise for Kelsey, but I watched him earlier. That crib doesn't stand a chance without some expert intervention."

"No problem. I'll volunteer tomorrow." He studied her. "I probably shouldn't take you away from your own party, but you don't seem to be having a very good time, anyway. Want to take a walk so we can talk?"

She was on her feet at once. "I thought you'd never ask. Let me just say good-night to everyone. I'll meet you outside."

"Keep them distracted," he said. "I'll try to pay the bill before Grandma Jenny can get to it."

While he took care of that, he saw Hannah carrying on over Lesley Ann's baby boy. Then she gave her grandmother, her daughter and Jeff quick hugs and headed his way. He couldn't seem to stop himself from dropping a quick kiss on her knitted brow. "Stop worrying. The news isn't that bad."

"I imagine that depends on your perspective. You weren't the one left behind."

They strolled down Main Street to the beach, then walked over the dunes to the hard-packed sand in silence. Luke almost hated to break it, but he knew this conversation couldn't be put off forever.

"How did you find out about your dad being close by, anyway?" he asked finally. "Did Jeff spill the beans?"

"No, he didn't even realize that's who you'd had him look for. Actually, when I was cleaning out my mother's room, I found some unopened letters addressed to me. They were all postmarked nearby."

Luke frowned at that. "You'd never seen them before?"

She shook her head. "Mom obviously kept them from me."

"That fits with what your dad said. He said he had tried to stay in touch for a while."

"But why didn't he call? Hearing his voice would have been so much better." Her gaze narrowed. "Or did he try that and no one would let him talk to me?"

"No, he didn't call."

Hannah sighed. "I guess I just want to blame someone for keeping us apart. How did you find out about all this, anyway? What made you go looking for my father?"

"It was something Doc said, so I asked Jeff to see if he could locate him."

"Why didn't you tell me then?"

"I was being protective. I wanted to know more before I filled you in. I'm sorry if that was the wrong way to handle it. I know this is about people keeping secrets from you and now I'm one of them."

"No, I get why you did it," she conceded. "Tell me what you found out."

Luke explained as much as he knew about what had happened all those years ago and the decisions that her father and mother had made. "He honestly believes they did the right thing."

Hannah clearly didn't agree. Her eyes sparked with real anger. "That's ridiculous! Nobody walks away from a wife and child he claims to love to keep from borrowing money against a stupid piece of property. What kind of woman puts a man she supposedly loves into that position, anyway? Did you meet her?"

Luke shook his head. "Your father says she's a hard woman who had a tough life before they met. I gather she had some issues with depression, too, that made him worry about what might happen to their child."

Her expression mystified, she asked, "How

could my father love someone who's mean enough to make threats and destroy a family? Do you think he does?"

"He's still with her," Luke said. "That's all I know."

"But why? I don't understand."

"Maybe losing one family was enough. Maybe he wasn't willing to lose another one. He says they've had a good life. You can ask him about all of that, if you decide to see him. And don't forget about your mother's role. I gather she'd finally had enough. I think she was the one who made the final decision that pushed him into leaving."

Pondering that, Hannah led the way back up to the edge of the road, then sat down on a bench under some palm trees that were rustling in the evening breeze. "I still can't believe I have a half brother. What was he like?"

"He seems like a nice-enough guy. He doesn't know any of this. In fact, all he knew about Seaview was that mentioning it upset his mother."

"Does he have children? Does Kelsey have cousins?"

"I don't know. We never discussed that." He studied her. "Any idea what you're going to do?"

"A part of me wants to go there right this second and rant and rave and create a major scene," she confessed ruefully, then added with more passion, "I'd even like to tear that awful woman's hair out."

Luke grinned. "Then isn't it a good thing that there's not another ferry until morning?"

"Probably, but venting could be good," she replied, then sighed. "Another part of me wants all of this to just go away. Years ago, it would have meant the world to me to see my dad again, but now? Maybe I should just let it go. Leave him to his life. Forget about having a half brother. What do you think I should do?"

"It's not really up to me. I will ask you this, though — can you really do that? Can you relock the box now that you've opened it?"

"I honestly don't know," she told him. "I wonder if I would have come down here or stayed so long if I'd had any idea how things would turn out."

"Hey, don't say that. Then we might not have hooked up," Luke reminded her. "I wouldn't have wanted to miss this."

She leaned against him, met his gaze, then smiled slowly, comfortable with the way their relationship was developing, even if it scared her. “Me, neither. Why don’t we drop all this for tonight and go home?”

He stood up and held out his hand. “Now, that sounds like a stellar idea. Think we can sneak up to my room without getting caught?”

Hannah stood on tiptoe and pressed a very promising kiss against his lips. “I’m counting on it. I missed being in your bed and in your arms the past few nights.”

He grinned at that. “Nice to know I’ve left a memorable impression.”

“Don’t gloat. It’s unseemly.”

Luke laughed. “Unseemly? Just stating a fact, darlin’.”

Hannah narrowed her gaze. “I haven’t heard you mention missing me. Am I not as memorable as you are?”

“You are, without question, the most memorable woman I’ve ever been with,” he replied solemnly.

“And how many would that be? Just in the interest of clarification, of course.”

“Oh, no, you are not catching me in that trap. And why are we standing here discussing sex, when we could be home doing it?”

Hannah considered the question. “Not a single reason I can think of. Want to race me home?”

“You’re only suggesting that because I still

have a bum knee," he accused.

"I'm suggesting it because I suddenly want to hurry," she countered. "Step it up, mister. That knee is getting better every day. You can't use that as an excuse when I beat you."

He caught her hand and spun her around. "Have I mentioned that I love you for not ever letting me off the hook?"

"I'll keep that in mind," she said lightly.

While she was still standing there, he winked and took off at a surprisingly brisk clip. She stared after him for a heartbeat.

"You cheating scoundrel," she shouted, and then she ran, though there wasn't a chance in the world she'd ever catch him. Then, again, maybe it didn't matter, because she knew he'd be waiting for her.

22

Hannah sat at the kitchen table in the morning mulling over everything she'd learned from Luke about her father and his new family. Did she really want to get involved in that drama after all this time? The little girl inside who still yearned for her dad screamed yes. The mature adult who'd managed all these years without him was less certain.

Did she want to see him because she genuinely still loved him and wanted to reconnect? Or did she, as she'd said last night, merely want to heap guilt on him and make him understand just how deeply he'd hurt her? Was this about revenge or reconciliation? Could she ever look at things from his perspective and understand the decision he'd made? Or would that only deepen the resentment she'd always felt toward the inn and Seaview Key? It was ironic that she'd always blamed the inn for driving him away, only to discover that it had, but not in the way she'd imagined. In his own way, he'd loved it enough to protect it. It was going to require a lot more thought before she could decide what happened next.

She was still pondering the enormity of it all when Grandma Jenny came into the kitchen. She made her own cup of tea, then sat down opposite Hannah.

"I thought you'd be happier having Luke back here again," Grandma Jenny observed. "The two of you looked pretty intense last night and here you are this morning looking as if you didn't sleep a wink."

Hannah flushed. There hadn't been a lot of sleeping going on last night, but she could hardly explain that. If Gran hadn't figured out that she'd been sleeping in Luke's bed for a while now, then Hannah wasn't going to tell her. "I just have a lot on my mind."

"Such as? Does this have something to do with your father? Did Luke see him?"

Hannah nodded. "Why didn't you and mom tell me what happened back then? I deserved to know."

"I've already explained that," Gran said impatiently. "You were too young."

"But later, you could have told me it was all some crazy, misguided attempt to keep the inn in the family. Was that what you meant when you told me how much he'd loved this place?"

Gran frowned then. "Is that what Clayton's saying?" She waved it off. "Nonsense. The inn was never in any real danger. That awful woman couldn't have gotten her hands on it. It was in my name, not Clayton's. She made her threats, that's true enough, but they were idle threats. What she really wanted was money."

"But if the inn was in no danger, then why did he give in to her demands? Luke said something about her suffering with depression, so he was worried about the baby she was carrying."

"So he said at the time. If you're asking for my opinion, I think that was the crux of it. She was carrying his child and your father had an honorable streak that made him want to do the right thing."

Hannah still didn't understand. "How was it more right to go with her than to stay here with us? If her mental health was that precarious, he could have fought her for custody."

Gran looked momentarily taken aback. "Your mother would never have stood for that and he knew it. That's exactly why he focused on the inn. The threat she'd made gave him the excuse he needed to run off with his floozy. At the same time, it helped him save face with your mother. She could tell herself that it wasn't about him leaving her at all, but saving our heritage. I know you probably don't want to hear this, but your father — for all of his decency and kindness, for all that he adored you — was a weak man. A foolish one, too. He honestly thought he could walk away and that everyone would somehow believe he was doing the right thing by all of them. He didn't want to turn anyone against him. I think he was taken aback when your mother told him she wanted him out of her life — and yours — for good."

"Mom told him that?" She couldn't imagine the kind of strength that must have taken. Unlike Hannah's eagerness to be rid of her own husband after she'd tired of his on-again, off-again commitment to their marriage, she'd always believed that her mother had remained wildly in love with her father. Had that been true? Now, she couldn't be sure.

Grandma Jenny nodded. "She loved him, but she'd had enough, you see. This hadn't been his first affair and it wasn't likely to be his last. I was never more proud of her than I was that day, when she sat right here in this kitchen and told him that once he walked out the door, it was over for good. There would be no turning back, no forgiveness."

"I had no idea," Hannah murmured.

"Of course not. She didn't want you to know. Just because she was through with him, she didn't want you to hate him. She didn't even hate him herself. She simply loved her self-respect more. And she wanted you to be able to hold on to the good memories. I suppose in a way, by cutting him out of your life at that point, she thought she was protecting you from ever finding out about his flaws."

"So, knowing all this now, what should I do?" Hannah asked.

Gran gave her a sympathetic look. "Your decision. You're an adult now. You can meet your father on your own terms, establish whatever kind of relationship you want with him." She hesitated, then added, "And you do have a half brother. If it were me, I think I'd want to meet him, at least."

"I do," Hannah said. "Almost as much as I want to see my father again. After all, my half brother is as much of a victim of all this as I am. From what Luke said, the story was kept from him, too."

"Then you'll go to see them? Or invite

them here?"

Hannah considered both scenarios, but neither seemed entirely right. There was her father's wife — her stepmother, technically — to be considered if they met in his home. Hannah wasn't anxious to cross paths with her. Here on Seaview, where she'd feel comfortable, there would be plenty of baggage for her father to face. "Neutral turf, I think," she said at last. "Maybe a restaurant on the mainland."

Gran looked dismayed. "In public?"

Hannah shrugged. "It's not as if this is going to be some tearful, dramatic reunion or an out-of-control shouting match."

"You sure about that?"

She shook her head. The truth was, she wasn't sure about anything at all when it came to her father, even whether he'd earned the respect that came along with that title.

Luke called Doc first thing in the morning after his return to Seaview. "When you have some time, I'm ready to sit down and talk about joining the clinic," he told him.

"Lunch at The Fish Tale," Doc said eagerly. "I'm buying."

"Does noon work for you?"

"Make it half past. I never get the last of

the morning patients out the door on time."

"Then I'll see you at twelve-thirty," Luke said. "Thanks, Doc."

He hung up his cell phone just as Hannah came outside. She studied him quizzically. "Why were you talking to Doc?"

"I was setting up a meeting. We're going to finalize our plans for me to join him at the clinic."

"Really?"

"That can't be a surprise to you. I've been talking about it for a while now."

She shrugged. "I suppose I thought you'd come to your senses. After living in Atlanta, how can you be happy here?"

"The more relevant question is how did I ever manage to be happy in Atlanta?"

She frowned. "Come on, Luke. You were married, you had two great kids and you had a thriving medical practice in a major metropolitan area. What's not to like about that?"

"I think it's pretty evident that my marriage wasn't all that solid and satisfying for either one of us. I was successful in my medical practice, but I wasn't really happy with it. And I was so busy I hardly had any time at all with my kids. I finally feel as if I'll be able to enjoy them now, even if we are separated some of the time."

"A lot of the time," Hannah corrected.

"Not compared to the separations that happened even when we were living under the same roof," he insisted. "This is a fresh start for me, Hannah. I'll finally have a real balance in my life. The slower pace will allow that. I'll be able to have real quality time with my kids, when I visit Atlanta or when they come here. I'll be able to practice the kind of medicine that can really make a difference." He regarded her speculatively and threw out a thought that had been coming to mind more and more frequently. "I'd have time to devote to a marriage now, too."

"Have you mentioned that to Lisa?" she asked irritably.

"She's not the one I'm interested in marrying."

She gave him a wary look. "What are you suggesting?"

"Nothing right this second," he said, backing down at the scared tone in her voice. Maybe he was rushing ahead too fast for her. "I'm just putting that out there, planting the seed, so to speak. Maybe it's something we could start considering."

"We?"

He chuckled at her stunned expression. "Yes, as in you and me."

"Luke, I can't live here," she protested.

"Can't or won't?"

"I don't want to," she said emphatically. "There's nothing for me here, except years of resentment and bitterness. A few weeks can't wipe away all the bad memories."

"Come on, Hannah! What about your grandmother? She's here. Kelsey and Jeff seem determined to settle here. Your grandchild is on the way. And, of course, there's me. I ought to sweeten the pot just a little, or have I gotten that all wrong?"

The question seemed to fluster her. "No, of course, you matter. A lot."

"I sense a *but* in there," he said. "Are you saying I'm not important enough for you to even consider moving back here?"

"It's not that," she protested. "You are important. The past few weeks have been amazing. I haven't felt this way in years. To be honest, I'm not sure I've ever felt this way."

"What way?"

"Loved. Cherished. Desired."

"And you are all of those things," he told her. "And I think you feel the same way about me."

"I do," she admitted. "But I can't."

"Can't? Why the hell not?" he asked, just not getting it. She sounded so determined to throw ice on the whole idea of marriage, but so far she hadn't said anything that made sense.

She gave him an impatient look. "I have cancer, Luke. I have to stay focused on that fight."

"Which means you can't have a relationship?" he asked incredulously. "Someone who can fight with you? You will beat this, Hannah. I believe that."

"You don't know that. I could *die,* Luke. There's not a day of my life now that I don't think about that."

"I could die, too," he said reasonably. "None of us have guarantees before we get married or get involved with someone." He sought more impassioned words to convince her. "So what if we only have a few months or a few years together? Isn't that better, having that time and living every second of it, than denying ourselves all of it, because fate might not let it last long enough? Come on, Hannah, if people worried about what fate *might* have in store, they'd never do anything, never love anyone."

He could tell she wanted to believe him, wanted to take that leap of faith with him, but he could also see that she wasn't quite ready to do it. He crossed to where she was sitting on the edge of her chair, looking as if she wanted to make a break for someplace safe, someplace where there were no hard choices to be made. He gathered her up and kissed her as if there truly were no tomorrow.

"I want that," he said. "I want it today and tomorrow and for however many days there might be. Just think about that, okay? That's all I'm asking."

She returned his gaze, her expression vaguely dazed. "Okay," she said, touching a finger to her lips.

Luke winked. "I'll see you later. I'm off to meet Doc."

And maybe after he'd settled that part of his future, he'd stop at the island's fancy new jewelry store and see if he could find just the right ring to seal that part of his future, too. Maybe if he had something concrete to show Hannah, proof that his intentions were serious — cancer or no cancer — she'd find a way to overcome her fears and give them a chance.

"Come with me," Jeff said, dragging Kelsey away from her desk in the office where she was noting several new reservations.

"Hey, I'm in the middle of doing something," she protested. "Do you realize we're booked up through the end of April? Isn't that amazing? And reservations are coming in for May and June, too."

"That's great," Jeff said with enthusiasm. "But that's not more important than what I have to show you. Stop fussing and just come. It'll take five minutes, more if you decide to reward me."

"Reward you?"

He grinned. "The surprise is that good," he assured her as he led the way upstairs.

Kelsey followed him toward his room, but instead of going there, he stopped at the room next door. "Close your eyes," he commanded. "And don't argue with me about that, too."

"Okay, okay." She dutifully closed her eyes.

She heard him unlock the door, then he took her hand in his and led her into the room.

"You can open your eyes now," he said, his voice laced with excitement.

Unsure what to expect and praying that she would react the way he so obviously wanted her to, she opened her eyes slowly, then blinked.

"Oh, my," she whispered, stunned. "Oh, Jeff, this is amazing." She spun around slowly, trying to take in everything. "It's a nursery for our baby. When did you have time to do this?"

"During your naps and whenever you had to go to the mainland for supplies," he said. "Do you really like it?"

She threw her arms around his neck. "Of course I do. How could I not love it?"

He'd painted the walls a pale shade of pink and added a border of ducks and flowers at the top. The crib was white and had a mobile of ducks above it. The comforter matched the border on the walls and the sheets were the same pink as the paint. There was a changing table and a dresser, as well as a lamp that coordinated with everything. There was even a toy box in the corner and half a dozen stuffed ducks in the crib. A rocking chair sat in another corner with a pin-striped pink-and-white blanket tossed over it.

"I hope I didn't overdo it with the ducks," he said worriedly. "You'd pointed out the border one day on the mainland and I kind of ran with it."

"It's absolutely perfect," she assured him.

"You're not disappointed that you didn't get to choose everything yourself? You have so much to do around here. I wanted to take one thing off your mind."

She gave him a resounding kiss. "This is exactly what I would have done, and the fact that you wanted to do it for us, for me and the baby, is the sweetest, most thoughtful thing anyone has ever done for me."

"Luke had to help me assemble the furniture," he admitted with a rueful expression. "He volunteered, but I think your mom was afraid it would all collapse if she left it to me. She was probably right. The instructions were incomprehensible."

Kelsey laughed. She could imagine how frustrating that would have been for him. "Obviously the two of you made a great team. Has my mom seen it since you finished? Or Gran? I assume they at least knew what you were up to."

"Of course they knew, but they haven't been in here since it's been finished. I wanted you to be the first one to see it," he said. "There's one more thing that goes with it."

"Oh?"

"It's in the toy chest."

Kelsey crossed the room and lifted the padded top of the chest, which could also be used as a window seat. Inside the chest was a small box. Her heart began to beat a little faster and harder. "Jeff," she asked, her voice breathless. "What is this? It's clearly not a toy for the baby."

"Well, the nursery is really for the baby, but I thought her mom ought to have something special, too, so that's for you." His gaze caught hers and held. "If you're ready to accept it."

She lifted the wrapped box gingerly and held it in a hand that shook. She hadn't expected to be so nervous when this moment finally came again. "I'm not sure I can open this," she said. "My hands are shaking."

"Want help?" he asked.

She thought about it, then shook her head. She wanted to savor every moment of this. It took a long time to remove the bow with her fumbling fingers and then what seemed like an eternity to unseal the paper. Then she was holding the small velvet box in her hand. She knew that once she opened that box, her life would change forever. Even though she'd reached her decision a while ago, even though she'd been anticipating this moment, she had to struggle with one last bout of uncertainty.

Then she glanced around the nursery and into Jeff's eyes, which were filled with hope, and she knew that this was right. Marrying him had been inevitable and the timing was irrelevant. She held the box out to him. "You open it," she said.

He took it from her and flipped open the lid to reveal a large, princess-cut diamond solitaire. When she would have reached for it, he captured her hand and held it, then dropped to one knee.

"Will you marry me, Kelsey? There is nothing in this world that I want more than to spend my life with you and our daughter and any other children we might have. That life can be right here in Seaview or anywhere else, because for me, wherever I'm with you will always be home."

The last flickering doubt was swept away by the sincerity of his words and the love shining in his eyes. She knelt down before him and captured his face in her hands.

"I hope you know how very much I love you, Jeff Hampton. It was never, ever about that. Me saying no was only because I didn't know who I was or what I wanted, and I needed to be absolutely sure about that before I could be sure we could share a life together. I found myself here and I think I even found a whole other side to you. I know that I'm more certain than ever that we belong together."

"Help me out here," he pleaded. "Was that a yes?"

She leaned forward and kissed him. "That was definitely a yes," she said when she pulled away.

Jeff took her hand and slid the ring on her

finger. "It looks good there," he said.

"And it will stay there forever," she promised him. "Now let's go tell Mom and Gran. They are going to be so relieved that there's going to be a wedding before I give birth to this baby."

"Do you think you can pull off the kind of wedding you've always dreamed of in just a few months?"

"With Mom and Gran on the case, no problem," she said at once. "We are the Matthews women, after all."

And after being in Seaview with her mother and grandmother for all these weeks, she understood just how amazing that really was. There was nothing they couldn't accomplish. She just prayed her mom would come to believe that, too.

Hannah was up to her eyeballs with wedding preparations. Kelsey had asked for the impossible, something with all the frills, and she wanted it to be at the beginning of June, now only a few weeks away.

"After that I'll be big as a blimp," she had told Hannah. "Do you think Dad will come to walk me down the aisle?"

Hannah hesitated, then forced a smile. "If you want him here, he'll come."

"Is it possible to do all this so quickly?"

"Of course," Hannah had assured her.

"I knew you wouldn't let me down. It means you'll need to stay here longer, though. You can't plan a wedding in Seaview from New York."

"I could," Hannah argued, though without much heat. She wanted to share every second of the excitement with her daughter and with Gran, who was already enlisting the help of everyone she knew at the church to make sure it was filled with flowers and decorated according to a picture Kelsey had torn out of a magazine.

"Dave's probably going to freak when you tell him," Kelsey said. "When was the last time you spoke to him?"

"It's been a while now," Hannah said evasively. "We have a deal. He knows I'll call whenever I'm ready to come back to work."

"He was okay with that?" Kelsey asked incredulously.

"He wasn't ecstatic, but I told him that was just the way things had to be."

"He's holding your job for you, though?"

"Yes," Hannah said. "Probably."

Kelsey had stared at her with dismay. "Probably? Does that mean he might fill it? Then what will you do? Mom, don't stay here if you need to be in New York. We'll manage here and between faxes and e-mails and phone calls, you'll be right in the thick of things."

"It won't be the same," Hannah had insisted. "My only daughter is only getting married once and I intend to share every second of it."

So, here she was in Seaview, months longer than she'd ever imagined she would be when she'd arrived back in January. She kept telling herself that she didn't hate it only because of Luke and the flurry of excitement over the wedding, but when she was being totally honest, she could almost admit that she was enjoying the relaxing rhythm of her days here, to say nothing of the passion Luke had instilled in her nights.

It had come as a jolt last week, though, when Luke announced that he was going to start looking for his own place. She'd come to count on him being at the inn. She'd even encouraged him to stay on there.

"I'm taking up a room that could be rented for a lot more," he'd reminded her. "This place is a business. Besides, the kids will be coming for the summer and I can't impose on Kelsey and your grandmother by having them stay here again."

"You know they wouldn't mind," Hannah had argued, but it was a losing battle. He'd made an appointment for this afternoon with a real estate agent. She wasn't entirely sure why she found that so upsetting. Maybe because it was a reminder that he was moving on with his life, while she was still in this self-imposed limbo, not quite ready to go back to her life in New York, not willing to embrace a new one here.

"Hey there, you busy?" the man in question asked from the doorway to the office.

"Not too busy to see you," she said, smiling at him. "I thought you were going to look at houses."

"I am. I thought you might want to come along."

"Why?"

He grinned at the question. "Because I value your opinion," he responded. "Because I want someplace that might entice you to consider sharing it."

His words and the allure of that prospect warmed her, even as she steeled herself against wanting it too much. Nothing had changed. She still had the prospect of a cancer recurrence looming over her, and with her next checkup just a few weeks away — the week after Kelsey's wedding, in fact — it was on her mind constantly.

"Come on, Hannah. Come with me," he said. "It'll be fun, and you can save me from buying the first place the agent shows me."

Since she knew how anxious he was to get this decision behind him, she understood the likelihood that he might do just that. "Okay, but only to save you from yourself."

"Thank you," he said solemnly, even though his eyes were twinkling at having won. "Have you had lunch? Want to grab something on the way?"

The truth was, she hadn't eaten all day, but the thought of food made her feel a little queasy. "I'm not hungry, but if you are, we can stop."

He studied her with a frown. "You skipped breakfast. Grandma Jenny mentioned it. Are you feeling okay?"

"Just a little off," she admitted. "Probably a touch of flu or something. Or maybe that fish we had for dinner last night."

"Maybe I should cancel the appointment and take you over to the clinic to get checked out."

"Don't be silly. You're a doctor. If I keel over, who better to be with me?" She forced a cheery note into her voice. "Let's go find you the perfect house."

"Okay," he said with obvious reluctance. "But if you're not feeling better by tomorrow, you are coming to the clinic."

"Fine, whatever."

He gave her a wry look. "You sound like Gracie, when she's patronizing me."

Hannah laughed. "Or Kelsey when she's patronizing me. Thanks for calling me on that. Should I rephrase?"

"Nope, just be at the clinic first thing tomorrow if you're not feeling a hundred percent."

"Thanks for worrying about me," she said with more sincerity.

"Just part of the package," he assured her. "Love, honor, cherish and worry."

"Luke," she protested.

"I'm going to keep reminding you of how I feel, Hannah," he said stubbornly. "Maybe one of these days you'll finally believe me."

"I do believe you," she told him. Why couldn't he see that that wasn't the point? It was cancer that stood between them and she honestly couldn't see that ever changing. Even after the checkups dwindled to once a year, there would always be the tiny, nagging fear of a recurrence. She knew firsthand what that could do to loved ones, the toll it would take. She wouldn't do that to Luke or his children and that was final. Saying no was an act of kindness. Someday he'd understand that.

He cupped her chin with his hand and met her gaze. "If you do believe me, then you should also understand that if the worst happens, I will still grieve for you. The only thing you will have accomplished is to rob us of the happiness we might have had. Promise me you'll think about that, Hannah."

With his words echoing in her head and his gaze locked with hers, all she could do was nod.

23

Luke didn't like the way Hannah had looked earlier. The whole time they'd been going through houses, he'd been paying more attention to her than their surroundings. Her color wasn't good and she seemed a little shaky. Then, again, she hadn't eaten all day.

"Luke, did you see the size of the yard out back?" Hannah said, snapping him back to the task at hand. "It goes right to the inlet and there's a dock. You could have a boat. The kids would love it."

"And the house probably floods every time there's a storm, much less a hurricane," he said, barely sparing a glance at the yard. "I've seen enough for today. Let's get out of here."

"But there are three more I wanted you to see," Sallie Bryce protested.

"Another day," he said firmly. "Hannah and I have somewhere we need to be."

Hannah regarded him blankly. "We do?"

"We do," he confirmed, steering her out of the house and into the car. "We'll talk tomorrow, Sallie."

"I'll look forward to it," the agent responded with forced perkiness.

Hannah frowned at him. "What is wrong with you? Why are you suddenly in such a hurry?"

"Because I have a craving for a late lunch. I never should have skipped it. How about you? Are you hungry yet?"

"Not really."

"Well, you can eat some conch chowder or something," he said, driving straight for The Fish Tale. If that didn't bring her color back, he was heading straight for the clinic next. He didn't know what was going on with her, but he intended to get to the bottom of it. For all he knew, she could be pregnant and trying to hide it from him. Something told him, though, that it was more likely that she was worrying herself sick about the cancer and trying to hide *that.*

At the restaurant, before Hannah had a chance to argue, he gave Jack their orders and led the way to a booth.

"You're awfully bossy this afternoon," she commented.

"Lack of food," he told her.

"That'll teach me to always make sure

you're well fed. I had no idea that hunger made you so cranky and autocratic." She took a sip of the iced tea he'd ordered for her, then broke off a chunk of bread and chewed it, her expression thoughtful. "So, did you like any of the houses we saw today? You didn't really seem to be paying much attention."

"Nothing knocked my socks off. How about you?"

"I liked the last one," she said. "Let's face it, anything on Seaview is at risk in a hurricane, but this was solid enough to have withstood quite a few storms over the years. The view and yard were amazing. The kitchen's been updated. So has the master bathroom. It's basically in move-in condition." She pulled a piece of paper from her purse and began making notes. "You'd have to paint, of course. Fix the screens on the back porch."

To Luke's relief, as she made her case, the color in her cheeks improved. When Jack set the bowl of chowder in front of her, she began eating almost without noticing what she was doing. Instead, she continued her enthusiastic recitation of all the positives about the house, jotting a note whenever she thought of a drawback.

"You liked it that much?" he asked finally.

"I didn't notice half that stuff."

"Which is why you brought me along," she said dryly. "Men! What do any of you ever do without us?"

"Live in hovels?" he suggested, not entirely in jest. He would have been content for years in the little starter house he and Lisa had bought in Atlanta, if she hadn't forced him into that showplace she insisted they needed. Was that when their marriage had started to unravel? On some level had he realized then how different they were? Or had there simply been so much room, it had become easier to avoid each other while still under the same roof?

"Hovels?" Hannah repeated. "More than likely." She tucked the notepad back into her purse. "I'll type all this up for you back at the inn. Then you should probably take another look at the house and pay attention this time. These problem areas will give you a stronger bargaining position when you put in an offer."

"Yes, ma'am," he said with a grin, relieved to see her spunk returning. "And since you're obviously feeling a bit feistier than you were earlier, mind if I ask you something?"

"What?"

"Have you made any decision about seeing your father? Every time I've brought it up before, you've changed the subject. I have no idea how you're feeling about him right now."

"Neither do I," she admitted. "I've been avoiding it. Planning the wedding has given me the perfect excuse not to think about him at all."

Luke knew he was treading into dangerous territory, so he chose his words carefully. "A wedding might be the perfect way to heal old wounds."

"No," she said fiercely. "I won't drag that drama into the middle of Kelsey's wedding and risk ruining it for her."

"Slow down. I wasn't suggesting that you see your dad for the first time at the wedding," he explained. "I thought maybe you could meet, try to work through a few things. That would make the wedding even more of a celebration, if your dad were there to see his granddaughter walk down the aisle."

"I don't know," Hannah said, her skepticism plain. "It could be a disaster."

"If you two talk and things go badly, then you certainly don't have to invite him."

She met Luke's gaze. "You think I *should* see him, don't you? And include him in the wedding."

"As long as you're still down here, I think you should take advantage of his proximity, yes, at least to meet with him."

"But why?"

"Because I don't think you'll ever be truly happy until you put the past behind you once and for all," he said. "I'm not saying you have to embrace him and make him a part of your life now, just see him and put old issues to rest. If you can reconcile, great. If not, I think you'll be able to make peace with that, too, but only if you've seen him and talked."

"Do you think that's possible? Can you honestly say you've done that with Lisa and Brad?"

"Lisa and I are getting there," he said. "Each visit's been a little easier. Brad's another story, but I imagine I'll make peace with him eventually. We'll never be friends again, but hopefully we can be civil."

"Okay," she said.

He blinked at her quick acquiescence. "What exactly are you agreeing to?"

"Call my father. Set something up. I want you to plan it and I want you there. As for inviting him to the wedding, we'll have to see how this meeting goes. I'm still struggling to accept the fact that Kelsey wants her father at the wedding. Dealing with both of them may be more than I can handle."

"I understand," he said. "Are you sure you want me there for this meeting with your dad?"

She nodded. "I need you there to remind me that I've had a life all these years without him, that it doesn't really matter how things turn out."

"Okay. I'll set it up. When?"

"Soon, before I change my mind. I have to go to the mainland tomorrow to see the caterer about the wedding. That appointment is at ten. We can see him afterward."

"What about your half brother?"

She shook her head. "One step at a time, okay?"

"The first one's always the hardest," he said. "But I'll be right there."

Tomorrow — and forever — if she'd let him.

Hannah had fought with the caterer over every little thing. Even as the curt words had left her mouth, she'd known that her irritation had nothing to do with the menu. It had everything to do with this upcoming lunch she was having with her father. With every minute that passed, she was sorrier that she'd agreed to do this. She had enough on her plate with the wedding and all the other decisions looming on the horizon. Lately, she'd been feeling a little off, too, though she had no idea why. Probably stress over the wedding and the cancer screening looming on the horizon just after the wedding.

"How did my father sound when you suggested this?" she asked Luke, twisting the scarf she'd worn on the ferry earlier into a knot.

"As nervous as you are," Luke said, resting his hand atop hers for a moment. "But he also seemed very eager to see you."

"He probably won't come," Hannah murmured to herself. "I wouldn't, if I were him."

"He'll be here," Luke said, turning into the parking lot of the restaurant they'd agreed on. "In fact, there he is, waiting right by the door."

Hannah turned quickly and, indeed, there he was, looking years older, yet much the same as she'd remembered. Her heart climbed into her throat and her eyes filled with tears. "He came," she whispered, not quite believing it, not quite believing how relieved she was to see him.

"You hop out and join him. I'll park the car," Luke suggested. "It will give you a minute alone together."

Hannah hesitated. "I almost feel as if you

should be there to introduce us." She forced a wobbly smile. "Crazy, huh?"

"Understandable. Now, go. He's seen us."

Hannah exited the car slowly. She took one step in her father's direction, and then something inside her broke free and she was running toward him. "Daddy," she whispered, launching herself at him as she had when she was younger.

He caught her and held her in a fierce hug, his shoulders shaking with silent sobs. "Oh, Hannah Banana, I never thought I'd live to see this day," he told her, his voice choked.

"Me, neither."

"I'm so glad you came. I was afraid you'd change your mind," he admitted.

"Me, too."

He took a step back. "Let me get a good look at you," he said. "You look like your mother, Hannah. You're as beautiful as she was."

"No, I'm not."

He smiled at that. "I imagine Luke agrees with me, don't you, young man?" he said as Luke joined them.

"I do, indeed," Luke said. "Shall we go inside?"

"I asked for a quiet table when I made the reservation," her father said. "I thought we might want a little privacy." He studied Hannah again, as if not quite daring to believe she was real. "I also have Clay on standby, in case you change your mind about meeting him today. He'll join us for dessert if you want. He's very excited about meeting you."

"I want to meet him, too," Hannah said, overwhelmed by the speed with which things were happening. "But give me a few minutes to decide, okay? All this is happening so fast. There's so much for me to absorb."

"Of course."

After they were seated in an alcove off to one side, she told Luke to order something for her and then faced her father. His face was lined now, but there was still the remembered warmth and humor in his eyes. His hair was gray, but he wore it in the same neatly trimmed style. Despite all the years they'd been separated, she would have recognized him anywhere. He was still the man she'd once loved with all her heart.

And she was still angry with him.

As if he sensed that, his expression was somber and his gaze steady as he met hers. "Where shall I begin?"

"Just tell me why it happened," she said, then challenged, "Why did you choose them over us?"

"There's not a good answer to that," he admitted. "I suppose I thought they needed me more. Your mother was a very strong woman and you two were surrounded by people who loved you. Lucy, that's her name, she had none of that." He glanced at Luke. "I imagine Luke told you that she had some mental health issues back then. I worried about how she'd care for Clay. I had no worries on that score with your mother and grandparents. I knew you were in the best possible hands."

Hannah was about to ask why he'd strayed in the first place, why he'd gotten another woman pregnant, but that offense hadn't been committed against her. It was between her father and mother. Besides, it didn't really matter now. It was over and done. She needed to leave it in the past where it belonged.

"Did you ever regret it? Did you miss me? And Mom, did you miss her?"

"Of course, but life goes on, Hannah. You're old enough to know that. You can't let the past cripple you. If you do, then you're destroying the present and the future. What good is there in that?"

"Mom died," she told him. "Did you know that?"

He nodded. "It was in the paper. I almost called your grandmother then, and you, but I decided it wasn't the right time. I wasn't sure there would ever be a right time."

"I have a daughter," she told him, pulling a picture of Kelsey from her purse to show him. "She's getting married soon."

He studied it closely, his eyes misty. "It's like looking at a picture of the way you must have looked at that age," he said. "She's lovely. I am so sorry I missed all those years with you."

"She's helping Gran run the inn," Hannah said, surprised by how proud she was of that. "And she's having a baby. You'll be a great-grandfather soon."

"Oh, my. I'm not sure I'm ready for that. I can't be *that* old."

"I'm still getting used to the prospect of someone calling me Grandma," Hannah admitted.

He started to hand back the picture, but Hannah shook her head. "You keep it, if you want to."

"Of course I want to."

She glanced toward Luke questioningly, knowing he'd understand what she was thinking. "Should I?"

"Up to you," he murmured.

She'd thought about including her father

in the wedding, and suddenly she couldn't think of a single reason not to. His presence wouldn't create the scene she'd worried about. She could count on Grandma Jenny to be polite, whatever her feelings might be. If there was a scene, it was far more likely to be between her and her ex-husband.

"Dad . . ." She drew in a deep breath, then asked, "Will you come to the wedding?"

He seemed startled by the invitation. "I would love to be there, but I have to ask, do you want me to come alone?"

She thought about that, thought about what she knew of his wife and the threats that had stolen her father from her life. "I won't have Kelsey's wedding ruined," she said fiercely, her attempt at being magnanimous forgotten.

He nodded. "I understand what you're saying. I'll think it over, okay? I think enough time has passed that it might be fine, but I won't take a chance on letting Lucy spoil the occasion. I promise."

"And Clay? Will you bring him and his wife, if you do decide to come? I don't think I'm ready to meet him today. I think I need to go home and think about all this." She turned to Luke. "We should go. The ferry will be leaving soon."

There was no mistaking the disappointment in her father's eyes, but the meeting had been overwhelming. She couldn't be here another minute. It had gone well, better than she'd hoped, in fact, but her emotions were raw and she'd tested the limits of her maturity.

Still, she leaned down and kissed her father's weathered cheek. "We'll talk soon, okay? I'll call you."

He nodded. "I love you, Hannah Banana."

"Love you," she said, then turned and ran from the restaurant.

She was barely holding back tears when Luke caught up with her in the parking lot. He pulled her into his arms.

"You okay?"

She nodded against his chest.

"Glad you came?"

She nodded again.

"It's all going to work out, you know. The two of you will forge a new relationship. I know that's what he wants."

"Me, too."

"Then you'll make it happen."

"I shouldn't have run out and left him sitting there," she said. "I just couldn't stay there another minute."

"He understood."

"Is he okay?"

"A little shaken, same as you. I insisted he

call Clay to come and join him. It will give him time to absorb what's happened. They'll talk over what to tell Lucy and how to handle the wedding."

"Thank you for setting this up, and for being here," she told him.

"Nowhere I'd rather be," he said.

Hannah looked into his eyes and knew he meant that with one hundred percent sincerity. If only she could find some way to allow herself to embrace his unconditional love and the future he was offering.

The weeks leading up to the wedding were increasingly hectic. Add the stress of trying to reestablish her relationship with her father, and Hannah was tense from morning until night.

"You sound exhausted," Sue said when she called.

"Too much to do, too little time," Hannah told her. "You are still coming for the wedding, right?"

"I'll be there," Sue promised. "So far the doctor hasn't thrown up any warning flags about me flying at this stage of my pregnancy."

"Well, if he does, then stay put. I don't want you taking any chances," Hannah told her.

"Believe me, I won't," Sue said. "How are things with you and Luke?"

"He bought a house," Hannah told her, then went on to describe it.

"Sounds tailor-made for a family," Sue commented slyly.

"His kids will love it," Hannah said, deliberately misunderstanding.

"And you? Do you love it?"

"It's a great house. It just had a good vibe the second we walked inside. There are lots of windows, so there's terrific light pouring into all the rooms. The views are amazing."

"Sounds like the perfect place for someone who wants to write children's books," Sue suggested.

"Will you give it a rest?" Hannah pleaded. "I'm not moving in, much less changing careers."

"Has Luke asked you to move in?"

"He's said a lot of things. So have I. It's not in the cards, Sue. Drop it, please."

"Just let me go on record as saying that you're crazy," Sue said. "And now I'll drop it."

"Thank you."

"At least until I get there and can size things up for myself."

Hannah chuckled ruefully. "I'm almost sorry I invited you."

"No, you're not," Sue retorted confidently. "See you soon. And I expect to see at least one of those children's stories written down on paper when I get there. If you want my opinion, the one about the mystical, magical mermaid seems like a good place to start. That's the baby present I want from you, okay? In hardcover and fully illustrated."

"I don't think publishing works that fast," Hannah said wryly.

"Okay, I'll wait for the illustrated version, but I want something on paper so it will be the first story I read to the baby."

"Since I know you're going to pester me until you have it, I'll see what I can do," Hannah promised.

After Hannah hung up, she went to take her shower. As part of the daily ritual, she also did a breast self-exam. The first tumor had been caught on a mammogram while it was still small enough that she hadn't even been able to feel it. Even so, even after chemo and radiation and the most recent all-clear report, she was still terrified all the time that there were other tumors that had somehow escaped detection. She was compulsive about checking.

Standing in her shower now, she diligently soaped up her hands and began to check around her scar and under her right arm. Instead of the slick, smooth surface she'd been feeling for weeks, though, there was . . . something. She sucked in a sharp breath, fighting almost immediate panic. Holding her breath, she stroked her fingers over the spot again. There it was, a clearly defined little bump. It hadn't been there yesterday or the day before. She was sure of it.

She thought of all the times lately she'd felt vaguely ill and rushed to the conclusion that cancer was suddenly rampant in her body. Bile crawled up the back of her throat.

"No," she whispered, pressing harder, trying to make the tiny lump disappear or dissolve or something. She couldn't seem to make herself stop touching it, willing it away, even as tears spilled down her cheeks, mingling with the spray of the shower.

Was this how it had been for her mother when the cancer had come back? Had she felt this searing sense of terror, this numbing dread that she was about to go through it all again — the mammogram in a cold, lonely room, then a biopsy and the endless wait for results, surgery, chemo, radiation, all of it with absolutely no certainty about the outcome? Could she face that again, especially knowing that the odds were starting to work against her?

This was exactly what had kept her from giving in to Luke, from grabbing at the future he'd offered. Cancer was unpredictable and cruel. Just as hope settled in, it could be snatched away. Leaning against the tiled wall of the shower, she let the tears flow, choking back sobs out of fear that someone would hear her.

A light tap on the bathroom door suggested that someone already had.

"Hannah?" her grandmother called. "Hannah, are you okay?"

She tried to speak, tried to squeeze out the words that would send her away, but she couldn't get anything past the boulder lodged in her throat.

"I'm coming in," her grandmother announced, opening the door as she said it, then peeking around the shower curtain.

As soon as she spotted Hannah, she must have known, because the worried frown on her face deepened and her own tears welled up.

"Another lump?" she asked, her voice tremulous.

Hannah nodded.

"It's okay," she said, her face a mask of grim determination. "We'll deal with it. It might not be anything at all."

"We both know it is," Hannah said. "It's

something."

"It doesn't have to be malignant," Grandma Jenny insisted. "We'll focus on the positive. I mean it, Hannah. Positive thoughts only."

Hannah wanted to be strong enough to put on a brave front. It must be horrible for Gran for this to be happening again so soon after her daughter had died from cancer. Hannah wanted to strike a positive note, but the fear was too great. All she could think about were the months of suffering her mother endured. Once again, she dissolved into tears, great gulping sobs that she couldn't seem to stop.

Her grandmother looked for a moment as if she might climb into the shower with her. Instead, though, she backed up a step. "I'm getting Luke."

"No," Hannah protested. "No, Gran. This isn't his problem."

"He's a doctor. He might have something that will calm you down." She gave Hannah a look of total understanding. "And he loves you. His place is here."

Hannah knew further argument was pointless. "Whatever you do, though, please don't let Kelsey know about this. Not until we know more."

"I'll do my best," Gran promised. She

spun away and left Hannah there.

Moments later, Luke was there. He didn't even hesitate. He merely stepped into the shower fully clothed and gathered her close.

"It's okay, Hannah. Gran told me about the lump, but everything is going to be okay."

Oddly, in his arms, she almost felt as if it might be. They stood there for what felt like an eternity, her head resting on his chest, the shower spilling over them, their hearts beating in tandem.

His hand, which had been stroking her back in a comforting gesture, slid lower, cupped her bottom. Despite herself and the dire circumstances, she giggled.

"What?" he demanded.

"I knew this wasn't entirely altruistic," she teased. "You've been trying to get me naked for days, but there have been too many people around the inn and too many guests arriving in town for the wedding, so I couldn't even sneak away to your place. I should have known that given the opportunity, you wouldn't be able to resist copping a feel."

He regarded her with hurt indignation for about two seconds, then shrugged and grinned. "Holding a naked woman is pretty irresistible. You can't blame me for taking advantage of the situation, can you? Besides, it made you smile."

"Because it's so totally male."

His gaze held hers. "And you're so totally female, Hannah. Don't forget that. No matter what happens, you will always be wonderfully, incredibly female."

He reached behind him and snatched a towel. "Here, wrap yourself in this. I'm going back downstairs to get some of the clothes I left over here."

She grabbed his hand, when he started to walk away. "Don't leave, Luke, please. Not yet. I don't want to be by myself. I'll start to think about what comes next."

"Okay, then," he said, scooping her up and carrying her to the bed. He sat her on the edge. "Where's your robe?"

"Hanging on a hook on the back of the bathroom door. You've seen me naked before, Luke, so it's a little late for modesty."

"Hey, I'm trying to behave myself here. Let's remove at least some of the temptation. Besides, your grandmother is probably right outside the door trying to decide if she made a mistake in bringing me up here."

"I'm sure she's had some idea of what's been going on between us for a while now," Hannah said. "I like to believe she's naive, but she sent you in here for a reason."

"Because I'm a doctor," Luke said.

"No, because she knew that you were probably the only person who could calm me down." She met his gaze. "She was right, too. I'm still scared, but not as much as I was a few minutes ago."

"You going to let me check whatever you found during your exam?"

"Is that just another way to get your hands on me?"

He grinned. "Of course."

Unbelievably she was able to smile at that, too. "Here," she said, guiding his hand to the lump.

She watched his expression closely, but it revealed nothing as he tenderly poked and prodded, then sat back.

"What's the verdict?" she asked when he said nothing.

"We'll need to do a biopsy to be sure," he said, holding tight to her hand. "But I'm ninety-five-percent certain it's just scar tissue."

She stared at him blankly, hardly daring to hope. "Scar tissue?"

"That's what it feels like to me, but we'll do the test to be sure, so your mind can be completely at ease."

She waited for relief to wash over her, but it didn't come. Ninety-five percent wasn't one hundred. She stood up.

"I'm getting dressed. I want you to do the test now. Can you do it at the clinic?"

"Are you sure? Would you rather go to New York and see your oncologist? He could do the whole battery of tests."

"That will take too long. Do it here, Luke. Send the results up there, if there's any question about what they show, but I need to know."

He nodded at once. "I'll get changed and meet you downstairs."

He started from the room, then came back and cupped her chin in his hand. "However this turns out, it changes nothing. I will still love you. I will still want to marry you. Understood?"

Hannah blinked back a fresh batch of tears. "Understood," she said softly. For right now, for just this one moment in time, she wanted desperately to believe that.

24

Luke made a pact with Hannah and Grandma Jenny to say nothing around Kelsey about the biopsy. Hannah wanted nothing to spoil Kelsey's wedding, which was on Saturday, just days away. The inn was already starting to fill up with wedding guests — a small cadre of friends from New York and Jeff's family, who'd taken the news of the wedding and the pregnancy with surprising delight. Even Hannah's boss and his wife had shown up, partly out of friendship, Luke was sure, but also because it gave him an opportunity to press Hannah about coming back to New York.

Luke was glad he'd closed on his new house, because Hannah had agreed to stay there to open up more rooms at the inn for all the expected company. It was also keeping her out of reach of Dave's pressure.

His kids were arriving on Friday, flying down on their own for the first time. Kelsey had wanted them to be part of the festivities.

For now, though, he and Hannah had some precious time to themselves. He knew she was freaking out over the anticipated test results and there was nothing he could say to reassure her. He just held her during the night when anxiety kept her awake.

She'd finally fallen asleep this morning around dawn. He was due at the clinic in an hour, so he slipped out of bed, showered, then went into the kitchen to brew coffee and fix breakfast. He hoped she'd keep sleeping, but he wasn't counting on it.

Sure enough, just as he put an English muffin in the toaster, she wandered into the kitchen, barefoot and wearing one of his shirts. He thought she'd never looked sexier, though he doubted she'd believe him if he told her. Her self-image seemed to have crashed with the discovery of that lump.

"You should still be in bed," he said, even as he handed her a glass of orange juice.

"Too much to do. I have to pick Sue up at the airport this morning, then run by the caterer's with a check. Then Kelsey and I are supposed to go by the church this afternoon and make sure everything's under control there."

"I thought the church was Grandma Jenny's domain." He scooped scrambled eggs and the muffin onto a plate and slid it in front of her.

"Try telling that to Kelsey. If she hasn't checked it for herself, then she can't check it off that endless list of hers."

Luke grinned. "Sounds like someone else I know."

She shrugged. "Family trait."

"Think you can find some time in there to drop by the clinic later?" he asked casually.

She looked up from the eggs, panic in her eyes. "The results?"

He nodded. "I should have them this afternoon. I can wait and tell you here tonight, if you'd prefer. I thought about waiting until after the wedding, but I know you'd prefer to have them sooner rather than later, right?"

She nodded, still looking stricken. "I'll come to the office. Is it okay if I bring Sue with me?"

"Of course," he said at once. "I feel good about the results, Hannah. I really do."

"From your lips to God's ear," she said.

"I'm sorry it had to be today."

"It's not like I haven't been thinking about them nonstop, anyway."

"I know, but still, this should be a totally

happy week when you can focus on Kelsey's wedding."

"And if you're right about the results being good, I'll be able to do that starting this afternoon," she said with more optimism than she'd shown since he'd done the biopsy.

"Now, that's the spirit." He dropped a kiss on her cheek. "Leave the dishes. Someone's coming in to clean this morning. I'll see you this afternoon. Any idea what time you can come by?"

"I'll be there by four. Will that work?"

"Absolutely." He started for the door, then turned back. "You okay? I can have Doc go into the clinic so I can spend the day with you."

"No need. I'll be fine," she assured him with a smile that seemed only slightly forced. "There are so many last-minute details to deal with, I won't have even a second to think."

"Okay, then. Later."

"Later," she responded.

Outside, Luke looked up toward the sky. "Please, God, give us later. Not just today, but years."

The thought of finding Hannah again, of having her in his life, and then losing her was enough to break his heart.

■ ■ ■ ■

Hannah put her hand on Sue's rounded belly and smiled. "Just look at you, all pregnant and motherly. You're beautiful."

"I feel frumpy and fat," Sue grumbled, then grinned. "But I've never been happier or more excited. And look at you, all tanned and fit. Seaview seems to agree with you, or do we have Luke to thank for the color in your cheeks?"

"He gets credit for some of it," Hannah admitted.

"So, what's on the agenda for today?"

"I have to run a check by the caterer's and then we'll catch the ferry out to the island. Grandma Jenny is planning lunch for us at the inn, then Kelsey has a meeting for the two of us at the church so she can hear for herself that the minister actually knows how to perform a wedding. I thought you could catch a nap then, if you want to."

"And when am I going to meet the gorgeous Luke? Will he be joining us for dinner?"

"Actually it could be a bit sooner than that," Hannah said carefully. "If you want to. I have to run by the clinic around four."

Something in her voice must have given

her away, because Sue's expression immediately filled with concern. "What's going on?"

Hannah swallowed hard, then forced out the words. "I found a lump."

Sue immediately reached for her hand and gave it a squeeze. "Why didn't you call me?"

"There was nothing you could do. You'd just have worried."

Sue didn't even attempt to hide her dismay. "It's been tested?"

"Luke did a biopsy. He'll have the results this afternoon. He thinks it's scar tissue."

"Then that's what we'll believe," Sue said at once. "Positive thoughts."

"Kelsey doesn't know," Hannah warned her.

"Got it. And of course, I'll go with you to the clinic, even though there's absolutely nothing to worry about."

Hannah clung to her hand, relieved to have her friend by her side. "I am so glad you're here."

"Me, too, sweetie. Me, too."

But despite Sue's attempt to be cheerful, there was no question that a pall had been cast over the visit.

Luke held the envelope with Hannah's test results. Across his desk, Hannah sat next to her friend Sue. The two of them were holding hands so tightly their knuckles had turned white. Hannah's eyes were dark with fear and Sue's were shimmering with tears.

"You ready?" he asked, his heart in his throat. He could have looked the moment the results reached his desk, but he'd waited. He'd told himself there hadn't been time to look them over earlier, but the truth was, he was as nervous as Hannah.

Hannah nodded. "Just get it over with," she told him.

Luke opened the envelope and read the lab report, a sigh of relief escaping. He barely resisted a desire to run around the desk and scoop Hannah up in his arms.

"Scar tissue," he announced. "Nothing else. Just scar tissue."

Hannah blinked back tears. "You're sure?"

"It says it right here." He tapped the paper. "When you see your doctor in New York after the wedding, there will be more-thorough tests, but this one came back clear."

"Thank God," Sue murmured. She gave Luke a fierce look. "If it had said anything else, I'd have had to kill you."

He laughed. "Yes — shoot the messenger."

"I know we glossed over the pleasantries, but I'm Hannah's very best friend in the world, Sue." She gave him a penetrating look. "And the way I hear it, you're more than a messenger."

He grinned. "That remains to be seen. I'm working on it, though."

"Don't give up," she said.

"Hey, you two, I am right here in the room," Hannah grumbled. "And I feel like celebrating. Let's go see if the grocery store stocks nonalcoholic bubbly and have a toast."

"Why don't you let me do that?" Sue said. "Just point me in the right direction and I'll pick it up and bring it back here. Then you two can do a little private celebrating of your own."

"Are you sure?" Hannah asked. "It's been years since you've been here. Will you be able to find the store?"

"It's an island. How lost can I get?" Sue asked.

Grateful to her for her consideration, Luke gave her directions. When she was gone, he walked around the desk.

"Told you it would be good news," he said, his knees brushing against Hannah's.

"It won't always be," she said direly.

"But it *could* always be," he stressed. "That's good enough for me. I'm a risk-taker."

"Some risks are too big to be taken," she argued.

He touched a finger to her lips. "My decision."

"Luke —"

He silenced her protest by kissing her. He did a thorough job of it, too.

"How could I not want more of that?" he asked afterward.

Though Hannah looked a little dazed, she gestured toward the report lying on his desk. "How could you possibly want more of those?"

"Sweetheart, it was good news. Focus on that."

"I want to," she said.

"What's stopping you?"

"Paralyzing fear."

"Waste of time," he told her. "It won't change anything. It will just rob you of the happiness you could have. Decide to live, Hannah. Reach out and grab every second you can. And I want you to do that with me."

He waited for her to think about that, waited for her to offer him at least a slim hope that they could reach for the future together.

"I'll try," she said eventually, touching a hand to his cheek. "It's the best I can do,

Luke. One minute at a time, I'll try."

He nodded. It wasn't all he'd hoped for, but it was a start. "Then we'll make those minutes count."

"I look like a blimp, a giant white blimp," Kelsey complained, turning this way and that in front of the full-length mirror.

Her father said solemnly, "You do not. You look beautiful. Doesn't she, Hannah?"

Kelsey rolled her eyes. "You have to say that. You're my parents and you want this wedding to happen. I should have waited until after the baby's born."

"This is better and you really do look beautiful," Hannah said. "I swear it. If you want, I can get Jeff in here. I'm sure he'll agree with me."

"Bad luck," Kelsey said succinctly. "Besides, he wants this wedding to happen even more than you do. He'll say whatever it takes to get me down the aisle today."

"True." Hannah smiled. "But I promise you that all I really want is for you to be wildly happy. I think you will be with Jeff."

Kelsey threw her arms around Hannah's neck. "I think so, too. I have no idea why I waited so long to say yes."

"You were taking the enormity of this step seriously," Hannah said. "I'm proud of you for that. And, in case I haven't said this enough, I am very proud of you for figuring out what makes you happy and going for it. You're doing an amazing job with the inn. Gran is ecstatic that you're here and want to keep it running. I'm also proud that you're generous enough to welcome your grandfather, his wife and my half brother for your wedding."

"And me," her father said. "I haven't spent nearly enough time with you, but I promise we'll change that."

"I did that for our family," Kelsey said. "I want my baby to be surrounded by every single person who will love her. As for the inn, I'm not doing it just for Grandma Jenny," she said firmly. "It's fun. I love getting to know all the guests and making sure they have a good time. There's something new every day. I think I might have realized sooner that this was what I wanted if I hadn't been so afraid you'd disapprove, Mom."

Hannah frowned at the suggestion that she might have stood in the way of Kelsey choosing her own future. "Why would I disapprove of anything, if it made you happy?"

"Come on, Mom. You always hated the inn and Seaview. Gran knew it. So did I."

She studied her mother intently. "But I think your attitude's changing a little bit, isn't it? At least toward Seaview?"

Hannah nodded slowly. "Being here with you and Gran has been wonderful," she admitted. "It's going to be hard leaving you here, especially with the little one on the way."

"Hold on," Kelsey said. "You're leaving before the baby comes? Dad, could I have a few minutes alone with Mom?"

"Of course," he said as he left. "Hannah, you did an amazing job with our daughter."

"Mom, you have to stay here," Kelsey said.

"I have to go back, sweetie. You know that. You've heard Dave badgering me ever since he arrived."

"I've also told him to butt out," Kelsey retorted. "What about Luke? I know he wants you to stay. Your home is here with us, Mom. What is there for you in New York?"

"My career," Hannah said flatly.

"Sit," Kelsey ordered.

"Baby, it's almost time for the wedding to start. We don't have time for this discussion now."

"Then I'll make it fast," Kelsey said. "Mom, all you have in New York is a boss who works you to death. I'm sure it's been very satisfying all these years to know that Dave counts on you and it certainly paid the bills, but you're not excited about it anymore, not the way you used to be. It turned into drudgery a long time ago. You're just scared to admit it, because it's all you have."

"It most certainly is not all —" Hannah began indignantly.

"It is," Kelsey said, cutting her off. "Until you and Luke hooked up down here, you hadn't been on a date in years. You certainly haven't met anyone as wonderful as Luke. You have one really good friend, Sue, and a lot of acquaintances. You don't even have me anymore. Your whole family will be down here. You've always defined yourself by being needed — I don't have to have a psychology degree to understand that. Well, where are you more needed? Here or New York? Just think about that, Mom. Promise me."

"If it will get you into church and down the aisle, I'll promise you anything," Hannah said in a flip tone.

"I'm serious," Kelsey said, not budging. "Promise and mean it."

Hannah regarded her, surprised by the somber tone. "This really matters to you, doesn't it?"

"It does. I want you here to be a part of my baby's life. And mine. And I want you to be as deliriously happy with Luke as I am with Jeff."

"Then I promise to think about it," Hannah said.

"I'll hold you to that," Kelsey warned her, then grinned. "Now, let's go get me married so I don't have this baby on the way down the aisle."

After a perfect wedding with no mishaps and everyone — Lucy included — on good behavior and with Kelsey and Jeff away on a three-day honeymoon on nearby Sanibel Island, Hannah pitched in to help at the inn. As soon as they were back, she planned to head for New York and another round of tests to be sure that the biopsy results hadn't been a fluke. While she was there, she also intended to speak to Dave about her job. Though he'd brought it up at every opportunity during the visit to Seaview, there hadn't been a moment for a serious conversation.

Despite everything Kelsey had said, Hannah was still clinging to the idea that her life was in New York. Maybe the truth was that she simply couldn't handle a change so huge at this point in her life when there was so much other uncertainty.

Leaving Luke and her family was going to be hard. She recognized that, but the past few months had been an unexpected gift, a chance to heal a lot of old wounds and spend time with people who meant the world to her. She couldn't find a label to pin on what she'd found with Luke, who was sitting beside her now as twilight fell.

With most of the guests out for the evening, they had the porch at the inn to themselves. Gran had actually gone off to her quilting circle for the first time in months. Her energy seemed boundless now that she knew the inn was going to stay in the family.

"This is the perfect way to end a day," Luke murmured contentedly. "Sitting here and unwinding with you."

"It is," Hannah agreed, not yet ready to tell him that moments like this would end soon.

When her cell phone rang, it was a jarring interruption to the serenity of the evening. "Sorry," she murmured to Luke when she saw that it was Dave. "I have to take this."

"Sure. I'll go in and pour some more tea."

"Thanks," she said as she flipped open the phone. "Hey, Dave. What's up?"

"That's what I want to know. I've given

you months to make up your mind, Hannah. Even when I saw you over the weekend, I tried not to do a full-court press, but the truth is I can't wait any longer for your decision. We just landed a major account and I need you back here, or I'll have to replace you. So, this is it. Are you coming back or not?"

"I'm flying up next week," she told him. "Can we talk about this then?"

"Sorry, no," he said. "I need to know now. Tonight."

She frowned at the reply. Obviously Dave was in crisis mode. Dave was always in crisis mode, but tonight she found it annoying. Nothing could possibly be so important that she had to made a decision in the next five seconds. This was either gamesmanship on his part, or he'd found her replacement and was looking for an excuse to hire the person.

"Who is it?" she asked quietly.

"Who? The new account?"

"No, the person you want to hire."

"The person I want is you," he insisted.

"Who is it?" she repeated.

He muttered a curse under his breath. "You know me too darn well. Max Carter's just become available. He's good, Hannah. He'd fit in here, but I don't have a spot for him if you want your job back."

Hannah gazed across the street at the calm waters glistening under the full moon. She listened to the music coming from inside the inn, an old favorite of Gran's, the Glenn Miller Orchestra, perhaps. Then Luke came through the door, two glasses of iced tea in hand, as well as some bruschetta he'd magically whipped up from fresh tomatoes and Merilee's sour dough bread. Suddenly it was no contest. All this stacked against the demands of a man who respected her for her capabilities, but didn't care about her needs as a human being.

Hannah swallowed hard and decided it was time to take a leap of faith. With Luke's gaze locked with hers and her heart fluttering as if she were nineteen again, there really wasn't any choice to make. As long as Seaview Key had Luke, New York had absolutely nothing she really wanted.

"Hire Max," she told Dave without the slightest hesitation. "You're right. He will fit in perfectly."

Dave gasped. "You're serious?"

"I am," she said, reaching for Luke's hand and twining her fingers through his.

"You're not just saying that because I pressured you into making a decision, are you? This is really what you want?" Dave asked, his voice filled with disbelief.

Hannah met Luke's gaze and saw that he'd picked up on enough of the conversation to understand the choice she was making. His lips curved. "This is really what I want," she said, holding Luke's gaze.

Dave was still talking when she clicked off the cell phone and tossed it aside.

Luke pulled her into his arms. "You're sure about this?"

"What is it with you men?" she asked. "You've been begging me to make a decision and now that I have, you don't seem to want to accept it."

Luke grinned at her feigned annoyance. "Just giving you one last chance to back out," he said. "Because once you say yes to me, I won't let you go, Hannah. This is it."

Her gaze never left his face as her expression sobered. "This is it," she said emphatically. "You, me, here, for as long as it lasts."

"Forever," he corrected. "I won't settle for anything less."

She touched his cheek as she had days earlier. "From your lips to God's ears."

The employees of Thorndike Press hope you have enjoyed this Large Print book. All our Thorndike and Wheeler Large Print titles are designed for easy reading, and all our books are made to last. Other Thorndike Press Large Print books are available at your library, through selected bookstores, or directly from us.

For information about titles, please call:

(800) 223-1244

or visit our Web site at:

http://gale.cengage.com/thorndike

To share your comments, please write:

Publisher
Thorndike Press
295 Kennedy Memorial Drive
Waterville, ME 04901